WHO

Brought together…by a baby!

Three passionate novels!

In April 2007 Mills & Boon bring back
two of their classic collections, each
featuring three favourite
romances by our bestselling authors...

WHOSE BABY?

With This Baby...
by Caroline Anderson
The Italian's Baby by Lucy Gordon
Assignment: Baby by Jessica Hart

MEDITERRANEAN
WEDDINGS

A Mediterranean Marriage
by Lynne Graham
The Greek's Virgin Bride by Julia James
The Italian Prince's Proposal
by Susan Stephens

WHOSE BABY?

WITH THIS BABY...
by
Caroline Anderson

THE ITALIAN'S BABY
by
Lucy Gordon

ASSIGNMENT: BABY
by
Jessica Hart

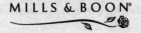

MILLS & BOON®

*MILLS & BOON and MILLS & BOON with the Rose Device
are registered trademarks of the publisher.*
Harlequin Mills & Boon Limited,
Eton House, 18-24 Paradise Road, Richmond, Surrey, TW9 1SR

WHOSE BABY?
© by Harlequin Enterprises II B.V. 2007

With This Baby…, The Italian's Baby and *Assignment: Baby* were
first published in Great Britain by Harlequin Mills & Boon
Limited in separate, single volumes.

With This Baby… © Caroline Anderson 2003
The Italian's Baby © Lucy Gordon 2003
Assignment: Baby © Jessica Hart 2001

ISBN: 978 0 263 85514 2

05-0407

*Printed and bound in Spain
by Litografía Rosés S.A., Barcelona*

WITH THIS BABY...

by

Caroline Anderson

Caroline Anderson has the mind of a butterfly. She's been a nurse, a secretary, a teacher, run her own soft-furnishing business and now she's settled on writing. She says, 'I was looking for that elusive something. I finally realised it was variety, and now I have it in abundance. Every book brings new horizons and new friends, and in between books I have learned to be a juggler. My teacher husband John and I have two beautiful and talented daughters, Sarah and Hannah, umpteen pets and several acres of Suffolk that nature tries to reclaim every time we turn our backs!'

CHAPTER ONE

'NOT again!'

Patrick slammed the phone down and shot back his chair, narrowly missing the dog's tail. Ever the optimist, the dog leapt to his feet, anticipating a walk, but Patrick shook his head.

'Sorry, Dog, not this time,' he muttered, snagging his jacket off the back of the chair and heading for the door. Still hopeful, those persuasive eyes watched him for the slightest encouragement, but Patrick lobbed him a biscuit and left him to it. This shouldn't take long. It never did—although last time he'd felt almost sorry for the girl.

He shook his head to dismiss thoughts of last time from his mind, and headed for the lift. If this young woman thought she was going to be any luckier than the other one at slapping a paternity suit on him, she had another think coming. She'd have more luck with the lottery.

Patrick knew every woman he'd ever had an intimate relationship with—knew, loved and had remained friends with, furthermore—and no stranger was going to be able to hoodwink him into believing she'd had his child.

The lift doors slid open to reveal a young woman standing in the foyer with a screaming baby in her arms, and Patrick sighed inwardly. Was this a change of tack for the paternity punters? The last one had

5

also come armed with a screaming baby—to wear
him down, or tug his heartstrings?

Either way, it wouldn't work. It hadn't then, despite
her haunted eyes, and it wouldn't now. He was made
of sterner stuff.

'Mr Cameron?'

Well, that made a change. At least she wasn't calling him 'Patrick, darling'. He studied her for a moment, taking in the soft silver-blonde hair scooped
back into a ponytail, the clear, challenging eyes, the
too-wide mouth devoid of lipstick, the snug jacket
that showed off all too clearly her softly rounded
breasts and slender waist.

'Do I know you?' he asked, knowing full well that
he didn't—and for some reason regretting it. Stupid.
She was just another money-grubbing little liar.

She shifted the baby in her arms and the screaming
settled to a steady grizzle. Still rocking the infant
gently, she looked up at him with those clear grey
eyes that seemed to search into the deepest recesses
of his soul and find him wanting.

'No—no, you don't know me,' she said, and her
voice surprised him, low and mellow and distracting.
'You knew my sister, though—Amy Franklin. She
came to see you a few weeks ago with the baby.'

Ah. 'And I told her I'd never seen her before in
my life.'

'And I don't believe you,' she said softly, her eyes
accusing. 'I've got evidence—'

'Excuse me—is that your car?'

They both turned and looked at his receptionist,
Kate, who was pointing through the plate-glass doors.
Right outside, and causing a chaotic traffic jam, a

recovery truck was busily winching the remains of an ancient lipstick pink Citröen 2CV up into the air.

'Good grief,' he said weakly. It looked straight out of the 1960s hippy era. The tatty paintwork was smothered in huge psychedelic flowers, and as it was raised into the air the driver's door fell open and swung gently in the wind, releasing a trail of paper cups and sweet wrappers that rained down like confetti on the man beneath.

'How dare he?'

Thrusting the baby at him, the young woman turned on her heel and headed for the door, marching out with hands on hips and haranguing the unfortunate truck driver, arms flailing like a windmill as she gesticulated wildly at the dangling car.

'Oh, good grief,' Patrick said again, and, handing the screaming baby to his bewildered receptionist, he went outside, extracting his wallet and wondering what this little fiasco was going to cost him. Far more than the car was worth, without a shadow of a doubt, but any minute now she was going to land the poor guy one by accident and get herself arrested.

'I'm sorry, this young lady was just trying to gain access to our car park, but the car stalled and she couldn't get it going again. She'd just come in to call a recovery vehicle,' he ad-libbed, shouldering her none too gently out of the way and stepping between them. 'Perhaps I could reimburse you for your trouble…'

The man, burly and immovable, gave a dismissive snort. 'Sorry, mate. Rules is rules. I have to remove it, it's causing an obstruction. She'll have to collect it from the pound—not that it's worth it. I mean, what is it worth? A tenner? Fifty quid for the rarity value? Personally, if it wasn't for the fact that you have to pay the fine anyway, I wouldn't bother.'

Personally, nor would he, but, then, it wasn't his car—thank goodness!

'How much will that cost—this fine you're talking about?' she asked, elbowing herself back in front of him with a sharp dig in the ribs.

Not as sharp as her intake of breath, however, at the driver's reply. 'That's obscene!' she exclaimed, but he just shrugged.

'Should have used a meter, love. Wouldn't've happened then.'

'But it broke down!' she wailed, latching onto Patrick's fabrication like a real pro. 'You heard the man!'

'And pigs fly. Look, love, I can't winch it back down, I've done the paperwork and it's more than my—'

'Job's worth,' she and Patrick said in unison. The man's face hardened into implacability.

'It's all right for you lot that don't have to worry about money,' he said.

Patrick sighed and rammed a hand through his hair, but his companion didn't pause for breath.

'You lot?' she snapped. 'Don't bracket me with him! I worry about money constantly, and I haven't got any to throw around—hence my worthless car! You can't take it!' And then, with a masterly touch of pathos, she added, 'Besides, it's got all the baby's things in it—I need them! She's hungry.'

'Baby? What baby?' The man eyed the car wor-

riedly, and Patrick could almost hear her mind working, but then she took pity on him.

'Don't worry, I had the baby with me—but all her
things are still in the car, you can't take them away,
I need to feed her.'

The driver sighed, clearly relieved that he wasn't
dangling a tiny baby in the car above their heads, and
winched it back down with a resigned shake of his
head. 'Look, lady, I shouldn't do this, but I'll give
you a minute to get what you want from it before I
take it away.'

'But I want my car.'

'Just do what he says,' Patrick advised her softly,
eyeing the huge traffic jam that was building up behind the truck. 'You can always get the car later.'

'If I can find the money, you mean,' she muttered.
'And anyway, how am I supposed to get the baby
home without a car?'

Patrick's heart sank. Here we go, he thought, feeling the contents of his wallet slipping further out of
his grasp with every second. 'Don't worry about that
now. Just get your stuff.'

Just? Huh!

Five minutes later, the elegant marbled foyer of his
empire was littered with a pile of junk which in total
was probably worth less than the loose change in his
pocket, and the Franklin girl was standing in the doorway with a ticket in her hand, staring dispiritedly after
her vanishing car.

In the background the baby was still grizzling, and
Patrick looked wonderingly at the pile of junk at his
feet. Ancient trainers, a jumper that had seen better
days, a ratty old blanket, half a dozen paperbacks, a

briefcase—curiously decent and quite incongruous—
and a whole plethora of baby stuff in varying stages
of decay. He met his receptionist's bewildered eyes,
rammed his hand through his hair again in disbelief
and sighed shortly.

'Now what?' he said, half to himself, half to Kate.

'I'll get a box,' she said hastily, recovering her
composure, and thrusting the baby back into his arms
she abandoned him with it and disappeared.

Patrick looked down into the baby's miserable,
screwed-up little face and felt a surge of compassion.
Whatever was going on, this poor little mite was innocent, and, judging by the feel of it, she needed a
dry nappy and probably a decent meal.

'Let me have her,' the young woman said, and took
the baby, cradling it against her shoulder and comforting it as if she'd been doing it all her life.

'All right, sweetheart. It's all right, Jess,' she
crooned, but Patrick wondered if it really was or if
they were just empty promises.

No. Dammit, he wouldn't fall for it.

The ticket the truck driver had given her had fallen
from her fingers, drifting to the floor, and he picked
it up and shoved it in his pocket. He'd deal with it
later.

Kate came back with a couple of cardboard boxes
and started packing the junk into them, and he
crouched down beside her to help, just as the baby
started to wail again in earnest.

Her hands stilled and she looked up at the baby
with sympathy in her eyes.

'I'll deal with this lot,' she said softly. 'Why don't
you take Miss Franklin up to your apartment so she

can see to the baby?' she suggested, and with a resigned sigh he nodded and held out his hand to usher
the young woman towards the lift.

'I'll need the baby seat and that blue bag,' she said,
and he scooped them up and led her to the lift, glancing over his shoulder at Kate still crouched on the
floor.

'Thanks, Kate. I owe you,' he said softly. 'Can you
ask Sally to deal with my calls?'

She nodded, and he turned his attention back to the
more pressing problem in front of him.

'Come on, let's get the baby sorted out and then
we can talk,' he said, reminding himself firmly that
she was just a blackmailer, even if she did have a
figure to die for and the most beautiful voice he'd
ever heard in his life...

'Right, now she's asleep, let's sort this out,' Patrick
said firmly, determined to take control of a situation
that showed every sign of disintegrating into chaos.
'As I said before, I don't know your sister. I told her
that when she came to see me, and I can't imagine
why she's sent you now, because nothing's happened
since I saw her to change anything.'

She looked up at him, those extraordinary grey
eyes filled with silent accusation. 'On the contrary,'
she said. 'Everything's changed, because three days
after she came to see you, my sister died of an overdose, and I'm holding you responsible—for that, and
for your child—so, you see, *everything* has changed.'

Patrick felt shock drain the colour from his face.
That poor girl, so tightly strung, her eyes haunted and
despairing, was dead, and her sister was here to take

up the cudgels on her behalf. No wonder she was so determined, but despite her assertions nothing had really altered, at least not as far as he was concerned.

The baby wasn't his, and never would be, and there was nothing he'd said or done that made him in any way responsible for the tragic death of that baby's mother, however regrettable.

'I'm sorry about your sister,' he said, gentling his voice but with no loss of resolve. 'If I could help you, I would, but it really isn't anything to do with me.'

'Nice try, but it won't work,' she said flatly. 'I've got the photographs.'

His heart sank. 'Photographs?' he asked. She'd been saying something downstairs about evidence just as the car thing had intruded, but it hadn't really registered. Oh, hell…

'Yes, photographs. Intimate photographs—if you know what I mean.'

He did, only too well, and he winced inwardly, even though he knew they must be fake like all the others. 'Anybody can achieve that these days with a digital camera and a bit of chicanery,' he argued, but she wasn't finished.

'Photographs taken in your apartment here? On that sofa, in front of the window? In the bedroom where I changed the baby's nappy? On your roof garden? Where and how would she have got those? Someone on your staff? Come on, Mr Cameron, you can't get out of it. All it will take is a DNA test to prove it, and if you won't submit to it willingly, I'll just have to take you to court, and, believe me, I fully intend to win.'

He didn't doubt it for a moment.

'Get the baby tested, by all means,' he agreed willingly. 'My DNA has already been tested for another of these bogus claims, and I can assure you it won't match this baby's any more than it's matched any other. Your sister isn't the first young woman to try this, and unfortunately I don't suppose she'll be the last. I'll see if I can find the information and send it on to you.'

'You do that. I'll give you a week, and then I'm taking action—starting with sending the photographs to the press.' She delved into the blue bag that seemed to contain her entire life's resources, and produced a slightly dog-eared card that she thrust at him.

'Here. If you don't contact me by next Monday morning, you'll be hearing from my solicitor and the tabloids, probably simultaneously. Now perhaps you'll be good enough to call me a taxi. I'll arrange to have my other things collected in the next few days.'

On the point of telling her to take a hike, he caught sight of the sleeping baby and his irritation evaporated.

Poor little scrap. She didn't deserve this, and it was a long way to—he glanced down at the card.

Suffolk. Ms Claire Franklin, Lower Valley Farm, Strugglers Lane, Tuddingfield, Suffolk. Nice address, but she didn't look like a farmer. A farm worker? Lodger? Nanny? Nothing too highly paid, judging by the car and her remarks about money.

Claire. He savoured it on his tongue. Interesting, how an ordinary name had suddenly become somehow musical.

'How are you going to get home?' he asked her,

refocusing. 'Have you got enough money for the train?'

The confidence in her eyes faltered for a moment, then firmed again. 'I'll manage.'

He sighed, opened his wallet and pulled out several notes. 'Here—that should be enough to get you and your things home in a minicab.'

She eyed the cash and her eyebrows arched eloquently. 'You must have a hell of a guilty conscience, Mr Cameron.'

He hung onto his temper with difficulty. 'On the contrary, Miss Franklin, I have a perfectly clean conscience—and I want it to stay that way. Now, are you going to take the money, or are you going to be stubborn and independent and make the baby suffer all the way home on the tube and the train?'

For a moment she hesitated, then she took it with a curt nod and tucked it into the bottomless blue bag. 'I'll pay you back,' she said, and something in her voice made him believe her against all the odds.

Drawing her dignity around her like a cloak, she picked up the carrier with the baby in it, slung the blue bag over her shoulder and stood patiently waiting.

'I'll call the cab,' he said, a trifle curtly because he didn't want to admire her for anything. Picking up the phone, he asked Kate to order a minicab. 'On second thoughts,' he added to his beleaguered receptionist, 'get George if he's free. Usual arrangement.'

He cradled the phone, then escorted his visitor and her now sleeping charge to the lift. 'I've ordered a minicab. He'll take your things, as well, so you won't have to get them picked up.' He stuck out his hand. 'Goodbye, Miss Franklin.'

She took it almost graciously, her palm cool, her grip firm and capable, and inclined her head. 'Goodbye,' she murmured, but he had a feeling she wasn't finished, and he was right. She carried the baby into the lift, turned and met his eyes with a steady look that held the promise of another skirmish to come. 'I mean it,' she said before the doors sighed shut. 'One week, and then all hell breaks loose.'

He didn't doubt it for a moment.

He held that clear grey gaze until the doors interrupted it, and then turned away with a shrug. Let her do her worst. There was no way the child was his, cute though she might have been, regardless of some bogus photographic evidence.

Of course, if Will had still been alive he would have blamed him. It wouldn't have been the first time his brother had got him in a scrape, by a country mile, and it was just the sort of damn fool thing he might have done, Patrick thought with a fondness touched with irony.

He could just imagine him now, pretending to be his richer and more successful twin, capitalising on his brother's success without bothering to earn the right to it. Had he entertained women here, told them his name was Patrick?

Surely he would have outgrown that kind of prank? They'd often pretended to be each other, with no thought of the consequences, driving their teachers and then later on their girlfriends mad, but then they'd grown up.

Or he had.

Will, on the other hand, had never considered the consequences of his actions—like getting the dog, for instance. It was just like Will to take pity on the poor, scruffy little black bundle he'd been and then all but abandon him when the responsibility for looking after a lively puppy got too irksome.

If it hadn't been for Patrick, Dog would have ended up being rehomed. Instead, he'd found a master who struggled in the midst of the city to find time to exercise his intelligent mind and his restless body, and who took his care seriously.

Even if he hadn't ever given him a proper name!

He summoned the lift, and as the doors opened he saw a small pink rabbit lying on the floor.

The baby's. It must have fallen out of the little baby seat. Damn. He'd get Sally, his long-suffering PA, to send it—or, better still, Kate. She seemed to have a soft spot for the child and Sally would ask him endless questions.

He went into his office, the pink rabbit in his hand, and dropped it in his desk drawer just as Sally came in.

'Everything OK?'

She tried hard to keep the curiosity out of her voice, but failed dismally. Dog, on the other hand, greeted him with cheerful and unquestioning enthusiasm, and seemed a much safer bet. He wasn't going to ask awkward questions about his visitor!

'Fine,' he lied. 'I'm going to take Dog in the park,' he added hastily as she started to open her mouth again, and picked up the dog lead. 'Hold my calls.'

'Still?' Sally said, but he pretended not to hear her. He went down to the now tidy foyer, Dog bouncing excitedly at his heels, and ignored Kate's frantic gestures as she dealt with a phone call that was obviously for him.

The park beckoned—the park, and peace and quiet, time to think, because a troubling thought was beginning to take shape in the back of his mind.

It was early April—and Will had been dead a little over a year. If that baby was more than four months old, it could have been his.

And—because they were identical twins—the DNA would match.

'No charge,' the minicab driver said. 'It's on Mr Cameron.'

'Oh.' Claire blinked, puzzled. 'Are you sure?'

'Quite sure. That's what Kate said when she called me. Anyway, I'm on a retainer. I'll just bill them.'

'But he gave me money.'

George laughed, not unkindly. 'Of course, if I was a real rogue, I'd take that off you, love, but I'm not, so don't argue, there's a good girl. Just say "Thank you very much," and be grateful. He can afford it.'

She opened her mouth, shut it again, then opened it and said, 'Thank you very much.'

Eyes twinkling, he carried her miscellaneous possessions into the cottage, wiggled his fingers at the baby and left her to her confusion.

She could feel the cash burning a hole in the side of the blue bag. She'd give it back to Cameron, of course, and repay the cost of the minicab—once she'd earned it, and the money to get her car out of the pound.

Huh! That was the rub, she thought as she fed the

grizzly, hungry baby and bathed her ready for bed. How on earth was she going to earn it? She couldn't afford to pay the phone bill, and without a phone she couldn't get work, at least not the sort of freelance stuff she did.

The irony of it was that Patrick Cameron was an architect, and there was probably room in his organisation for another draughtsperson, doing some of the donkey-work on the less important contracts. Maybe that was it. Maybe she should ask him for work, so she could support the baby and herself and be independent?

Independent? She snorted. She'd be more dependent on him than ever like that, and it wasn't what she wanted. Nor did she want him taking any interest in the baby. Not that it seemed likely, because he certainly hadn't shown any interest in her today!

No. All she wanted—needed—from him was enough money to pay for child care so she could concentrate on her job for a few hours a day and work herself out of this financial hole. Earn enough money, perhaps, to fund a bank loan to convert the barn and turn it into a studio so she could run the painting holidays she'd dreamed of.

She'd got it all worked out. She could live upstairs, with a farmhouse kitchen downstairs big enough to do all the catering, and she'd have a huge studio at one end, and the cottage could be the guest accommodation. Then she'd be able to earn money, indulge her creative streak *and* look after the baby, all at the same time.

Oh, yes. She'd thought it all through—all except how to pay for it, but Patrick Cameron had plenty of money, and giving his baby a future was little enough to ask of him under the circumstances.

And in less than a week she'd see him again, she was sure of it. He couldn't afford all the mud-slinging the tabloids would get up to, not in his position, so he'd have to co-operate to a certain extent. He couldn't continue to deny knowing Amy once he'd seen the photographs, and he'd have to start playing ball.

First off was the DNA check, of course, and then there would be no question about it.

It would be interesting to see how he dealt with that, she thought. In so many ways he'd been a real gentleman, but his stubborn refusal to acknowledge his relationship with Amy gave the lie to that. So which was the real Patrick Cameron? Her curiosity was piqued, and she realised with a shock that she was looking forward to seeing him again.

Not that she was interested in him in any personal way—of course not. He'd been Amy's lover, and that made him strictly off limits. Besides, that dark hair, unruly even though it was short, and those curious green-grey eyes that should have been soft and yet were strangely piercing—they didn't appeal to her in the least, except academically, because he was Jess's father.

And that body—not that she'd seen much of it, of course, except in the photos which she'd been reluctant to study in any detail.

Liar!

Claire ignored her honest streak in favour of self-delusion. Much more comfortable, because acknowledging her interest in a man rich enough to buy her out hundreds of times over, a man whose work she respected and admired, a man who, if she allowed herself to be honest for once, was the most attractive man she'd seen in years—actually, make that two and a half decades—acknowledging her interest in him would only underline just how fruitless that interest would be.

She was nobody. Nothing. Just a frustrated interior designer and graphic artist making a tenuous living freelancing at her drawing board, working for anyone who needed her draughtsmanship and visualising skills, with no future, no hope of career advancement, no pension prospects.

She laughed silently. Pension prospects? She was twenty-six—but suddenly, since she'd become responsible for this little scrap, that seemed to matter.

And without Auntie Meg's unexpectedly generous bequest, they'd be homeless as well.

'Oh, Auntie Meg, I wish I knew what to do,' she sighed, staring out of the window at the dark shape of the barn just fifty or so paces away. She could sell it, of course, but that would mean the end of her dream.

Oh, well. Maybe Patrick Cameron would prove himself to be a guardian angel in disguise. She could only wait and hope.

Patrick looked at the letter from the DNA lab that had performed the last paternity test for him a year ago— a test that had proved unnecessary, because the woman had broken down in the end and confessed she'd just wanted to get some money.

Nevertheless, the test had been done, and, in case

it should happen again, the lab had agreed to keep his profile on record, the details of the individual barcode that identified each and every one of his cells as his and his alone.

He sighed. Until last year, he couldn't have said that, but now Will was gone.

His clone, Will used to joke, but last year he'd been serious. It had been just before he'd gone away, and he'd said, very quietly and with some considerable dignity, that it was time to move on and stop living in his brother's shadow.

'It's as if I'm a clone of you, and they left some vital nutrient out of the Petri dish—that extra *je ne sais quoi*. Still, without you standing beside me, who would ever know? And not even you, dear bro, casts a shadow long enough to reach Australia.'

And his smile had been wry and sad, and Patrick had hugged him hard.

'Don't be a fool,' he'd said, choked, but Will had meant every word of it. He'd gone to Australia, bent on making himself a new life, and two weeks later he'd been dead, drowned in a stupid accident with a surfboard.

And now it seemed he might have had a child.

Patrick dragged in a deep breath and filed the information in its envelope, then tucked it into his jacket pocket. The car—the psychedelic 2CV—was sitting in the underground car park beneath the building, and it was time to go.

As he strapped Dog into his harness and fastened him to the front seat belt, he wondered if the car would make it. By the time he reached the M11, he was almost certain that it wouldn't. Despite its service, it ran like a pig, it was hideously noisy and uncomfortable, not to mention terrifyingly vulnerable amongst the heavy lorries, and he decided the truck driver who'd winched it away had had excellent judgement.

Paying her fine was just doing the decent thing. Bothering to have the damn car serviced and valeted and returning it to her, on the other hand, seemed a ludicrous waste of money, because he was convinced it was destined for the crusher.

Still, maybe she'd be grateful. She'd seemed sorry enough to see it go—though why he wanted her gratitude he couldn't begin to imagine. He certainly wasn't sure he wanted it enough to risk his life in this bit of pink tin foil she called a car!

On second thoughts, tin foil might be better—it didn't rust. This clapped-out old heap might be a classic, but it must be thirty years old if it was a day, and it was well and truly past its sell-by date. Hell, it was at least as old as him, and considerably older than Claire Franklin.

Claire.

He rolled it round his tongue, savouring the shape of the word, remembering her eyes, her mouth, that soft, lush figure, the delicate fragrance that had still been lingering in the air when he'd gone back up to his apartment with Dog at the end of the day.

Was it really only two days ago? It seemed like a lifetime.

He could feel the little bulge of the pink rabbit in his pocket, and he wondered if the baby had missed it. Jess, she was called. Jessica? Jessamy? Jessamine?

The realisation that he was looking forward to seeing her again shocked him. He hated babies! Smelly, leaky little things—but this one could be Will's, his last gift to the world, and for that reason alone he wanted to see her again.

The fact that she came with a rather attractive young aunt attached was nothing at all to do with it!

CHAPTER TWO

CLAIRE heard the car coming long before it pulled up on her drive.

Of course, if things had been going right, she wouldn't have heard it at all, but she'd hit something in the long grass in the meadow behind the barn and the cutting deck on the little tractor mower had collapsed, and so it was silenced.

Silenced and broken, yet another thing in her life that was going wrong.

Hot and cross from struggling about underneath the mower to try and see what had happened, she rolled over and stared up—and up. Up endlessly long legs clad in immaculately cut trousers, up past a sand-washed silk shirt in a lovely soft green-grey the colour of his eyes, up to a face she hadn't expected to see again quite so soon.

Great. Just when she was looking her dignified best!

'Mr Cameron.'

'Ms Franklin.'

She scrambled to her feet, taking advantage of his outstretched hand to haul herself up, and gave her back a cursory swipe to dislodge some of the chopped grass that was no doubt sticking to it like confetti.

There on her drive again, like a bad penny, was Amy's car come back to haunt her—and haunt Patrick Cameron, if the look on his face was anything to go by. Oops. He didn't look as if he'd enjoyed his journey.

'Where's the baby?' he asked without preamble, and she felt the hairs on the back of her neck bristle. Just like the dog's—only the useless thing was sleeping inside with Jess, and ignoring her duty with not a bristle in sight.

'She's asleep. Why?'

He shrugged, but there was nothing casual about his incisive tone. 'Just wondered. I mean, you're out here—who's looking after her?'

'I am,' she retorted, the irritation spreading from the back of her neck to permeate her voice. 'I'm hardly far away. Do you have a problem with that?'

'I just expected you to be right beside her, within earshot.'

'I am right beside her. She's in the house, about thirty yards away, and the dog's with her.'

Or she had been until that moment. Pepper, belatedly cottoning on to the arrival of their visitor, came barrelling out of the back door, barking furiously.

'It's OK, Pepper,' she said, and the lurcher skidded to a halt, lifted her head and then ran to the car, jumping up and scrabbling at the door.

'Ah. Dog,' he said, and Claire felt her eyebrows shoot up.

'Dog?'

He gave a slight, humourless smile. 'In the car. My dog. Well, my brother's dog, actually. It was as far as we ever got with naming him. Will Pepper be OK if I let him out?'

'*She'll* be fine, she loves other dogs. She's too

trusting. Is *he* OK, though? I don't need a vet bill.' To add to all the other bills on her list.

'He's fine. We meet other dogs in the park all the time.'

He went over to the car and released the dog called Dog, and he and Pepper sniffed round each other and wagged cautiously.

Claire, used to Pepper with her shaggy blonde coat and little neat ears, stared at Dog in amazement. Black, with a white splash on his chest, and smaller than Pepper, he had the biggest ears she'd ever seen except on a German shepherd, and his body couldn't seem to decide if it was terrier, Labrador or collie.

Pepper didn't seem to care, however. She was just enjoying the attention and his lineage was obviously the last thing on her mind.

'So much more direct than people,' his owner said, watching them circle with their noses up each other's bottoms, and she laughed, surprised by the dry flash of humour.

'I think I'll settle for being human.'

His smile was slow and lazy, and crinkled his eyes. It crinkled her stomach, too, and she felt as if she'd been punched by the force of that latent sexual charm. Good grief! No wonder Amy had fallen for him.

Amy. That's what this was all about, she reminded herself before she could get totally sidetracked by his charm. Amy.

She brushed her hands together and looked up at him again. 'Um—you brought the car. Thank you. What do I owe you?'

'Owe me?' he said, sounding surprised. 'You don't owe me anything. I had to get here somehow.'

'And getting that heap out of the pound and driving here in it was your preferred choice of transport? Give me a break!'

He chuckled softly. 'OK. I'll admit I'm glad I don't have to drive it back, but it made it, which I have to say surprised me.'

It surprised Claire, too, but she wasn't telling him that! It would no doubt collapse on her the very next time she took it out—just like the mower and the strimmer and everything else.

'Having problems?' he asked, jerking his head towards the mower, and she rolled her eyes and sighed.

'You don't want to know. I hit something, and the cutting deck's dangling now. Goodness knows what I've broken. I'll get John to look at it.'

'John?'

'A mechanic-cum-miracle-worker. He keeps my bits and pieces going.' When I can afford to pay him, she added to herself silently. 'By the way, George wouldn't take any money from me on Monday for bringing me back, so I owe you for that, too, and the cash you gave me.'

He shrugged. 'I'll let you pay it back in kind. I didn't dare stop the car in case it wouldn't start again, and it's been a long morning. I reckon a cup of coffee should settle the score.'

'That's a very expensive cup of coffee,' she told him, 'and anyway, you're in luck because I haven't got any. I've only got tea, but no milk, so you'll have to let me pay you back.'

'Tea will be fine,' he said, cutting her off. 'Shall we?'

He held out a hand, gesturing for her to lead the

way, and with a shrug of defeat she took him into the house through the boot room—as untidy and scruffy as ever—and through to the kitchen, where Jess was beginning to stir in the pram. 'Have a seat,' she said, pushing the cat off the only decent chair, and he sat and looked around curiously.

'What a lovely kitchen,' he said, and she nearly choked. It was ancient, the cupboards were all chipped and scratched, and it needed a match taking to it—or at the very least a bucket of hot, soapy water followed by a paintbrush.

'I thought you were an architect,' she said with a thread of sarcasm, and he chuckled that lovely, deep, sexy chuckle again.

'I am. I spend my life specifying high-tech glass and stainless-steel kitchens, somewhere between an operating theatre and the control room of a spacecraft, and you daren't touch them for fear of leaving a fingerprint. You could come in here with a muddy dog and feel at home—it reminds me of my childhood, visiting my grandmother. Homely. Restful. Soothing.'

She looked around her and saw it with his eyes— saw the old black Aga that she couldn't afford to run, and the deep butler's sink with its mahogany draining board, the painted solid timber cupboards—all the things that everyone wanted, by all accounts, only new, of course, and made to look old. Distressed. Claire nearly laughed aloud. It was certainly distressed!

Still, the blue and white Cornishware china on the dresser shelves was highly collectable now, and the brightly coloured mugs hanging on the hooks above the kettle brought a vivid splash of colour to the room. And through the gap in the hedge opposite the kitchen window, you could see across the meadow and right down the valley to the church in the distance.

Yes, it had charm, and she loved it—which was just as well, because she was no more likely to be able to fly than refit it. She'd been working her way steadily through the house until Amy had died and she'd had to give up her job. Now there was a huge list of essentials ahead of the kitchen, and the mower was tacked right onto the top as of today. Really, April was not a good time for the darned thing to fall apart.

'How strong do you like your tea?' she asked, dropping a teabag in a mug and pouring on the water.

'Not very. Have you got lemon? No, forget it.'

She snorted. 'I don't have it anyway. I'm sorry, you're not getting a very good return on your investment here, are you?'

'That's not why I'm here.'

No, it wasn't. He was here because she'd given him very little choice, and all these smiling pleasantries were just exactly that. Any second now, she guessed, the gloves would be off.

She fished the teabag out of his mug, dunked it up and down in her own and wished, for the hundredth time that day, that she'd got milk. She'd tried some of Jess's formula in it, but it hadn't been the same, and, anyway, she was running out of that, too.

She turned to face him, mugs in hand. 'So, where do you want to start?' she asked, taking the bull by the horns.

'I'd like to see those photographs.'

'Ah.'

She set the mugs down in front of him and turned away. She hated looking at the photos. They weren't sordid, thank God, but they were intimate—hugely intimate, emotionally revealing. Things no one should see except the participants—things Amy should have taken with her to the grave, locked up in her heart.

Still, he'd been there, so it hardly mattered if he saw them, did it? She didn't have to look again and upset herself with the painful images of her sister with this undeniably attractive man.

She went to the study and pulled out the packet of photos from the bottom drawer, and gave them to him.

'Here.'

He took them, opened the envelope and eased them out, a strange expression on his face. Cradling her tea, she watched him as he sifted through them slowly, over and over again.

Then, without a word, he put them away in the envelope and looked up at her, his eyes curiously sad.

'You'd better sit down,' he said, and she sat, wondering what it was that had put that look on his face. Had he loved Amy? Was that it?

It wasn't, and if she'd had a lifetime, she couldn't have guessed what was coming next.

'The man in those photographs isn't me,' he said. 'It's my twin brother.'

She stared at him blankly, then laughed. 'Oh, very good. How clever—except, of course, that Amy called you Patrick. And now you're going to tell me he was also called Patrick?'

Patrick—this one—shook his head. 'His name was

Will. He sometimes used to pretend to be me—a sort of prank we used to play as kids, except he apparently never grew out of it. He died a year ago, in Australia.'

'Died?' she echoed, and her hopes crumbled to dust. There was no way he'd pay for his brother's child, and so she'd have to sell their home and move, or at least sell the barn, and Amy's debts would eat up so much of that.

'Tell me—what date were these taken?'

'It's on the back of the envelope,' she said woodenly. 'March, I believe.'

He turned the packet over, and nodded. 'That fits. I wondered if it would. I was away—in Japan, on a contract. Will was using my flat for a week—and apparently masquerading as me. It must have been then. So, tell me, when was the baby born?'

'Two weeks before Christmas.'

He nodded, then he turned his head slightly and studied Jess in the pram.

'She doesn't look like him.'

'She's very like Amy.'

He nodded again, and let out a quiet sigh. 'I wish she'd looked more like him—a sort of reminder. That would have been nice.'

'You could always look in the mirror,' she said, and his mouth kicked up in a sad smile.

'Not quite the same. Still.'

He stood up. 'I've got something for you—I'll just get my jacket,' he said, and went out to the car.

She followed him, propping herself up in the doorway and watching as his long legs ate up the path. The dogs were playing now, having a tug of war with one of Pepper's knotted bones, and he paused to ruffle their coats.

They wagged at him and carried on, growling and pretending to be fierce, and after one last pat he straightened up, pulled open her car door and reached in for his jacket.

As he closed the door, it bounced open again, as she'd known it would.

'It does that,' she told him, going over to yank the handle and bang the door. 'It's a knack you have to acquire.'

He flinched and muttered something along the lines of not in this lifetime, and she stifled a laugh. Poor baby, he'd really had to slum it! Oh, well, it would do him good—let him see what she was up against. She could do with all the sympathy she could get, the way things were panning out.

They walked back to the house, past the broken little tractor with its drooping cutting deck, past the barn with its door hanging half-open on rusty hinges to reveal the strimmer that had gone on strike over the winter and steadfastly refused to start.

She wondered what else could go wrong, and decided she didn't want to think about it. She had more than enough to think about—like the fact that it seemed he wasn't Jess's father after all, although proving it could be tricky, because, of course, the DNA would match if he and his brother were identical twins. If that really was his brother in the photos and not him, then they were like two peas in a pod.

And, of course, because of that it would be the easiest thing in the world for him to pass off his child as his brother's, now that Will and Amy weren't there

to argue the case. It would absolve him of all responsibility. How convenient.

And yet he didn't seem dishonest.

She gave a silent snort. Like she was such a good
judge of character! She'd let Amy hoodwink her for
years, bleeding her dry in one way and another and
now leaving her with Jess to bring up, safe in the
knowledge that, of course, she, Claire, the sensible
one, would do the right thing.

So he could be a liar and a smooth talker, quite
easily, and how on earth would she know?

Oh, rats. It was too confusing, too involved, too
difficult to deal with. She didn't want to doubt him,
but now it was there in the back of her consciousness,
this insidious little doubt, niggling away and destroying her peace of mind.

Not that she had much of that these days.

'Here,' he said, pulling an envelope out of his
jacket pocket and handing it to her as they went back
into the kitchen. She eyed it warily.

A letter from a solicitor threatening her with legal
action if she revealed the photos? A cheque—no, she
didn't get that lucky.

'It's the information about the DNA lab,' he told
her, putting her out of her suspense and puncturing
the last little bubble of hope. 'They've got my profile
on record. The instructions are all in there. You just
have to take the baby to the GP for a cheek swab,
and get it sent off to them with the enclosed covering
letter and the cheque that's in there, and then they run
the test. It should match if she's Will's daughter—
and that's definitely Will in the photos.'

'How do I know that?' she asked.

His brow pleated. 'How do you know? Because we're identical.'

'Exactly. So how do I know it isn't you?'

He stared at her, clearly taken aback. 'Me? I've told you, I was out of the country.'

'I've only got your word for that.'

'It's usually good enough,' he said drily, and if she hadn't known better, she would have said he sounded hurt. Then he went on, 'Anyway, it's easy. Apart from the passport stamps and minutes of the meetings I attended in Japan, I haven't had my appendix out—unlike Will. And there's a scar in the photos.'

And before she had a chance to say anything, before she could challenge him or express her scepticism, he tugged his shirt out of his trousers, hitched a thumb in the waistband and pushed it down, revealing a taut, board-flat abdomen without so much as a crease in it. 'See? No scar.'

Her shoulders dropped. Well, at least she knew he was telling the truth. There was no way a surgeon's knife had ever scored that skin. She dragged her eyes away from the line of dark hair that arrowed down under that dangerously low waistband, and looked back up at him.

'OK, so it isn't you in the photos,' she agreed.

'No—but it might as well be,' he said quietly. 'If the baby is Will's, then she'd be as closely related to me as she would be if she were my own, and I would feel the same obligation towards her. I never thought I would, but it seems blood *is* thicker than water, after all, and if she's Will's child, then in his absence she's mine, and I'll do what's right by her.'

He ground to a halt, the long speech seeming to

open up more than he'd intended to reveal, and he firmed his lips together and looked away—at Jess, awake now and waving her arms and legs happily in the pram.

'You don't have to explain that to me,' she reminded him. 'Why do you think I'm looking after Jess instead of handing her over to Social Services for adoption?'

He nodded slowly. 'Yes, of course you understand. You're in the same boat. Lord, what a coil.'

His jacket was hanging over the back of his chair, and she could just see one pink ear sticking up against the rumpled grey-green linen.

She inclined her head towards it and smiled, deliberately lightening the tone. 'So, Mr Cameron—is that a rabbit in your pocket, or are you pleased to see me?'

For a second of startled silence she wondered if she'd gone too far, but then he gave a soft huff of laughter and pulled it out.

'I'd forgotten all about it. I found it in the lift. I didn't know if she'd miss it—if she was old enough yet to have fixated on it. I gather babies can be funny like that.'

'Not this young, not at four months, but she does like it. Thank you.'

He handed it to her and their fingers brushed, sending sparks up her arm. She snatched her hand away, feeling a little silly, and gave the rabbit to Jess, who grabbed it and stuffed one ear in her mouth.

'Instant hit,' she said with a smile, and scooped the baby up. 'Here, it's time to get to know her. Jess, this is your Uncle Patrick. Say hello.'

She dumped Jess on his lap, and for the first few seconds he looked dumbstruck and awkward.

'She won't break, you know,' she told him, taking pity on him after a minute, and he shot her a slightly desperate smile.

'Do I have to support her head?' he asked. 'It's the only thing I can remember.'

'No, she's fine now. She can stand up if you hold her, and jump on your lap, but she shouldn't do it for too long.'

'How on earth do I know what's too long?' he asked with a thread of panic, and she laughed.

'Don't worry, she's not made of glass. She's just a baby. Don't drop her on her head and she'll be fine. They're tough as old boots.'

She headed for the door, needing a moment to herself to let it all sink in, and his eyes tracked her like a laser.

'Where are you going?' he asked, his voice rising slightly with alarm.

'The loo. You got a problem with that?'

He relaxed visibly. 'Um—no. That's fine. I just thought—'

'I was going out? One step at a time, cowboy,' she said with a smile, and left him to it.

'Well, little Jess. So you're Will's baby,' he said softly, staring into her solemn brown eyes. 'And like the lady said, I'm your Uncle Patrick. What do you think of that?'

Not much, from the expression on her face. Her lip wobbled, and instinctively he jostled her gently on his knee and smiled at her.

'Hey, hey, I'm not so bad. I may not know anything about babies, but we can learn together. I don't
suppose you know too much about architects or un-
cles, either, but you'll learn, just like I will about
babies. Oh, yes, you will.'

He nodded at her, and she blinked, so he did it
again, his smile widening, and all of a sudden her
face transformed. Her eyes creased up, her mouth
opened to reveal one tiny white tooth in a gummy
smile, and she giggled.

Patrick swallowed. There was a lump the size of a
tennis ball lodged in his throat, and he had to blink
hard to keep her in focus.

'So you think I'm funny, do you?' he said, his
voice a little scratchy, and she giggled again, one arm
flailing out to grab at his nose.

'Ouch! Sharp nails!' he chided gently, easing her
surprisingly strong little fingers off while he still had
skin. Instead of his nose, she fastened her hand on his
finger and clung, pulling it to her mouth and gnawing
it.

'I'm not sure that's clean enough to chew,' he said
doubtfully, but Claire came back into the room at that
moment and stood right beside him—close enough
for him to smell the new-mown grass that clung to
her—and suddenly the germs didn't seem to matter.

Instead, the sharp, sweet scent of grass teased his
senses, heady as an aphrodisiac, and he had to force
himself to concentrate on her words.

'Don't worry,' she was saying, 'children shouldn't
be brought up in a sterile environment, it's bad for
them. I'm sure your fingers aren't that grubby.'

'Doggy, probably,' he said, struggling for common sense.

'She'll live. Did I hear her laughing?'

He looked up at her, suddenly self-conscious. Had she heard him making a fool of himself with her?

'She giggled,' he said, still slightly awestruck by that manifestation of personality in someone so very young, and Claire smiled.

'Oh, she does. The sillier you make yourself, the more she likes it. I think it appeals to her sense of humour, watching adults turn themselves into fruit-cakes on her behalf.'

Fruitcakes, indeed! So she *had* heard. Oh, well, it might be a point in his favour, and he had a feeling he was going to need all the Brownie points he could get!

I'll still want to be involved in her upbringing, to see her first steps, to hear her first words.

The words had been going round and round in Claire's head since Patrick had spoken them, and, watching him with the baby now, she still had no clear idea what that implied. What did 'involved' mean, exactly? He wanted to see videos of her from time to time? Visit her occasionally?

Or go for custody?

As the thought popped into her mind, she felt the chill of fear run through her, and her heart started to pump.

Surely not. He couldn't. Anyway, he wouldn't win, he was a man.

And his DNA was an exact match with Will's.

What if he said it *was* him, after all? What if he claimed she was his baby, and not his brother's?

Her eyes went to the photos, the only proof she had that the man who had fathered her sister's baby had been the one with the appendix scar. There were no negatives, and no other copies. If the photos were to fall into the wrong hands...

'Claire, what's wrong?'

She jumped, swivelling her eyes from the photos to him, and met his clear, steady green-grey gaze.

'You said you wanted to be involved in her up-bringing,' she said, her voice a little taut.

'That's right. I do.'

'How involved? What exactly did you mean?' she asked, unable to prevaricate. She'd always been direct, always gone for the jugular. If he planned to take the baby from her, she needed to know.

'I don't know,' he said, and she could see the confusion and honesty in his eyes. 'I suppose it means I want to see her as often as possible, but she lives here with you, and I live and work in London. That's not really very straightforward.'

'You can visit her whenever you want,' she said, trying to make it easy so he wouldn't try and take her from him. 'You can stay here—there's room. I won't try and stop you seeing her.'

He cocked his head on one side and regarded her keenly. 'You think I'm going to go for custody, don't you?' he said, his voice deceptively soft, and she swallowed and looked away.

'I don't know. I just know I can't lose her. She's all I've got of my sister.'

She broke off, the wound still too raw, and he tsked softly.

'Silly girl, I'm not going to take her from you. How can I? I'm not married, I live in a flat at the top of my office block with a tiny roof garden and a hell of a long drop to the street below. You're a woman, you've cared for her since she was born, you live in the country in a totally safe setting. What judge in their right mind would rule in my favour?'

She closed her eyes briefly and nodded. 'I suppose so. I was just...'

'Panicking?' he finished for her, his voice gentle. 'Don't. On the other hand, don't expect it all your own way. My parents will want to be involved in her life as well, and they'll want to have her to stay—there'll be birthdays and Christmases and all sorts.'

Claire nodded again. He was right, it wouldn't be easy, but if they were able to work together, perhaps they could dream up a solution that would help them all.

'First things first, though,' he said, his mouth kicking up in a wry grin. 'There's a strange smell coming from this little bundle of laughs, and I think she needs her auntie.'

I want to be involved with her upbringing.

Claire smiled, some of the tension easing away. 'Time for your first nappy-changing lesson, then,' she said, and stood up. 'Come on.'

'But—I can't!'

'Oh, you can. You'll be amazed what you can do. And once she's washed and changed, it'll be time for her next feed—and then, of course, there'll be another nappy.'

The look on Patrick's face was priceless, and it was all Claire could do to stop from laughing out loud.

'I'll make the feed up,' he said, flailing for an excuse, but she was adamant.

'They're all made up,' she assured him. 'But you can do the next lot. I promise.'

Funny, he didn't look in the least bit grateful…

CHAPTER THREE

AN HOUR later, Jess was back on his lap, sweet and fresh after her feed and second nappy change, and the dogs were hanging around looking hopeful.

At least, Pepper was looking hopeful, and Dog, head cocked on one side and those ridiculous ears at attention, was watching his master like a hawk. He'd clearly taken to his new playmate, but he wasn't keen on Patrick being too far out of sight in this strange place, and he certainly wasn't sure about that funny little thing on his lap.

Patrick looked down at the dog and gave his ears a gentle tug. 'It's all right, boy,' he said softly, 'she's just a baby.'

Just a baby. Huh! The very idea of this cataclysmic development in his life being described as *just* anything was laughable, and his brother's baby was about as complicated as it got.

The photos leapt into his mind again, the girl he'd seen once a few weeks ago with the man he'd never see again—he'd grown up with him, played with him, fought with him, loved and hated him alternately until, with maturity and understanding, love had won.

They were probably the last photographs taken of Will alive—certainly the last ones Patrick and his family would have access to—and he'd cut his throat before he'd let his parents near them.

Not that they were sordid—far from it. They were

tender and touching, little intimate cameos, private thoughts and feelings captured, frozen in time. They were good photographs, which didn't surprise him. Will had always been a keen photographer and he'd had a gift for somehow distilling the essence of a moment.

However, this time he'd used his skill to capture feelings that should have remained private between the two of them—which, of course, they would have done, had Amy not died. The photos of her revealed her vulnerability with painful clarity, and the naked emotion in some of the shots made Patrick's heart contract.

Others, however, were more playful, and they'd made him want to smile. In one, Amy had obviously sneaked up on him with the camera and caught him sleeping. The next one showed him reaching out towards her, his eyes warm and laughing.

It was almost like a silly holiday snap, fun, less private than the others, and for a moment he considered doctoring it up for his parents and then dismissed it. No. They didn't need to know about the photos. It would only provoke a barrage of questions, and they didn't need the answers. He certainly hadn't.

Will's interlude with Amy was none of his business, and he heartily wished it had remained that way, but it hadn't. Still, the time they'd spent together had brought Jess into the world, a fitting memorial to them both, a sweet, happy little thing who made his throat close with emotion every time she smiled at him.

For that alone, he could forgive her parents almost anything.

'Patrick?'

He looked up, dragging himself back into reality, and met Claire's worried grey eyes.

'Are you OK?'

His smile was twisted, he could feel it, but too much had happened and he needed time to assemble his emotions.

'Yeah. Yes, I'm fine. I'm just…'

'How about a breath of fresh air? I usually take Pepper out about this time, and Dog looks as if he wouldn't mind a run.'

Fresh air sounded good. 'He'd love it—but what about the baby? Shouldn't one of us stay here with her?'

Claire stared at him. 'You think I'd leave her? She comes too. She loves our walks. I put her in the baby sling, although I must say she's getting a bit heavy. When she's bigger she can have a backpack, and then she can see where she's going, but for now, it's this.'

She reached down a padded blue canvas contraption, and Pepper leapt to her feet and ran to the door. Claire laughed softly. 'She knows, don't you, darling?'

Pepper gave one sharp bark and wagged furiously as Claire sorted out the straps and shrugged into the sling.

Patrick looked down at Jess happily gumming a plastic keyring on his knee, and suddenly didn't want to hand her over. He realised he was enjoying her, to his enormous surprise, and even the nappies hadn't been too grim.

'I'll take her,' he offered.

Claire paused. 'Are you sure? She's heavy and she dribbles.'

'I'm sure I can cope,' he said drily, and the next minute Claire had let out the straps on the sling and clipped him into it. Then the baby was threaded in, clamped firmly against his chest, her little arms pressed against his ribs and her feet kicking—ah. Just about safe, but a fraction lower and she might be the only child he ever got to hold.

'I've made the straps too long,' Claire said, and hoisted the baby up a little. He gave a quiet sigh of relief and shrugged into his jacket, catching a smile on Claire's face before she turned away.

'What?'

She shrugged, still smiling. 'Nothing—it's just not exactly your average dog-walking coat.'

He looked down at his pale linen jacket, the sort of thing that passed for casual in the city, and one side of his mouth kicked up in a wry smile.

'I have to give you that, but it's the only one I've got with me and it's a bit chilly outside for shirt-sleeves.'

'Didn't you bring a jumper?'

He had, of course, and it was in the bag in her dreadful car still, but now he had the baby all strapped on and the dogs were dancing about with excitement.

'I'll live,' he said, and with a shrug she pulled on a fleece and headed through the door and off down the drive, abandoning him.

He closed the door behind them, looking for a key without success. 'Aren't you going to lock it?' he asked, and she turned and stopped in her tracks, looking at him in amazement.

'Lock it? Apart from the fact that there's very little in there worth stealing, this is the country.'

'And knowing that, don't the thieves target it?'

She laughed. 'If they can find me. Strugglers Lane isn't called that for nothing, you know. Come on, the dogs are getting a head start.'

And heaven knows what Dog will be like if he sees a rabbit, Patrick thought. He forgot about the unlocked house and set off after Claire, quickly settling into a rhythm beside her.

The baby, snuggled against his chest, soon fell asleep, her little body surprisingly heavy after a while. Still, it was a good feeling—extraordinary, really.

A few days ago he'd been a single man with no commitments, walking his dog alone in the park. Now, suddenly, he was walking the same dog, but with a baby on his chest and another dog and a beautiful woman by his side.

That thought brought him up short, and he looked at Claire keenly. Yes, she was beautiful. Of course she was—he just hadn't really registered it amongst all the other information. Desirable, yes. Feminine, undoubtedly. Her sense of humour he had discovered to his cost, but—beautiful?

Oh, yes, she was beautiful. Lush and soft and slender, yet athletic and graceful, with an innocent charm that could knock a guy's defences for six. And that voice!

Oh, yes. No question about it, if it hadn't been for the package that she came with, he'd be negotiating for their first date right now.

He forced himself to concentrate, to consider the ramifications of this new twist in his life and work out how it could be accommodated without totally dislocating his lifestyle.

He snorted softly under his breath.

Not a chance! All of a sudden, because of one foolish and ill-considered escapade of his brother's that had probably been too brief to be called an affair, Patrick now found himself responsible for a baby. And not only the baby, but Claire as well, he realised.

He didn't know what she did for a living, but from the little he'd seen he was sure it wasn't paying enough to maintain her. And there had been that briefcase, totally out of character with all the other things in her car. It had sat there aloof in the middle of his foyer, surrounded by the ancient trainers and other piles of junk, a silent declaration of a different lifestyle.

So which was the real Claire? The battered trainers, or the smart leather briefcase?

She turned, looking back over her shoulder and pausing until he came up beside her, and he found his curiosity growing.

'Tell me about yourself,' he said, without preamble.

She looked surprised. 'What do you want to know?'

'Anything you want to tell me. We're going to have to work together on this for a long time, Claire. We might as well be friends.'

A fleeting smile crossed her lips and then faded, driven out by a lingering hint of worry in those expressive grey eyes. 'Yes,' she said thoughtfully, and turned back to the path. 'It's a bit rough here, you have to be careful,' she warned, and led the way for a moment in silence.

Then, once they were past the bad patch, she turned

back to him and hesitated once more so he could catch up.

'You want to know about me?' she said, and gave a wry smile. 'It's nothing exciting. I'm twenty-six, I'm a graphic artist and I've got a degree in interior design. I can't bear commercial work, though, and there aren't very many local opportunities for domestic stuff—not enough rich people, and most of the big stores now offer advice which is more than adequate for the average punter.'

'Which leaves you out in the cold.'

She laughed softly. 'Yes—well, I would have been, quite literally, but Auntie Meg left us a home.'

'Us?'

She smiled at him again, sadness touching the depths of those lovely grey eyes. 'Me and Amy. She didn't have anywhere to live either, so we lived together, but it just meant she didn't have to make any effort at all to find work, and I ended up supporting her.'

She shrugged, just a tiny movement but so expressive, and he knew exactly how she felt. Will had done the same, allowing his brother to shoulder the burden of responsibility while he concentrated on having fun for both of them.

'Been there, done that,' he said, sharing his feelings with her a little reluctantly. He didn't like to say anything that might be construed as criticism of his brother, despite his private feelings, because at the end of the day nothing Will had done had really made much difference to Patrick's life.

Until now...

'So Auntie Meg left you the house—any money to look after it?'

Her laughter was a little desperate. 'I wish! No, just the house in need of—well, you've seen what it's in need of. A new kitchen, a new bathroom—the wiring and plumbing's done, and the roof's now sound, but then the baby came—'

She broke off, her eyes straying to Jess asleep against his chest, and he saw the weariness in them.

'Were you working until then?'

'When Jess was born? Yes—until Amy was ill. She had postnatal depression. Well, I don't know if it was postnatal depression or if that was just when it happened—perhaps an inescapable dose of reality, for a change—but she'd got problems. Debts and things, and her personal life was a mess. I cut back so I could look after her, but she was on self-destruct...'

'She looked terrible when she came to me,' he said, wondering not for the first time if he was, in fact, responsible in some way for her decision to take her life, but Claire shook her head as if she realised his train of thought.

'She always looked terrible. She had done for years. It was part of her image, I think. She cultivated the tragic look—it was her bread and butter. People felt sorry for her and helped her out.'

'Except I didn't.'

Her smile was gentle and forgiving. 'No. No, you didn't, and I can't blame you—not now I know the truth. I know I said I held you responsible, but that was before I knew Jess wasn't yours, when all I had to go on was the photos and what Amy had told me. But you'd never seen her before, she was meaningless to you. Just another paternity hunter. Why should you help her? You weren't responsible.'

'Except, of course, that she genuinely believed that I was the father of her baby, and thought I was just denying knowing her to avoid the responsibility.'

Claire stopped and turned towards him again, searching his face with eyes that seemed to see right through him to the doubt inside.

'Don't hold yourself responsible for her death,' she said quietly. 'You aren't. It wasn't the first time she'd tried this stunt—she's been in hospital several times with an overdose. It was just that this time I'd taken some work I'd been offered. I couldn't afford not to, and she came back from you and threw herself down in floods of tears and told me about all her debts.'

'Debts?'

'Oh, credit cards and loan sharks and things. She was a silly girl, and she'd got herself in a right mess. You were her last hope, apparently.'

'And I told her to go away.' He stabbed a hand through his hair, struggling with guilt even though he knew it wasn't his fault. Should he have done more? He'd given her enough money to get home, but that had been all. Had it been too little, even for a total stranger?

'Don't—it really wasn't your fault, any more than it was mine. I know that.'

'But you still feel guilty.'

Her eyes flicked away, but not before he saw the raw flash of pain in them. 'Of course. Anyway, I went to the bank the day after she told me about the mess she was in and arranged a loan against the house, and paid off her debts.' She gave a tiny huff of laughter heavy with irony. 'And two days later, while I was at work trying to find the money to pay it back, she killed herself.'

'Leaving you with her debts.'

'Yes—and, of course, they would have died with her, ironically. She killed herself because she couldn't see a way out, and I'd already found it for her—or I thought I had. Maybe I hadn't. Maybe it wasn't really anything to do with the money. Maybe she just felt even more guilty because she'd dumped it all on me. I really don't know.'

'Did she leave a note?'

'Oh, yes. Nothing more than an apology for leaving me with the mess, though. No explanation, but it wasn't really necessary. Let's face it, I knew her well enough and it could have been any one of a dozen things that triggered it—none of them justification for taking her life, though. Nothing was that dreadful on its own, I didn't think, but perhaps I just didn't understand.'

She turned away, drawing in an unsteady breath, and Patrick realised how she must be hurting still. It had only been a few weeks since Amy had died— six? Seven? It had been a year since Will had gone, and the pain was still as fresh as the day he'd heard the news.

He gave her a moment to pull herself together, then looked at his watch. 'Should we go back? Time's getting on, and we've got a lot to sort out.'

'And you need to get back to London.'

'Ideally. And I could do with some lunch. It's two o'clock and I'm starving.'

Claire laughed a little bitterly. 'Well, I don't know

what we'll find. A few shrivelled potatoes in the bottom of the sack and not much else.'

'Perhaps we need to go to the pub and get a meal, and then do a shop.'

'I can't afford to do a shop—'

'And you can't afford not to eat. You have to look after the baby, and you need your strength. She needs you, Claire—and I need you. I can't look after the baby, and if you can and will, then I will happily pay whatever it takes to make that possible. Let's face it, what you're giving her is beyond price, and I'm only too conscious of that.'

She stared at him, and then without warning her eyes filled and she turned away.

'Thank you,' she said, her voice choked, and without pausing to think he reached out and wrapped an arm around her shoulders, hugging her to his side.

'Don't cry, it'll be all right,' he murmured, but that just seemed to make it worse. For a moment she clung to him, her slender body shaken with sobs, but then she drew herself up and eased away, scrubbing at her tears with a battered tissue that had seen better days.

'I'm sorry,' she said. 'It's just—it's all too much, and sometimes I just feel so trapped. I mean—I want to look after her, but I can't, because I can't get enough work, and without working I can't afford the phone, and without the phone nobody can ring me with work anyway, and—oh, I don't know, it's just a mess.'

'You haven't got a phone?' he said, stunned. 'You live in the middle of nowhere—what if the baby's ill?'

'I take her to a doctor.'

'What—in that death trap you call a car?'

'It's Amy's,' she said woodenly. 'Well, it was Auntie Meg's, but Amy commandeered it because she didn't have one. I sold my car when I had to give up work, because I couldn't afford the payments on it. It was lovely—a VW Golf, not new, but not very old, and it was my pride and joy, but it wasn't mine, so it had to go.'

Such a simple statement, and it tore at his heart. He didn't know what it was like to be poor. His father had been a successful architect, and he'd inherited the gene. He'd gone into the family firm as soon as he'd qualified, and within a few years he'd won numerous awards and taken the firm from strength to strength.

Lack of money wasn't a problem for him, never had been and hopefully never would be. He could imagine the fear, though. He'd lost his wallet once and been unable to cross London without it. His mobile phone battery had been flat and he'd thought of getting a taxi, but he'd had no cash at home, the office had been closed and he would have had no way of paying.

He'd walked, and as he'd walked, he'd passed young people begging on the street, their eyes hollow.

He'd never taken his money for granted again.

'Don't worry about the car,' he said now. 'I'll sort something out. And the phone. I need to be able to contact you, and vice versa.'

'I'll pay you back,' she began, but he silenced her with a look.

'You can't do everything. I can't give the baby physical day-to-day care, you can't earn the sort of money I can. We need a sensible division of labour here, a sharing of resources. Don't argue.'

She opened her mouth again, then shut it and smiled.

'Thank you,' she said.

He snorted. 'Don't thank me. I get the distinct feeling I've got the easy option here. This baby weighs a ton, and unless I'm very much mistaken, she's just peed all down my shirt.'

Claire felt slightly helpless and out of control. She wasn't used to being looked after, and she wasn't sure she liked it.

Not that Patrick was domineering or anything, he just…took control, calmly and competently, and before she knew what was what, her phone was reconnected, the old fridge was groaning with goodies, its replacement, a big fridge-freezer, was on order, and he was whisking her off out again.

'Where are we going?' she asked, firmly taking control of the steering-wheel of Amy's car. Not that she liked driving it, but she was running out of ways to exercise her authority, and this was one of the few left to her.

'The nearest VW garage,' he said, and she looked at him in astonishment.

'Why?'

'Because this thing's a death trap, and I don't want my niece travelling in it any more. Besides, when I come up for the weekend, I'll need a car, and I don't intend to drive up from London every week and fight with that traffic on Friday nights. So, I'm going to buy a car, and during the week it will be yours to do what you like with, all expenses paid, and in return I'll expect you to pick me up from the station on Friday evening and drop me back at stupid o'clock on Monday morning. OK?'

She stared at him, stunned. He was coming up every weekend?

'What if I can't?' she said, struggling for excuses. 'What if I'm working?'

'Late Friday night and early Monday morning? Unlikely—and if you are, I'll get a taxi.'

She started the engine—at the third attempt—and pushed the clutch down. There was a horrible scraping noise from the gearbox, and she winced and rammed it into gear.

Patrick flinched, and she wondered what kind of car he drove. A Mercedes, probably. Big and fast and dripping with accessories.

Or a Porsche or somesuch—a little pocket-rocket for nipping through the London traffic and eating up the miles.

'What car have you got in London?' she asked, not being one for idle speculation when a direct question would do, and he turned slightly in the seat, angling his big body towards her, and his mouth crooked up in a teasing smile.

'Guess,' he said, so she did, and he gave a surprised cough of laughter.

'A Porsche?' he said, his voice incredulous, and laughed again. 'Not me. Will might have done, but not me. Besides, they don't have enough ground clearance. I go on site, remember? Try something more practical.'

'OK. A Mercedes.'

'Closer.'

'BMW.'

'Nope.'

'Audi.'

He sighed, his smile quirking. 'Am I so predict-able?'

'It's OK,' she said, forgiving him. 'It was a pretty safe bet—and, no, you're not. For instance, I would have had you pegged for a designer dog—you know, a Hungarian Visla or a Weimaraner or something like that, not, well, you know—a mutt.'

He made a rude noise. 'Dog isn't my dog,' he re-minded her. 'He is—or was—Will's. He bought him from a girl begging by the side of the road. She had a little bitch with three puppies, and he gave her fifty pounds for him because he felt so sorry for them all. It was freezing cold, and the puppies were shivering, and he had a soft heart.'

'Unlike you, of course.'

He shot her an assessing look and then his mouth kicked up in a smile. 'Unlike me, of course. Anyway, he was living with me at the time because he was between jobs, as he would put it, and he brought the miserable little scrap in to see me in the office. The first thing he did was pee on a set of client's drawings, and he hasn't really looked back.'

Claire laughed, picturing the scene, and thought of the loyal and obedient dog he'd turned into.

'He loves you,' she said, and he pulled a face.

'I feed him. He's not stupid.'

'And play with him, and talk to him. I bet he sits in your office with you and goes with you on site.'

Did she imagine it, or did he colour slightly? How very revealing.

He cleared his throat and stared straight ahead. 'I hope he's all right with Pepper in the kitchen.'

'They'll be fine. I've never known her put a foot wrong. She'll look after him.'

She turned onto the garage forecourt and pulled up. 'Right. About this car,' she said.

He paused, half in, half out of the car, and turned towards her. 'What about it?'

'I'll pay you back. If you can pay enough to cover my child care, I can work and pay for the car.'

'I'd thought I'd explained this,' he said patiently. 'I need a car at the weekends—'

'So borrow it.'

'I'd rather own it.'

'Well, so would I.'

'But you won't buy a new one.'

She felt her jaw drop, and yanked it back up again. 'Fine,' she said, giving up. If he wanted to throw his money away, let him!

She got out of the car and slammed the door— twice, because, of course, it didn't shut the first time—and followed him into the showroom, the baby in her arms. She could see the salesman looking over Patrick's shoulder at the 2CV, a slightly doubtful look on his face, and as she reached them she heard the tailend of his specification.

'Turbodiesel for economy, and an estate, because we've got two dogs and a baby to accommodate.'

Good grief. How incredibly…married-sounding. The salesman smiled vaguely at her, then blinked.

'Miss Franklin?' he said, and she returned his smile, amazed that he'd recognised her.

'Hello,' she said.

He stared at the baby, then at Patrick, and recovered himself with a start. 'Um—lovely baby,' he said, and Patrick cleared his throat slightly and brought the man's attention back to business. 'Now, how soon were you looking to do this?' he asked, flicking through some paperwork.

'Now,' Patrick said. 'Preferably this afternoon.'

'Ah.' He put his paperwork down and looked at them over the top of his glasses. 'Of course, you won't have a colour choice.'

'Do you have one available?'

'Well, as a matter of fact, if you don't mind a dark metallic blue, there's the demonstrator...'

'That's fine,' Patrick said, and the deal was done.

Half an hour later, the car was paid for, the insurance was arranged and he'd transferred Claire and the baby into it.

'I'll see you back at home,' he said, and there was something so natural and nice about the sound of it that she nearly cried.

Stupid. It was just a figure of speech, she told herself, but in many ways it was more than that, because he was going to be there three nights out of seven. Like it or not, Patrick Cameron was about to become a very important feature in her life.

CHAPTER FOUR

IT WAS strange how, in just three short weeks, Patrick's trips to Suffolk to see Claire and the baby had become such an important feature in his life.

This would be his third weekend there, and he and Dog were falling comfortably into a routine of commuting at the weekend.

At least, he was. Dog was less happy. He didn't like the train, even though George delivered them to the station and Claire picked them up. It was still too noisy, too crowded, too stressful for him, and Patrick had to agree.

Of course, travelling first class made it slightly better, but Dog still didn't like the motion of the train and spent the entire journey trying to get onto Patrick's lap. If he'd been happy on the floor it would have made a hellish journey slightly less grim, but nevertheless the rewards made it all worthwhile, for both of them.

Having got there, though, Dog loved his weekends in the country with Pepper, and for Patrick, just the sight of Claire's smile when she picked them up made him forget everything else.

She was waiting for them now, parked near the exit from the station, and she flashed the lights so he could find her.

Not necessary. He seemed to have radar where she was concerned, and so did Dog. Whining softly, he trotted eagerly at his side, and when Patrick opened the tailgate he leapt in, tail lashing, to greet Pepper.

Patrick knew just how the dog felt.

Stowing his case behind the passenger seat and buzzing Jess with a quick kiss hello, he flashed Claire a smile.

'Hi, there. Sorry to keep you waiting—the train was on the drag.'

'It's OK. We've only just got here. I had to change Jess's nappy before we could leave, and it was a lulu.'

'Excellent. Hopefully she will have got it out of her system for the weekend, just in time for Uncle Patrick,' he said with a grin, and slid in beside her. 'So, how's it been?'

Her smile was wry. 'Oh, you know—up and down. I've got some work—it's the first time in ages, and I'm having difficulty getting back into it.'

'You don't have to work,' he told her, but she shook her head in disagreement.

'I do, I can't freeload off you indefinitely.'

'It's not freeloading.'

'Yes, it is. Well, it feels like it, anyway. I want to pay my way.'

'But you are, more than, just by looking after Jess.'

She shrugged, and pulled out into the traffic. 'I feel beholden, and I don't like it. In fact, I've made a decision. I'm going to put the barn on the market.'

He stared at her, shocked. 'The barn?'

'Yes. I'm sure someone will buy it to convert it.'

'But you can't sell it,' he protested. 'It's so much a part of the property. Anyway, will you get planning permission?'

She nodded. 'I've already got it—detailed permission for conversion to a four-bedroomed dwelling. I can show you the plans, if you like.'

'You'll have neighbours,' he said, instinctively knowing how she'd hate that, and she shrugged again.

'I can't help it. I've got a bank loan against the house to clear Amy's debts, and I can't afford the payments. It's that or move altogether, and it's probably the lesser of the two evils, even though—'

She broke off, and he swivelled in his seat so he could watch her face more easily. 'Even though what?'

Again, those slender shoulders lifted, despair evident in the slight movement. 'Oh, I had a stupid dream.'

'Tell me,' he said softly.

'It was nothing. A pipe dream. It was never going to happen.'

'Tell me,' he said again, and with a sigh, she did.

'I thought about running painting holidays—you know, watercolour, landscape, pastel, life drawing—all sorts of things. I could have different activities each week, to give people a variety of options. Jess and I could live upstairs, with a big kitchen downstairs to feed everybody, and the rest of the ground floor could be a studio, perhaps with a darkroom so we could do photographic screen-printing. That way I could be independent, and look after Jess, and do what I really want to do instead of what other people want all the time.

'But, like I said, it's just a pipe dream. The cottage needs a fortune spent on it before it could conceivably be used for guests, and as for the barn—well, you've seen it.'

He had. He'd seen it and thought what a beautiful building it was and what an amazing home it would make.

Brick built, with lovely oak roof trusses and tie beams and great thick walls, it could be wonderful if it was sympathetically restored and converted to take advantage of those features. In his mind's eye he'd already started working on the plans, even though he knew there was no point because it wasn't for sale.

And yet here out of the blue was his chance, and maybe the answer to Claire's problems.

'Sell it to me,' he said, and she nearly ran a red light.

'Excuse me?' she said, turning towards him with a stunned look on her face.

'I said, sell it to me.'

She looked away again, shaking her head slightly as if to clear it. 'I thought you said that. Why?'

Patrick shrugged, trying to keep the little quiver of anticipation in check. 'Because you need the money, and I need somewhere to stay when I come up. It isn't fair to expect you to put me up for the weekend for the next eighteen years or so.'

'I don't mind.'

'But I do. I feel as if I'm encroaching on your privacy, and it isn't fair. Neither of us asked for this, Claire, but we're stuck with it. Maybe this would make it better. If I bought it, it would be the best of all worlds—you wouldn't have a neighbour during the week, I'd have a proper base up here, you'd get your house back to yourself again, you'd get the money to clear your debts and regain your independence, which seems so important to you. There are all sorts of good reasons.'

She was silent for ages, except for the sound of the cogs grinding inside her brain. Her thought processes were transparent, he thought. She'd make a lousy poker player. Eventually she turned to him.

'You don't know how much it is,' she said.

He pulled a face. 'I can hazard a guess, and the cost of the conversion is much more significant. Think about it, and let me look at it and do a few doodles.'

'I've got the plans,' she said, and then rolled her eyes. 'Of course, you're an architect. You'll want to do your own.'

'Of course. I'll look at the others, but their only real relevance is in showing me what I can get past the planners. And I guess I won't really know the answer to that until I ask them.'

'I haven't said I'll sell it to you yet,' she reminded him, and he wondered how hard it would be to persuade her. Not too hard, he thought. It made too much sense, for both of them. They were stuck in this relationship for years because of Jess, and this seemed such a tidy option he wondered why they hadn't thought of it before.

He felt the familiar shiver of anticipation that came whenever a design project really caught his imagination, and warned himself to slow down.

She hadn't said yes yet—but she would. He was sure of it. She had to.

Claire was confused. She'd had it all worked out— she'd even spoken to the estate agent—but now

Patrick had thrown her a curve and she didn't know what to do.

Did he really want the barn, or was he just bailing her out yet again? She didn't really know—all she knew was it seemed like a very good idea on one level, and a truly lousy idea on another.

It would lock them together in a way that at the moment they weren't, although, if she was sensible about it, she'd have to admit that, in fact, they were locked together anyway, and would be until Jess had grown up.

Good grief, she'd be forty-four by the time Jess was eighteen! Married, with children of her own? She hoped so, but there wasn't anyone on the horizon, and, trapped at home as she was with the baby, there wasn't likely to be, either.

Suddenly the weight of responsibility seemed unbearable, until she remembered that she now had someone to share it with—someone who seemed more than happy to be involved.

Patrick was putting the baby to bed, and she was making their supper. She was ravenous, but she always waited for him on Friday evenings, because it seemed churlish not to, and besides, she enjoyed the company. It was nice to have someone to talk to who could actually return the conversational ball, instead of just grinning and waving and dribbling.

Tonight they were having a chicken pasta dish with salad, and she was just putting the cheese on top when he came back into the kitchen.

'Everything OK?' Claire asked him.

He nodded. 'She's gone out like a light,' he said, and came over to where she was working, sniffing appreciatively. 'Smells gorgeous—I'm starving. Anything I can do?'

'No, not really, it's all done.'

He stole a bit of cheese off the top, and she smacked his hand lightly and put the dish under the grill. He cleared up the tiny bits on the worktop instead, and then shrugged away from the units and headed for the fridge.

'Fancy a glass of wine?'

It was a habit they'd got into, if you could get into a habit in such a short time. Claire rather thought you could, and there was something curiously comforting about the little ritual.

He would put the baby to bed, she would cook the supper, he would open the wine and they would sip the first glass while the supper finished cooking. Then, after they'd finished, they'd take their coffee through to the sitting room and sit by the fire.

Very cosily domestic—and frighteningly addictive.

And, of course, if he bought the barn, once it was converted it wouldn't happen any more. He'd come back at the weekend and go into his own house, taking the baby, and she'd have the entire weekend to herself.

What an appallingly lonely thought...

'Here,' he said, appearing at her elbow with a glass of rosé suspended from those long, strong fingers.

'Thanks.' She took it, their fingers brushing, and she felt a strange little shiver run over her skin. Hastily she turned back to check the pasta under the grill, hugely conscious of his lean hips propped against the worktop beside her.

The pasta was fine and clearly didn't need her attention, so there was really nothing to do to distract her from the long, rangy length of his legs, or the breadth of his shoulders, or those firm, sculpted lips as they closed on the rim of the wineglass.

Patrick tilted the glass, and she watched his throat work as he swallowed. Good grief! Since when had *swallowing* been such a turn-on?

A tiny moan rose in her throat, and she stifled it ruthlessly. Crazy! She was going crazy, driven mad by the proximity of this much too attractive man in her kitchen, in her personal space, so close—and yet not close enough.

'So you want to buy it?' she said without preamble, and very carefully he set down his wineglass, folded his arms and gave her a level look.

'What brought that on?'

Claire shrugged. There was no way she was telling him what had been going through her mind—not if she wanted to keep even a shred of her dignity.

'I've been thinking about it while I was getting the supper, and I've decided you're right. It would solve both our problems, and it's the obvious solution. So, do you, or don't you?'

'Want to buy it? Yes, I do.'

'Fine. I'll show you the plans after supper, if you like.'

He nodded, still watching her thoughtfully, and she picked up her glass and took a gulp.

Well, she'd done it now—sold off Auntie Meg's barn for development. Sorry, Auntie Meg, she said silently, but I don't really have a choice, and better Jess's uncle than a total stranger.

The pasta was done now, so she turned off the grill

and pulled it out of the tiny little cooker that sat on the worktop.

'Why don't you use the Aga?' Patrick asked her, and she gave a hollow laugh.

'Firstly, because it's solid fuel and doesn't work very well, and secondly, because I can't afford to. Anyway, it doesn't have a grill.'

'If I buy the barn, then you'll be able to pay to get it reconditioned and converted to oil or gas,' he said.

'And I still won't be able to afford to run it.'

She set the pasta down in the middle of the kitchen table next to the salad, and picked up the serving spoon, meeting his eyes defiantly.

He held her gaze, his own level and searching, and after a moment she looked away. She'd never stare him down, and anyway, it was all rather silly and pointless. It was hardly his fault they were in this mess, after all.

She scooped out a dollop of pasta and slapped it on his plate, then handed it to him abruptly.

'Help yourself to salad,' she said, equally abruptly, and served herself a smaller portion, the fire going out of her.

She sat down, prodding the pasta with the fork, and after a moment he reached across and covered her left hand where it lay on the table. His fingers closed around hers, squeezing gently, and she felt tears well up in her eyes.

How stupid! There was nothing to cry about. Just because she was selling the barn...

'Claire, it'll be all right,' he said, and it sounded like a promise.

It would have been fine if she hadn't stopped believing in promises years ago.

The plans of the barn were interesting, if only because they gave the exact dimensions and showed Patrick the sort of thing that the local planners would accept. Other than that, he found them pedestrian and unimaginative, but, then, he was probably unnecessarily picky.

Still, if this was going to be his home—and he felt it would be, in every way that mattered—then it was very important that it was right.

He swallowed his coffee, champing at the bit because it was dark outside and he would have to wait until morning before he could walk around the barn and really study it closely. In the meantime he could look at the plans again, or talk to Claire—and just at the moment, she looked as if she needed to talk.

'Tell me about Auntie Meg,' he said, and she tucked her feet up under her bottom and curled further into the corner of her chair.

'She was my great-aunt—ancient and really the nearest thing I ever had to a grandmother. We used to come and visit her when we were little, and she used to let us play in the barn. She kept sheep and goats, and they slept in the barn, but we were allowed up in the hayloft above if we were careful, and it was our secret place. It was wonderful—such a change from London where we were brought up, and I always vowed I'd live in the country when I grew up. I never dreamt it would be here.'

No wonder she was so reluctant to part with the

barn, he thought—and no wonder she'd had dreams for it.

'How much input did you have into the plans?' he asked her, and she pulled a face.

'Oh, practically none. I was told my ideas were unworkable and the planners wouldn't allow them, but it was only speculative anyway and I just wanted it agreed in principle, so I let him get on with it.'

That encouraged him. He hadn't wanted to think she was party to such a boring conversion, when there was so much scope for something better.

'What about the land?' he asked, and she shrugged.

'I don't know. I haven't really thought about it. The estate agent was coming over on Monday.'

Monday. Did he have anything inescapable to do on Monday, or could he be here to sort the whole thing out?

'Do you need to involve the estate agent?'

She looked a bit surprised, but then shook her head after a moment. 'No—no, of course not. I haven't signed anything. It's only to get it valued, but they did that last summer anyway. I don't imagine it will be hugely different.'

He nodded, his eyes flicking back to the plans again. It needed a great open space in the centre, vaulted right up into the roof, with the stairs rising up to a walkway that ran from side to side bridging the gap. Two rooms and two bathrooms at each end, if there was room, and then storage over the breakfast area in the lean-to on the front, but the study on the other side of the hall would be nice vaulted up to the ceiling…

'I can hear your mind working,' she said, and he gave her a wry grin.

'I'm just itching to see it in daylight. There are so many things I can't remember in enough detail.'

'Tell me about your work,' she said, changing the subject, and he looked at her in surprise. Of course, she was an interior designer, so she probably was genuinely interested.

Most people weren't, at best pretending a polite interest, at worst getting him off the subject as fast as possible.

'I've done a lot of stuff in London, obviously—restoration and regeneration in the Docklands area, of course, but other things—art galleries, houses, offices—all sorts of stuff, some of it a bit wacky. It's fun. Very varied. I won't do routine stuff, I hate it. I don't think it's good for the reputation of the firm, for a start, but obviously we do a bit of bread-and-butter design, you have to. You can't expect every project to win you an award.'

'That's not what I hear.'

Patrick felt warmth creep up his neck and he gave a little huff of embarrassed laughter. 'People exaggerate.'

'I've been doing some research on the internet, since I've had the phone back on. I think it's all pretty much deserved.'

'So does that mean you liked what you saw?' he asked, and could have kicked himself for trawling for her approval so blatantly.

Claire smiled, a slow, teasing smile, and he felt his guts tighten. Lord, she was gorgeous.

'I liked what I saw,' she admitted.

'And do you trust me to do the barn?'

She shrugged, still smiling. 'Probably. At least it will be different, and almost inevitably better than that…'

She inclined her head towards the untidy pile of plans, and he chuckled.

'I should hope so. I'm sure, though, if he was going to live there that guy would have made more effort. He just didn't want to have to redraw them. Which reminds me, do you have a drawing board?'

'Of course—how do you think I work? At the kitchen table?'

'Stranger things have happened.'

She smiled. 'No. I've got a drawing board—two, actually, because the ruler on one sticks a bit at one side and it's hard to get it totally accurate. Why?'

It was his turn to shrug. 'Just wondered. I thought I might doodle out a few ideas in the morning,' he said, and she nodded.

'Sure. It's in my study. Feel free.'

'I will—thank you.'

A peaceful, companionable silence fell for a while, and he rested his head back against the wing of the old chair and closed his eyes. It was so quiet, with only the occasional hiss from the fire and the soft snoring of the dogs at their feet to break the silence.

He loved it—loved the contrast to his hectic life in London, loved sitting here like this with Claire and the dogs, while the baby slept peacefully upstairs. It somehow felt so right, like—like being married, he thought with a shock, and nearly laughed aloud at the notion.

He was going crazy. They were just sharing the

responsibility for the baby, that was all. Nothing more.

And certainly not *that*, no matter what his dreams might tell him to the contrary!

The sooner the barn was done and he was in it, the better...

Saturday was one of those gorgeous late spring days, gloriously hot and sunny, the air heavy with the scent of flowers and the hum of bees feeding on the nectar.

Patrick was up early, showered and dressed and out in the garden by seven o'clock, while the air was still fresh and the grass drenched with dew.

It was long, he noticed, and wondered if Claire had had the mower fixed yet. Probably not, if the state of the lawn was anything to go by.

He walked over to the barn and opened the huge, heavy door with difficulty. It groaned on its hinges, and he wondered how on earth Claire managed to open it. Sheer, stubborn bloody-mindedness, probably, he thought, feeling absurdly proud of her.

She had guts, he had to give her that. It couldn't have been easy dealing with her sister's death and shouldering the burden of a tiny baby, and yet she'd done it without hesitation or question, and would continue to do so, he was sure of it.

He wondered what the legal ramifications of Jess's guardianship were, and decided he'd have to look into it. In the meantime, there was the barn to explore.

He opened both doors wide, then the matching doors on the far side, so that the sun poured through the centre of the building and filled it with light. Dust motes danced in the sunbeams, and he stood in the centre of the barn and gazed through the opened doors straight down the valley to the church in the distance.

What a fabulous view, he thought, and vowed to use it to the maximum advantage. The stairs, he decided, needed a half-landing, a gallery on which to pause and fill up the senses. It would be a wonderful place to sit and read, with a comfortable chair and perhaps a cat curled up on his lap.

He'd have to borrow Claire's, he decided, because although he could take Dog backwards and forwards to London, a cat would be quite a different proposition.

There was a ladder at one end of the barn, reaching up to a hole in the floor above, and he climbed up it to the hayloft, walking cautiously and testing each board before he trusted it with his weight.

He looked around, studying the roof timbers at close range and wondering how many of them could be preserved. Most of them, probably, although he might have to put in some additional supports.

The roof really was very beautiful, and it would be a tragedy to board up the ceiling and conceal it, as the previous architect had intended. No, he would leave it open, almost to the apex, with just a small area of loft in which to hide services.

He went cautiously down the ladder again and out into the lean-to section. It was well named. It was leaning more than a little, and would need some serious structural repair if it was to be preserved, but that could be done. There was nothing that couldn't be done if he threw enough money at it, and with its unrivalled setting the investment would certainly be justified.

Even if it wouldn't, he didn't care. That wasn't what this was all about.

He didn't analyse too carefully what it was all about, because he had a feeling that he didn't really want to know the answer.

He went back out into the garden and stood, head tipped back, looking up at the roof. Hopefully the slates could be preserved. It would be nice to reuse them, and there were some York stone flags inside that he would have to work into the scheme somehow.

Calling the dogs, he went back into the kitchen to find Claire there with the baby propped on one hip, while she heated her bottle of milk and tested it one-handed.

'Want me to take her?' he said, reaching for the baby, and Jess gave him a beaming smile as he lifted her from Claire's arms. 'Morning, gorgeous,' he said, kissing the tip of her nose, and Claire grinned at him.

'I thought you were talking to me,' she teased, and suddenly the atmosphere between them became electric.

After a moment of tense silence, Claire turned away, a gentle tide of colour sweeping over her cheeks, and Patrick drew in a quiet, steadying breath and stepped back.

'Did you sleep all right?' she asked, hastily filling the silence, and he groped about for something sensible to say.

'Um—yes, fine,' he said, and rolled his eyes. He sounded like a total idiot, which was hardly surprising, because, as he was beginning to discover, being too long in Claire's company was enough to completely addle his brain.

Not to mention playing hell with his hormones!

Claire tested the milk against the inside of her arm, shook the bottle and tested it again, and then finally, when there was absolutely no way she could prevaricate another moment, she turned to take the baby from him.

'I'll feed her,' he said softly, and took the bottle from her hand. 'Why don't you go and get dressed while I do this. And I'll make us a cup of tea.'

'What a fine idea,' she said, and fled for the sanctuary of the stairs. She'd already showered before the baby had woken, but nevertheless she took her time getting ready before she went back downstairs again.

What on earth had possessed her to make a remark like that? She must have been mad—and Patrick had quite clearly been as embarrassed as she was. Idiot.

Finally unable to justify dithering around any longer, she went back downstairs to find Patrick and Jess nose to nose, both laughing, and between one second in the next she went from longing to have him out of her house to dreading the time when the barn would be done and he wouldn't need to stay.

She would miss watching the interaction between them so much. It was a real joy, watching the man and the baby getting to know and love each other, and she wondered what Patrick's parents would make of Jess.

'Have you told your parents about her yet?' she asked, but he shook his head.

'No. I thought I'd wait until the result of the DNA analysis came back, make it all a bit more official. What do you think?'

What she thought was that she'd still not got round to taking Jess to the doctor for the test, and she felt a pang of guilt. 'Why don't you just tell them?' she suggested. 'I think the DNA is just a formality, don't you? I mean, what with the photographs and every-thing...'

He nodded, blowing a raspberry on Jess's round little tummy. 'You're probably right,' he said with a heavy sigh. 'The thing is, I just don't know how to bring the subject up. They were devastated when Will died, and they won't talk about him.'

'Surely they'd be pleased?'

He looked up at her, his eyes sad, and for the first time she considered what he himself had gone through. She knew all about it—the shock, the guilt, the hurt, and then the terrible empty sadness.

'You're right,' he said. 'They'll be thrilled. I'll tell them the next time I ring. In the meantime, Tuppence here needs a fresh set of pants and a nap, and I could do with talking through the barn with you.'

'So where's my tea?' she asked, fully aware that he hadn't had time to make it.

He shot her a cheeky grin as he headed for the stairs with Jess.

'Keeping fresh in the kettle,' he said, and winked.

Her heart, stupid thing that it was, did a back-flip in her chest, and she pressed her hand against it and gave it a good talking-to when he was out of earshot.

'Mad, crazy woman! He's just being friendly! All these winks and grins—they don't mean anything. He's just a man—they flirt without thinking, just like they breathe and watch football on the telly, and if you let yourself believe anything else, you're in for a serious disappointment.'

Even if he did have a particularly *nice* grin…

CHAPTER FIVE

FOR the rest of the morning they crawled around the barn, looking in every nook and cranny, while Claire told Patrick stories from her childhood, like the time she and Amy had hidden from Auntie Meg, giggling and shushing each other while she'd searched and searched in vain for them.

In the end she'd called the police and they'd got into terrible trouble, but Auntie Meg had hugged them when Amy had cried, and had forgiven them, and they'd made drop scones on the hotplate of the Aga.

Telling him about it, she could even taste them, and she thought, yes, it would be nice to get it fixed. She could make drop scones with Jess when she was older...

She told him about the time the cat had had kittens in the hayloft and they'd sat up all night with Auntie Meg and watched, and about the boy she'd met in the village when she was fifteen, who'd followed her back to the barn and tried to kiss her.

'I screamed and ran away,' she told him, chuckling, and Patrick looked at her thoughtfully, a half-smile playing around his lips.

'And would you scream and run away if I tried to kiss you?' he said in a gentle, teasing voice that only an idiot would take seriously, and she conjured up a laugh.

'Of course!' she said, and wished he would try,

because absolutely the last thing she would have done was run away.

He didn't, though, he just smiled a little wryly and said, 'Very wise,' and walked off, prodding at a crack in the wall. He crouched down to get a better look at it, while she just stood there with her mouth hanging slightly open and wondered if she'd imagined the entire conversation or if he really would have kissed her if she'd given him any encouragement.

'A surveyor's had a look at the cracks,' she told him, gathering her scattered thoughts, 'and it will need underpinning in places, and the cracks stitching, but none of it needs to be taken down apparently, apart from the corner of the lean-to.'

He nodded and straightened up, flexing his legs. 'I'm not worried about the cracks,' he said. 'I've seen far worse.' He glanced at his watch. 'Time to take the dogs for a walk?'

It was—and time to stop fantasising about what the kiss would have been like if it had ever materialised.

She had to remain friends with Patrick for the next eighteen years, and doing something stupid like kissing him was hardly the best way to go about it.

Anyway, he clearly had no intention of kissing her, he had just been teasing—another thing men did like breathing and watching football.

You need to get out more, girl, she told herself firmly, and followed him back to the house.

He must be crazy, flirting with her like that, but he just hadn't been able to help himself.

They walked the dogs, Jess in the sling on his front, and when they got back he played with the baby for a while on a blanket in the garden until she was hungry again. After he'd fed her and put her down for a nap and they'd eaten the sandwiches Claire had made, he went into the study and doodled for a while at the spare drawing board, playing with some ideas for the barn, while Claire pottered in the kitchen just behind him.

The window was open, and he could hear the bees buzzing in the honeysuckle just outside. It was headily distracting, and when Claire brought in a cup of tea midway through the afternoon, he was sitting staring into space.

'Having a break?' she asked him, and he turned to her and smiled.

'Soaking up the bucolic atmosphere,' he said with only a trace of irony.

'Oh, we've got lots of bucolic atmosphere round here,' she said, perching on the desk beside him. 'More than you can shake a stick at.'

He chuckled and, pushing his chair back from the drawing board, stretched hugely. 'I'm hungry.'

'I've made a cake,' she told him.

'I know, I can smell it,' he replied. 'I suppose you're now going to tease me and tell me that it's for tomorrow.'

Her mouth quirked in a little smile. 'Of course. Anyway, you shouldn't eat cake while it's hot, it gives you indigestion.'

'So why bother to mention it?'

'Just so you know how wonderfully domesticated I am,' she said sassily, and went back to the kitchen.

He picked up his tea and followed her, standing

over her while she cut a big chunk of the moist, steaming gingerbread and waved it under his nose.

He didn't know whether to strangle her or kiss her, so in the end he took the easy option, removed the cake from her fingers, put it down on the worktop and cupped her face in his hands. Her eyes widened in surprise, then fluttered closed as his mouth covered hers in a chaste, controlled kiss that nearly killed him.

'That's for teasing me,' he said, his voice a little gruff. Picking up the cake, he took it and his tea back into the study and shut the door firmly behind him.

Claire stared at the closed door of the study in aston- ishment. Her fingers traced the outline of her lips, still tingling from the slight, undemanding pressure of his mouth.

Well, what on earth had that been all about?

She shook her head to clear it, and cutting herself a chunk of the cake, she took it and her tea out into the garden and sat down with her back against the trunk of a tree and thought about it.

As kisses went, she decided after a while, it wasn't much of one—hardly qualified, in fact—so perhaps she was making too much of it and it had just been a joke.

Yes. That was it. A joke.

Funny, she didn't feel like laughing. She felt like throwing herself face down on the grass and scream- ing and drumming her feet in frustration, but that was just silly.

Instead she sat there, and ate the cake that had started it all, and wondered how on earth she was going to get through the next eighteen years.

* * *

The next week was chaotic. Patrick was busy at work, rushed off his feet sorting out one problem after another, and none of it was helped by his inability to concentrate on anything except the barn.

He got an independent surveyor to inspect it and come up with a price, and when he was sure that Claire was happy with it, he got his legal department to sort out the purchase and get the wheels in motion.

One of the first things he wanted to do was talk to the planners, and after he'd spent twelve to fifteen hours a day in the office, he went upstairs to his apartment and spent another two or three hours on the plans for the barn, so that he'd have something to show them at the end of the week.

In fact, it was late on Friday before he could get away, but by then he'd arranged a meeting with the planners for Monday morning and had rescheduled his entire week to clear Tuesday and Wednesday as well. Finally, with a sense of anticipation he hadn't felt for ages, he loaded his suitcase and the dog into his car and set off.

By the time he'd caught the train, he'd decided, it would be too late to expect Claire and the baby to turn out, and anyway, if he was going to be there for several days he'd need his own car. Claire seemed to have taken to the Golf like a duck to water, and there was no way he was driving Amy's 2CV again unless his life depended on it, so it made sense.

He'd told her not to wait up for him, but when he eventually pulled up on her drive at midnight, the light was still on in the sitting room and he could see her in there, fast asleep on the chair.

Pepper was at the window, tail lashing, barking furiously, and as he watched Claire stood up, shaking sleep off and running her hand through the soft, shining tresses of her hair, lifting it back from her face and yawning as she stumbled to the door.

He felt something stir deep inside him, something elemental, not desire, exactly, but related to it—something warm and cosy and totally unexpected, that warded off the loneliness and sadness that was his constant companion.

'I'm sorry to wake you,' he said, but she just smiled sleepily up at him, and without thinking he bent and brushed his lips over hers. 'Hi, there,' he said softly, and her cheeks flushed softly with colour and she stepped back.

'Hi. Have you eaten? I've left you some casserole. I can heat it up if you like.'

'I've eaten,' he said, thinking of the stale teacake and indifferent coffee he'd picked up in a roadside café on the way. 'I could murder a cup of tea, though.'

'I'll make it. The kettle's hot.'

He followed her into the kitchen, accompanied by the dogs who were milling happily around his feet, and while Claire pottered with the kettle and mugs, he stretched and leant against the worktop and watched her.

I've missed you, he nearly said, but he stifled it in the nick of time. 'How's Jess?' he said instead, and she looked up at him with a smile.

'Lovely. She's got another tooth—that's three now. Her smile's really cute.'

So was hers, but he didn't say so. Instead he tried

not to stare at the way her sweater pulled across her breasts, outlining their lush fullness and making his hands ache to cup them.

'I'll go in and see her on my way to bed.' He shifted so she wasn't directly in his line of sight, but turned his head anyway, too spineless to overcome the need to watch her. 'So, apart from the tooth, how's your week been?' he asked, groping for normality.

'Oh, you know. I did that freelance work on Monday, and took it in to them on Tuesday. They seemed pleased enough, so maybe there'll be some more to follow. Be nice, wouldn't it?'

'You don't have to—'

'I do,' she said firmly, and he just smiled and let her have her way.

'So, how was your week?' she asked, and he gave a tired laugh.

'Hell, thank you for asking. Still, it's over now, and none of the clients have your number, and someone else can deal with it all next week. I'm having a few days off to sort the barn out and talk to the planners— if it's OK with you having me here?'

It had just occurred to him that he should have asked her before assuming he could stay for longer, but she didn't seem to mind. On the contrary, it seemed she had a use for him.

'Actually, that's brilliant,' she said. 'Could you look after Jess on Monday afternoon? I've got a dental appointment at four and I was going to have to take her.'

'Of course,' he said, his conscience relaxing again, and then suddenly there was nothing to say.

Claire stared into her tea for a while in silence, and Patrick watched her, wondering why it was only now that he'd noticed the little tilt to the end of her chin and the light dusting of freckles over the bridge of her nose. Had she been out in the sun? Probably. It had been a glorious week, by all accounts.

He'd missed it, trapped in the office in meetings or phone conferences or stuck in a site hut baking in the sun. He wondered why people thought architecture was glamorous, and decided they just knew nothing about the realities of it.

All they saw was the awards, the unusual, the wacky. They never saw the daily grind.

He realised with sudden perception that he was jaded, tired of the whole thing, bored with it. He'd worked for years without a proper holiday, unless you counted business trips to Japan and New York, or going to Australia to collect Will's body and escort it home, which frankly he didn't.

He'd take some time off, do the barn, oversee it himself. They could manage without him in the office, and if they couldn't, well, they could ring him and he might—just might—answer the phone.

Sometimes.

'How would you feel about having me here for a while?' he said to Claire.

'A while?' she asked, looking puzzled.

'A couple of months, say. I'd get a caravan and live in it, I wouldn't expect you to put me up, but I'd like to oversee the barn conversion—get a bit of a break from the city, have a little hands-on, if you know what I mean.'

'You don't have to live in a caravan!' she protested. 'That's silly—they're always either too hot or too cold, and there's plenty of room in the cottage. I mean, by all means get a caravan if you would rather, but don't do it on my account.'

He looked at her, all warm and sleepy and tousled, and wondered how sane it would be to stay here day after day for so long. Would he be able to keep his hands to himself? He'd have to, he decided, and sighed inwardly.

Oh, well, a bit of physical labour on the barn should settle his libido—starting right now, if there was any lighting out there. Unfortunately there wasn't, so it would just have to wait for the morning. Another long, hard night, he thought, and stifled a despairing laugh.

Oh, Claire, if you only knew...

The following morning, though, instead of tackling the barn, Patrick phoned his parents in Cambridgeshire, unable to put it off any longer.

'I've got something to tell you,' he said. 'Are you in later if I come over? About an hour?'

'Of course we'll be here, if you're coming,' his mother said. 'It sounds exciting.'

Whether she'd think that when she knew, he had no idea, but he couldn't tell them over the phone. He went and found Claire, pottering in the garden with a pair of shears, hacking down the little front lawn.

'What are you doing?' he asked.

'Cutting the grass. What does it look like?'

'The mower not mended?'

'No. Apparently it needs so much doing to it it's

not worth repairing, and the strimmer's broken, so it's the shears or nothing, I'm afraid.'

He went back inside, found the *Yellow Pages* and hunted down a local mower supplier. 'I need a small tractor mower, with big squashy tyres for soft ground, capable of cutting lawns and topping a meadow,' he said. 'What have you got?'

He was given a choice, and decided on the one with the grass collection facility, just in case Claire ever wanted to pick it up. He could picture Jess crawling around on the grass, getting covered in little bits, and it seemed like a good idea.

He gave them the address, paid by credit card and asked them to deliver it. 'I don't suppose there's any chance of it coming today?' he asked, and after a bit of muttering and an outrageous additional delivery charge, they agreed.

He went back out to Claire. 'I've ordered a new mower—it's on the way. If it isn't what you want, send it back and go and choose the right one, but the grass is getting silly and I'll need a mower for the barn.'

She sat back on her heels and looked up at him crossly. 'You love it, don't you? Playing Mr Fixit?'

He sighed and stabbed a hand through his hair, too weary for another fight. 'It's a mower, Claire. We need one, between us, it's no big deal.'

'Well, it is to me!'

He stared at her, frustrated by yet another show of independence. Was she going to be like this for ever? 'Why?' he asked, trying to keep the irritation out of his voice. 'You like crawling around on your hands and knees and cutting the grass with shears? Doing that meadow would be like cutting a lawn with nail scissors!'

'I could just get a goat.'

'Oh, good idea. Another mouth to feed.'

'They eat grass.'

'They eat everything. It would eat your honeysuckle, and the roses, and all the bark off the trees, and every shrub and twig your Auntie Meg planted, and then in the winter it would need hay and feed—you need a mower,' he ended emphatically. 'Just accept it, Claire. It doesn't make you beholden or anything. It can be my mower. I'll lend it to you, OK?'

She sighed and looked away, and he thought her eyes seemed to sparkle in the sunlight.

Tears? He hoped not. He hated it when women cried. He never knew if it was just a put-on or if it was genuine, although with Claire he knew it would be genuine, but that just made it worse.

And he couldn't comfort her, because apparently it was his fault. Again.

Mr Fixit, indeed!

'I'm going to see my parents, and tell them about the baby,' he said, crouching down beside her. 'They'll probably want to see her, but they only live an hour or so away, so I thought I might bring them back and we could go out for lunch somewhere.'

She stared at him in horror. 'You're bringing them here? Without warning? Patrick!'

She leapt to her feet, abandoning the shears, and ran into the house. He followed her and found her in the kitchen, furiously slamming things around, putting stuff away, wiping down the worktop where he'd made his toast.

'Don't you ever—*ever*—do that to me again!' she stormed. 'Look at the place!'

He looked, and he couldn't see anything wrong with it, but, then, he was a man, what did he know? He liked it just the way it was, but telling Claire that when she was in this mood wasn't likely to endear him to her. He'd probably get a wet mop round the ear, and that he could live without.

'Shall I take Jess with me instead?' he suggested, and she glared at him.

'No—she doesn't need an unnecessary car journey, and anyway, you ought to tell them first, not just dump her on their laps.' Her voice softened. 'They're going to have a shock, Patrick. It's going to be quite hard for them.'

'I know.' He scrubbed a hand through his hair and met her eyes ruefully. 'Look, I'm sorry about this, but I just rang them on impulse. I should have done it ages ago, but I just didn't get round to it. Putting it off, I suppose, but then I decided I couldn't put it off any longer. I'm sorry. I should have warned you.'

She shook her head. 'Don't worry, the place could do with a good clean. Jess is sleeping now, I'll do it while she's in bed, and then she can sit in her chair and watch me clean the sitting room. With any luck it'll still be nice and we can sit outside—oh, and don't get any ideas about going out for lunch, I'll cook something. Don't want them thinking I can't look after their granddaughter properly.'

He wanted to hug her, but her last comment had been delivered just a bit crisply, and he thought he might still get that wet mop round the head, so he just thanked her and beat a hasty retreat.

* * *

'What? A baby—oh, Patrick! So, what's the mother like? Do you know her? Had you met her before? We didn't know there was anyone in his life…'

'She's dead,' he told them, watching yet another shock register.

'Dead?'

He didn't want to go into details, so he just nodded.

'How awful. So who's looking after it—is it a boy or a girl?'

'She's a girl—Jess—and her aunt's bringing her up—her name's Claire Franklin. Amy—the mother—was her younger sister.'

His mother turned, tears in her eyes, and gazed pleadingly at her husband. 'Oh, Gerald—could we take her? We could give her a home.'

Patrick shook his head. 'No, Mum, you can't. She's got a home. Her place is with Claire—and me, at the weekends. I'm buying Claire's old barn next to the cottage and converting it, so I can come up every weekend to look after her and see her. You can come and see her there, or she can come to you sometimes, but, no, you can't have her and bring her up.'

'But why?'

'Because we're too darned old to start that nonsense again,' his father said firmly. 'I've retired, we're free—the last thing we need is to be tied to a tiny baby, it wouldn't be fair on any of us, and anyway, it sounds like these two young people have got it all sorted out. They've got the energy for it, darling. We haven't.'

His mother subsided, her face crumpling. 'It's just—she's our grandchild. Will's baby…'

She started to cry softly, and Patrick sat beside her and hugged her.

After a moment she straightened up and searched Patrick's face. 'Does she look like him?'

'No, not really. She's like her mother, Amy.'

'Oh. What a shame she's dead. What happened to her?'

Patrick hesitated, then told them, sparing them too many of the details.

'And you feel guilty, hence all this running round after the child,' his father said, hitting the nail firmly on the head as usual.

Patrick sighed, scrubbing his hand through his hair. 'Yes and no. It's more than that. She's a real little sweetheart. I never thought I'd like babies, but she's…lovely.'

'I want to see her,' his mother said, rallying.

He smiled. 'I knew you would. Claire's expecting us for lunch.'

How she was supposed to feed two extra people without warning, Claire didn't know. She threw all the contents of the fridge on the table, studied them and threw what she didn't need back in.

A quiche, she decided—bacon and tomatoes and asparagus, if there was any yet, with a scattering of herbs from the garden and some fresh new potatoes from the vegetable patch. It was too early for home-grown salad, but she'd got some at the supermarket yesterday, so that would do.

And for pudding, she'd take an apple pie out of the freezer. It was made with home-grown apples from the tree behind the cottage, and if she thawed it in the microwave, she could crisp it in the oven when the quiche was finished.

Two lots of pastry, but it was just too bad, that was the best she could do at such short notice.

She chopped and sliced and kneaded while her anger bubbled under the surface, and as she worked, she plotted all the ways she could kill Patrick. Something slow, she decided. Slow and painful.

She scraped the bacon and vegetables into the pastry case, spread them around and poured in the egg and cheese and milk mixture—itself practically beaten to death—and a sprinkling of fresh herbs. More cheese on top, and into the oven.

And now, she thought, for the sitting room.

Except that Jess cried, and even though Claire fed her and changed her nappy and walked her up and down, she still cried, grizzling and scrubbing at her gums. Teething again, Claire thought, and carried her on her hip while she hastily tidied the sitting room with one hand and picked the worst bits of fluff off the carpet.

And then Patrick's car turned onto the drive, before she had time to worry any more, followed by another car. She went to the front door, Jess on her hip and the dogs rushing on ahead, Pepper wary but Dog wagging furiously and darting from Patrick to his parents and back again.

Claire stood in the doorway, suddenly stupidly apprehensive, and Jess buried her face in Claire's side and howled.

'Oh, baby, come on, they've come to see you,' she said softly, but Jess was inconsolable.

She met Patrick's eyes in desperation. 'I think she's

teething again,' she said, and he reached for her, tucking her up against his chest and rubbing her back gently.

'It's all right, baby, it's all right. Uncle Patrick's got you.'

His mother put her hand over her mouth and watched, eyes filling, as Patrick soothed and rocked the baby until she was quiet, and then he turned her in his arms so she could see her grandparents.

'Mum, Dad, this is Jess.'

Jess stared at them, her brown eyes like saucers, and her lip trembled again.

'Oh, dear. Teething?' his mother said, and took the baby from him, carrying her up and down the garden and singing to her until she was distracted from her gums.

'Dad, this is Claire,' Patrick said, and his father shook her hand, his clear green eyes so like Patrick's assessing her kindly.

'Lovely to meet you, my dear. Gerald Cameron— and that's my wife, Jean. I'm sorry to descend on you like this without warning—I gather you've kindly offered us lunch. It's very good of you.'

'It's a pleasure,' she said, realising with surprise that it was the truth. Then the word 'lunch' dropped into her consciousness and her eyes widened. 'I just have to take something out of the oven, if you'll excuse me. I'll put the kettle on.'

She all but ran back to the kitchen and yanked the oven door open, rescuing the quiche in the nick of time. She put the apple pie in to crisp, put the potatoes on to boil and filled the kettle again.

Patrick materialised behind her and peered over her shoulder.

'That looks good.'

'Of course,' she said, cockily confident now she knew it wasn't burnt. 'How's the baby?'

'Quiet. My mother's in her element.' He paused for a moment. 'Thank you for doing this,' he said quietly. 'They were quite shocked, but their first instinct was to come and see her, and it's much easier here, especially if she's miserable with another tooth. They really appreciate it. *I* really appreciate it.'

Claire forgot her plans for his demise. 'No problem. I like your father. He's very like you.'

'I think it's supposed to be the other way round,' he said with a smile. 'So, where are we eating?'

'In the garden? We can carry the table and chairs outside and sit under the apple tree, if you like. Otherwise it's in here or the dining room, which is a bit dark and gloomy. You choose.'

'Outside?' he said, and hoisting the table up, he carried it out, manoeuvring it through the door and coming back a moment later for the chairs.

'Did the mower come?' he asked, pausing in the doorway on his second pass, and she shook her head.

'No. You didn't expect it today, did you?'

Just then his father stuck his head round the door. 'There's a lorry here with a lawnmower on it,' he said, and Patrick put down the chairs and shooed Claire out to the front.

She was expecting it to be wrong—too big, too top-heavy for the slope by the river, tyres too narrow for the soft ground down there by the ditch—but it wasn't. It was perfect, a modern version of the one she had, but with a grass collector so Jess wouldn't get covered in little bits all the time, and exactly the sort of thing she would have chosen—if she'd had the money.

'Will it do?'

She nodded, a stupid lump in her throat. Ridiculous. It was just a mower, for heaven's sake! 'It's perfect. You can make a start after lunch,' she said, and went back to the kitchen with his father's chuckle following her down the hall.

CHAPTER SIX

LUNCH was a great success.

Jess spent the entire time on her grandmother's knee, chewing furiously on her plastic keyring and enjoying all the unexpected attention. And because they were in the garden and the weather was wonderful, there was a lovely alfresco party feel to the whole thing.

Patrick heaved a silent sigh of relief and sat back, leaving them to it. Claire was coping fine, and his parents were managing not to ask searching and insensitive questions, and the baby was quiet. What more could a man ask for? he thought, and relaxed.

The food had been wonderful. Nothing complicated, just fresh ingredients simply cooked and served in the fresh air in the dappled shade of the gnarled old apple tree—the tree from which Claire had picked the fruit for the apple pie the previous autumn, she'd told him.

There was something incredibly satisfying about that, he thought. Satisfying, basic and fundamental. He could understand why farmers carried on against all odds and in all weathers, working the land, reaping the rewards.

Had the old hunter-gatherers felt like that, too, when they'd found a tree full of ripe, soft fruit, or hunted down a mammoth? He laughed softly to himself. The nearest he ever got to hunting down a mammoth was a quick sortie to the local supermarket, crammed in between endless site meetings and arguments with planners.

So *safe*, so reliable, so remote from the precarious reality of famine and crop failure—even when they were out of stock of the things he wanted!

Not that he'd want his livelihood to be precarious, but he'd often thought that there should be a more simple life, some happy medium between the chaotic mouse-in-a-wheel existence of today and the hand-to-mouth existence of his early forebears.

There was just something so profoundly peaceful about sitting there in the shade of the tree with the taste of the apple still fresh on his tongue and the quiet hum of bees in the blossom, ensuring the next crop.

It might be nice to have some chickens, he thought absently—or then, perhaps not. It wouldn't be fair to Claire, with him away so much, but the idea was tempting. The baby could help feed them, when she was older, and watch the chicks scratching in the dirt. She'd love that.

He nearly laughed. There was a way to go before Jess was ready for that, he reminded himself, and found his eyes drawn to her yet again.

She had finally stopped chewing on the plastic ring, and was sleeping peacefully in her pram just beside the table. He met his mother's eyes and she smiled at him mistily, and he wondered why he'd waited nearly five weeks before telling them about Jess.

They'd been so pleased to meet her, and they'd really taken to Claire, as well. He was hugely relieved about that, because if they liked her and trusted her, then they wouldn't worry about her being responsible for Jess's upbringing—which meant they wouldn't be permanently on his case.

Well, not about that, anyway. There were plenty of other areas of his life where they found room for a little parental nagging, but that, fortunately, didn't seem destined to be one.

While Claire and his mother were busy discussing the baby's sleeping pattern, he caught his father's eye. The other man, blatantly not as fascinated as his wife by the intricacies of his granddaughter's daily routine, looked across at the barn and inclined his head towards it.

'So—is this the project?' he asked quietly, and Patrick nodded.

'Yes. Fancy a look?'

He nodded agreement, and Patrick glanced at Claire. 'Are you OK if we slide off for a minute?'

'Sure. Tea or coffee?'

'Whichever. Thanks. We won't be long.'

They strolled over to the barn and he opened the door—more easily since he'd oiled the hinges and the heavy wheel that it ran on—and his father looked around thoughtfully and nodded.

'Mmm. Interesting. What's the view like?'

He opened the other door, and his father threw him a wry smile. 'I might have known. You always were a sucker for a good view.' He pretended interest in a particularly boring bit of timber, his voice a study in innocence. 'So, you'll move up here, and live next to Claire. She's a nice girl.'

Innocence, my foot, Patrick thought. 'Well, I'll live

next to Jess, in fact, and it's only for the weekends,' he pointed out, but his father just carried on smiling.

'We'll see,' he said, and Patrick rolled his eyes.

'Dad, this is about Jess, and Will, not about me and Claire.'

'Of course,' his father agreed, the smile fading at the mention of his other son, but Patrick had the feeling he was just being agreeable and didn't believe a word of it.

Funny, that, he thought. He'd been wondering himself just how much his decision to move up here and convert the barn was to do with Jess, and how much was because of Claire, and he'd tried to convince himself his motives were entirely honourable and connected to the baby's welfare.

Nothing at all to do with her aunt, and why should it be? She'd shown no interest in him, and any slight move he'd made had been met with a firm put-down—like his silly suggestion in the barn last weekend, when he'd asked if she'd run away if he kissed her.

Of course, she'd replied. He'd done it later, anyway, over the gingerbread, and the feel of her lips was seared on his memory for ever.

She hadn't screamed and run away, though. Perhaps he should have pursued it.

And perhaps not. It was a difficult enough situation, without his father egging him on. He refocused his father's mind on the barn, and showed him his plans, getting them from the car and spreading them out on the bonnet of the brand new lawn tractor and poring over them.

'So this is where you've got to,' his mother said,

coming into the barn behind him with the baby on her hip a while later.

He turned and smiled. 'Sorry, I was just showing Dad the plans.'

'Claire's made tea,' she said. 'Are you going to come in?'

He nodded and folded up the blueprints. 'So, what do you think, Mum?'

'I think she's lovely.'

'I'm talking about the barn, not the baby.'

'And I was talking about Claire.'

Et tu, Brute?

'Mum, Claire and I are just related to Jess. That's all. There's nothing going on between us, and there won't be, ever. We're friends, nothing more, nothing less, and that's the way it's staying.'

He turned towards the door, and found Claire there, a tray in her hands and a curious expression on her face.

'I thought I'd come to you, since you were clearly not coming in,' she said lightly, but there was something in her eyes that he couldn't read.

'We were just coming.'

'I'll take it back, then,' she said. Turning on her heel, she walked back across the drive to the cottage and disappeared inside.

'I think we're in the sitting room,' his mother said, shooting his father a quick glance that Patrick wasn't supposed to see.

He sighed under his breath. Oh, hell. They were going to start matchmaking, he could feel it in his bones, and then things between him and Claire would get really awkward.

He shook his head in despair. He really didn't need their help. He had the distinct feeling he could manage to mess up his relationship with Claire all by himself!

Well, that was her told, as if she'd needed telling.

What did you expect? Claire asked herself. You've always known he's out of reach.

But he kissed me, she thought, and stopped herself before the fantasy took flight. It had just been a peck. Well, last night. But then, there'd been the kiss over the gingerbread a week ago. That had been more than a peck.

Not much more, though, and still meaningless, she told herself firmly. You're just turning into a desperate old maid. You'll have to get out more.

'So, what do you think of Patrick's ideas for the barn?' Gerald asked her as they settled into the sitting room with their tea.

What she thought was that she hadn't been shown them, but she disguised her hurt with a casual little shrug. 'I haven't seen them. They're nothing to do with me, really, and anyway, there hasn't been time. Patrick didn't get here until late last night, and then this morning—'

'You had to cook for us without warning. That was a lovely lunch, by the way, my dear,' Jean said appreciatively. 'Thank you for going to all that trouble.'

'It was no trouble,' she replied, putting aside her hurt that Patrick hadn't shared his thoughts with her yet. 'It's lovely to meet you, and to see you with Jess.'

Jess, wide awake again, was cuddled up on her

grandmother's knee with a bottle, and Claire wondered why she'd been so worried about meeting them.
Because she'd feared they'd want to take her away?
Possibly, but now, having met them, she didn't think
they would, even if they wanted to. A small baby's
routine was gruelling for the carer, and it would get
worse before it got better, Claire was sure. And she
was equally sure that, having been parents, the
Camerons would have worked that out for themselves
and decided to leave it up to her.

She hoped.

'Well, I'd like to see the plans,' his mother was
saying. 'Go on, Patrick, let's have a look, talk us
through them.'

'They're only rough, really—just ideas,' he said,
but she laughed.

'I don't want a structural engineer's report, darling,
just an idea of what you've got in mind, for interest's
sake,' she teased, and with a wry chuckle he got to
his feet and fetched the plans from the study.

He spread them out on the floor, kneeling down on
the carpet covered in little bits of fluff and dog hair
that Claire hadn't had time to vacuum off, and went
through his ideas and thoughts.

And Claire, amazed that two people could come up
with two such different designs for the same building,
forgot to feel slighted that she hadn't been shown the
plans until now and allowed herself to be fascinated.

It sounded lovely—light and airy and spacious,
with hugely high ceilings open to the roof wherever
possible, and just a few big rooms, not the fussy little
collection of this and that that the previous architect
had worked into the scheme.

As if he'd read her mind, he said, 'It's only for me and Jess, and the occasional visitor, so I don't really need lots of rooms. I'd rather have a feeling of space in the rooms I have, and anyway, large multifunction rooms are the way it's going. People want much less formality these days.'

'And this?' his mother asked, pointing to a roughly sketched bit that didn't exist at present.

'That's an extension. A cart lodge for parking, and another room—perhaps a studio? You never know, I might find I end up working here some of the time, especially in the school holidays when she's older.'

Claire's heart jumped at the prospect, and she studied the plan of the extension more closely. It was at the back, taking advantage of the view, and out of sight of her cottage.

So she wouldn't be able to watch him at work, she thought, and the thought was curiously depressing.

Still, it was easy to see why he'd done it like that, because the view would be stunning, of course. If it wasn't for the barn being in the way, she'd have the same view from her study, but of course she didn't.

She would have done from her studio in the barn, if her plans for the future had ever worked out, but they'd been pipe dreams. She knew that in her heart of hearts, and so she stifled the little pang of regret and focused on the difference Patrick's money and support was going to make to her life.

No more worries, no more struggling alone, and every weekend she'd have his company.

Her heart lurched at the thought, and she told herself not to be silly.

Friends, nothing more, nothing less, and that's the way it's staying.

Oh, rats.

The mower was great—simple to operate, easy to start, and a huge improvement on the last one, he was sure. Patrick backed it out of the barn, studied the instruction manual again and then set off around the front garden.

Hmm. Trees everywhere, in the way, and not a sensible route to be had. Still, he managed, and then he headed round the side of the cottage to the back, and cut the grass there around the apple tree where they'd had lunch the day before and under the big oak in the corner where he thought he'd make a swing for Jess when she was bigger.

Again, no sensible route presented itself, and after about ten minutes of retracing his tracks over and over again to get to the missed bits, Claire appeared in the doorway, arms folded, and propped herself against the frame and watched him, a smile twitching her lips.

'What?' he asked, feeling a bit silly.

She shrugged. 'I normally start over there, otherwise it's difficult,' she said, pointing towards the barn, and he ground his teeth.

'I'd noticed,' he said, wondering how much damage the machine would do to her if he ran her over with it. Too much, he decided, and turned off the engine. 'I tell you what, why don't you demonstrate—since it's your garden and I'm only a mere interloper?'

'Mere nothing,' she mumbled under her breath. At

least, that's what he thought she said, but it could have been anything.

Whatever, she took the wheel of the machine, sliding onto the seat with considerably more grace than he'd achieved, and with a quick flick of the key she started it, engaged the cutting deck and set off across the lawn, whisking through it in no time flat and irritating him to bits.

Until, that is, he noticed the way the uneven ground jostled her breasts and made them undulate gently.

Is that a rabbit in your pocket or are you pleased to see me?

He groaned and turned away. There were easier ways to torture himself—like pulling out his toenails. He went into the study, turned his back firmly on the window and spread the plans out again on the drawing board.

Claire had hardly said anything about them, and a little bit of him was piqued and—yes, really— wounded at her lack of interest.

'It's nothing to do with me,' she'd said, and he'd felt the excitement go out of it at that moment.

But why? He wasn't doing it for her, it wasn't really anything to do with her, and maybe her lack of interest wasn't really that so much as a lingering hurt that she'd had to sell it at all.

Damn. He hadn't thought of that, and he should have done.

He turned on the swivel chair and studied her out of the window, flying up and down the meadow on the little tractor with her breasts jiggling and her face flushed by the sunset.

She was truly gorgeous, and not for the first time

he wished they weren't involved in this inescapable relationship. They were, though, and as a result there was too much at stake to risk muddying the waters with something so transient and irrelevant as desire.

He had to admit that his feelings didn't seem to be transient, though—far from it. Claire was getting further under his skin with every day that passed, and keeping his hands to himself was getting more and more difficult.

She went over another bump and her breasts jiggled again, and with a low snarl of disgust he spun the chair back to the drawing board and forced himself to pay attention. He was meeting the planners the next day, and he really, *really* didn't have time to fantasise about how her body would feel under his hands!

'So, how was the mower?' Patrick asked her, and she didn't know if she'd imagined it or if he sounded just the tiniest bit offhand with her.

'Fine,' she said, and then noticed the wry arch to his brow.

'Only fine?'

She rolled her eyes. 'OK, it's wonderful, you were right, thank you very much, it's a brilliant mower, we really needed one between us, I love it, you're perfect—better?'

He laughed, a soft huff of sound that rippled over her nerve endings and made her knees go weak.

'A little insincere, but I dare say I can forgive you for that, since you seem to have registered all the important points.'

He shrugged away from the study door and came

towards her, hands rammed in his pockets, a slightly diffident look on his face.

'Um—I've been fiddling with the plans. I wondered if you wanted to see.'

Her heart lurched a bit, and she filled the kettle to give herself time. 'If you like,' she said, unsure how to react, not wanting to stick her nose in where it wasn't needed but curious nevertheless—even though it wasn't any of her business and it wasn't her barn any more.

Stop it, she told herself. You had to sell it. Better an award-winning absentee architect than a noisy family with no taste and hundreds of teenagers having wild parties.

Even so...

'Claire?'

She turned, pasting a smile on her face, but he didn't smile back. Instead he studied her thoughtfully, and shook his head.

'I'm sorry. I've been really insensitive about this, haven't I? It was your dream, and I've taken it away.'

'No. No, you haven't. It was only a dream. Reality took it away—reality and Amy, and I can't blame her for that,' she said, feeling tears well in her eyes. 'She didn't mean— Oh, hell.'

Breaking off, she ran away, out of the house and over to the barn, her retreat, as always—and then realised that it wasn't hers any more, or soon wouldn't be, and then where would she go to lick her wounds?

A sob caught in her throat, and she leaned against the wall of the barn and stuffed her hand in her mouth to stifle the noise.

She needn't have bothered. Patrick was right be-

hind her, turning her gently into his arms and cradling
her against his chest while she howled her eyes out.

'It's all right, baby, it wasn't your fault. You did
everything you could. She was on self-destruct,' he
murmured, and she realised what he'd already known,
that she wasn't crying about the barn at all, but about
Amy, and the waste of it, and so, giving herself up
to the luxury of being comforted, she slid her arms
round his waist and hung on tight.

When the storm had passed, Claire stood there for
another couple of minutes, wallowing in the feel of
his firm, strong arms around her, his chest hard beneath her cheek, his legs straddling hers so she was
pulled into the cradle of his thighs.

He was leaning against the barn, and she could feel
the brickwork on her wrists, so she eased away, wriggling her arms out from behind him and straightening
up reluctantly.

Not far, though, because he didn't release her, just
slackened his hold and dropped his linked hands
down to rest on her bottom while his eyes searched
her face.

'Don't look at me, I must look a fright,' she said,
scrubbing her nose with the back of her hand, and he
smiled and pulled out a clean tissue from his pocket
and blotted her eyes and wiped her nose and then
pulled her back into his arms.

'All right now?' he murmured, and she nodded,
avoiding his eyes. However nice he was to her, it
didn't stop her looking awful, and the bit of her that
wasn't wallowing in self-indulgence wanted to run
away and hide.

He wasn't having any, though. He brought one
hand round from behind her back, the other still hold-

ing her in place, and with a firm, blunt fingertip he tipped her chin up.

'I know what you're going through,' he said gruffly. 'I've worn out the T-shirt. Just remember, she was an adult. You're not your brother's keeper, Claire.'

She nodded, knowing he was right but not really believing him.

'Stop it,' he said, and then cut off her train of thought with devastating effectiveness by lowering his mouth to hers and kissing her.

It was still relatively chaste, a carefully controlled kiss, not platonic by any stretch of the imagination, but not overtly passionate either.

She eased away before she welded herself up against him and disgraced herself, and walked slowly but fairly steadily back to the cottage. He fell into step beside her, not touching her but close enough that if she just moved her hand a fraction, his would be there.

'Jess is crying,' he said, and went ahead of her to get the baby up. She'd been sleeping for hours, exhausted after yesterday, and Claire had wondered when she'd wake. She'd been surprised she was still asleep after she'd done the mowing, but it hadn't taken nearly as long as usual, thanks to the new machine.

She gave a wry smile. It was wonderful, and she'd been singularly ungracious about it, but it was just so easy for Patrick with all his money to fling it around like that. It made her feel even more inadequate and beholden, but she was learning to live with it. Between the car and the mower and the money for the barn, she was getting quite good at it, in fact.

Oh, rats. So much money, so beholden—and the car was a total fraud, because now he'd got his own up here anyway and was going to be here for months!

She groaned quietly. She could still feel the imprint of his body on hers, hard and solid and very masculine, and even though the kiss had been quite tame, nevertheless his body had reacted unmistakably. So had hers, but her reaction was invisible, thank goodness, and she'd got away from him in the nick of time before she'd lost all restraint.

He was only a man, after all, only human, and if she'd flung herself at him, he would have been a fool not to take her up on it. It wouldn't mean anything, though, not to a man like that who could have anyone he wanted. It was only her heart that would be broken, and she couldn't run away.

Thank heavens she'd had the sense to back away!

Why had he kissed her like that?

Or, more precisely, why had he kissed her at all? So near and yet so far. Damn. He was an idiot.

Jess cried, and he focused on her little face as she lay on the changing mat. 'Oh, baby. What's the matter? Are you hungry? I won't be a moment, but your nappy's sopping wet. Come on, let Uncle Patrick sort you out.'

She squirmed on the mat, trying to roll over, but he held her down with one large hand in the middle of her tummy while he opened out the new nappy and slid it under her bottom. Baby wipes, stick the tapes, and off we go, he thought, scooping her up against his chest and talking to her all the way down the stairs.

Claire was in the kitchen, making tea in mugs, and

Jess's bottle was standing on the table, already warmed, with a bowl of cereal and a bib.

'Cereal, Jess,' he said, and tucking her bib round her neck, he sat her on his knee and fed her. He was getting almost competent, he thought. All this practice.

He looked up as he put a spoon of cereal in Jess's mouth, and Claire's mouth closed as if around a spoon. He arched a brow, and she blushed and turned back to the mugs, fishing out the teabags.

'It's a reflex,' she said. 'You do it, too.'

'No, I don't,' he said, and then a second later felt his mouth open and close as Jess's did. Well, damn!

Claire laughed at him, and it was so good to hear her happy again that he gave a wry chuckle and let it go. He'd get her back for something later, he had no doubt.

In the meantime, he had his hands full making sure the cereal went into Jess's mouth and not all down his shirt.

Or in his hair, he thought flatly, as Jess, deciding she'd had enough, blew a huge raspberry and splattered him with goo.

Claire laughed, and so did Jess, a lovely little giggle, and he forgot the indignity and laughed with them.

The dogs were at his feet, licking up the little splatters, and the cat was watching from the sidelines, and he could hear a bird singing in the apple tree.

Paradise?

It felt very close to it, he thought, and yet it was just an illusion. He was sitting here with his brother's baby on his lap, with his brother's dog at his feet, next to his brother's girlfriend's sister, living the life his brother should have been living.

Damn you, Will, he thought sadly. You should be here, doing this, and Amy should be here, and Claire and I should be—what? Where? Not here together, forced into a relationship we daren't compromise.

He gave a short sigh and stood up, handing the baby to Claire.

'I'll go and sort myself out. I'll be back in a minute,' he told Claire. Heading up the stairs again, he went into the little room he was using, closed the door and rested his head against it.

If Amy and Will were still alive, he and Claire would have met on a level playing field, and maybe now they'd be having an affair, instead of tiptoeing round each other and aching for things they couldn't have.

Well, he was, he didn't know about her. She wasn't interested in him. If she had been, she would have kissed him back just now instead of standing there and letting him kiss her and then walking away.

Damn, damn, damn.

He went back downstairs, dressed in a clean shirt and jeans and with the cereal rinsed out of his hair, and Claire was sitting on a chair, giving Jess her bottle.

'Fancy soup for lunch?' she asked, but he couldn't stay there another minute.

'I'm not hungry,' he said. 'I think I'll take the dogs for a walk.' And without waiting for a reply, he whistled for Pepper and Dog, picked up their leads and headed for the door.

CHAPTER SEVEN

MUCH to Claire's surprise, Patrick invited her to the meeting with the planning officers the following morning.

It was a surprise because he'd been in such a strange mood yesterday after he'd come back from his walk—well, no, in fact, after Jess had spat cereal all over his head and he'd gone upstairs to change.

Because of the kiss? She had no idea. She'd given up trying to figure out what made his mind work, it was a complete mystery to her. All she knew was that every now and again he seemed to be able to read her mind, sometimes even before she did, and she found it thoroughly disconcerting when she never had a clue what he was thinking.

Now, however, he simply said to her, 'I'm sure they won't mind if you bring Jess, and as it's your property and you put in the initial planning application, it might work better with you there. Anyway, I thought you might be interested to see what they said.'

She nodded cautiously, wondering if he really wanted her there or not, and then decided he shouldn't have made the offer if he didn't mean it. 'Yes, I would be interested,' she agreed, 'although I don't know that my presence will make a great deal of difference—I mean, my opinion won't carry a lot of weight, will it, not compared to somebody like you?'

'Somebody like me?'

One eyebrow was arched slightly, and there was a cynical twist to his lips.

She met his look with a level stare. 'You know what I mean.'

'Only too well. They'll look at it with a microscope, because they'll be expecting me to push the envelope.'

'And have you?'

He shrugged. 'Not really. I did think of going for a totally self-contained steel structure within the building, but I thought they'd probably have a fit. Actually, I've been boringly moderate, because I thought the building should be allowed to speak for itself. Let's just hope the planners see it that way.'

He gathered the plans together, put them into his briefcase and snapped the locks shut. 'How long will it take to get to the council offices?' he asked her.

'I don't know—about twenty-five minutes?'

'Time for a coffee?'

She thought quickly. Jess was sitting in her chair, playing with a string of brightly coloured little plastic people suspended in front of her, but Claire knew that any minute now she'd be getting hungry.

'You make the coffee, I'll feed the baby, otherwise we won't get through this meeting without a barrage of opinion from Titch here.'

It was fascinating, being a fly on the wall in many respects while Patrick and the planners duelled.

And watching him talk about his ideas and vision for the barn, watching his face become animated as he talked about how it would look, she felt the whole project come alive, and as it did, her regret that she had sold it to him faded away, replaced by a curious excitement at the prospect of seeing it take shape.

They argued, of course, disagreeing about certain aspects of his design, and Claire sat back and watched as he skilfully engineered the meeting and reasoned away their objections one by one.

There was only one point on which they completely refused to back down, and that was the glass stairway that she hadn't even known about.

'Inappropriate, it should be oak,' one of them said.

'It would be wonderful, of course, in a city apartment, but in a barn in the country...' The speaker left his comment hanging in the air, and the others nodded.

To her surprise, Patrick simply shrugged. 'OK. I take your point, we'll go for oak,' he said totally reasonably, and then laid his hands flat on the table and looked around at them all. 'Are we all right otherwise?' he asked them.

'Well, in theory, but, of course, it'll have to go through all the appropriate channels,' the spokesperson said.

'Of course—but since the plan is agreed in principle and planning permission has been granted, I'd like to start immediately.'

They blustered for a moment or two, but then conceded. Provided he didn't work too quickly, and liaised with them at every turn, then—grudgingly—they agreed that he could start the groundworks.

They left the meeting room, and it was only when they were outside in the car park that he turned to her and smiled.

No, he didn't smile, he positively grinned, a cheeky, little-boy grin that made her laugh aloud.

'Excellent,' he said, and she could feel the smug self-satisfaction coming off him in waves.

'But you didn't get your glass staircase,' she said, puzzled that he should be so pleased, but he simply laughed.

'I never expected to get it. I had to work in something to concede, and I thought that was the sort of thing they'd be expecting from me—so I gave it to them. A really simple oak one will look much better. It's what I'd always intended, anyway.'

'How sly,' she said, and he chuckled.

'Of course. There's no point in having all this experience if I don't put it to good use. Now, how about lunch?'

The next few days were hectic. Patrick went back to London in the Golf estate, and left the Audi TT and Dog behind with Claire. It felt odd going back without him, but he had so much to do and, anyway, the animal was much happier with Pepper for company. And Claire didn't seem to mind the idea of driving the Audi, either!

Kate smiled at him when he walked into Reception, and propped her elbows on the desk. 'So, how's it going?' she asked him.

'Good. The planners are being very reasonable, and I think the barn should look really good.'

'And Claire and the baby?'

Leave it to Kate to get straight to the point. 'They're fine,' he said, refusing to indulge his receptionist's curiosity. 'Is Sally in?'

'Yes, she's in her office. She said you weren't coming in today.'

'I wasn't, but I've had a change of plan. Are Mike and David in?'

'Mike is, David's in a meeting. He'll be back in about an hour.'

Patrick nodded and headed for the lift. He had plenty to do for the next hour, but then he really needed to talk to Mike and David, and tell them his plans. They wouldn't like it, but that was tough. He'd given the firm enough over the years, and the last year, especially, had been very difficult. It was time for him now, and if that meant his partners had to pick up some of the slack, well, so be it. It wouldn't kill them to take a little more responsibility, and David in particular was under-using his talent.

Anyway, he was hardly leaving the country. He'd only be two hours away by car and a matter of seconds on the phone. They'd cope.

The lift doors slid open, and he walked into Sally's office and grinned.

'Morning, Sally,' he said brightly, and she stared at him in amazement.

'I thought you weren't in today—and where's the dog?'

'I wasn't—and he's in Suffolk. I've come back to do one or two things, and didn't think it was worth dragging him back.'

Sally stared at him as if he'd grown two heads. 'Not worth it?' She shook her head slightly, as if to clear it, and stared at him again. 'I don't quite understand,' she said a little weakly. 'I thought you were coming back tomorrow for the rest of the week—I'm sure that's what you said!'

He shot her a slightly crooked grin. 'I was,' he confessed, 'but I've had a change of plan.' He hesitated for a moment, and then went on, 'Actually, I've decided to have a couple of months off, to supervise this barn conversion.'

Sally's jaw dropped, and he leant across the desk, put his finger under her chin and closed her mouth.

As soon as he released it, it opened again, but only because she'd recovered her powers of speech.

'You're doing what?' she said, but before he could reply, she carried on, 'You've got meetings arranged into the hereafter, the new project south of the river is just about to take off, you've got to finish the house in Hampstead, the offices in Ealing are getting to crisis point with the builders—and you're going to slope off to Suffolk and supervise this barn conversion?'

Her voice rose towards the end of the sentence, and Patrick just raised an eyebrow and stepped back and nodded.

'Something like that,' he said, and smiled at her. 'Any chance of a coffee?'

He walked into his office, and closed the door behind him with a soft click.

On the count of three, he heard a tiny, muffled scream from the other side of the door, and then a thump. He smiled, shrugged out of his jacket and hung it over the back of his chair, then sat down with his feet crossed on the edge of the desk, locked his hands behind his head and smiled.

She'd calm down in a minute, and then she'd bring in his coffee and the diary, and they'd go through it and sort out the most pressing of the problems. Some of his appointments, of course, couldn't be rescheduled until he'd spoken to Mike and David, because the various projects he was involved in would have to be reallocated to them.

He decided David could take the new Battersea project—it was just the sort of thing to test his talent and, given enough room to stretch his wings, Patrick was sure he was ready for it.

Please, God.

The door opened, and Sally appeared with a mug in one hand and the diary in the other.

'Do Mike and David know?' she asked, and he shook his head.

'Not yet.'

She raised an expressive eyebrow. 'It's going to really hit the fan, you do know that, don't you?'

He grinned. 'They'll live,' he said unsympathetically. 'They've been spoonfed for years, and it's time they learned to stand on their own two feet. It's not going to kill them.'

Sally snorted softly under her breath. 'No, but they might kill you,' she pointed out, and flicked open the diary. 'Right, about these appointments.'

Twenty-four hectic and somewhat difficult hours later, Patrick loaded his car with clothes, a fax machine, a photocopier and a drawing board that worked smoothly, and headed back to Suffolk.

Dog and Pepper came bouncing out to meet him, followed at a rather more dignified pace by Claire, with Jess on her hip.

He had a terrible urge to say something corny, like,

'Hi, honey, I'm home!' but stifled it and simply smiled instead, patted the dogs and reached for the baby who was waving her arms madly at him and leaning right over.

'How's my little sweetheart?' he asked, and she giggled and bounced up and down in his arms.

'She's got another tooth,' Claire told him with what sounded suspiciously like motherly pride, and he duly inspected Jess's gummy little mouth and congratulated her on the tiny new arrival.

Just one day, he thought, and she'd changed. She was changing so fast now, every day bringing something new, and she'd even started to crawl after a fashion. He wondered how men in the forces coped, coming back after a posting abroad to find their young children altered almost beyond recognition.

And Jess wasn't even his.

What a peculiar thought.

He handed her back to Claire and unloaded the car, taking all the office equipment into her study and trying to find somewhere to put it.

'You could always take over the dining room,' she suggested, but he didn't fancy the idea. For a start, it didn't have a view of the barn, which might be handy when the builders started work, and for another thing, she would never be in there.

He didn't analyse that one too closely, just shook his head.

'I'm sure we'll manage, and I'd like to be able to see the barn,' he said. 'Anyway, you might find some of the stuff useful for your work.'

She snorted under her breath. 'What work?' she muttered, and he realised that for the last couple of weeks, at least, she hadn't seemed to have done anything.

By choice, or because there was nothing available? If it was the latter, and he was almost sure it was, then what on earth would she have done without him?

He'd discovered during the course of their weekends together that she and Amy had lost their parents four years ago, just a year before Auntie Meg, so she was quite alone now. He wondered how that felt. His parents, for all their interference, were very loving and supportive, and the thought of them not being there and having no one else to take their place was chilling.

Patrick resolved to use his influence to put some work her way, because he sensed that she was worried about her recent loss of earnings even though he'd told her that he would happily support her as well as the baby. Although, of course, once she got the money for the barn she should be able to live much more comfortably.

'So, how was London?' Claire asked him over a cup of tea a few minutes later.

'OK. My partners were a bit shocked that I was disappearing off the face of the earth for so long, but I'm sure they'll cope. They're both highly qualified, after all, they just like having their hands held.'

'Well, they'd have to cope if anything happened to you,' Claire pointed out reasonably, and he nodded.

'Absolutely,' he said, and, stretching out his legs, he balanced his mug of tea on his belt buckle and sighed with satisfaction. It was good to be home, he thought, and the thought startled him.

Home? Was that what this was now? And where? The barn, or this kitchen, with Claire and the baby and the dogs and the cat all piled in together in glorious confusion?

He didn't want to dwell on that. There was a lot he didn't want to dwell on these days, and Claire seemed to be in the middle of all of it.

'I've spoken to a builder—a man from near here that I've used in the past. He's coming over in the morning to have a look, and if he can, he'll start work immediately. One of his clients has gone belly-up and he's got a team standing idle at the moment, so we might just be lucky.'

Claire nodded, but she didn't say anything, and he wondered if she was still having trouble with the thought of him doing up the barn.

'Claire? Are you OK about this?' he asked gently, studying her face for any sign of distress, but there was none.

'I'm fine,' she said, and smiled a little ruefully. 'In fact, you might have to throw me off your site,' she confessed, 'because I'm itching to see how it turns out.'

He laughed, and felt the tension drain out of him. 'It's not my site,' he told her firmly, 'and I have no intention of throwing you off it.'

'Don't speak too soon,' she said with a laugh. 'You don't know how bad I'll be yet.'

Bad? He wasn't expecting her to be bad. He would be only too happy for her to take an interest, even if it was critical, because for all she denied it, it was something to do with her, a part of her inheritance, part of her upbringing, and she had every right to like it—or, at the very least, to voice her objections.

*   *   *

By the middle of the next day, it was all happening. The builder had moved in his team, the scaffolding was going up, and the roof was coming off the lean-to.

Claire watched it with interest, doing her best to keep the dogs out of the way in case something should land on them, and besides, not wanting to incur the workmen's wrath when the dogs ate their sandwiches. At first she was concerned that the banging would keep the baby awake, but her room was at the other end of the house, next to Claire's, and the noise didn't seem to penetrate.

Predictably, Patrick was outside with his sleeves rolled up getting in amongst it, and the moment the scaffolding was secure, he was at the top, a hard hat on his head, climbing about on the scaffold boards as if he'd been born up there.

She smiled. Hands on, he'd said, and it seemed that he really meant it. Claire, knowing how these things worked, spent her day filling the kettle and plying everyone with tea and coffee and chocolate biscuits.

'You're spoiling those lads,' the foreman told her, but she just smiled, because she knew he didn't mean it, and he took another biscuit.

'Don't I get tea?' Patrick asked, appearing at her shoulder.

'You missed it, mate,' the foreman said with a chuckle, and, taking another biscuit, he wandered off towards the rest of the workforce, leaving her alone with Patrick.

'Did I?' he asked her, but she shook her head.

'Of course not,' she told him. 'I put the kettle on again before I came out. I was going to have one in the kitchen, and I wondered if you wanted to join me.'

She heard her voice, and could have groaned aloud.

I wondered if you wanted to join me. You sound like a pathetic old maid, she told herself in disgust. She didn't wait for his reply, just headed back to the kitchen and hoped he'd follow.

He did, of course, and she was pragmatic enough to realise it was for the tea and not her company. Running around on the scaffolding in full sun was thirsty work, after all. Of course he wanted tea. He'd probably take it straight back outside.

He didn't. Instead, he hooked out a chair with his foot, twirled it round and sat astride it, resting the mug on the back and regarding her steadily over the top of it.

'So, what do you think? Are you going to be able to cope?'

She blinked in surprise. 'With what? The builders?'

He grinned. 'Just remember, when you're making tea twenty-five times a day, day after day for the next three months, that you were warned.'

She smiled back and shrugged. 'We can't have people passing out from dehydration and toppling off the top of the scaffolding,' she replied lightly. 'It wouldn't do your reputation any good at all.'

'It probably wouldn't do the toppling people any good, either,' he retorted, and buried his hand in the biscuit tin.

'You don't look as if you're complaining, anyway,' she teased, only too glad that he'd decided to stay and keep her company after all. She'd missed him quite ridiculously, the night he'd spent in London, and she'd found herself wondering if, in addition to sorting out his business interests, he'd also been sorting out personal ones.

As far as she knew, he was single. At least, when

he'd been up at the weekends, he hadn't had any phone calls that she knew of from women—excluding his mother, of course, and his secretary, Sally, and she'd only rung once. That had definitely been about work, and it had sounded from their conversation as if they hadn't any kind of personal involvement.

Of course, she could always just ask him, but even she, direct as she usually was, drew the line at that. If Patrick wanted her to know, he'd tell her, and he seemed to tell her quite a lot about his life, so, thinking about it realistically, if there was a woman she would have known about it.

Not that it was relevant, of course. He'd already told his parents, loud and clear, that she was only a friend. *Nothing more, nothing less, and that's the way it's staying.*

More's the pity.

It was late on Saturday evening that Claire heard the cat crying. She hadn't seen her all day, but that didn't usually worry her, because the cat was a pretty independent creature anyway.

She was out in the garden, tidying up around the beds in the front, and she lifted her head and listened.

There it was again, a definite plaintive cry that seemed to be coming from the barn.

She looked up at it, shrouded in scaffolding and green mesh, but she couldn't really see anything, and there was certainly no sign of her funny little tortoiseshell cat. She went in search of Patrick, and found him in the study, hunched over the drawing board with his brows drawn together in a frown.

'I can hear the cat crying and I think she's stuck in the barn,' she told him.

He straightened up and swivelled round to look at her. 'Have you looked for her?'

She shook her head. 'I know you're a bit of a pedant about people going in there without hard hats on, and anyway, she sounds high up. I don't really do heights.'

Patrick rolled his eyes. 'Great. I expect she's got up on the scaffolding somehow. I'll come and have a look.'

They went back outside, and as they approached the barn, they could hear the cat crying pathetically. Patrick sighed and picked up the ladder, resting it up against the scaffolding and testing it to make sure it was secure.

'Hold the bottom while I go up,' he told her, and put his foot on the first rung.

'You haven't got a hat on,' she told him, but he just shrugged.

'I'll have enough to deal with, carrying the cat, without worrying about a stupid plastic hat falling off.'

So she took up her position at the bottom of the ladder and watched him as he climbed up to the top and walked around, calling the cat.

'She's gone up on the roof,' he called down. 'I'm not sure if I can get her. I'll have a go.'

Her heart in her mouth, Claire stood in the middle of the front garden and watched him as he climbed up onto the fragile roof structure. He must be mad, she thought, he could fall through it and kill himself. He was nearly there, he just needed to reach out his arm...

'I've got her,' he said, and her heart started to beat again as together they made it down onto the top of the scaffolding and slowly back down the ladders to the bottom.

She closed her eyes and swallowed hard against the nausea that was rising in her throat. If that roof had given way...

'Thank you,' she said fervently, and took the ungrateful cat from him. 'Shh,' she said, soothing the struggling cat, but she wouldn't be soothed, so Claire put her down and let her go.

The cat fled across the garden and up the apple tree, and sat there on a branch, licking herself and eyeing Patrick suspiciously.

Claire laughed and turned to Patrick, and then the smile faded.

'Are you all right?' she asked him.

He was wincing, and he had his hand down the back of his shirt collar, feeling his shoulder gingerly.

'I don't think she appreciated that,' he said, his voice dry, and he withdrew his hand, the fingertips stained with blood. 'Ouch. I thought she'd got me.'

'Come inside, let me look at that,' Claire said firmly, and pushed him back into the kitchen.

He stripped off his shirt and turned around, exposing several long, fine scratches beaded with blood to her worried eyes.

She clicked her tongue. 'Bad little cat,' she murmured, and rummaged in her first-aid cupboard, such as it was.

'This is where you're going to tell me it's going to sting a little, and I'm going to go through the ceiling,' Patrick said in a wry voice, and she smiled behind his back.

'That's the one,' she said, the smile evident in her voice, and he mock-glared at her over his shoulder.

'You don't have to sound so cheerful about it.'

She poured a little antiseptic onto a bit of cotton wool and dabbed it onto the first of the scratches.

He flinched, swearing copiously under his breath, and she apologised and bit her lip to stop the giggle. It really wasn't funny, she shouldn't laugh. If that roof had given way...

The thought sobered her instantly and, laying her other hand on his shoulder to comfort him, she gently cleaned the rest of the scratches and then smeared antiseptic ointment on them.

'All done,' she said, and he turned to face her.

'Thanks,' he murmured, and then their eyes locked.

She knew what was going to happen. It was almost like watching it in slow motion. His hands came up to cup her face, and his head lowered until his lips settled gently against hers. This time, however, when he lifted his head, he didn't move away.

Instead, with a muffled groan, he pulled her into his arms, cradled her between his long, hard thighs and kissed her thoroughly.

Her mouth parted for his, and his tongue swept hers, searching, exploring, teasing her until her legs were weak and she just wanted to lie down.

With him.

Now.

She pushed him away, and after a moment he lifted his head and released her. She stumbled back out of his reach, her fingers pressed against her lips, and stared into his turbulent eyes.

Desire, hot and heady, stared back at her, and she swallowed and stepped away again, then again, until she was nearly at the bottom of the stairs.

She couldn't handle this. She was going to make a

fool of herself, and he was only playing with her, just passing the time.

Just friends.

Yeah, right.

Claire turned and ran up the stairs to her room and stood there, heart pounding, wondering what on earth would happen now.

Not what she wanted, that was for sure. Patrick was too self-controlled for that—although he hadn't looked so self-controlled a moment ago, and he certainly hadn't felt it.

She heard his footsteps on the stairs, and he appeared in her bedroom doorway, a guarded look on his face. He'd pulled his shirt back on so he wasn't quite so nakedly tempting, but it didn't really help, because she'd seen him now, she knew what that naked skin and rippling muscle felt like under her hands...

Oh, lord!

'It's all right, I understand, you don't have to give me the ''We're just good friends'' speech,' she said crossly, but he just smiled, a strained, taut smile, and shook his head.

'I wasn't going to,' he said, and then took her breath away. 'I was going to suggest we finish what we started.'

CHAPTER EIGHT

CLAIRE'S heart wedged in her throat, and she stepped backwards into the room, her legs coming up against the side of the bed so that she sat down abruptly.

'But— I thought you said we were just friends.'

'I was a fool,' Patrick said gruffly.

Nothing else. He didn't try and persuade her or touch her in any way, he just stood there and waited until she thought she'd choke from the lump pressing in the back of her throat.

Then after what seemed like for ever but was probably only a matter of seconds, he shrugged and turned away.

'Wait!' she cried, her voice strangled. She swallowed, took a deep breath, tried again. 'Patrick, please—wait.'

He turned back and waited, and when her arm would obey her, she lifted her hand and held it out to him. The baby was down for the night, the dogs were curled up in the kitchen fast asleep in their beds, and there was nothing to stop them.

Nothing except common sense, and that seemed to have been totally abandoned for now.

Slowly—painfully slowly—he reached out and took her hand and pulled her to her feet.

'Thank God,' he said gruffly, and drew her into his arms.

His mouth found hers again, gentle and undemanding, and he feathered soft kisses over her lips, her cheeks, down over the beating pulse in her throat and into the hollow at its base. His tongue traced the line of her collar-bone, leaving a trail of fire in its wake, and then his hands slid up around her sides and cupped her breasts.

A deep groan erupted from his throat, and he bent his head and nuzzled at them, his breath hot through the fabric of her T-shirt.

'I want to see you,' he said gruffly, and, stepping back, he caught hold of the hem and peeled it up away from her.

Claire felt a moment of self-consciousness, but the warmth in his eyes and the tenderness of his touch washed it away. 'Oh, Claire, you are just...' he said, his voice catching, and she slid her hands inside the open edges of his shirt and slipped it off his shoulders.

'Just what?' she asked a little breathlessly.

'Beautiful. Exquisite. Gorgeous.'

How odd. She was just thinking the same thing about him. Her hands lay flat on the sculpted muscles of his chest, feeling the pounding of his heart against her palms, and she looked up into his eyes and swallowed hard.

She tried to say his name but it came out as a ragged whisper, and with a muffled oath he pulled her into his arms and wrapped her tight against his chest.

'I need you,' he said roughly. 'I've wanted to hold you like this for so long.'

Patrick's mouth found hers again, plundering it, searching out the hidden recesses with the urgent velvet sweep of his tongue, and then he lifted his head and she thought she'd die without him.

She didn't have the chance to find out because he didn't go anywhere. He scooped her up into his arms, laid her gently on the bed and came down beside her, his mouth finding hers again for a moment, then leaving it to trail fire over her shoulders and down over her breasts, suckling the aching nipples through the fine fabric of her bra.

She arched up, bucking against him and crying out, and he soothed her with trembling hands—clever hands that knew just how to touch her to reduce her to putty.

'Please,' she sobbed breathlessly, and he kissed her again, soothing her, quieting her, then he knelt up on the bed beside her and undid her jeans, drawing them carefully, slowly down over her legs, his eyes tracking their progress with smouldering intensity.

Then the last little scrap of lace that passed for underwear was gone—not, by a miracle, her usual boring old cotton knickers, she thought with relief bordering on hysteria—and she was naked beside him and he was feasting his eyes on her body.

One hand trailed over her skin, leaving goose-bumps in its wake. 'You are so lovely,' he said, his voice taut and raw with need. 'I knew you would be.'

He put his hand into his back pocket and pulled out a foil packet, handing it to her. 'Here, hang onto that for a minute.'

For a moment she stared at it, then she coloured as she realised what it was.

Lord, she hadn't even thought!

She looked up at him and her breath caught. His jeans were gone, his underwear too, and he lay down beside her and met her eyes, wry humour jockeying for position with urgent need.

'Are you going to hold that all day, or are you going to do something with it?' he asked, teasing her gently, and she gave a ragged little laugh and handed it to him.

'Here—you do it. I'll probably do something silly.'

'I doubt it,' he said, but he took it from her anyway and dealt with it, then rolled towards her, wedging one long, heavy thigh between hers and finding her mouth in a searing kiss that left her weak and shaken.

'Please,' she whispered, her voice cracking, and he moved over her, cupping her face in his hands and staring deep into her eyes as he entered her.

A low groan tore itself from his chest, and his lids fluttered shut. His mouth sought hers again, and then he started to move, slowly at first, then faster, harder, sweeping her along with him until the wave crested and she clung, sobbing his name as the wild storm thrashed around them and then moved away, leaving her weeping and shaken in his arms.

'It's OK, baby, it's OK,' he murmured, cradling her against his heart, and for the first time in as long as she could remember, she dared to believe that it might be.

Patrick lay beside Claire in her bed, staring at the ceiling and desperately trying to crush down the wave of emotion that threatened to engulf him.

He hadn't felt anything since Will had died, hadn't allowed himself to feel anything because it was all too raw, but now, with Claire at his side and little

Jess in the room next door, the feelings wouldn't be held back.

He squeezed his eyes hard shut against the scalding tears that suddenly formed in them, but they wouldn't be held back either, and they leaked out of the corners and dribbled down into his hair.

It was Claire's gentleness that had undone him, her tender reticence, the kindness of her touch. It had been so long—more than eighteen months—since he'd been in a relationship, and he'd forgotten just how healing a woman's touch could be. A sob caught at his throat, and he stifled it ruthlessly. Claire was asleep, exhausted after the emotion of the last few months, still grieving for her sister, and she needed her rest.

He turned his head and looked at her, at her lashes lying soft against her cheeks, the faint trails of tears dried now on her pale skin, and his heart contracted. He didn't quite know how it had happened, but she had got past his guard somehow while he hadn't been paying attention, and he'd fallen in love with her.

So, what now? he asked himself.

Claire made a funny little noise in her sleep and snuggled closer to him, and his arms tightened around her and he pressed his lips to her hair.

He'd worry about it in the morning. For now, he was content just to hold her.

Claire woke up to the sound of Jess crying and the dull ache of muscles unaccustomed to love-making. She realised she was naked, and finding her nightshirt under the pillow, she pulled it on and padded down the landing, following the sound of the fretful baby down the stairs and into the kitchen.

It was still early, about five o'clock, but Jess was grizzly and hungry and Patrick, naked except for a pair of jersey boxer shorts, was busy warming her bottle in the microwave and rocking her on one hip.

'Hi, there,' he said, his eyes smiling, and she smiled back uncertainly.

'Hi. Can I do anything?'

He shrugged. 'Not really. I've changed her nappy and I'm warming her milk, and I've put the dogs out—you could make a cup of tea, if you like.'

She nodded and put the kettle on, then tried not to watch him too obviously while he took care of the baby. It was hard, though, because he looked so good and her eyes were just drawn to him. She studied him over the rim of her mug, blowing on her tea and watching him through the steam, pretending that he just happened to be in her line of sight.

She coloured, though, when Patrick looked up and caught her staring at him, and a slow, lazy smile of satisfaction curved his lips.

'Want a closer look?'

Claire gulped and brazened it out. 'How much closer?'

He eyed the gap between them. 'Oh, about ten feet?'

She laughed softly and went over to him, bending to kiss the top of his head as he sat at the table, Jess in his arms sucking hungrily on her bottle.

'I wonder if she'll go down again?' he said, his voice low and husky, and she met his smouldering eyes and felt her colour rise again.

'Probably,' she said, feeling the anticipation beating a tattoo at the base of her throat.

'Good,' he murmured. 'I was looking forward to waking up with you. Slowly.'

Her heart stopped and then started again, lurching against her ribs and unsettling her. She'd gone crazy. Nobody else had ever made her feel like this. She hadn't known it was possible, and yet she supposed it must be, or else why would people stay together when things got tough?

There must be something there to hold them, apart from habit, she thought.

Love.

The word popped into her mind and stopped her in her tracks.

Love? But—she hardly knew him. How could she love him?

Easily. He was kind and funny and generous— hugely generous—and he knew just how to touch her...

Lust, that was what it was. Just a physical thing, because she was such a sad case and never went out, never had affairs, never let anybody close to her.

Unlike Amy. Amy had had endless men after her, and all too often she'd woken up in the morning with a massive case of guilt and a man beside her she couldn't even remember.

Will, though, had made an impression on Amy, and since they were identical twins, and she knew just how big an impression Patrick had made on *her*, she could quite see why Amy had fallen for his charm.

But she, Claire, didn't do that kind of thing. She'd never in her life woken up with a man beside her that

she didn't recognise. She'd hardly ever woken up
with a man beside her at all—including this morning,
of course. Maybe going back to bed with him was a
bad idea, she thought, and then he looked up and
caught her eye again, and she changed her mind.

Suddenly it seemed like an excellent idea, and she
couldn't understand why she was trying to talk herself
out of it.

Making love with Patrick was a voyage of discovery.

Nothing was hurried, nothing skimped, and by the
time he finally allowed her to reach that tormenting,
elusive release, she was begging for mercy and so was
he.

It was wonderful, and they spent the whole of that
Sunday either making love or playing with the dogs
and the baby and talking about what they were going
to do to each other next.

Well, Patrick talked, his voice soft and sultry, and
Claire just tried to remember to breathe. Even that
was almost beyond her at times.

Then finally, by the evening, they were content to
sit in the sitting room, arms round each other, and
watch television while they ate a hastily-thrown-
together pasta dish on their laps.

The dogs were walked, the baby was in bed, and
an hour later so were they, content now to lie nestled
like spoons against each other as they slept.

'Claire?'

She opened her eyes to find him sitting beside her
on the edge of the bed, dressed in his jeans and an
old shirt, a mug in his hand.

'I've brought you tea. The builders will be here in a minute, and I thought you might like a chance to come to before they arrive.'

She sat up against the pillows, scraping her hair back off her face and blinking against the light. 'Oh—I was fast asleep. I'm sorry. What time is it?'

'Seven. I've given Jess her bottle and put her back down again, and I'm just going to take the dogs out for a run. I'll be back soon.'

He leant over and kissed her, just a slow, tender kiss, passionless at first, but by the time he stood up her heart was pounding and his grin was wry.

'Later,' he said, and made it sound like a vow.

For the rest of that day Claire watched Patrick while he worked on the barn with the builders, and the feelings she had were terrifying. She'd never felt anything remotely as powerful as this in her life, and she didn't know how to deal with it.

She'd never really thought they'd end up in bed like that. She really hadn't thought he was that interested in her, and in her heart of hearts, she knew he couldn't be, not properly interested, not happy-ever-after, roses-round-the-door kind of interested. They were too different, worlds apart. He could have anyone he wanted, and she was just a passing distraction.

He'd soon get bored with her, she was sure, and then the game would be over.

If indeed it was a game to him, but she was almost convinced it was. And if he was just playing with her, she thought, she'd die, and by the end of the day, she knew she couldn't allow it to happen. No matter what their personal feelings, they had to deal with Jess and her upbringing, and Claire knew she had to protect both herself and the baby from anything that could make that untenable.

And if that meant distancing herself from Patrick, then she would.

Starting right away, that evening, just the moment he came in.

Patrick walked through the door and his heart sank.

She'd had second thoughts—and third and fourth thoughts, if the look on her face was to be believed.

Warily, he offered her a smile and sat down, taking the mug of tea she pushed across the table to him and swallowing half of it before she managed to get out the first word.

'I've been thinking,' she said, and he almost nodded.

'About?'

'Us.'

He put the tea down carefully and met her eyes, and they slid away, then came back, then slid away again.

'I think it's a bad idea,' she said, and even though he'd known it was coming, he still got that sinking feeling.

'Why?' he asked, deliberately keeping his tone mild when what he really wanted to do was shake some common sense into her.

Except, of course, that she was talking common sense and he was talking hormones—raging, adolescent, foaming-at-the-mouth hormones, coupled with a hefty dose of something that was going to hurt like hell any time soon.

'Because of Jess,' she said, as if he was an idiot. 'We have to be friends. We have to live together at the weekends, and when it all goes wrong, it'll just be so much harder.'

'It might not go wrong,' he dared to suggest, but she just looked at him as if he was mad.

'You don't really believe that,' she told him flatly, and he had to concede the point. It had never lasted before, why should this time, this woman, be any different? He'd cared very much for all the other women in his life over the years, not that there had been many, but none of them had been able to hold his heart for long.

Perhaps because he'd never given it, he thought, and with a stab of pain he realised that this time he was ready to.

'Anyway, I think we should try and forget this…this…'

She was floundering, and he stepped in and helped her.

'Fling?' he offered, aching just at the casual sound of it when it had been so far from casual, but she nodded.

'Yes, fling,' she agreed. 'I think we should forget this *fling* ever happened,' she went on, avoiding his eye again. 'For Jess's sake, if not for ours. She's the one that matters.'

Patrick couldn't argue with that, and he didn't bother to try. He'd just have to try a different tactic—patience.

Never his strong suit, but if it killed him, he'd win her round.

Starting by giving her the first point.

'OK,' he said, and her head whipped up and she stared at him blankly for a moment.

'OK?'

'We'll forget it.'

'Oh. Um—right. Um—fine. OK. Are you hungry?'

Claire was so shocked he nearly laughed. He would have done if he hadn't been ready to cry, or scream, or smash something.

'Not really,' he said. 'Actually, I think I might go into town—pick up a paper, maybe take a walk on the dock. I'll see you later.'

He went upstairs and showered, changed into clean jeans and a T-shirt and went out without seeing her again. He could hear her in Jess's bedroom, and he saw the curtain move as he drove off, but he couldn't talk to her.

Not yet, not until he'd got his head into order and all his ducks in a row.

Patrick drove to Ipswich and took a stroll along the new regenerated Waterfront area, indulging his architectural curiosity and trying not to think about Claire, but he ended up sitting in a bar by the water's edge, staring down into the murky water at the twinkling lights reflected off it and wishing life could—just for once—be easy.

He was so *sick* of his emotions being pulled every which way, and always having to be the strong one.

He'd thought, when Will had died, that maybe now he wouldn't have to act as a nanny any more, but then Jess had come into his life, with a real, genuine need of him, and he'd had to be strong again.

Well, it wouldn't really hurt him, and it wasn't as if he wasn't used to it. Besides, he could forgive little

Jess anything. He loved her to bits—loved her so much he couldn't imagine loving her more if she'd been his own child.

He'd do whatever it took to keep her safe and happy—and if that meant, in the end, that he lost Claire, well, it would have to be.

But he'd go down fighting. She might have won this first skirmish, but he hadn't given up yet. He'd go to the ends of the earth and back before he'd give up on her, because he was sure she loved him, too. She was just running scared, for some reason, but if he could convince her that he was going nowhere, he was sure they could have a future together.

He just had to woo her, slowly and steadily, and let her think it was all her own idea.

The alternative was unthinkable.

Claire went downstairs once she'd settled Jess, but she couldn't seem to settle herself. She ate some beans on toast, simply because she really ought to eat and not in the least because she was hungry, and then she washed up and went into the sitting room, but nothing in there held any appeal.

Fling, she thought to herself. Was that really how he'd seen it? As a fling?

Oh, lord, that hurt, even though she'd known it was true.

She found herself wandering into the study and sitting on Patrick's swivel chair, just to be near him.

She spun the chair round so she was facing the drawing board, and looked at the plans for the barn with sightless eyes.

Hopeless. She couldn't see a thing, everything kept

blurring, and she scrubbed her eyes and they blurred again.

Damn.

She got a tissue from the kitchen, blew her nose and wiped her eyes once more, and with the fortification of a glass of wine, she went back into the study and sat on his swivel chair again and looked around.

It was a mess in there, she realised, hopelessly overcrowded and cluttered. He needed more room to spread out his paperwork, and he might as well have the desk. Goodness knows, she seemed to have precious little use for it.

She walked over there and perched on the chair in front of it, sifting through the papers scattered on the top, and there in the middle of it was the envelope with the DNA information.

Oh, no. What with Jess to look after and the whole barn thing to think about, she'd totally forgotten to take Jess to the doctor for the test. Guilt stabbed at her, and she put the envelope in her bag and made a mental note to phone the surgery in the morning and arrange a time for the test.

Not that it mattered, of course, because she was sure Jess was Will's baby, and Patrick seemed happy enough. He hadn't mentioned it for weeks.

Still, she supposed it ought to be officially confirmed, just to keep everyone happy.

Then, just in case she'd overlooked anything else important lurking under the top layer, she went through the paperwork sheet by sheet, throwing out the junk mail, filing anything relevant, and putting the unpaid bills on one side to be dealt with later.

She was just on the point of retreating to her bedroom to avoid running into Patrick later when he arrived home.

He came in through the back door, greeted the dogs and then sauntered into the study.

Perversely, she was cross with him because he looked so calm and relaxed. At the very least, she thought, he should be a bit upset, if not as gutted as she was.

Which just proved, of course, that she'd done the right thing.

'Hi, there. What are you doing?' he asked.

'Just clearing up the desk for you,' she said, remembering the letter with another guilty twinge. 'I've moved all my paperwork—mostly into the bin,' she confessed, making him smile, 'and you can have it. The drawers are still full, of course, but I can clear them if you need them.'

'One might be handy, but don't worry. Won't you need the desk?'

'With the amount of work I'm taking on at the moment? Hardly.'

Her eyes flicked to the bills, and she caught her lip in her teeth. If she didn't get work soon, she'd have to pay the bills out of Patrick's money for the barn, when it came through. He'd said it would be soon, but how soon?

'What is it?' he asked, coming up behind her and resting his hands on her shoulders.

She tensed, and after a moment he lifted his hands away.

'Relax, I'm not going to jump on you,' he said gently, and she felt suddenly full of regret, because it might have been rather nice.

Till it all went wrong.

After all, it had just been a fling, she reminded herself.

'I was looking at the bills,' she said, not wanting to mention it but deciding it was a safer topic than him jumping on her.

'What bills?'

'Household bills—electricity, water rates, that sort of thing. I'm just wishing I had more work.'

'I'll pay the household bills, Claire, that was the deal.'

'But they're old.'

'Older than Jess?'

She stared at him. 'No, of course not.'

'Then I'll pay them. Leave them on the desk, I'll get to them in the morning.'

'There's a garage bill, as well, for Amy's car. Leave that. I'll talk to John—maybe give him the car in settlement.'

'How much is it for?'

'Twenty-five pounds.'

'The guy in London seemed to think it was worth a lot more than that. Perhaps you should put it in a classic car auction—maximise your assets. I'll pay the garage bill—and before you say it, you can pay me back when you've got the money. All right?'

Outmanoeuvred, she laughed quietly and nodded. 'Thank you, Patrick. You're being very reasonable about all this.'

'All what?'

She looked up, and caught a curiously unguarded look in his eyes.

Or did she? It was gone now, gone so quickly she

wasn't even sure it had existed outside her imagination.

'The bills, the money—us.'

'Ah. Us.' His mouth twisted into a wry smile. 'Don't worry, Claire, it's OK. You're probably right. Still, it was fun. If you change your mind at any time...'

'I won't,' she vowed, and she wasn't sure if she was promising him or herself. Either way, it did nothing to make her any happier. She stood up.

'I'm going to bed now,' she told him. 'I'll do Jess in the night if she wakes.'

'OK. I'll see you in the morning.'

She expected him to carry on sitting there at his drawing board, but he didn't. He stood up, and as she drew level with him, he put his arms around her and hugged her gently.

'Sleep well,' he said, 'and don't torture yourself with regrets. It was a good experience, even if it was a mistake.'

She nodded, acknowledging the truth in what he'd said, and then before she could break down and cry or change her mind and throw herself back into his arms, she backed away, turned on her heel and all but ran to the sanctuary of her room.

Some sanctuary. She could smell the faint tang of Patrick's aftershave on the sheets, and she could have kicked herself for not changing them. Sliding between them and lying there cocooned in the scent of his body was a sublime torture, and probably no more than she deserved.

She'd been a fool, given in to something she'd

known was a mistake. And so what if it had been a good experience, as he'd said? It was still the silliest thing she'd ever done in her life, and she had no doubt she'd regret it for ever.

CHAPTER NINE

PATRICK wasn't playing fair.

He could have given her a bit more space, been a little more distant, but no. He was just *there*, on the very fringe of her personal space, driving her nuts.

He was all over her study, for a start, and of course for the last few weeks it wouldn't have mattered because she hadn't had any work, only now, suddenly, just when she wanted to crawl into a corner and howl all the time, she had more than she knew what to do with.

Like buses, Claire thought in frustration. You wait ages and ages, and then they all come at once.

Where the work had come from she had no idea, but there was piles of it, and whenever Jess was asleep she was at her drawing board, furiously trying to get something done before the baby woke.

And where was Patrick? Right there, at his drawing board on the other side of the room, or working at the desk, or on the phone chasing up suppliers or talking to the planning department.

As if that wasn't bad enough, he started cosseting her, bringing her cups of tea and coffee, looking over her shoulder at her work and praising it, taking Jess off her hands and sorting her out if Claire was getting too close to a deadline.

His parents appeared on the scene quite often, as well. His father would disappear with him to the barn or pore over the plans, and his mother would cuddle Jess and play with her and feed her so Claire could get on.

Jean obviously adored her granddaughter, and it was mutual. Jess loved Jean and never failed to smile and gurgle and chatter all the time she was with her.

She was starting to talk, just odd little words here and there, like 'dog'—and 'Mummum' or 'Dada', which made Claire want to cry. Not, oddly enough, because Amy wasn't there, but because she and Patrick weren't Jess's mother and father, and had no real right to be called Mummy or Daddy by the little girl they'd come to think of as their own.

It would have seemed so natural.

She'd started to think about adoption—something Social Services had told her wasn't necessary, since she was Jess's only living relative and therefore automatically her legal guardian.

But if anything happened to her, she thought, Jess would inherit the cottage and any cash that was left from the sale of the barn, but beyond that, and certainly for her day-to-day care, she'd be dependent on Patrick's generosity. Although, of course, he would legally assume the same responsibility that she had now, and he wouldn't shirk it.

At least, she didn't think so, but she wasn't sure, and anyway it didn't seem concrete enough. What if Patrick died, too? Stranger things had happened, she thought, her imagination running riot. After all, Will and Amy had both died, so why not Patrick and her?

And who would look after Jess then? Would the little girl automatically inherit Patrick's money, too—and thence security? And who would ensure it?

Would she be taken into care and put up for adoption? And all that money would make her an easy target for fortune-hunters. What would protect her from them?

I need a will, Claire thought, worrying about it in the middle of the night, and she got up and went down to the study and rummaged around in the drawers. Nothing. Damn. She was sure there had been a DIY will form kicking around somewhere, but perhaps she'd thrown it out by mistake.

There was no point in going back to bed. It was too hot to sleep, and she was restless and unsettled. If it hadn't been for Patrick asleep in the room next to the bathroom, she would have taken a shower, but she didn't want to disturb him. The middle of the night was the only time she managed to get away from him these days, and it was the only time she found any peace.

She went into the kitchen and put the kettle on, bending to stroke the dogs asleep in their baskets under the table. Their tails thumped, and she sighed and sat down, her toes on the edge of Pepper's basket while Dog leant over and washed her ankle thoroughly.

His tongue was hot and rough, but she didn't have the heart to stop him, or Pepper when she rested her hot, heavy head on the other foot. There was something hugely comforting about their unquestioning affection.

No strings, no limitations, no qualifications.

If only Patrick loved her half as much.

If only she could trust him to be there with them, regardless of whether he loved her or not.

The ideal solution would be for them to adopt Jess together—it would solve any future problems and ensure her security. But in order for them to be able to do it, they'd have to be married, of course.

And that just wasn't going to happen. A man like Patrick Cameron wouldn't want to marry her, no matter how good they might be in bed together. She was far too boring and provincial by his international jet-set standards to be a suitable wife for him.

A little bit of her realised she was being unfair, because he didn't exactly belong to the international jet-set and anyway he seemed quite happy buried here in rural Suffolk, but nevertheless she didn't think she had what it would take to keep him.

Not long term, at least, and that was what was needed to give Jess stability. And yet…

'I think Patrick and I should get married,' she said to the dogs.

'Sounds good to me.'

She spun round, her hand flying to her chest, and her mouth dropped open.

'You gave me such a fright,' she said, and then realised what he'd said, and why he was saying it, and wanted to die.

'Oh, lord, I don't believe this,' she said, and buried her burning face in her hands.

'What's the matter? I think it's a wonderful idea.'

Claire lifted her head and eyed him through a crack in her fingers.

Patrick was sitting down on the other side of the table, regarding her with clear, steady eyes, and he didn't look as if he was winding her up. She lowered her hands.

'What?' she croaked.

'I said, I think us getting married is a wonderful idea.'

'Patrick—I was joking,' she said, trying desperately to get out of it because she didn't want to look a fool when she realised he actually *was* teasing her.

He shrugged. 'OK, we won't, then. Are you making tea?'

Tea? When the hell had *tea* come into the conversation? She stood up, suddenly desperate to get away. 'Um—no, I want a shower. Help yourself, though, the kettle's hot. I'll see you in the morning.'

And she left the room, her heart still crashing around at the top of her chest, and it didn't settle until she heard his light go out about an hour later.

It was an interesting idea.

Not that it was the first time it had occurred to him, but he'd dismissed it because he hadn't thought Claire would even consider it.

Now it seemed she might—for all her protestations—and the more he thought about it, the more the idea appealed.

It would solve so many of their problems at a stroke—not least the one which plagued him every time he got within ten feet of her, and could smell the delicate fragrance of her soap or shampoo or perfume, whatever it was.

Nothing strong, nothing overpowering, just enough to tease his senses and remind him of the night—and day, and night—that they'd spent together just a few weeks ago.

Remind him, and torment the hell out of him.

Patrick ached for her, and night after night he went to bed and had to force himself to stay in his room and not walk down the corridor and into her room and kiss some sense into her before he died of frustration.

Like right now, for instance. He just needed to hold her, to touch her, to bury himself in her...

He let out his breath on a sharp sigh. He couldn't go on like this, but if he could persuade her to marry him, he wouldn't have to. They'd be together every night, wake up together every morning, and it would be as amazing as it had been that one weekend, every day for the rest of their lives.

He stared at the ceiling, watching it grow paler as dawn approached, and tried to work out the best way to convince her. He was sure she hadn't been joking. What he couldn't work out was why she'd said it then, but she had, and the very fact that it was in her mind was progress of a sort.

Content with that for now, he fell asleep.

Patrick was going to drive her crazy. He was just *there*, all the time, right underfoot, and he was going to drive her crazy.

Claire had the distinct feeling he was laughing at her, as well, about her stupid remark in the kitchen, and she felt so humiliated and cross she wanted to strangle him.

He came into the study, humming softly, and put a long, tall glass of juice down beside her.

'That's coming on,' he said, eyeing her design thoughtfully, and she put her pencil down and turned to pick up the juice.

He was too close, though—again—and as she turned her arm brushed his chest and sent shock-waves up into her shoulder.

'Could you give me some space?' she snapped. 'Every time I turn round, you're just *here*!' She held her palm just a scant inch from her nose, and he stepped back, throwing up his hands in surrender.

'Sorry. I was just looking—'

'Well, don't bother,' she growled. 'I've got more than enough to do without you hanging over me. I can't think straight with you buzzing around in here, driving me mad.'

'Fine. I'll move,' he said, his jaw tight, and the next minute he was lugging all his stuff out of the study and down the hall to the dining room.

Good, she thought, draining her juice and turning back to her drawing board, but it wasn't.

It was horribly lonely and quiet in there without Patrick's presence, and she began to regret it by the end of the day. Still, she wasn't asking him back, so it was just tough. She'd have to learn to live with it.

Or rather, without it—without him, and the distracting way he tapped his pencil on the edge of the ruler when he was thinking, and the slight squeak of his chair as he swivelled back and forth. She was better off without him, she told herself.

Repeatedly.

The tea and coffee stopped flowing—well, not for the builders. He still made theirs if she was busy, but he stopped bringing her one every few seconds, and she found she missed his interest in her work.

She missed seeing his drawings of the inside of the barn, as well, and missed him involving her in the design details of the interior. Just trying for free advice, she thought, but even she had to admit to herself that he was probably only being polite, because his ideas were usually better than hers.

Well, of course they were, he was doing this kind of thing all the time. She was more into the finishing touches, the superficial things that set the scene. He was making the scenery itself.

Different skills, different requirements.

And he didn't require hers any more, apparently.

You can't have your cake and eat it, she told herself, but it didn't help. She still missed him, and being involved with the barn, and just generally having his company.

And then on the Friday evening, at the end of that long and lonely week, just as she came downstairs from her second cool shower of the afternoon he came in from the barn, the dogs at his heels. She'd been watching from the house during the day, and had seen him out there with the builders, working alongside them, and she'd felt ridiculously left out.

It isn't yours, she kept telling herself, but she still felt left out. Even the dogs had been out there, and Jess was too hot to be much company. Even the cat had taken herself off. She was lurking in the shade under the hedge, waiting for the cool of the evening and watching the birds, and wasn't in the least interested in Claire or her problems.

And now Patrick was in, and as usual he'd take himself off and she still wouldn't have any company!

He was washing his hands at the sink, and as he reached for the towel, he winced.

'Are you all right?' she asked without thinking, and he gave her a wry smile.

'Caught the sun. I've been up on the scaffolding this afternoon without my shirt for a while. It's my own fault.'

She knew that, but she hadn't thought about him getting sunburnt. She'd been too busy watching him. She felt herself frown. 'Take that off, let me see,' she said, and after a second's hesitation he shrugged off the soft blue cotton shirt and turned his back to her.

'Ouch,' she murmured, pressing her finger to the glowing skin.

'Mmm. It's a bit sore from this side, too. Of course,' he went on, sending her a slow, lazy grin over his shoulder, 'it would have been better if I'd had sunscreen on, but I couldn't do it on my own, and I didn't have anyone to do it for me.'

'That's nonsense,' she said crossly. 'I would have done it, you only had to ask.'

'But you wanted me out of your way,' he said, his voice mild. 'You said so.'

Claire scowled at him. 'I still would have done it. I'm going to have to put aftersun on it now, aren't I?'

'Let me shower first,' he said, and disappeared upstairs, leaving her fuming gently. To try and say it was her fault was ridiculous, and she wouldn't—*wouldn't*—feel guilty.

Still, it wasn't that bad. He'd be sore for a few hours, but the gel would take the heat out of it.

Patrick came back down just as she'd fed the dogs, and the sight of him in his jeans with the zip tugged up but the stud left hanging open below that bare expanse of smooth, tanned skin and rippling muscle took her breath away.

He'd grown leaner since he'd been working on the barn, she realised. Leaner and harder and even more delicious.

Damn. And she was going to have to touch him.

She reached for the tube from her first-aid cupboard, squeezed a dollop out onto her hand and smeared it firmly across his shoulders. He muttered something rude and flinched under her hand, and she felt a pang of guilt.

'Sorry,' she said contritely, gentling her touch, and she smoothed it carefully over the rest of the reddened area. 'It's really caught it up here,' she said, smearing the gel lightly over the top of his shoulders, 'but the rest doesn't look too bad.'

Too bad? She nearly laughed aloud. He was the best thing she'd seen in years.

'What about my front?' he asked, turning slowly towards her, and she looked at the red-brown tinge to his chest, the blush on the sensitive skin over his collar-bone, the dark copper coins of his nipples beneath the light scatter of hair that arrowed down to that unfastened stud…

'I think you can do that,' she said, thrusting the tube at him and backing away.

He caught it, and her hand, but he didn't release her. Instead he lifted her hand and pressed her fingers to his lips. Her eyes flew up and met his, warm and searching, and that was it.

She heard the tube fall to the floor, but after that the world narrowed to the two of them standing there in the kitchen, their arms around each other, their mouths brushing, sipping, tasting...

'Where's Jess?'

'In bed. She's just had supper and her bath.'

He let her go and eased away, his eyes burning with need.

'Come to bed with me.'

She couldn't speak. All the arguments against it were still there, and every bit as sound as they'd ever been, but they deserted her with those few simple words.

He held out his hand, and she slipped hers into it and followed him up the stairs to her room. He closed the door with a soft click, and then drew her into his arms, raining kisses over her face, her hair, her shoulders.

He didn't say anything, just undressed her with slow, patient fingers, kissing and caressing every inch of skin as it was revealed, and then he made love to her with a blistering tenderness that would have taken away any last resolve that remained if she hadn't already surrendered to him, body and soul.

And afterwards, as she lay beside him on the damp, tangled sheets, he turned his head towards her and smiled. 'There. That wasn't so bad, was it?'

Claire looked away. 'I thought we weren't going to be doing it again. I thought we'd agreed it was a mistake.'

'It didn't feel like a mistake to me,' he said softly.

She let out her breath on a shaky sigh. 'No—but it's still a bad idea. I don't do affairs.'

'Funny, nor do I. So, I've been thinking...' Patrick trailed a finger over her arm, down to her wrist, and picked up her hand, threading their fingers together. 'We could make it permanent. I know you said you were joking, but we could get married. It's not such a crazy idea.'

She turned her head, unable to believe what she was hearing.

'Why would we do that?' she asked, her voice not quite even, and his lips quirked into a fleeting smile.

'Because it would be the best thing for Jess, and it would solve the problem of this thing between us...' He paused, and then went on, his voice slightly rough. 'And because I love you?'

She stared at him, stunned, and saw the truth in his eyes for the first time.

'You love me?'

He laughed softly, a wry and rueful sound that warmed her heart. 'For my sins,' he replied. 'I have done, I think, ever since I saw you waving your arms like a windmill at that man when he was taking your car away.'

'Amy's car,' she corrected automatically, and then felt a bubble of happiness rise up inside her.

'Oh, Patrick—are you sure? You aren't teasing?'

His smile faded. 'Absolutely not. I love you, Claire. I want to be married to you, and have babies with you, and live here with you for the rest of our lives. I'm not teasing, darling. I've never been more serious in my life.'

Tears filled her eyes and overflowed, and she threw herself into his arms and hugged him, laughing and crying all at once. 'Oh, Patrick. I love you, too,' she said in a choked voice.

'Is that a yes, then?' he said, his voice muffled by her shoulder.

She lifted herself away from him and looked down into his beloved face. 'Of course it's a yes. Of course I'll marry you.'

Relief filled his eyes and, drawing her back down into his arms, he kissed her.

They went down to the kitchen later and raided the fridge, throwing together an impromptu salad and eating it in the kitchen with the dogs at their feet.

There were questions in Claire's mind that needed answering—things like where they would live, and if he'd want to adopt Jess—all sorts of important details that would keep, but she was impatient and wanted answers now.

'Where are we going to live?' she asked first, and he looked at her as if she was mad.

'Here. Well, you will, I imagine, unless you want to come down to London, but I'll have to spend at least part of the week in the office. I can work up here, though, some of the time, so you shouldn't be alone too much.'

She nodded. 'But—what about the barn?'

'It's up to you, but I rather thought we'd live in it. I'd like to.'

'So what about the cottage?'

He shrugged. 'You wanted to do your painting holiday thing. We could do it up for that, or you could let it, or we could use it as a drawing office for the two of us, or we could build a link from the barn and connect the two.'

'It would be huge!' she said in amazement.

'Well, maybe, but we could use it for work and as a guest annexe, or something. The kids could have a playroom or den in it.'

'Kids?' she said, laughing, swept along on his dream, and he grinned.

'Oh, yes. Lots of kids. I wouldn't want Jess to be an only child—and I'd like to adopt her. Give her the same rights as the others. What do you think?'

Claire nodded, only too pleased that they were in agreement. 'Sounds wonderful. Will the planners let you build a link?' She met his eyes and laughed. 'Of course they will. You'll tell them you want to build it out of stainless steel, and then when you come back down to brick and green oak and pantiles, they'll go belly up in no time.'

Patrick's lips twitched and he suppressed a chuckle. 'I don't know what you mean,' he replied, and standing up, he put his plate in the sink and scooped up the wine bottle and glasses from the table.

'Come on, we're going back to bed. We've got lots of catching up to do.'

'With sleep?'

'Amongst other things, but it wasn't top of my list,' he admitted with a smile.

She stood up and followed him, happier than she'd ever been in her life.

'I'm going to town. I've got to get some plans copied. Why don't we go in later on to pick up the copies and have lunch, and maybe go and look for a ring— or do you want one from Hatton Garden?'

She stared at him as if he was mad. 'Hatton Garden?'

'Diamonds?'

'Oh.' She shook her head, unable to contemplate such extravagance. 'Why do I need diamonds?'

'I thought all women needed diamonds on these occasions.'

She smiled, the baby squirming in her arms. 'I don't need anything except you and Jess,' she told him.

'We'll see. My mother won't forgive me if I don't do this properly.'

Claire chuckled. 'Well, we can't have that. Perhaps a tiny diamond, then, just for your mother's sake.'

She kissed him goodbye on the doorstep, then waited for the postman to hand her the letters.

'Lovely day,' he said. 'Barn's coming on.'

'Yes, it is,' she said, smiling because she couldn't help herself. 'Thanks.'

Claire closed the door and went through to the study, sifting through the letters absently, then one caught her eye and she ripped it open and pulled out the single sheet.

It was from the DNA laboratory, the paternity test report that showed that Will was the father of Amy's baby.

Except that it didn't.

She scanned it, then read it again, word for word, unable to believe what it said.

Four words stood out, four simple words that would turn their beautiful rosy world upside down.

Not the biological father.

There must be a mistake, she thought. There must be.

The words leapt out at her again, and she dropped

the letter as if it was red-hot. Not the biological father. And if Will wasn't Jess's father, that meant that Patrick wasn't Jess's uncle, and Jean and Gerald weren't her grandparents.

A cold chill swept through her, and she read it again, and then again, just to be sure she hadn't got it wrong. But, no, there it was in black and white. 'No match was found, therefore the late identical twin of the man tested was not the biological father of the tested child.'

Jess squirmed to get down, and numbly Claire put her on the floor and sat down at the desk. What on earth was she to do? How could she tell them? They loved Jess to bits. How could she take her away from them all?

She'd have to tell Patrick, but how? And why? Did it really matter? He loved her, he loved Jess—would it matter if he never knew? He hadn't asked about the test, hadn't mentioned it for weeks. Had he forgotten? Disregarded it?

If he didn't care one way or the other, then of course she could tell him, but if he did care—if buying the barn and asking her to marry him was all for Jess's sake—would he still feel the same?

She could lose him, she realised, staring dry-eyed at the letter. Oh, Patrick. What am I to do?

Nothing yet. She stuffed the letter into the back of the bottom drawer, out of sight and out of mind, retrieved Jess from the waste-paper basket and took her into the kitchen.

She'd put the baby in the buggy and take her and the dogs for a walk, and then, when she'd had time to think it through and find the right words, she'd tell Patrick, gently, at the right moment.

She wished she didn't have to, and a part of her wondered if she did. Would it be better not to tell him? Did he need to know? He loved Jess so much, and to take all that away from him seemed so cruel.

She opened out the buggy and scooped Jess up out of the dogs' water dish. 'Come on, Jess, let's take the dogs for a walk, shall we, before it's too hot? We'll worry about the silly letter later.'

Patrick was almost in town when he realised he was missing one of the documents he wanted to get copied.

'Oh, damn,' he said, and, turning round, headed back to the cottage. They might as well all go in now together, he thought, if Claire was back from walking the dogs. That way they could do their ring-shopping before it got too hot, and they could go somewhere nice by a river or something for lunch.

He turned onto the drive and went in via the back door, finding it unlocked as usual, but the place was deserted. She must still be out with the dogs, he thought, and went into the dining room, hunting through the paperwork to find the document.

Nowhere, he thought in exasperation, and then realised he'd last had it in the study before he'd moved out. In the desk, perhaps?

He opened the drawer he'd been using, but it wasn't there. Where, then? Had it fallen down the back of the drawer into the one below? It was possible, it had happened before. He checked it, and then pulled out the bottom drawer, and there in the back was a crumpled piece of paper.

'Here we go,' he said, pulling it out and straightening it on the desk, and then as he registered what it was, he froze and read it, then reread it.

'My God. She's not Will's baby,' he said under his breath, and then read it again, unable to believe it. There was no arguing about it, it was there in black and white, the result he'd fully expected at the start of this whole thing, before he'd known the baby was Will's.

Except that she wasn't, and so Jess wasn't his niece, and she wasn't his parents' grandchild.

Hell, they'd be gutted. *He* was gutted. He loved her—adored her, thought of her as his own, wanted to adopt her—but she wasn't Will's.

And Claire had known.

She must have known for weeks, and kept it from him. It only took a few weeks at the most for modern paternity tests to come back with a result, and it was now late July. She'd had all the stuff to get the test done in April, so she must have had the results— May? And so, of course, she must have known about it last night, when he'd asked her to marry him, when they'd talked about adopting Jess.

And she'd known that night in the kitchen, when she'd said they should get married. OK, she had been talking to the dogs, but it must have been because she'd been thinking about the result of the test and had realised she had no further hold on him.

He heard the latch on the back door, and then the dogs came in, tails lashing, and licked his hands. He waited, and Claire came into the room with Jess on her hip and smiled at him.

How could he not have noticed before that the smile didn't reach her eyes?

He didn't smile back, just pushed the letter across the desk towards her and watched as all the colour drained out of her face.

'Ah. You found it,' she said, her words damning her, tantamount to a confession that she'd hidden it.

'I was looking for a document. I went through the desk.'

Patrick stood up, his whole body trembling with reaction.

'I'm going back to London. I don't know what I'll do about the barn—sell it, probably, when it's finished. You can keep the car, but otherwise, I'm afraid, the gravy train just hit the buffers. And don't expect to get any more work from your recent sources, because it won't be forthcoming.'

Emotions chased across her face one after the other, and she stared at him helplessly.

'Gravy train? Recent sources? Patrick, what on earth are you talking about?' she said, her voice unsteady, and he thought what a damn fine actress she really was. In bed, too? Lord, that hurt, and it put a bitter edge to his voice.

'Where did you think all that work you've suddenly got came from? A fairy godmother? Wake up, Claire.'

She took a step back, her eyes suddenly filled with tears.

'I don't understand. Patrick, talk to me! What's going on?'

'What's going on? I don't know, why don't you

tell me? You seem to be the one in possession of the facts!'

He threw the letter in her face and stalked past her, running up the stairs two at a time and throwing his clothes into his bags.

He'd never get the drawing board and other things into the TT, but they were replaceable. No doubt Claire could sell them for a nice fat profit.

Raw, aching with hurt and betrayal, he flung his bags into the car, called the dog and put him in the front seat, then gunned the engine and shot off down the drive, away from it all—from the barn that had become more than just a project, from the child he'd grown to love as if she were his own.

And from the woman who had come to mean more to him than he could ever have imagined possible…

CHAPTER TEN

PATRICK went to his parents' house. He couldn't bear to go back to London, not to the empty apartment that he'd hardly been in for the last few weeks, at the top of that empty office block deserted for the weekend with not a soul around to distract him from the terrible ache inside.

So he went to his parents', and he told them, as gently as he could, that Will wasn't Jess's father.

'Well, we knew that,' his mother said matter-of-factly. 'We've known for weeks.'

'Did Claire tell you?' he asked, stunned, but his mother just shook her head.

'No, she didn't have to. It's obvious, darling, if you remember your school biology. She's very fair, like Claire and Amy. Everyone in our family's got dark hair, on both sides, for generations. To have fair hair, you need a recessive gene from each parent.'

'So? Will could have had a recessive gene.'

She shook her head again. 'No. If we'd had a recessive gene in the family melting pot, it would have come out by now. I mean, it is possible, but most unlikely, and anyway, she isn't in the least like any of the family babies—no resemblance at all.'

Patrick stared at her, totally confused. 'But—you kept on coming over, and seeing her, and making a fuss of her, just as if she was Will's.'

'Well, of course we did. It was no hardship, believe

me, and anyway, apart from our own selfish reasons, you're bringing her up with Claire.'

'Was,' he said, his voice catching. 'I *was* bringing her up. I'm not any more.'

His mother's face creased with concern, and she reached out a hand to him. 'Oh, darling. Oh, no. What's happened?' She looked at him keenly, studying his face, and he swallowed hard and looked away.

'She didn't tell me. She had the result, and she didn't tell me. She hid the letter—and last night I asked her to marry me,' he said lightly, but his voice cracked. 'What an idiot—and all I was to her all along was a meal ticket.'

'Oh, darling, no, I don't believe it. So when did she tell you?'

'She didn't. I found the letter.'

'Ah,' his father said, nodding thoughtfully. 'And what did she say?'

'Say?'

'What did Claire say, when you talked to her about it?' Jean asked, that patient tone in her voice as if she were dealing with a delinquent six-year-old. He remembered it well from his childhood. 'Did she say why she hadn't told you?'

He stared at her blankly. 'I didn't ask her.'

'You just walked out—with the dog, and all your stuff?'

'Pretty much.'

'I see.'

He sighed shortly and rammed a hand through his hair. 'Mother, I really don't need this. She kept it from me deliberately. Why do I need to discuss it with her—and why do I need you telling me off like a child? I'm dying inside, for God's sake.'

He broke off and stood up, crossing to the window and dragging in a great lungful of air, but it didn't seem to help. The garden swam into a blur, and he squeezed his eyes tight shut and pressed his fingers against them.

He felt the comforting presence of Dog at his side, and opening his eyes he headed almost blindly for the door. 'I'm going to walk the dog,' he said abruptly, and headed out, Dog at his side, leaving his parents to discuss the mess he'd made of his life to their hearts' content.

He walked for hours, through the woods behind the house and out into the countryside, and finally he came home hot and exhausted and suffering from dehydration some time in the middle of the afternoon.

His mother took one look at him and sat him down with a big jug of iced water and a slab of home-made gingerbread, and all he could think was that it wasn't as nice as Claire's. Stupid, really, because he loved his mother's gingerbread. He ate it half-heartedly, wishing it had been lemon Madeira so it didn't remind him of Claire, and then told himself he was being ridiculous.

How could anything remind him of Claire? To be reminded, he had to have her out of his mind, and just at the moment there wasn't a chance of that. *He* was out of his mind, but she was well and truly in it.

His mother was sitting on the other side of the table with a cup of tea, and she pushed a glass of water towards him to encourage him to drink. He drained the glass, and she refilled it and he drained it again, and then he started to feel more human.

Human, and ashamed of the way he was treating them.

'I'm sorry,' he said. 'I'm not behaving very well. I didn't mean to be rude earlier, I know you're only trying to help.'

'You're upset. I can understand that. What I can't understand is why you imagine that lovely girl is after a meal ticket.'

He stared at her as if she'd gone mad. 'Why? It's obvious why! Look at everything I've given her—the car, the fridge, the lawnmower—the money for the barn, for heaven's sake.'

'But that was your idea—and, if I remember rightly, so was the car, and the fridge. And the lawnmower was definitely nothing to do with her, so don't start being unfair, Patrick. And anyway, no matter why she didn't tell you about this letter, it's obvious she genuinely loves you.'

He shook his head fiercely. 'No, she doesn't. She was just using me. Believe me, Mother, she's a brilliant actress. She thought we ought to get married. I overheard her talking to the dogs one night a couple of weeks ago, telling them. At least, I thought she was talking to the dogs, but the whole thing could have been put on for my benefit, if she heard me coming down the stairs.

'I think she'd just realised she had to move things on with me, because once I found about Jess she knew the gravy train would hit the buffers. I hadn't even asked about the DNA result for weeks. I'd forgotten about it. Hell, she must have thought she was home and dry.'

His mother shook her head despairingly. 'You aren't making any sense. I know Claire, and you aren't talking about her at all.'

'Mother, she hid the letter!'

'And have you had your copy?'

He stared at her. 'What?'

'Have you had your copy of the report?'

'No. I expect it's gone to London.'

'And none of your post is being forwarded?'

'Don't be silly, it's all being forwarded.'

'So why haven't you had the letter?'

He shrugged. 'Because she's intercepted it?'

'Is that likely, or possible? Who gets to the post first?'

He shrugged again. 'Either of us, I suppose. But if it had come on a day when she was there first, she could have removed it.'

'Or perhaps it just hasn't arrived yet?'

He frowned. 'But, I gave her the stuff weeks ago. Months. All she had to do was go to the GP, and the results would be through in a couple of weeks, three at the most. She should have heard in May.'

'And what if she didn't get round to it for a while? She's a bit like that—a little bit chaotic. Is that possible?'

Of course it was possible—but he didn't think it was likely. He didn't want to think it was likely, because that meant he'd been an even bigger fool than he'd thought he was.

He shook his head. 'No. I think it was all a scam

for the money. In fact, if it wasn't for the photo-graphs—'

'What photographs?'

He looked at his mother blankly, then swore softly under his breath. 'Nothing.'

'Patrick, what photographs?'

He sighed and closed his eyes. He recognised that voice. It was the same voice she'd used earlier, and there was no escaping it this time. She hadn't been a primary school headmistress for nothing.

'Of Will and Amy. He took them—the time they were together.'

'I'd like to see them.'

'No. Mother, they're…' He closed his eyes, seeing them again. 'They're private. Personal.'

'Sordid?'

He shook his head. 'No, they're not sordid. They aren't like that, thank God. No, they're tasteful. Some of them are very beautiful.'

'Then I'd like to see them.'

'Mother, they're…intimate.'

'Patrick, I'm an adult. It's not going to shock me. I want to see them. They're photographs of my son, or taken by my son, just before he died. We've got little enough of him, especially now we haven't got Jess. I want to see them.'

He shook his head again, slowly and with regret this time. 'You can't, anyway. Claire's got them.'

'Then I'll ask Claire to show them to me the next time I'm over there.'

His head snapped up and he stared at her. 'Over there? You can't go over there, Mother.'

'Yes, I can—and so can you. I have no intention

of losing touch with her and Jess—and you have to talk to her, Patrick,' his mother said gently. 'You have to find out her side of the story—if you love her.'

He met her eyes, his heart agonised. 'Of course I love her,' he said unevenly. 'That's why it hurts so bloody much.'

'Then go and talk to her. Go now, straight away, and see what she says.'

He shook his head. 'I can't. I need time. I can't think clearly.'

'Maybe having the facts would make that a whole lot easier, son,' his father said, coming in behind him and resting a comforting hand on his shoulder. 'Go and see her. Sort it out. You've got too much at stake to let pride get in the way.'

It was cool in the barn, cool and calm and soothing in the fading light. Claire sat on the floor in what would be the master bedroom, right where the bed would go, and stared sightlessly down the valley.

She felt empty inside, hollow, gutted. Patrick had left her, just like that, because the baby wasn't Will's.

Left her, and taken her source of income, and now the barn would be finished and sold to strangers, and she would have lost everything.

And the worst thing was, she didn't know why. Not if he really did love her, as he'd said last night. It must have all been for Jess, but it hadn't felt like that when he'd been making love to her. That hadn't been for Jess. It hadn't been just for him, either, he'd made sure of that.

So if he loved her, if he wanted to marry her for herself, then the fact that Jess wasn't Will's really shouldn't make a difference, not to them, not to their relationship.

And yet it had made enough difference for him to walk out without discussing it, without talking it over with her or explaining anything.

And so maliciously! What was all the talk about the gravy train? She'd protested about nearly every penny he'd spent on her or the house, and kept trying to give it back and earn enough so that at least she could be independent, even if he wanted to support Jess.

She sighed and swallowed hard, fighting back tears.

She hadn't realised that the work she'd done recently had all come via him. She should have worked it out, but she'd been too busy to think rationally or she would have smelled a rat.

She looked around at the half-finished interior, the high vaulted ceiling, the beautifully restored beams spanning the roof, with replacement beams he'd had cut from old oak where necessary. It was going to be wonderful, and someone else's family was going to be living here.

Not her, with Jess and Patrick and the cat and dogs and all the other children that would come with time, because there wouldn't be any other children. Not with him, at least, and probably not with anyone, because it would be a cold day in hell before she let anyone near her again.

'Claire?'

She turned her head, her heart jamming in her throat, and in the fading light she saw Patrick's head and shoulders at the top of the ladder.

'May I join you?'

She shrugged, her heart pounding now. 'It's your barn.'

He climbed the last few rungs, swinging himself up onto the walkway and walking over to her, his footfalls echoing in the empty barn. He paused, then lowered himself down beside her on the rough chipboard floor, just a few feet away, one leg drawn up, his hands linked over his knee.

For a while he said nothing, just sat there, staring down the valley, a muscle working in his jaw. Then he spoke, his voice carefully controlled and emotionless.

'Can we talk?'

'About the letter?'

'Amongst other things.'

She shrugged. 'I don't know what there is to say. I thought you loved me. Now I find you don't, and you think I'm just after your money. I find that very difficult to deal with.'

'Why didn't you tell me?'

Claire turned to stare at him, confused and angry. 'Tell you what? That I'm not a fortune-hunter?'

'About the letter. About the result. About the fact that Jess isn't Will's baby.'

She was astonished. 'I didn't get a chance!'

He gave a short huff of humourless laughter. 'Don't give me that. You've had weeks.'

'No. No, I haven't. It only arrived today.'

It was his turn to stare. 'Today? You're telling me it took three months for the result to come back? I don't believe you.'

She coloured and looked away. 'I didn't get round

to taking Jess to the doctor for ages. I don't know—
it didn't seem to matter. It seemed almost irrelevant.'

'Where is she, by the way?' he asked, and she was
oddly reassured that he still cared.

'Asleep. Pepper's with her. She'll bark if she wakes
and cries.'

Patrick nodded, then his brows pulled into a frown.
'So—you didn't know yesterday? Last night, when I
asked you...' His jaw worked again. 'When we talked
about adopting Jess?'

'No, of course not! I was going to tell you when
you got back from town. I just—I didn't know how.'
Her voice softened, her anger draining.

'I know how much you love her, and how much
she's come to mean to your parents, and I couldn't
take that away from you, so I hid the letter to give
me time to think. I'm sorry, I shouldn't have done
that, I should have rung you on your mobile, but I
didn't know how to say it, how to take her away from
you like that. Your last link with Will.'

Tears spilled down her cheeks, and she brushed
them angrily aside. 'I'm sorry, Patrick. I'm so sorry
I've dragged you all through this for nothing. I was
really sure, when Amy told me—and the photos.
There just seemed to be so much evidence that
pointed at Will being her father, and you were happy,
you didn't mention the test.'

'I'd forgotten,' he admitted gruffly. 'I'd just got so
used to thinking of her as Will's baby, and then somehow she was just...ours.'

Claire nodded slowly, closing her eyes against the
tears.

'I know.'

'Do you have any idea whose baby she could be?'

She shook her head. 'No. There might be a clue in Amy's things, but I don't really want to know. I can't go through all this again with anyone else.'

'I wouldn't suggest you do, but Jess might ask when she's older, and she has a right to know.'

She nodded. 'I could look. She had a diary. I've never— It just seems so personal.'

'I know. I had the same thing when Will died. All sorts of personal stuff, aspects of him I'd never known and would have loved to talk to him about, but it was too late. It's always too late.'

Patrick turned away. 'Claire—for what it's worth, I'm sorry, too. I said some unforgivable things this morning, all unjustified. I just— By the time you got back with the dogs, I'd managed to convince myself you'd had the letter for weeks and you'd manipulated me into asking you to marry me, because you thought when I found out about Jess I'd leave you.'

'And will you?' she asked, her voice carefully controlled even though her heart was breaking. 'Is that what you're going to do? Leave me?'

He turned back to her, and his eyes were agonised. 'Not if you'll have me back. I wouldn't have left if you'd told me. It was the deception, not Jess. I thought you'd lied to me, kept it from me, and that was what hurt. If I'd been there when the letter came, I would have told you that it didn't matter, not really. Not to us. I love you anyway, regardless. Jess is just the icing on the cake, but deep down, it's you I love, you I want to be with—if you'll have me.'

She wanted to say, Yes, of course I'll have you, but she couldn't.

'You hurt me so much,' she said instead, pressing her fingers to her lips to keep in the sobs. 'I couldn't believe what you said—that you could think that of me. I just didn't understand—'

She broke off and jumped up, running over to the ladder and scrambling down it, running into the house away from him. She shut the door, wanted to lock it, but of course the key wasn't there and she couldn't find it. She could never find it.

'Claire?'

Patrick pushed the door open and came in, gathering her into his arms and cradling her against his chest.

'Hell, I've been such a fool, I'm so sorry.'

'So you damn well should be,' she said, her fists pounding on his chest. 'How could you think that?'

'I don't know. That's why I was so confused.'

'And what unconfused you?' she asked, pushing out of his arms and going over to the sink to stand staring down the valley at the last rays of the sun.

'My mother. She asked if I'd had my copy of the letter, and, of course, I haven't. I thought you might have intercepted it, but she told me I was crazy and that it was obvious you loved me. She reminded me about how much fuss you've made over every little thing I've tried to do for you—and, of course, she was right.'

'Well, hurray for your mother. At least one person in your family has some sense. And to think I was worried I wasn't good enough for you. I suppose I should be grateful Jess isn't related to you, because at least this way I won't be reminded of you every few minutes for the rest of my life.'

There was silence for a moment, then she heard the door open and he clicked his fingers for Dog.

'Claire, all I can say is I'm sorry, and I love you, and if you ever change your mind—well, you know where to find me.'

The door closed with a soft click, and Pepper pressed her nose into Claire's hand. She looked down, and the dog looked up at her with mournful eyes.

'Oh, darling, I know,' she said. Crumpling onto the floor, she buried her face in the dog's fur and sobbed her heart out.

The diary was revealing. Amy had recorded her time with Will in painful detail, ending with the simple words, 'I love him.'

The next day she'd tried to ring him, but she'd been told Patrick was in Japan on business. Then, a few days later, had come the discovery that she was pregnant.

'Hope it's Patrick's, but don't think so. He was too careful, except for that one time, but don't think the dates are right. It must have been someone at the party. Oh, hell, what do I do? A baby.'

She'd mentioned a party in her dairy, a few days before her weekend with Will, and it all seemed to fit. Claire turned to the pages at the end, the last things Amy had written, and she found a poignant entry after her meeting with Patrick.

'He didn't even seem to recognise me. He gave me money for the train—a ridiculous amount, but nothing like enough to sort out my debts—and he was very kind, but he didn't seem the same. It was weird—like there was something missing. He didn't seem like the man I loved. Anyway, it was worth a try, but I know the baby isn't his. I was just hoping—but that isn't fair, really, is it? God knows who Jess's father is, but I'm grateful to him, because she's the most beautiful thing that's ever happened to me. What a shame I won't be here to look after her, but Claire will do it, and do it better, like she does everything better. She'll be safe with you, Claire, if you're reading this now I'm gone. Thank you for everything. I love you—and I'm sorry.'

And that was it. The last entry, made the day she'd died.

Claire, who had thought all her tears were gone, closed the book and wrapped it against her heart. Curling up on her side on Amy's bed, she wept the healing tears of grief, and as the dawn light crept across the ceiling, she fell asleep.

The phone woke her, the shrill ringing finally penetrating the haze of sleep and grief, and scrambling to her feet she ran downstairs to the study and picked it up.

'Hello?'

'Claire? It's Jean Cameron. I'm sorry to phone so early, but Patrick's been in an accident. He's in Ipswich Hospital. Can you come? He keeps drifting in and out of consciousness, but he's asking for you.'

Claire sat down abruptly, her blood running cold. 'Is he all right? What's he done?'

'They don't know yet. They found the car an hour ago in the hedge. He's got head injuries and broken ribs, but they don't know the extent of the head injury yet.'

'I'm on my way,' she said. 'Tell him I'm coming. Tell him—' She broke off. 'Tell him I love him.'

'Tell him yourself. Drive carefully, darling. We'll see you in a minute. Oh, and Dog's safe, by the way. The police have got him.'

Claire dragged a brush through her hair and scooped Jess out of bed, changing her nappy and grabbing a bottle from the fridge as an afterthought. 'Pepper, stay,' she said, but Pepper wouldn't, as if she knew something was wrong, and so she took her, too.

She tried to drive slowly, but the needle kept creeping up. She kept expecting to be stopped by the police, but finally she was there, turning into the car park and pulling up as near as possible to the A and E entrance. She needed to put money in a meter, but she'd forgotten to bring her handbag, so she scribbled a note on the inside of a chocolate wrapper, stuck it in the windscreen and grabbed Jess from the car seat.

'Pepper, stay,' she said, and ran towards the entrance, Jess grizzling in her arms.

'I'm looking for Patrick Cameron. I understand he was brought in—'

'Claire.'

She spun on her heel and saw Patrick's father there, holding out his arm. 'Come with me—I'll take you to him.'

They went down the corridor and into a room at the end, and there he was, wired up to all sorts of equipment, his mother sitting at his side holding his hand and talking softly.

She looked up, and tears flooded her eyes.

'Claire—thank God you're here safely. Give me the baby—come to Grannie, darling.'

Grannie. Oh, God.

'Patrick? Patrick, it's me. Claire. Wake up. Talk to me.'

His eyelids fluttered, and he stared at her blankly for a moment, then he smiled, a tiny movement more of a grimace than a smile, but it was enough.

'You came,' he said, his voice rough and slurred, and tears filled her eyes.

'Of course I came. I love you.'

'Love you, too. Head hurts.'

'That's because you tried to think. You're not good at it. You're an idiot. You should leave it to me.'

The smile widened slightly, almost turned into a grin.

'I know. Stay with me.'

'Always.'

His eyes locked with hers, recognition and understanding in them, and then with a sigh his eyes slid shut.

She looked up at the nurse on the other side of the bed in horror. 'Oh, God, is he...?'

'He's asleep. He's all right. He's had a scan, and it's fine. He's just had a nasty knock on the head and he's got concussion. He'll be OK. We'll continue to monitor him for the next few hours, and then depending on his progress he can probably go home in a day or two.'

Claire sat down before she fell, then realised she had a death grip on Patrick's hand. She relaxed it, but the grip didn't change, and she realised he was holding her just as hard.

She lifted his hand to her mouth and kissed it, and his fingers relaxed a little, easing the pressure but still there, still hanging on. She wrapped his arm against her chest, rested her cheek on his fingers and closed her eyes.

'So she did sense I wasn't Will.'

Patrick put the diary down and rested his head back against the pillows, relieved to know the truth at last. 'I'm glad. Glad for him that he made enough of an impression, glad she loved him, glad she didn't blame me. I don't feel so bad about her now.'

'And we still don't know who Jess's father is, and I don't suppose there's any way of finding out.'

He took Claire's hand. 'It doesn't matter. She's got a mother and a father, and given time she'll have brothers and sisters. Did I tell you my parents had already worked it out?'

She shook her head. 'No. How?'

'Hair colour. Our entire family has dark hair, and besides, she didn't look like any of the others. I don't think they care, though, not really. They still love her to bits. They love you to bits, as well.'

'And you?'

'Oh, they love me, too.'

She punched him gently on the shoulder, and he winced. 'Careful. That's a bruise.'

'Well, don't tease.'

He smiled. 'Yes, I love you to bits,' he relented. 'You know that. Come here and I'll show you.'

'You're injured. It's only two days since your accident.'

'I'm better. I want to check my progress. Come here.'

He reached out and pulled her down against his side, but he only kissed her. In truth, he didn't feel up to anything more strenuous, but he was improving fast. Another day or so, he thought.

'The baby's awake,' she murmured.

'I know. I can hear her chatting. Go and get her.'

So she did, and they lay there on the bed together while Jess chatted and played with a little stacking toy, and Patrick couldn't believe his luck.

Dog was downstairs in the kitchen curled up with Pepper, none the worse for his ordeal, and he was back with Claire and the baby, alive and reasonably well despite his accident.

He turned his head and met Claire's eyes searchingly. 'Tell me something. If I hadn't had the accident, would you have come to see me?'

She nodded slowly. 'Yes, because once I'd calmed down I realised it was all just one of those stupid things, but there are conditions.'

He felt a flutter of fear in amongst the relief. 'Conditions?'

'Never jump to conclusions again. Talk to me. Trust me.'

He nodded, emotion clogging his throat. 'I'm sorry. I'm not very good at this, but I'll get better, I promise. And I'll never doubt you again.'

'Oh, you will,' she assured him, 'because you're human, but, then, so am I, so that's fine. Just talk to me first, then fly off the handle.'

He smiled. 'Done. Now, I think the baby needs your attention.'

Claire slid off the bed and threw back the covers. 'I think you're looking better,' she said with a smile. 'And it must be your turn.'

He sighed and shook his head, but he got up, flexing his shoulder gingerly, and scooped the baby off the bed.

'Come on, trouble, let's sort you out.'

Jess grabbed his ears and kissed him, a great, wet, sloppy kiss that made his heart swell with love. To think he'd nearly lost her—nearly lost all of it.

What a fool he'd been, but never again. With Claire at his side he changed the baby, then carried her downstairs to the kitchen. He could hear hammering and sawing from outside. The builders were working on the barn, bringing his dream to fruition, and just as soon as he was better he'd be out there overseeing it, because it was Claire's dream, too, and their home, and it was too important to delegate.

He was going to take care of it, of all of them, because dreams could be elusive and slip away, and he was going to make absolutely certain that he hung onto this one for the rest of his life...

THE ITALIAN'S BABY

by

Lucy Gordon

Lucy Gordon cut her writing teeth on magazine journalism, interviewing many of the world's most interesting men, including Warren Beatty, Richard Chamberlain, Sir Roger Moore, Sir Alec Guinness, and Sir John Gielgud. She also camped out with lions in Africa, and had many other unusual experiences which have often provided the background for her books. She is married to a Venetian, whom she met while on holiday in Venice. They got engaged within two days.

Two of her books have won the Romance Writers of America RITA® award, SONG OF THE LORELEI in 1990, and HIS BROTHER'S CHILD in 1998 in the Best Traditional Romance category.

You can visit her website at www.lucy-gordon.com

PROLOGUE

SHE was seventeen, as pretty as a doll, and as lifeless, sitting in the window, staring out, unseeing, over the Italian countryside.

She didn't turn when the door opened and a nurse came in, with a middle-aged man. He had an air of joviality that sat oddly with his cold eyes.

'How's my best girl?' he greeted the doll by the window.

She neither replied nor looked at him.

'I've got someone to see you, precious.' He turned to a young man standing behind him and said curtly, 'Make it quick.'

He was twenty, little more than a boy. His hair was shaggy, he looked as though he hadn't shaved for days, and his eyes were wild with pain and anger. He went quickly to the girl and dropped on his knees beside her, speaking in an imploring voice.

'Becky, *mia piccina*—it is I, Luca. Look at me, I beg you. Forgive me for everything—they say our child is dead and that it is my fault—I never meant to hurt you— can you hear me?'

She turned her head and seemed to look at him, but there was no recognition in her eyes. They were lifeless.

'Listen to me,' the boy implored. 'I am sorry, *piccina,* I am so sorry. Becky, for pity's sake, say that you understand.'

5

She was silent. He reached up a hand to brush her light brown hair aside. She did not move.

'I did not see our baby,' he said huskily. 'Was she pretty like you? Did you hold her? Speak to me. Tell me that you know me, that you love me still. I shall love you all my life. Only say that you forgive me for all the pain I have brought you. I meant only to make you happy. *In God's name, speak to me.*'

But she said nothing, merely stared out of the window. He dropped his head into her lap, and the only sound in the room was his sobs.

CHAPTER ONE

THE words stood out starkly, black against the white paper.

A boy. Born yesterday. 8lbs 6oz.

A simple message that might have been the bringer of joy. But to Luca Montese it meant that his wife had given a son to another man, and none to him. It meant that the world would know of his humiliation, and that made him curse until there was nobody left to curse, except himself, for being a blind fool. His face was not pleasant at that moment. It was cruel and frightening.

Fear of that face had made Drusilla leave him as soon as she knew she was pregnant, six months ago. He had arrived home to find her gone, leaving him a note. It had said that there was another man. She was pregnant. It was no use trying to find her. That was all.

She had taken everything he had ever given her, down to the last diamond, the last stitch of couture clothing. He'd pursued her like an avenging fury, not in person but through a battery of expensive lawyers, nailing her down to a divorce settlement that left her nothing beyond what she had already taken.

It galled him that the man was so poor and insignificant as to be virtually beyond the reach of his revenge. If he had been a rich entrepreneur, like himself, it would have been a pleasure to ruin him. But a hairdresser! That was the final insult.

Now they had a big, lusty son. And Luca Montese was childless. The world would know that it was his fault that his marriage had been barren, and the world would laugh. The thought almost drove him to madness.

Three floors below him was the heart of Rome's financial district, a world he had made his own by shrewdness, cunning and sheer brute muscle. His employees were in awe of him, his rivals were afraid of him. That was how he liked it. But now they would laugh.

He turned the paper between his fingers. His hands were heavy and strong, the hands of a workman, not an international financier.

His face was the same; blunt-featured, with a heaviness about it that had little to do with the shape of features, and more to do with a glowering intensity in his eyes. That, and his tall, broad-shouldered body, attracted the kind of woman—and there were plenty of them—who gravitated towards power. Physical power. Financial power. All kinds. Since the break-up of his marriage he hadn't lacked company.

He treated them well, according to his lights, was generous with gifts but not with words or feelings, and broke with them abruptly when he realised they did not have what he was seeking.

He could not have said what that was. He only knew that he'd found it once, long ago, with a girl who had shining eyes and a great heart.

He barely remembered the boy he'd been then, full of impractical ideas about love lasting forever. Not cynical, not grasping, believing that love and life were both good: a foolishness that had been cruelly cured.

He brought himself firmly back to the present. Dwelling on lost happiness was a weakness, and he always cut out weakness as ruthlessly as he did everything else. He strode out of the office and down to the underground parking lot, where his Rolls-Royce—this year's model—was waiting.

He had a chauffeur but he loved driving it himself. It was his personal trophy, the proof of how far he'd come since the days when he'd had to make do with an old jalopy that would have collapsed if he hadn't repaired it himself.

Even with his best efforts it was liable to break down at odd moments, and then *she* would laugh and chatter as she handed him spanners. Sometimes she would get under the car with him, and they would kiss and laugh like mad things.

And perhaps it was a kind of madness, he thought as he headed the Rolls out of Rome to his villa in the country. Mad, because that heart-stopping joy could never last. And it hadn't.

He'd brushed the thought of her aside once, but now she seemed to be there beside him as he drove on in the darkness, tormenting him with memories of how enchanting she had been, with her sweet gentleness, her tenderness, her endless giving. He had been twenty, and she seventeen, and they'd thought it would last forever.

Perhaps it might have done if—

He shut off that thought too. Strong man though he was, the 'what if?' was unbearable.

But her ghost wouldn't be banished. It whispered sadly that their brief love had been perfect, even though it had ended in heartbreak. She reminded him of other things too, how she'd lain in his arms, whispering words of love and passion.

'I'm yours, always—always—I shall never love any other man—'

'I have nothing to offer you—'

'If you give me your love, that's all I ask.'

'But I'm a poor man.'

How she had laughed at that, ripples of young, confident laughter that had filled his soul. 'We're not poor—as long as we have each other...'

And then it was over, and they no longer had each other.

Suddenly there was a squeal of tyres and the wheel spun in his hand. He didn't know what had happened, except that the car had stopped and he was shaking.

He got out to clear his head, looking up and down the country road. It was empty in both directions.

Like his life, he thought. Coming out of the empty darkness and leading ahead into empty darkness.

It had been that way for fifteen years.

The Allingham was the newest, most luxurious hotel to have gone up in London's exclusive Mayfair. Its service was the best, its prices the highest.

Rebecca Hanley had been appointed its first PR consultant partly because, as the chairman of the board had said, 'She looks as if she grew up with money to burn, and didn't give a damn. And that's useful when you're trying to get people to burn money without giving a damn.'

Which was astute of him, because Rebecca's father had been a very rich man indeed. And these days she didn't give a damn about anything.

She lived in the Allingham, because it was simpler than having a home of her own. She used the hotel's beauty salon and gymnasium, and the result was a figure that wasn't an ounce overweight, and a face that was a mask of perfection.

Tonight she was putting the final touches to her appearance when the phone rang. It was Danvers Jordan, the banker who was her current escort.

They were to attend the engagement party of his younger brother, held in the Allingham. As Danvers' companion and a representative of the hotel, she would be 'on duty' in two ways, and must look right, down to every detail.

As she checked herself in three angled mirrors Rebecca knew that nobody could fault her looks. She had the slim, elegant body that could wear the tight black dress, and the endless legs demanded by the short skirt. The neckline was low-cut, but within relatively modest limits. Around her neck she wore one large diamond.

Her hair had started life as light brown, but now it was a soft honey-blonde that struck a strange, distinctive note with her green eyes. Small diamonds in her ears added the final touch.

On exactly the stroke of eight the knock came on her door and she sauntered gracefully across to let Danvers in.

'You look glorious,' he said, as he always did. 'I shall be the proudest man there.'

Proudest. Not happiest.

The party was in a banqueting room, hung with drapes of white silk interspersed with masses of white roses. The engaged couple were little more than children, Rory twenty-four, Elspeth eighteen. Elspeth's father was the president of the merchant bank for which Danvers worked, and which was part of the consortium that had financed the Allingham.

She was like a kitten, Rebecca thought, sweet, innocent and intense about everything, especially being in love.

'I didn't think people talked about "forever and ever" any more,' she said to Danvers when the evening was half over.

'I suppose if you're young enough and stupid enough it seems to make sense,' he said wryly.

'Do you really have to be young and stupid?'

'Come on, darling! Grown-ups know that things happen, life goes wrong.'

'That's true,' she said quietly.

Elspeth came flying up to them, throwing her arms around Rebecca.

'Oh, I'm so happy. And what about you two? It's time you tied the knot. Why don't we make the announcement now?'

'No,' Rebecca said quickly. Then, fearing that she had been too emphatic, she hastened to add, 'This is your night. If I hijacked it I'd be in trouble with my boss.'

'All right, but on my wedding day I'm going to toss you my bouquet.'

She danced away and Rebecca heaved a secret sigh of relief.

'Why did she call you Becky?' Danvers asked.

'It's short for Rebecca.'

'I've never heard anyone use it with you, and I'm glad. Rebecca's more natural to you, gracious and sophisticated. You're not a Becky sort of person.'

'And what is "a Becky sort of person" Danvers?'

'Well, a bit coltish and awkward. Somebody who's just a kid and doesn't know much about the world.'

She put her glass down suddenly because her hand was shaking. But she knew he wouldn't notice.

'I haven't always been gracious and sophisticated,' she said.

'That's how I like to see you, though.'

And, of course, Danvers wouldn't be interested in any other version of her than the one that suited himself. She would probably marry him in the end, not for love, but for lack of any strong opposing force. She was thirty-two and the aimless drift that was her life couldn't go on indefinitely.

She rejected his suggestion of dinner, claiming tiredness. He saw her to her suite and made one last attempt to prolong the evening, drawing her close for a practiced kiss, but she stiffened.

'I really am very tired. Goodnight, Danvers.'

'All right. You get your beauty sleep and be perfect for tomorrow.'

'Tomorrow?'

'We're having dinner with the chairman of the bank. You can't have forgotten.'

'Of course not. I'll be there, at my best. Goodnight.'

If he didn't go soon she would scream.

At last she had the blessed relief of solitude. She turned out the lights and went to stand in the window, looking out at the lights of London. They winked and glittered against the darkness, and in her morbid mood it seemed as if she was looking at her whole life from now on: an endless vista of shiny occasions—dinner with the chairman, a box at the opera, lunch in fashionable restaurants, entertaining in a luxurious house, the perfect wife and hostess.

It had seemed enough before, but something about tonight had unsettled her. That young couple with their passionate belief in love had reminded her of too many things she no longer believed.

'Becky' had believed them, but Becky was dead. She had died in a confusion of pain, misery and disillusion.

Yet tonight her ghost had walked through the costly feast, turning reproachful eyes on Rebecca, reminding her that once she had had a heart, and had given that heart freely to a wild-eyed young man who had adored her.

'A kid, who doesn't know much about the world,' had been Danvers' verdict on 'Becky', and he was more right than he knew. They had both been kids, herself and the twenty-year-old, Luca, thinking that their love was the final answer to all problems.

Becky Solway had fallen in love with Italy at first sight, and especially the land around Tuscany, where her father had inherited the estate of Belleto from his Italian mother.

'Dad, it's heavenly!' she said when she first saw it. 'I want to stay here forever and ever.'

He laughed. 'All right, pet. Whatever you say.'

He was like that, always willing to indulge her without actually considering what she was saying, much less what she was thinking or feeling.

At fourteen all she saw was the indulgence. It had been just the two of them since her mother had died two years before. Frank Solway, successful manufacturer of electronic products, and his bright, pretty daughter.

He had factories all over Europe, continually moving
the work to wherever the labour was cheapest. During
her school vacation they travelled together, visiting the
outposts of his business empire, or stayed at Belleto. The
rest of the time she finished her schooling in England.
When she was sixteen she announced that she was finished with school.

'I just want to live at Belleto from now on, Dad.'

And, as always, he said, 'All right, pet. Whatever you
like.'

He bought her a horse, and she spent happy days exploring the vineyards and olive groves that formed part
of Belleto's riches.

She had a quick ear, and had learned not only Italian
from her grandmother but also the local Tuscan dialect.
Her father spoke languages badly and the servants who
ran his house found him hard to understand, so he soon
left the domestic affairs to her. After a while she was
helping with the estate as well.

All she knew of Frank was that he was a successful
businessman. She never suspected a darker side, until
one day it was forced on her.

He had closed his last factory in England, opened another in Italy, then taken off for Spain, inspecting new
premises. During his absence Becky went for a ride and
found herself confronted by three grim-faced men.

'You're Solway's daughter,' said one of the men in
English. 'Frank Solway is your dad. Admit it.'

'Why should I deny it? I'm not ashamed of my father.'

'Well, you damned well should be,' another man
shouted. 'We needed our jobs and he shut down the
English factory overnight because it's cheaper over here.

No compensation, no redundancy. He just vanished. Where is he?'

'My father's abroad at the moment. Please let me pass.'

One of the men grabbed the bridle. 'Tell us where he is,' he snapped. 'We didn't come all this way to be fobbed off.'

She was growing nervous, sensing that they would soon be out of control.

'He'll be next week,' she said desperately. 'I'll tell him you called; I'm sure he'll want to speak to you—'

This brought a roar of ribald laughter.

'We're the last people he wants to speak to—he's been hiding from us...won't answer letters.'

'But what can I do?' she cried.

'You can stay with us until he comes for you,' the most unpleasant-looking man snapped, still holding the bridle.

'I think not,' said a hard voice.

It came from a young man that nobody had noticed. He had appeared from between the trees and stood still for a moment to make sure they had registered his presence. It was an impressive presence, not so much for his height and breadth of shoulder as for the sheer ferocity on his face.

'Stand back,' he said, starting to move forward.

'Get out of here,' said the man holding the bridle.

The stranger wasted no further words. Turning almost casually, he made a movement too fast to see, and the next moment the man was on the ground.

''Ere...' said one of the others.

But his words died unspoken as the stranger scowled at him.

'Leave here, all of you,' he said sternly. 'Do not come back.'

The other two hastened to help their companion to his feet. He was trying to staunch the blood from his nose and although the look he cast his assailant was furious he was too wise to take the matter further. He let himself be led away, but he turned at the last moment to glare back at Becky in a way that made the young man start forward. Then they all scuttled away.

'Thank you,' said Becky fervently.

'Are you all right?' he demanded abruptly.

'Yes, thanks to you.'

She dismounted, and immediately realised just how tall he was. Now his grim face and dark, intense eyes were looking down at her, the traces of cold rage still visible.

The angry little crowd had been alarming because there were three of them. But this man was dangerous on his own account, and suddenly she wondered if she was any safer than before.

'They've gone now,' he said. 'They won't come back.'

It was a simple statement of fact. He knew nobody would choose to face him twice.

'Thank you,' she said, speaking English, as he had done, but slowly. 'I've never been so glad to see anyone. I thought there was nobody to help me.'

'You don't have to speak slowly,' he said proudly. 'I know English.'

'I'm sorry. I didn't mean to be rude. Where did you appear from?'

'I live just past those trees. You had better come with me, and I will make you some tea.'

'Thank you.'

As they walked he said, 'I know everybody around here, but I've never seen them before.'

'They come from England. They were looking for my father, but he's away and that made them angry.'

'Perhaps you should not have ridden alone.'

'I didn't know they were there, and why shouldn't I ride where I like on my father's land?'

'Ah, yes, your father is the Englishman everyone is talking of. But this is not his land. It belongs to me. Just a narrow strip, but it contains my home, which I will not sell.'

'But Dad told me...' She checked herself.

'He told you that he'd bought all the land round here. He must have overlooked this little piece. It's very easily done.'

'Oh, that's lovely,' she said involuntarily.

They had turned a corner and come across a small stone cottage. It nestled against the lee of a hill in the shadow of pine trees, and her first thought was that it looked cosy and welcoming.

'It is my home,' he said simply. 'I warn you, it is not so picturesque inside.'

He spoke the truth. The inside was shabby and basic, with flagstones on the floor and a huge old-fashioned range. He was evidently working hard at improving it, for there were tools lying about, and planks of wood.

'Sit down,' he said, indicating a wooden chair that looked hard but turned out to be surprisingly comfortable.

There was a kettle on the range, and he made tea efficiently.

'I don't know your name,' she said.

'I am Luca Montese.'

'I'm Rebecca Solway. Becky.'

He looked down at the small, elegant hand she held out to him. For the first time he seemed to become uncertain. Then he thrust out his own hand. It was coarse and powerful, bruised and battered by heavy work. It engulfed hers out of sight.

His whole appearance was rough. His dark hair needed cutting and hung shaggily about his thickly muscled neck. He wore worn black jeans and a black sleeveless vest, and he was well over six feet, built on impressive lines.

Hercules, she thought.

The frightening rage in his face had disappeared entirely now, and the look he turned on her was gentle, although unsmiling. 'Rebecca,' he repeated.

'No, Becky to my friends. You are my friend, aren't you? You must be, after you saved me.'

For the whole of her short life, her charm and beauty had won people over. It was unusual for anyone not to warm to her easily, but she could sense this young man's hesitation.

'Yes,' he said awkwardly at last. 'I am your friend.'

'Then you'll call me Becky?'

'Becky.'

'Do you live here alone, or with a family?'

'I have no family. This was my mother's and father's house, and now it belongs to me.'

The firm tone in which he said the last words prompted her to say, 'Hey, I'm not arguing about that. It's yours, it's yours.'

'I wish your father felt the same way. Where is he now?'

'In Spain. He'll be home next week.'

'Until then I think it's better if you don't ride alone.'

She had been thinking the same thing, but this easy assumption of authority riled her.

'I beg your pardon?'

He frowned. 'There is no need to beg my pardon.'

'No, that's not what I meant,' she said, realising that his English was not as good as he'd claimed. '"I beg your pardon" is an expression that means "Who the heck do you think you are to give me orders?".'

He frowned again. 'Then why not just say so?'

'Because...' But the task of explaining was too much. She abandoned English in favour of Tuscan dialect.

'Don't give me orders. I'll ride as I please.'

'And what happens next time, when I may not be there to come to your aid?' he asked in the same language.

'They'll have gone by now.'

'And if you're wrong?'

'That's—that's got nothing to do with it,' she floundered, unable to counter the argument.

A faint smile appeared on his face. 'I think it has.'

'Oh, stop being so reasonable!' she said crossly.

The smile became a grin. 'Very well. Whatever pleases you.'

She smiled back ruefully. 'You might be right.'

He refilled her cup and she sipped it appreciatively. 'You make very good tea. I'm impressed.'

'And *I* am impressed that you speak my dialect so well.'

'My grandmother taught me. She came from here. She used to own the house where we live now.'

'Emilia Talese?'

'That was her maiden name, yes.'

'My family have always been carpenters. They used to do jobs for *her* family.'

That was their first meeting. He walked home with her, coming into the house, instructing the servants to take good care of her, as if he'd been commanding people all his life.

'Will you be all right?' she asked, thinking of him walking back alone in the gathering dusk. 'Suppose they're waiting for you?'

His grin was answer enough. It said that such fears were for other men. Then he walked out, leaving behind only the memory of his brilliant self-confidence. It was as strong as sunlight, and he seemed both to carry it with him, and leave it behind wherever he had been.

CHAPTER TWO

NEXT day Becky left the house early and rode down to find him. She had gone to bed thinking of him, lain awake thinking of him, finally slept, dreaming of him, then awoke thinking of him. She saw his face, young yet forceful, the mouth that was too stern for his years, until he smiled and became suddenly charming.

His mouth haunted her. With everything in her she wanted to kiss it, and to feel it kissing her back. And his arms, as powerful as steel hawsers, belonged around her. She knew that, as certainly as she had ever known anything, knew it with the conviction of a girl who had never seriously been denied anything she really wanted.

She had never even kissed a man before. But now that she'd met Luca she wanted him completely, in every way. It was as though her body had come alive in an instant, sending a message to her brain: this is the one.

The only question was how and when. It was impossible that the world, or Luca himself, could deny her.

As she approached he heard the hoof beats and looked up. She jumped down from the horse, facing him, and she knew at once, with joyful certainty, that he too had lain awake all night. But he turned away from her.

'You shouldn't be here,' he said. 'I told you not to ride alone.'

'Then why didn't you come for me?'

'Because the *signorina* did not give me orders to do so,' he said proudly.

'But I don't give you orders. We're just friends.'

She stood looking into his face, willing him to let her have her wish. He gave the slow smile that already made her heart beat strongly.

'Why don't you go and make the tea?' he suggested.

She did so, and spent the rest of the day helping him work on the house. He made rolls with salami, which was the most delicious food she'd ever tasted. But she hadn't given up her determination to make him kiss her. Sooner or later he would yield.

It took her three days to crack his resistance. During that time she came to know the man a little. He had a touchy pride that could make his temper smoulder, although he always reined it in quickly for her sake.

On the first day he had said, 'Whatever pleases you,' and that became his mantra. Whatever pleased her was right for him. This big man, who could be so ferocious to others, was like a child in her hands. It gave her a delicious sense of power.

But she couldn't make him do the one thing she wanted above all else. She created chance after chance, and he wouldn't take any of them, until one day he said, 'I think you should go home now.' He added in slow, awkward English, 'It has been very nice knowing you.'

Her answer was to pick up a bread roll from the table and hurl it at him. He ducked, but didn't seem disconcerted.

'Why don't you like me any more?' she cried.

'I do like you, Becky. I like you more than I should. That is why you must go, and not come back.'

'That doesn't make any sense!'

'I think you know just what I mean.'

'No!' she cried, refusing to understand what didn't suit her.

'I think you do. You know what I want with you, and I can't have it. I *must* not. You're a child.'

'I'm seventeen. Well, I will be in a couple of weeks. I'm *not* a child.'

'You talk like one. What you want, you must have. For the moment you want me, but I'm a man, not a toy to be played with then cast aside.'

'I'm not playing.'

'But you are. You're like a kitten with a cotton reel. You haven't yet learned that life can be cruel and bitter, and God forbid that you should learn it through me!'

'But you said you wanted me. Why can't we—?'

'Becky, my grandfather was your grandmother's carpenter. I'm still a carpenter. Sometimes I make a little money repairing cars, getting dirty.'

'Oh, nobody cares about that any more.'

'Ask your father if he cares about it.'

'This has nothing to do with my father. Just you and me.'

Suddenly he lost his temper. 'Don't be stupid!' he shouted.

'Don't call me stupid.'

'You are stupid. If you weren't, you wouldn't come down here and be alone with a man who desires you as much as I do. If you called for help there's nobody to hear you.'

'Why should I need help against you? I know you and—'

'You know nothing,' he said, in a rage. 'I spend my nights lying awake, thinking of you in my bed, in my arms, naked. I have no right to think these things but I can't stop myself. And then you come here, smiling and saying ''Luca, I want you'', and I go insane. How much do you think one man can take?'

Out of all this only one thing made any impact.

'You desire me?'

'Yes,' he said curtly, turning away to stare out of the window. 'Now go.'

'I'm not going,' she said softly, almost to herself. It was more than a decision. It was a declaration that she had chosen her path and would follow it.

She went close behind him, slipping her arms about his body. As she had known he would, he turned instantly, and fell straight into her trap. She had removed her upper clothing and he found himself holding her bare skin, her arms, her shoulders, her breasts.

He made one last, agonised effort.

'No, Becky—please—'

But the words were drowned by her lips on his, and then it was too late. It had always been too late.

He kissed her tenderly, then with increasing urgency, while his hands explored her and hers explored him. He was wearing a shirt, the front partly unbuttoned. It took her only a moment to rip open the remaining buttons so that she could press her breasts against his body. Inexperienced though she was, she knew at once that the sensation was too much for his self-control. When she moved to pull the shirt right off, he did it for her.

She was completely trusting, without caution or defences, and he seemed to know it even through his passion, for his movements were as controlled as he could make them.

At first all she felt was his tenderness, leading her forward gently. She was already in a fever for him, helping him remove the last of her clothes, then his, following his every move, trying to anticipate, so that he gave a shaky laugh, saying, 'Don't be in such a hurry.'

'But I want you, Luca, *I want you.*'

'But you don't know what you want, *piccina,*' he said hoarsely. 'I have no right—we must stop—'

'*No!* I'll thump you in a minute.'

'Little bully,' he whispered.

'You'd better let me have my own way, then, hadn't you?' she teased.

That was the end of his control. After that, no power on earth could have stopped him exploring her, enchanted by her sweetness and her young, blazing passion for himself.

As soon as he entered her she gave a little cry of excitement and began to move against him, urging him on. Her frank eagerness to make love and her lack of false modesty delighted him, and he gave everything without holding back.

It was a swift, unsubtle mating which came to a climax almost at once. Becky felt dizzy. One moment she was simply enjoying herself, and the next moment something tossed her up to the stars in a fine frenzy of pleasure, before sending her swooping back to earth, wondering which planet she'd landed on. Because it wasn't the same one that she'd started on.

'Oh, wow!' she said breathlessly. 'Oh, wow!'

The next moment she leapt on him again, ignoring his laughing protests. This time he loved her more slowly, or at least as slowly as she would let him, teasing her breasts with lips and fingers, until she wrapped her legs about him, demanding fulfilment, and he could do nothing but yield.

Afterwards they lay entwined while they drifted down from the heights, rejoicing to find each other still there.

'Why did you try to warn me off?' she whispered. 'It was beautiful.'

'I'm glad. I want everything to be beautiful and wonderful for you, always.'

'It *is* wonderful, and you're wonderful, and everything in the world is wonderful, because you love me.'

'I didn't say I loved you,' he growled.

'But you do, don't you?'

'Yes, I do.' He tightened his arms, pulling her naked body hard against his. 'I love you, *piccina*. I love you with my heart and soul, with my body—'

'Yes, I know *that*.' She giggled, letting her fingers run races over his skin.

'Don't tease me,' he groaned. 'I can't endure it.'

'I don't want you to endure it, I want you to give in.'

'Don't I always give in to you?' he asked with a touch of sombreness in his voice.

But that mood couldn't last. She wanted him to make love to her again, and he could never deny her anything.

On the day of Frank's return Becky drove to Pisa Airport to meet him in her own car, delivered as an early birthday gift during his absence.

'I thought you wouldn't want to wait,' he explained now as she thanked him.

'You spoil me, Dad.'

'That's what daughters are for,' he said cheerfully. He was on a 'high' of success, as he told her during the drive home.

'Got everything I wanted at less than I expected to pay. *Yessir!*'

Becky had heard him talk like this many times before, but now the memory of the Englishmen, and their desperation, made it sound different.

'Will anyone be put out of work?' she asked.

'What was that?'

'If you're making such a profit, someone has to lose out, don't they?'

'Of course. Someone always loses out, but they're the wimps, the people who deserve to lose because nature made them losers.'

'But is it nature that makes them losers, or you?'

'Becky, what is this? You've never had such ideas before.'

The thought flashed across her mind, *Or any ideas at all!* But all she said was, 'You closed down a place in England, and some of the people who lost their jobs came out here to find you.'

'The devil they did! What happened?'

'They found me instead. I was out riding alone and three men appeared from nowhere.'

'Did they hurt you?'

'No, but only because a man appeared and saved me. His name's Luca Montese and he lives near by. He was working on his cottage when he heard them shouting. He squared up to them, knocked one of them down and after that they all scurried away.'

'Then I must meet this man and thank him. Where exactly did this happen?'

She described the spot and he frowned.

'I didn't know I had any tenants there.'

'He isn't a tenant, he owns that bit of land. He says you tried to buy him out but he wouldn't sell.'

'Montese?' he muttered. 'Montese? Good grief, that's

him? Carletti, my agent, told me of some fellow who'd been making trouble.'

'He's not making trouble, Dad. He just wants to keep his home.'

'Nonsense, he doesn't know what's good for him. Carletti says the place is little more than a hovel. Squalid, unsanitary.'

'Not any more. He's done a wonderful job of rebuilding it.'

'You've been there?'

'He took me there after he rescued me, and made me some tea. It was nice and cosy. He's worked so hard on it.'

'Well, he's wasting his time. I'll get it in the end.'

'I don't think so. He's determined not to sell.'

'And I'm determined that he will, and I reckon I'm stronger than some peasant lad.'

'Dad!' she cried in protest. 'A moment ago you were going to thank him for saving me. Now you're planning to bully him.'

'Nonsense,' he said with his easy laugh. 'I'll just show him where his best interests lie.'

He visited Luca that same day, full of *bonhomie*, thanking him for his care of Becky while contriving to patronise him in a way that embarrassed her. Luca's response was a quiet dignity.

Then Frank looked around.

'Carletti tells me you've been holding out for more than this little place is worth,' he said.

'Then your agent has misinformed you,' Luca said quietly. 'This place is worth everything to me, and I will not sell.'

'All right, look, here's the deal. Because you helped my daughter I'll double my last offer. I can't say fairer than that.'

'Signor Solway, my home is not for sale.'

'Why make such a fuss about this tatty little place? It's barely half an acre.'

'Then why trouble yourself with it?'

'That doesn't concern you. I've made a more than fair offer and I don't like being trifled with.'

Luca gave his slow smile. It drove Frank Solway mad.

'Have I said something funny?' he snapped.

'*Signor*, I don't think you understand the word no.'

This was so completely right that Frank lost his temper and bawled indiscriminately until Becky said, 'Dad! Have you forgotten what he did for me?'

Frank scowled. He hated to be in the wrong, but neither could he back down. He stomped off without another word, yelling, 'Becky!' over his shoulder.

'Go with him,' Luca said gently when she didn't move.

'No, I'm staying with you.'

'That will make it worse. Please go.'

She yielded to his quiet insistence where her father's blustering only filled her with disgust.

The following day Frank said uneasily, 'I may have gone a little too far with Luca yesterday.'

'Much too far,' Becky said. 'I think you should apologise.'

'No way. That would make me look weak. But you're another matter. Why don't you drop in on him and tell him I'm not such a bad fellow? Don't make it sound like an apology but—well, keep on his right side.'

She left the house with a light heart. Now she could

spend the day with Luca without having to think of an excuse.

He observed her approach from a distance, a quizzical expression on his face.

'Does your father know you're here? Don't get into trouble for me.'

'Are you telling me to go away?' she demanded, hurt.

'It might be better if you did.'

'You sound as if you don't care one way or the other.'

'My back is broad, but yours isn't. I don't want you hurt.'

'In other words you're giving me the brush-off.'

'Don't be stupid,' he growled. 'Of course I don't want you to go.'

She ran into his arms, kissing him again and again.

'I'm not going, my darling. I'm not going to leave you.'

He kissed her long and deeply, and she responded with fierce, young passion. It was he who pulled away first, trembling with the effort it took to rein his desire back, but determined to do so.

'I would die rather than harm you,' he said in a shaking voice.

'But, darling, you're not harming me. Dad told me to come and see you.'

He looked at her wryly. 'And why would he do that?'

She chuckled. 'Can't you guess? He wants me to soften you up for his next offer.'

He grinned. 'And are you going to?'

'Of course not. But he's told me to keep on your right side, and while he thinks that's what I'm doing he won't make a fuss about me coming here. Aren't I clever?'

'You're a cunning little witch.'

'I'm only putting Dad's own theory into practice. He

says when you think someone's acting for you they're always pursuing their own agenda. Well, you're my agenda, so come here and let me get on your right side.'

She took his hand and he went with her, unresisting, because neither then nor later could he deny her anything. It was to be the ruin of both of them.

'Damn you, Luca! You duped me.'

Luca Montese's face showed no relenting.. 'Nonsense! You sleepwalked into this without checking.'

'I thought I could trust you.'

'More fool you. I warned you not to trust me, and goodness knows how many of my enemies warned you.'

The man glaring across the desk was in a fury at the thought of the money he'd coveted and lost. His name was—well, no matter. He was the latest in a long line of men who had thought they could put one over on Luca Montese, and found that they were wrong.

'We were supposed to be in this together,' he snapped.

'No. You thought you'd use me as a tool. I was to get the information, then you planned to make a deal behind my back. You should have been more suspicious. When you think a man's acting for you he's always pursuing his own agenda.'

Then a strange thing happened.

As Luca said the words a feeling of malaise came over him, so strong that he had to take a deep breath. It was as though the world had changed in a moment from a place where he was in control to a place where everything was strange and threatening.

'Get out!' he said curtly. 'I'll send you a cheque to cover your expenses.'

The man left fast, relieved simply to recover his expenses, which was more than anyone had got out of Luca for years. He wondered if the monster was losing his touch.

Left alone, Luca held himself still for a long time. The walls seemed to converge on him and suddenly he couldn't breathe.

When you think a man's acting for you he's always pursuing his own agenda.

The words had come so naturally that he'd never doubted they were his own. Yet they had carried a sweetness so unbearable that it had almost destroyed him.

He was choking. He got up and opened the window, but the terrifying memory wouldn't go away.

She had said it, and then she had pulled him down on the bed and loved him until his head was spinning. And he had loved her in return, making her a gift of everything that was in him, heart, body and soul, everything he was or hoped to be.

And that had been his mistake.

It was a mistake he'd never made again in the fifteen years since, when he had piled up money and power. He'd commanded his heart to harden until he could feel nothing, and he had been a success in that, as in everything else.

Now something frightening was happening. More and more the past was calling, tempting him back to a time when he was alive to feeling. But if he worked hard he reckoned he could kill it.

Only one person did not tread carefully when Luca was around, and that was Sonia, his personal assistant. Middle-aged, cool and efficient, she viewed her employer with eyes that were half motherly, half cynical. She was the only person he totally trusted, and with whom he could discuss his personal life.

'Don't waste time brooding,' she advised him over a drink that evening. 'You always said it was a weakness. You've got your divorce, so forget it, and marry again.'

'Never!' he snapped. 'Another barren marriage for people to snicker at? No, thank you.'

'Who says it'll be barren? Just because you didn't have a child by Drusilla doesn't mean a thing. Some couples are like that. They can't have a baby together, but each of them can have a baby by somebody else. Nobody knows why it happens, but it does.

'This hairdresser is her ''somebody else''. Now you have to find yours. It shouldn't be hard. You're an attractive man.'

He grinned. 'Not like you to pay me compliments. Normally, according to you, I'm an impossible so-and-so with an ego the size of St Peter's dome and—I forget the others but I'm sure you remember them.'

'Selfish, monstrous and intolerable,' she supplied without hesitation. 'I've called you all those things and I don't take back one word.'

'You're probably right.'

'But it doesn't stop you being attractive, and there are millions of women out there.'

He was silent for so long that she wondered if she'd offended him.

'It could work the other way too, couldn't it?' he said at last.

'How do you mean?'

'Suppose there weren't millions of women? Suppose there was only one woman with whom I had any hope of having children?'

'I've never heard of it working that way round.'

'But it might,' he persisted.

'Then you'd have to find her, and it would be like looking for a needle in a haystack.'

'Not if you knew who she was.'

Understanding dawned.

'You've already made your mind up, haven't you? Luca, you don't believe this because it's true, you believe it because you want to. It's rather comforting to know that you can be as irrational as the rest of us.' She regarded him curiously. 'She must have been very special.'

'Yes,' he said heavily. 'She was special.'

He was a man of action. A few phone calls and a representative of the best private-enquiry firm that money could buy was in his office next morning.

'Rebecca Solway,' he said, speaking curtly to hide the fact that his stomach was churning. 'Her father was Frank Solway, owner of the Belleto estate in Tuscany.

'Find her. I don't care what it costs, but *find her*.'

It was a successful evening. Philip Steyne, chairman of the bank, treated Rebecca with honour, and was clearly as impressed as Danvers had hoped he would be. When Rebecca left them for a moment Steyne said,

'Congratulations, Jordan. She'll do the bank credit. When can we expect the announcement?'

'Any day, I hope. Nothing's been said precisely, but of course she understands where we're heading.'

'Well, in good banking it pays to be precise,' observed Steyne with a grin. 'Don't take too long.'

When Rebecca returned he said, 'Rebecca, let me have the benefit of your expertise. You're a quarter Italian, right?'

'Yes, my father's mother came from Tuscany.'

'And you speak the language?'

She gave him her cleverest smile, a little bit teasing, but not too much. This was Danvers' boss.

'Which language do you mean? There's *la madre lingua*, the official language that they use on radio and television, and in government. But there are also the regional dialects, which are languages in themselves. I speak *la madre lingua*, and Tuscan.'

'I'm impressed. Actually Tuscan might be handy. This firm has its head office in Rome, but I believe it started in Tuscany, and it's all over the world now.'

'Firm?'

'Raditore Inc. Property, finance, finger in every pie. Suddenly it's buying a huge block of shares in the Allingham, and the bank's interested in closer contact. I propose a dinner party at my house—you, Danvers, their top brass. Let's see what there is to be gained from them.'

Driving her home, Danvers was lyrical in his praise.

'You really impressed the old man tonight, darling.'

'Good. I'm glad I was a help to you.'

She answered mechanically and he shot her a quick sideways look, thinking that this was the second time she'd been in a funny mood and he hoped it wasn't going to become a habit.

Again she didn't invite him into her suite, which he found annoying. He would have found it convenient to discuss the forthcoming dinner party. Instead Rebecca bid him an implacable goodnight and shut her door.

When he was out of sight she closed her eyes in relief, then stripped off hurriedly and got under the shower, wanting to wash the evening away. She was on edge tonight, just as she had been the night before. The mention of Tuscany had unsettled her, and the ghost had walked again.

CHAPTER THREE

As soon as Becky was certain, she hurried to tell Luca the news. He was thrilled.

'A baby? Our own little *bambino*! Half you, half me.'

'Your very own son and heir,' she said, snuggling blissfully in his arms.

How he laughed.

'I'm just a common labourer. Labourers don't have heirs. Besides, I want a girl—just like you. I want another Becky.'

Her pregnancy brought out the best in him, and she discovered again that he was a marvellous man, loving, tender, considerate as few men knew how to be. Later, when joy was replaced by anguish, it was his tenderness that Rebecca remembered most wistfully. How gently he took care of her, how worried he always was about her health. Nothing was ever too much trouble for him to do for her.

Her father was away a lot that summer, visiting his various interests, and there was little chance to tell him. When he did return it was only for a few days, filled with phone calls. Becky didn't want to break the news until she was sure of having all his attention, so she waited until she knew he would be home for at least two weeks. By that time she was three months gone.

'And you will tell him this time?' Luca asked.

'Of course. I only want everything to be right when I do.'

'I want to be with you. I won't have you face his anger alone.'

'What anger? Dad will be thrilled,' she predicted blithely. 'He loves babies.'

It was true. Like many bullies Frank Solway had a streak of sentimentality. He cooed over babies and the world said what a delightful man he was.

'Honestly, darling,' Becky said, 'this will make everything all right.'

How stupid could you be?

Her father was almost out of his mind with rage.

'You got yourself knocked up by that...?' He finished on a stream of profanity.

'Dad, I didn't get "knocked up". I got pregnant by a man I love. Please don't try to make it sound like something dirty.'

'It is dirty. How dare he lay a finger on you?'

'Because I wanted him to. To put it plainly, *I* dragged *him* into bed, not the other way around.'

'Don't ever let me hear you say that again,' he shouted.

'It's true! I love Luca and I'm going to marry him.'

'You think I'm going to allow that? You think my daughter is going to marry that low-life? The sooner this is fixed the better.'

'I'm going to have my baby.'

'The hell you are!'

She ran away that night. Frank followed her to Luca's house and tried to buy her back. But the mention of money only made Luca roar with laughter. Later Becky was to realise what her father heard in that laughter. It was the roar of the young lion telling the old lion that he no longer ruled. Perhaps her father's real hatred dated from that moment.

He tried to enlist the help of the locals, but he was thwarted. Frank Solway was powerful but Luca was one of them, and nobody was ready to raise their hand against him.

But Becky knew he wouldn't give up, and in the end it was she who suggested they leave.

'Just for a while, darling. Dad'll feel better about it when he's a grandfather.'

He sighed. 'I hate running away, but all this quarrelling is bad for you and the baby. We'll go for the sake of some peace.'

They fled south to stay with his friends in Naples. After two weeks he bought an old car, repaired it himself, and they set off again, heading south to Calabria. Two weeks there, then north again.

They talked about marriage but never stayed anywhere long enough to complete the formalities, just in case Frank's tentacles reached them. Wherever they went his skilled hands found him work. It was a good life.

Becky had not known that such happiness was possible. She was over the first sickness of pregnancy, feeling well and strong, spending her life with the man she adored. Their love was the unquestioning, uncomplicated kind that inspired songs and stories, with a happy-ever-after always promised at the end. She loved him, he loved her, and their baby would arrive soon. What more was there?

The thought of Frank was always there in the background, but as week followed week with no sign of him he faded and became unreal, a 'maybe' rather than a genuine threat.

She began to understand Luca better, and herself. It was Luca who revealed her body to her, its fierce responses, its eagerness for physical love. But it was also through him, and the life they lived, that she was able to stand outside herself, and look with critical eyes. What she saw did not please her.

'I was horrid,' she said to him once. 'A real spoilt brat, taking everything for granted, letting Dad indulge me and never wondering where the money came from. But it actually came from men like the ones who stopped me that day. He practically stole from them. You can't really blame them, can you?'

'You can't blame yourself, either,' he insisted. 'You were so young, how could it occur to you to ask questions about your father's methods? But when your eyes were opened you didn't try to look away. My Becky is too brave for that.'

There was always a special note in his voice when he said 'my Becky', as though all the best in her was a personal gift to himself, to be treasured. It made her feel like the most important person in the world. And in the world they made together, that was true.

She gradually came to understand that Luca was one person to her, and a different man to everyone else. The attackers who had fled him, filled with fear, had seen the side of him that others saw.

He was a potentially frightening man who carried with him an aura of being always on the edge of ruthlessness, even violence. It took time for Becky to understand this, because he never showed that side of himself to her.

They had their arguments, even outright rows, but he

fought fair, never turning his ferocity on her, and always bringing the spat to a speedy end, often by simply giving in. It hurt him to be at odds with her.

In their daily life he was tender, loving and gentle, setting her on a pedestal and asserting, by his actions, that she was different from all other human beings on earth.

His love for her carried a hint of worship that awed and delighted her, even while it sometimes made him over-protective to the point of being dictatorial. It was he who decided, in her sixth month, that their lovemaking must cease until after the baby was born, and she had fully recovered.

Torn by desire, she wept and pleaded. 'It's too soon. The doctor says we've time yet.'

'The doctor is not the father of your baby. *I am*, and *I* have decided that it is time to stop,' he declared in the most arrogant statement she had yet heard from him.

'But what will you do? It's months and months, and you'll—well, you know.'

'What are you saying? That you don't trust me to be faithful to you?'

'Well, I don't know, do I?' she cried.

There was a flash of temper on his face, for he had never given her a moment's cause for anxiety. But anger was gone in a instant, dissolved in laughter.

'Oh, stop that,' she said, thumping him in frustration.

But he roared aloud with laughter, holding her carefully against him.

'*Amor mia,* I promise to be home at the proper time every evening, and you may put a collar and lead about my neck,' he said with a grin.

'And every man in the place will say you're living under my thumb, and laugh at you.'

'But I don't care what they think, only what you think,' he said, serious again. 'You and our child are everything in life to me.'

He stuck to his resolve, keeping an iron control over himself, and spending all his spare time at home. Becky, talking to other expectant mothers in doctors' waiting rooms, knew just how lucky she was.

For most of the time she could push serious matters aside to enjoy their life. Everything was fun. Being poor, learning how to shop so that she got the best out of his wages, living in old jeans and letting them out as she put on weight—all this was fun.

It was Luca who finally decided that they should settle in one spot. She was now more than six months gone, and he said, 'I want you under the care of the same doctor from now on.'

They had reached Carenna, a small town near Florence, where he had found work with a local builder. It was a pleasant place to put down roots. He located a good doctor, found some birth classes, and attended them with her, mastering all the exercises, to her tender amusement. At home they practised together until they collapsed with laughter.

Perhaps so much happiness could never last. Sometimes it seemed as though she'd used up her lifetime's allowance in those few glorious months.

Philip Steyne's house was on the edge of London. As befitted his money, it was a mansion, set in its own grounds, with far more rooms than he needed.

The dinner party was for twenty, a number just large

enough to allow a mix, but small enough for the right people to home in on each other.

Rebecca knew what was expected of her and dressed accordingly in a dress of wine-red velvet that hugged her slender figure. Black silk stockings sheathed her legs, finishing in dainty black sandals. Tonight she let her long blonde hair flow freely in a 'natural' style that had taken the beauty parlour three hours to perfect, and which set the seal on her glamour. Her solid gold necklace and earrings were Danvers' gift 'to mark the occasion'.

'We still don't know who's actually coming tonight,' he remarked as the car purred into the drive. 'Raditore has played coy as to whether it'll be the chairman, chief executive or managing director.'

'Does it matter?' she asked. 'I know my job, and I it'll be much the same whoever it is.'

'That's right. Just make his head spin. I must say, you're dressed for it. I've never seen you looking so good.'

'Thank you.'

'I'm always proud of you.'

'Thank you,' she said again, speaking mechanically. It was hard to respond in any way, since Danvers paid compliments as though ticking off a list.

The car glided silently through the gate, down the long drive to the house. When they were nearly there Rebecca had a moment of strange and disturbing consciousness.

Suddenly the luxurious car was every luxurious car she had ever journeyed in, the huge, moneyed house was the end of a long line of moneyed houses, the dinner party to meet rich men, and charm them, was indistinguishable from so many—too many—others.

There was the house, the front door being pulled open, her hosts coming out onto the step, welcoming smiles in place. Philip Steyne's suit had been tailored in Savile Row, his wife's dress was haute couture. Like so many others.

'Danvers, Rebecca, how *lovely* to see you. Come in, come—Rebecca, you look *lovely* as always—what a *lovely* dress...'

The same words said a hundred times by a hundred people. And her own response, indistinguishable from before. The same smiles, the same laughter, the same emptiness.

Philip Steyne murmured in her ear, 'Well done. You'll reduce him to jelly.'

'Is he here?'

'Arrived ten minutes ago. Just through here.'

Again, just as before. But then, thankfully, the moment passed and she was free again to live her life on the surface, without thinking or feeling too much. Because only in that way was existence tolerable.

It had been a bad few minutes, but she was all right again now.

It was in this mood that she walked into the next room and saw Luca Montese for the first time in fifteen years.

Now they were settled they could plan the wedding.

'*Carissima,* you don't mind a simple ceremony with no gorgeous bridal gown?'

She chuckled. 'I'd look a bit odd in a gorgeous bridal gown and a seven-month bulge. And I don't want fuss. I just want you.'

They were going to bed and he tucked her up, then knelt down beside her, taking her hands in his and speaking in a low, reverent voice that she had never heard before.

'The day after tomorrow we will be married. We shall stand before God and make sacred promises. But I tell you that none of them will be as sacred as those I make to you now. I promise you that my heart, my love and my whole life belong to you, and always will.'

He spoke like a man uttering a prayer.

'Do you understand?' he urged. 'Whether my life be long or short, every moment of it will be spent in your service.'

He laid his hand gently over her bulge.

'And you, little one—you too I will love and protect in every way. You will be safe and happy, because your *mama* and *papa* love you.'

Becky tried to answer him, but no words would come through her tears.

'Oh, Luca,' she managed to say at last, 'if I could only tell you—'

'Hush, *carissima*. You do not need to tell me what I see in your eyes.'

He took her face between his hands and looked down at her searchingly.

'You will always be to me as you are at this moment,' he whispered before kissing her with heart-stopping gentleness.

She slept in his arms that night, and awoke to his kiss in the early morning. He was going to work sooner than usual, so that he could come home early to help with last-minute preparations for their wedding.

Becky spent the day tidying the house, and making

sure they had enough food and wine for their friends. She was just putting the kettle on for a much needed cup of tea when the doorbell rang.

It was almost a relief to find Frank standing there. She felt safer now, because surely her bulge would make him accept the inevitable?

'Hello, Dad.'

'Hello, Becky. Can I come in?'

He entered without seeming to notice her shape. He had a gift for not noticing what didn't suit him.

'You're on your own, I see. Got tired of you already, has he?'

'Dad, it's three in the afternoon. He's at work, but he'll be home any minute.'

'So you say.'

She'd known then that it wasn't going to be easy after all. But she tried.

'It's nice to see you—'

'Yes, I expect you're fed up with all this.'

'No, I'm not. This is my life. Look around you at all this food and wine. It's for our wedding reception tomorrow.'

He shot her a sharp look.

'So you're not married? Good, then I'm in time.'

'I'm having Luca's baby, and I'm going to marry him,' she said firmly. 'Won't you come to the wedding and drink our health, and be our friend?'

He looked down at her with an expression that might have been tenderness.

'Darling, you're living in a dream world. Trust me, I know what's best for you. He's deluded you.'

'Dad—'

'But I'm here to make it right. Just let me take care of you. Everything will be fine as soon as we're home.'

'This *is* my home.'

'This—this hovel? You think I'm leaving you here? Stop arguing *and come on.*'

Abruptly he dropped the pretence of kindness, and seized her arm. She shrieked. Luca, approaching the house, heard her and rushed the rest of the way, flinging open the door to find them struggling.

'Let her go,' he roared.

'Get out of my way,' Frank snapped.

Luca stood there, barring the door. 'I said let her go.'

Frank ignored him, trying to drag her towards the back door by sheer force. Becky struggled as hard as she could, but her size made it difficult.

With a curse Luca strode forward and placed one powerful hand on Frank's arm.

'Don't dare touch her,' he said, and there was the same menace in his eyes that she had seen before, when they had first met.

'I'm taking her home,' Frank repeated.

Luca's voice was infused with contempt.

'You are not only a bully but a deeply stupid man. Only a *cretino* would do this, knowing that he was threatening the well-being of the child she carries.'

Frank's answer was to try again to drag Becky away. Luca did not move, but his hand, grasping the other man's arm, was impossible to dislodge.

'Luca, don't let him take me,' she begged.

That sent Frank over the edge, and he began to rant and rave. Luca said nothing, merely standing silent and immovable. Perhaps it was that quiet dignity that infuriated Frank most, for he shoved Becky aside to contend with Luca.

Then the nightmare started. Heaving with distress, Becky suddenly found the world retreating and returning alarmingly. Everything seemed to spin around, culminating in a feeling of knives searing through her.

She screamed and doubled over as agony engulfed her like a furnace. The sound got through to the two men, halting their fight, although even then Frank had to put himself centre stage. Her last clear sight was of him shouldering his way ahead of Luca to lean over her.

But it was Luca she wanted. She reached out, calling his name, but Frank was there, leaning close, grasping her tightly, imprisoning her, blocking out everything but himself.

'Luca,' she screamed. *'Luca!'*

But suddenly he vanished. She never saw him again.

An ambulance came to whisk her off to hospital. Her daughter was born quickly and died within a few hours.

When the physical pain ceased there was another pain waiting, in her mind. Fire turned to ice as a merciless darkness enclosed her. The only thing she knew for sure was that she called repeatedly for Luca, but he was never there.

How could he not be there? His daughter had been born, and had died without his ever holding her in his arms. He had promised to love and protect her, but he hadn't been there when she needed him.

'She was so little and helpless,' she whispered into the void. 'She needed her father.'

But he did not hear. The darkness had swallowed him up.

Scenes changed about her. Somehow she knew that

she was back in England, and living in a new place, a large, pleasant house where there were people in white coats and everyone spoke in kindly voices.

Sometimes the voices were brisk and hearty. 'How are we feeling today? A little better? That's good.'

She never answered, but they didn't seem to mind. They treated her like a doll, brushing her hair and talking about her as though she wasn't there.

'There's no way of knowing how long she'll be like this, Mr Solway. She has profound post-natal depression, aggravated by terrible inner wounds, and they need time to heal.'

She never reminded them that she was a living being with thoughts and feelings, because she no longer felt like one. It was easier this way because they didn't expect her to respond, and the soul-deep exhaustion that possessed her made answering seem like climbing a mountain.

Often the words she heard were a meaningless jabber, but one day the world righted itself and she began to hear and see it normally. Frank was in the middle of one of his monologues, and the words made sense.

'...Not easy coming back to England—wrong time of the financial year—left me with a hefty tax bill, but I said only the best was good enough for my girl. And this place *is* the best. Oh, yes, no skimping.'

'Where is he? Where's Luca? Why doesn't he come to see me?'

'Because he's gone, for good. I bought him off.'

She turned her head slowly and stared at him with a look that made even that thick-skinned man flinch.

'What do you mean?' Even to her own ears her voice sounded dead and metallic.

'I mean I bought him off. He demanded money to go away and never trouble you again.'

'I—don't—believe—you.' The words came out like hammer taps.

'Then I'll prove it.'

His proof was a cheque for the euro equivalent of fifty thousand pounds, made out to Luca Montese, with the record, on the back, of the bank where it had been cashed.

She wanted to say that it was false, it proved nothing. But she knew the bank Luca used in Tuscany, and it was the same one.

Whether my life be long or short, every moment of it will be spent in your service.

How long after saying those words had he sold her back to her father for cash?

She had thought she was dead already, but there must still have been some feeling left alive, because she sensed the last remnants die at that moment. And was glad of it.

Everyone agreed that the meal was superb. The wine was a hundred-year-old vintage and the brandy even older.

Luca Montese had been the centre of attention from the start. As the guests entered, one by one, they were introduced to him—presented to him, Rebecca thought—in a way that left no doubt he was the guest of honour. But even without that he would have held attention by the magnetism that seemed to surround him like a force field.

His eyes were like flint. His smile was wolfish. He was a predator, coolly surveying the prey around him, counting them off in order of their importance to him.

They all knew it, of course they did. And each of them was courting him.

Except herself.

'Luca,' Philip Steyne said jovially, 'let me introduce you to one of my favourite people, Rebecca Hanley, who takes care of PR for the Allingham.'

'Then Mrs Hanley is a most important person to me,' Luca responded at once.

'Good evening, Signor Montese,' Rebecca replied coolly.

He felt different. The hand that engulfed hers was no longer the rough paw that had held her in passion and tenderness, and which she had loved. It was smooth and manicured, a rich man's hand. A stranger's.

She forced herself to meet his eyes, and found nothing there. No warmth, no alarm, no amazement, no recognition. Nothing.

Relief and disappointment warred, but neither won.

She disengaged her hand at once and murmured something about the pleasure of meeting him. There were people behind her, agog for an introduction, and they provided an excuse for her not to linger.

'You might have been a bit more gracious,' Danvers complained under his breath when he too had been introduced and passed on. 'These self-made men can be so touchy if they think they're being patronised.'

'But you're the one who's patronising him,' she pointed out.

'What?'

'The way you said "these self-made men" was deeply patronising. As though they're all alike.'

'They are, more or less. Full of themselves. Always wanting to tell you how they did it.'

Rebecca maintained a diplomatic silence. It would have been ill-natured to point out that Danvers had been born to money and therefore had nothing to tell.

She was getting her second wind. There had been the shock of meeting him without warning, but that was over now, and she could study him while he talked with somebody else.

She would hardly have known him. His height and breadth of shoulder were the same, but his hair, which had always been shaggy, tempting her to run her fingers through it, was cut back neat and short, revealing the lines of his face. The large nose with the hint of a hook was the one she knew, but the rest was strange.

'A rough diamond,' Philip Steyne murmured in her ear. 'But very rich. And when you think that he came from nowhere, and started with nothing!'

'Nobody really starts with nothing,' Danvers observed. 'Somehow, somewhere he got his hands on a lump sum of money to begin with. One can only speculate on what he had to do to get it.'

'Perhaps he'll tell you,' Rebecca said sharply. 'That's what ''self-made men'' do, isn't it?'

Danvers shared a grin with Steyne. 'Maybe it's best if we don't know,' he observed. 'He looks as though he could be an ugly customer.'

Rebecca said no more. She knew what Luca had done to get his start.

She had last seen him penniless. Now he was so rich and powerful that one of the biggest merchant banks in the country put itself out for him.

That alone revealed part of the story. She had mixed with financiers long enough to know the kind of men who prospered in that atmosphere. Luca's success told her that he had become everything he had once despised.

What his prosperity didn't tell her, his face did. The open, generous candour that had made him lovable was gone. In its place was hardness, even ruthlessness, eyes that glinted with suspicion where once they had shone with joy. An ugly customer.

Her father had said, 'He demanded money to go away and never trouble you again.'

Even after seeing the cheque she had sometimes repeated to herself that it couldn't be true. If he had returned she would gladly have believed any explanation. But she never heard from him again, and at last she had stopped crying the words into the darkness.

Seeing him now, she knew that the worst was true. Luca had needed money, and he had sold their love to get it.

As they entered the dining room she braced herself, knowing that she would be sitting next to him.

The bait in the trap, she thought wearily. Oh, what does it matter?

He did everything correctly, like a man used to dining amid wealth. After making a few brief, meaningless observations to her, he paid courteous attention to the lady on his other side, who was his hostess.

So far, so good. Nothing to alarm her.

Then Philip Steyne said jovially, 'Luca, in case you're wondering why we sat you next to Rebecca, it's because she speaks Italian, even Tuscan.'

'That was very kind of you,' Luca said. 'So, *signora*,' he turned his attention to Rebecca and slipped into Tuscan to say, 'are we going to go all evening pretending not to know each other?'

CHAPTER FOUR

So HE had known all the time, and picked his own moment to reveal it. Taken by surprise, Rebecca couldn't control a swift gasp.

The others were watching them, smiling, enjoying what they thought of as the joke.

'What did he say, Rebecca?' Philip asked. 'It must have been quite something to make you gasp like that. Come on, tell.'

'Oh, no,' she said brightly. 'I know how to keep a secret.'

Everyone laughed as if she'd made a brilliant witticism. Still smiling, she met Luca's eyes.

'Do we know each other?' she asked, also in Tuscan.

'Yes,' he said flatly. 'Why pretend?'

'Have you told anyone else?'

'No. That wouldn't suit me. Or you, I imagine.'

He was right, but it was intolerable that he took her reaction for granted.

'No,' she said briefly.

'No problem, then.'

'You're a remarkably cool customer.'

'Not now.'

'What did you say?'

'We can't discuss it now. There are too many people about. We'll talk later.'

His assumption that the decision was only his infuriated her.

54

'We will not talk later,' she said in a low voice. 'I shall be leaving early.'

He gave her an unexpected grin.

'No, you won't,' he said.

'Are you trying to give me orders?'

'No, just saying that you don't really mean it.'

'You're damned sure of yourself,' she said.

'Am I?' He seemed surprised. 'I couldn't go away without talking to you. Not after all this time. I just thought maybe you couldn't, either. Am I wrong?'

'No,' she said, annoyed with herself because it was true.

Luca addressed the rest of the table with an expansive smile.

'I can't fault this lady. Her Tuscan is perfect.'

Everyone applauded. Rebecca saw Danvers and Philip exchange triumphant glances.

She got through the rest of the meal somehow. When it came to the coffee everyone left the table and went into the huge conservatory. The double doors were wide open and many people drifted into the beautiful grounds, where the trees were hung with coloured lights.

'Come outside and show me the grounds,' Luca said.

Wanting to get this meeting over with, she followed him out and along the path that the lights dimly outlined. As they went she talked of trees and shrubs, pointing out the features of the landscaped garden in a voice that gave nothing away.

But at last he paused under the trees and said in Tuscan, 'We can drop the polite nothings now.'

'I really should be going back—'

'Not yet.' He put out a hand to restrain her, but she

withdrew before he could make contact, and he let his hand drop.

'Did you think we would ever meet again?' he asked.

'No,' she said softly. 'Never.'

'Of course. How could we ever meet again in the world? Everything was against it.'

'Everything was always against us,' she said. 'We never really stood a chance.'

He took a step closer and looked at her face in the light from the moon and a pink lamp hanging above them.

'You've changed,' he said. 'And yet you haven't. Not really.'

'You've changed in every way,' she said.

He rubbed the scar awkwardly. 'You mean this?'

'No, I mean everything about you.'

'I'm fifteen years older. A good deal has happened to me. And to you.'

'Yes.' She was being deliberately monosyllabic, refusing to give anything away. In some mysterious way he alarmed her now, as he had never done before.

'Your name has changed,' he said, 'so you've been married. But the man with you isn't called Hanley.'

'Yes, I'm divorced from Saul Hanley.'

'Were you married long?'

'Six years.'

'Did your father approve of him?'

'He was dead by the time I married. I didn't see him much in the last years of his life. We had nothing to say. He couldn't look me in the eye.'

'No wonder.'

The words brought them to the edge of dangerous ground, and she shied away.

'And you?' she asked lightly. 'I'm sure you have a wife at home.'

'Why should you be sure?'

'Because every successful man needs a wife to host his dinner parties.'

'I don't give dinner parties. Drusilla used to enjoy them, so we had a few, but we're divorced now.'

'Because she wanted dinner parties?' she asked, trying to make a joke of it.

'No,' he said abruptly. 'Other reasons.'

'I'm sorry, I didn't mean to pry.'

'No problem. Tell me what else you've been doing.'

The words sounded abrupt, ungracious, but she doubted if he had meant them that way. She guessed that Luca Montese's social skills were only skin deep.

'I sold the estate and went travelling. When I came home I did some book translating, using my Italian. That was how I met Saul. He was a publisher.'

'Why did you divorce him?'

'It was a mutual decision,' she said after a moment. 'We weren't suited.'

They had been strolling around the paths, and now the house was in view again.

'Perhaps we should go inside,' she said.

'I have something to say first.'

'Yes?'

He seemed to be having difficulty, then he blurted out, 'I want to see you again. Alone.'

'No, Luca,' she said quickly. 'There's no point.'

'That doesn't make any sense. Of course there's a point. I want to talk to you. It all happened too abruptly. We never even had the chance to say goodbye. We've each spent years not knowing what happened to the other, and there's a lot I want to explain. I'm entitled to the chance.'

'Don't talk to me like that,' she said, offended.

'Like what?' He was genuinely puzzled.

'Making demands, talking about what you're entitled to. You're not addressing a board meeting.'

'I just want you to understand.'

Did he think any explanation would make things better? she wondered.

'Luca, if it's about the money, you don't have to say anything. I'm sure it was all for the best in the long run. I should congratulate you. You must have used it very shrewdly.'

A strange look came over his face. 'Ah, your father told you about the money? I wondered.'

'Of course he did,' she said, feeling a pang of pain that he could speak about it so casually. 'So we can draw a line under it.'

'And that's all you have to say? Good God, Becky, have you no questions to ask me after all this time?'

'The girl I was then had questions, and the boy you were might have answered them.'

'He'd have tried. He always tried to do what you wanted, because he had no pleasure but your happiness. Have you forgotten that?'

She hadn't forgotten it but she had put it away in darkness, hoping never to think of it again.

'No,' she said at last. 'I hadn't forgotten. But it's too late now. We're not those people any more. We last saw each other fifteen years ago, the day before our wedding, when my father burst in. And I'm really glad you've made a success of your life—'

He stared at her. 'What was that you said?'

'I'm glad you've been successful—'

'No, before that, about our last meeting.'

'It was on the day before our wedding—or what should have been our wedding.'

'Then you don't remember...?' He checked himself. 'Well, perhaps it's not surprising. But it's even more important to see each other again. We have unfinished business, and it's time to take care of it.'

She gave a little shudder. She wanted nothing to do with this man who had Luca's name and a face that resembled his but had nothing else of him. Luca had been tender and gentle. This stranger barked his orders even when he was trying to make human contact. If this was what Luca had turned into, she wished she had never known.

'I'm sorry,' she said, trying to speak calmly. 'But I can see no point in a further meeting.'

'But I can,' he said bluntly.

She took a deep breath, trying to keep her temper.

'Unfortunately both sides need to be willing, and I'm not.'

'*They* won't be pleased if you snub me,' he said, jerking his head towards the house.

So he knew that she'd been told to charm him. Of course he did.

'*They* can conduct their business without my help,' she retorted crisply, and began to walk away from him.

'Are you going to marry Danvers Jordan?' he called after her.

She turned and asked, 'What did you say?' in a tone that was meant to warn him.

'I want to know.'

'But it does not suit me to tell you,' she said slowly and emphatically. 'Goodnight, Signor Montese.'

She hoped she could slip back into the conservatory without attracting attention, in case someone should wonder why she was alone. But Luca caught up and entered behind her, just close enough to make it look as if they were still together. To her relief he did not try to talk to her again for the rest of the evening.

But when they said goodbye he held her hand a little too long and said softly, *'Arrivederci per ora.'* Goodbye for now.

And she answered swiftly, *'Mai piu.'* Never more.

She would not see him again, and it was best that he knew it now.

He said nothing but released her hand and turned away.

On the way home Danvers said, 'Well done, darling, you made a hit with Montese. He couldn't speak highly enough of you.'

'I wish I could say the same,' she said, sounding bored. 'I thought he was an impossible man. Rude, vulgar, graceless—'

'Oh, of course. What can you expect? But as a money man he's got no equal.'

'I just hope I don't have to see him again.'

'I'm afraid you will. Apparently he's going to be living at the Allingham.'

'But why?' she cried in protest before she could stop herself.

'He has no home in this country. It makes sense for him to live in a hotel, and naturally he picks the one where he owns stock. It's perfectly reasonable.'

Of course it was reasonable. It was so reasonable that it alarmed her.

'When did he tell you this?'

'Just before we left. That's why I say you did a brilliant job. And Steyne is bowled over by you. He keeps dropping hints about my "acquiring a prize asset".'

The right response would turn this into a proposal, one that had been long expected. She took a deep breath and said, 'That's nice of him.' She yawned. 'Oh, dear, I hadn't realised I was so tired. Just drop me at the door, and I'll go straight up to bed.'

He accepted his dismissal without complaint, although his goodbye was rather chilly. She couldn't help it. When they reached the Allingham she said goodnight and walked quickly away.

Nigel Haleworth, the hotel's managing director, was a genially cynical man. Rebecca got on well with him, and at their regular weekly meeting next morning, when routine business had been dealt with, he said with a grin, 'You've met King Midas, I gather. He's arriving today. Penthouse suite, of course.'

'King Midas?'

'Luca Montese. Do you remember the story of Midas?'

'Yes. He made a wish that everything around him should turn to gold,' she remembered. 'But he forgot his beloved daughter, and when he touched her she too turned to gold. He was left with nobody to love.'

'Right. That's what they say about Montese—not the daughter bit, because he has no children. But there's nothing in his life but money.'

'I believe he's divorced.'

'A few months ago. Touchy subject. A "king" likes to have an heir, but he never managed to make her pregnant in six years of marriage. Then she had a baby by another man.

'You can imagine what that did to him. I gather he's a very frightening man if you're on his wrong side. He's made a thousand enemies, and they're all jeering at him behind their hands—what's wrong with "the king" that he can't do what any other man can do? That sort of thing.'

'It's nonsense,' said Rebecca sharply. 'They may just have been incompatible.'

'Or maybe he simply can't father a child. That's what they're whispering.'

Rebecca shrugged. 'If they're his enemies they'll believe what they like.'

'What did you think of him?'

After a moment she said, 'Let's say that I can understand why he has enemies.'

'Why not research him a bit before he arrives?'

Back in her suite she logged on to the internet.

English websites carried little about Luca or his firm, but Italian ones were more informative. Raditore had swiftly risen from a small outfit to a huge conglomerate with a speed that spoke volumes of its owner's skill and lack of scruple. But there was nothing about his personal life. He might never have had one.

And that was it, she realised suddenly. The man she had met the previous evening had seemed to have no hinterland beyond his fixation on herself, as though he'd shut down every part of himself except one.

Now she could feel something for him, and it was

pity. She had frozen to protect herself from insupportable pain. Had he done the same?

She found a multitude of urgent tasks to prevent her from being in the hotel when Luca arrived that afternoon. When she returned she was in a more settled frame of mind, even willing to concede that they needed to talk.

Doubtless he would call her and they would meet for a sedate dinner. They would bring each other up to date, after which she would be freed from ghosts. Feeling calm and prepared, she waited for the phone to ring.

Instead there was a knock on the door. Frowning, she opened it.

'This is for you, ma'am,' said the man with the package. 'Please sign here.'

When he had gone she opened the package cautiously, and found a jewel case.

Inside lay the most fabulous set of diamonds that she had ever seen. A necklace of three strands, earrings, bracelet, brooch. All of the very best. Rebecca's experienced eye told her that there was nearly a hundred thousand pounds' worth of jewels here.

The small card bore only the two words. *Per adesso.* For now.

She sat down, alarmed to find that she was trembling.

For now? It was almost a threat, implying that he would not accept her dismissal.

Why couldn't he leave her to her hard-won peace? Didn't he want peace himself?

At last she pulled herself together and headed out of the door. It took her five minutes to reach the penthouse suite, and her anger rose with every step.

'How dare you?' she said when he opened the door.

'Please take this back, and don't ever do such a thing again.'

He backed away from her, forcing her to come into the room to find somewhere to set the case down.

'I mean what I say. I don't want these things. Luca, what were you thinking of? You can't send something like this to a stranger.'

'You're not a stranger. You can't be.'

'I must be after all these years. Too much has happened. We're different people. I don't accept this kind of gift.'

'You mean not from me, because I'm not good enough?'

'Don't be absurd. Of course you're good enough. How can you say such a thing to me, after our past?' She lost her temper. 'I think I've earned better than that from you.'

'All right, I'm sorry,' he said gruffly. 'Maybe I'm not so different from what I was. Maybe, inside, I'm still the bumpkin your father looked down on. I can change the outside but not in here.' He pointed to himself. 'I hear the sneers, even when they're whispered.'

'But I never sneered at you.'

'So what's wrong with me giving you something?'

'This isn't "something", it's a fortune.'

'Do you take diamonds from him?' he demanded abruptly.

'Luca, stop that. I'm not answerable to you.'

He scowled, and she wondered how long it had been since anyone stood up to him, and said no. A long time, she suspected, since he didn't know how to cope with it.

'It's a simple question,' he grated.

'And I'll give you a simple answer. Mind your own damned business. Who do you think you are to turn up in my life after fifteen years and take anything for granted?'

'All right.' He threw up his hands. 'I've managed it badly. Let's start again.'

'No, let's just leave it here. We met again and found that we're strangers. There was no lightning flash. The past doesn't live again and it certainly can't be put right. Love dies, and once dead it can't be revived.'

'Love?' he snapped. 'Have I asked for your love? You flatter yourself.'

'Well, you certainly wanted something in return for diamonds. And I don't flatter myself, because it doesn't flatter me to be pursued by a man who approaches a woman as though he were buying stocks and shares. I am not a piece of property.'

'Aren't you? Well, it sure as hell looked like it last night.'

'What do you mean by that?'

'They paraded you in front of me, didn't they? First you sat next to me, then you led me out into the garden. Did you think I didn't know what was going on? Sweet-talk him! That's what they told you. Make his head spin so that we can milk him of his money. Wasn't it something like that?'

She faced him defiantly. 'It was exactly like that. What else would make me go out into the garden with you?'

It was cruel, but she was desperate to make him back off. He threatened the stability it had cost her too much to achieve.

But she was sorry when she saw the colour drain from

his face, leaving it a deathly grey. She had meant only to stab at his pride, as a warning. She might have thought he was hurt to the heart, if she believed that he still had a heart.

'Look, I'm sorry,' she said. 'That was cheap and unjust. I didn't mean to hurt you—'

'You can't,' he said curtly. 'Don't worry yourself.'

There was a knock on the door, and a faint call of, 'Room Service.'

Luca made a sign that he would be back and went to the door. Left alone, Rebecca looked around for somewhere to leave the diamonds so that there would be no more arguing about them.

The door to the bedroom was open and she could see the small chest of drawers against the bed, with a heavy lamp on top. Luca was still at the front door, and she had time to slip into the bedroom and pull open the top drawer, ready to thrust the box inside.

She had to move some papers aside to make room for it. Some were in a large open envelope that spilled its contents as it was moved. What Rebecca saw made her stop dead.

A photograph had fallen out. It showed a young girl with windblown hair and a young, eager face. She was sitting on the top rail of a fence, laughing at the cameraman, her eyes full of love and joy.

Luca had taken it on the day she told him about the baby. Even if she had not remembered, she would have known that from the look on her own face. This was a girl who had everything, and was sure she could never lose it.

And Luca had kept this picture with him.

It was as though someone had given him back to her.

Suddenly her anger at him melted and she wanted to find him and share the moment.

'Luca...'

She turned eagerly and saw him standing, watching her, his face defenceless, possessed by a look that mirrored her own feelings. He was there again, the boy she had loved, and who still lived somewhere in this harsh, aggressive man.

'Luca,' she said again.

And then it was gone. The light in his eyes shut down, the mask was back in place.

'What are you doing in here?' he snapped.

'I wasn't prying—'

'Then why are you here?'

She realised that he was really angry.

'I was putting the diamonds in here for safety, but never mind that. You kept this picture, all these years.'

'Did I? I hadn't realised.'

'You couldn't have kept it by accident, or brought it all these miles *by accident*.'

'There are a lot of papers in that drawer.'

'Luca, please forget what happened a moment ago. We were both angry and saying things we didn't mean—'

'You, maybe. I don't say things I don't mean. I'm not a sentimentalist, any more than you are.'

She looked at the picture. 'So you didn't keep this on purpose?'

'Good lord, no!'

'Fine, then let's dispose of it.' She tore the picture in half, and then again. 'I'll be going now. The diamonds are there. Goodbye.'

Luca didn't move until she'd walked out. But as soon

as the door had closed behind her he snatched up the four pieces of the picture and tried to put them back together with shaking hands.

Nothing was going right. The look she had surprised on his face, before he could conceal it, had been his undoing. Without meaning to she had breached his defences, and he had instinctively slammed them back into place, bristling with knives.

Deny everything, the picture, its significance, the power it had over him! That was the best way. It was done before he could stop himself, and now he would give anything to call the words back.

He'd thought himself prepared in every detail, but the glamorous sophisticate she had become had taken him by surprise the night before, making him flounder. After that he had made one wrong move after another.

But it wasn't his fault, he reasoned. Her stubbornness hadn't been part of the plan.

He wanted to bang his head against the wall and howl.

CHAPTER FIVE

IN THE early hours of the morning Rebecca heard something being pushed under her door.

She looked down at the envelope without touching it. Then she lifted it and stared longer, while thoughts and fears clashed in her mind.

'Destroy it, unread. If you read it you're embarking on uncharted seas. Play safe.'

She opened the letter.

His handwriting hadn't changed. It was big and confident, an assertion in the face of life. But the words held a hint of something else, almost as though he was confused.

You were right about almost everything. But the day your father arrived wasn't our last meeting. If you want to know about the other one, I'll tell you. Otherwise I won't trouble you again.

Luca

He was playing mind games, was her first thought, but she dismissed it, in fairness. Mind games demanded a subtlety that he didn't have.

She decided to go back to bed and think about it.

An hour later she was knocking on his door. He answered at once.

He was in a white shirt, heavily embroidered down the front, as though he'd spent the evening at a smart function. Now he'd returned and tossed aside his black jacket and torn the shirt open at the neck.

'I'm glad you came,' he growled.

'I want to hear what you have to say, Luca, but then I'm leaving at once.'

'My God, you won't give an inch, will you, even now?'

'No, because whatever you tell me can't really make any difference. How could you ever imagine that it would, after what you did?'

'After what I did?' he echoed. 'What did I do?'

'Oh, please, don't pretend you don't know. We talked about it the first evening. You took my father's money.'

'Naturally. I had every right to it.'

'Of course you did,' she said scornfully. 'After all, you'd given me several months of your valuable time, and I didn't even reward you with a living child. There had to be some recompense for that. But what do you think it did to me to hear my father crowing with delight because you'd lived down to his worst expectations?'

'That I...?' He frowned. 'What did he tell you?'

'That you'd taken his money to go away and never see me again. That's another reason I wouldn't touch those diamonds. Did you think I'd want to take anything from you after you sold me back to him? Besides, you overpaid. I know what those diamonds are worth, and it must be twice what he paid for me. *Or is that interest added on?*'

For a thunderous moment Luca was so silent that she had an eerie feeling that he would never speak again. Then he swore violently, turning away and smashing a fist into the other palm while a stream of invective flowed from him.

'And you've believed that, all these years?' he raged when he turned back.

'What else was I to believe? He showed me the cheque when it had been cashed and returned to him. It was your bank account. Don't pretend it wasn't.'

'Oh, yes, it was mine. He paid me that money, I don't deny it.'

'Then what more is there to say?'

'He lied to you about why. I left because, when Frank had finished, I was sure it was all my fault, the state you were in, the baby's death—I felt guilty about the whole thing.

'Then he had you whisked off to England, to a place I didn't know. I couldn't reach you. I went back to the cottage, and found him there, setting fire to it.'

She stared at him, trying not to believe.

'My father burned our home?' she whispered.

Something flickered across his face.

'Our home. Yes, that's what it was. I'm glad you remembered. He burnt it with his own hands. Luckily there were witnesses. On their evidence he was arrested and put into the cells. He could have faced a long stretch in prison if I hadn't told the police that it was a "misunderstanding" and I wouldn't press charges.'

'Why would you do that?'

His grin flashed out again, cynical, jeering.

'Why, for fifty thousand pounds, of course. That was my price for letting him off. I sold him back his freedom. *Nothing else.*'

'I don't believe it,' she whispered, just as she had done long ago.

'He got caught in the fire himself and burned his arm. Did you never notice that?'

And it came back to her, the memory of Frank arriving one day with his arm in a sling. He said he'd broken it, but months later she'd seen the ugly mark and thought it looked like a burn. When she'd asked him about it, he'd become angry and evasive.

'All these years,' she murmured, 'he told me that you—'

'You heard him offer me money once before,' he reminded her, 'and you heard my reaction.'

'Yes, I remember. He said you'd turned against me when I lost the baby and lost my looks.'

'You never lost them,' he said simply. 'Never. And did you really believe that of me?'

She nodded dumbly.

'You should have had more faith in me, Becky.'

His voice was sad, but not reproachful. He had never blamed her for anything.

'Oh, God,' she whispered. 'All these years, I thought that you—oh, God, oh, God!'

She had thought she'd touched bottom long ago, but now she knew that this was far worse. She went to the window and looked out into the darkness, too confused to think.

'I should have known,' she said at last, 'but I wasn't myself.'

'No, you were never yourself after the day your father came,' he said. 'I saw you once after that. Do you really not remember when I came to the hospital?'

Distressed, she shook her head. 'I always wondered why you never came near me again.'

'Do you think he would let me? He was your father, your next of kin, and I was nothing. If he'd arrived a day later we would have been married, but we weren't, and I had no rights.'

'Yes,' she said, suddenly struck. 'I remember him saying, "Then I'm in time." He meant in time to stop us marrying. But you were the baby's father.'

'Before he came to our door your father had approached the police chief, and got him in his pocket. I was arrested and held in the cells for a week.'

'Dear God! On what charge?'

He shrugged. 'Anything they could think of. It didn't matter, because they never meant to keep me inside for long, just long enough to suit Frank Solway's purpose.

'I thought you were dying. I begged to be allowed to see you, but nobody would listen. And then, at last, your father came to me and told me that the "little bastard" as he called our child, was dead.

'He said it was all my fault, that I'd caused you to lose the child by my "rough behaviour"—'

'But that's not true,' she burst out. 'He was the one who was rough. You didn't fight him back, you just stood there like a rock. I do remember that.'

'Of course I did, because I was afraid to harm you.'

'Then how could you have felt guilty when you knew it wasn't your fault?'

He tore his hair. 'Why does an innocent man ever confess to a crime he hasn't committed? Because they torture his mind until he thinks lies are truth and truth is a lie. I was in such torment, with our child dying, longing for you, not able to get near you, it wasn't hard for him to make me feel that I was entirely to blame.'

She looked at him, torn with pity.

'And then he took me to see you. I thought my chance

had come, that I could take you in my arms and tell you that I loved you. But you weren't in your right mind.'

'I had post-natal depression, very badly, and I think they gave me some strong medication.'

'Yes, I understand that now, but at the time I just walked in and saw you staring into space. I didn't know what had happened. You didn't seem to hear or see me.'

'I didn't,' she breathed. 'I had no idea you'd even been there.'

'I wasn't able to be alone with you. There was your father, and a nurse, in case I ''became violent''. I begged you to hear me. I told you over and over how sorry I was. You just stared at me. *Don't you remember?*'

Dumbly she shook her head. 'I never knew,' she said. 'I must have been completely out of it.'

'And your father knew the state you'd be in while I was there. I wonder what he persuaded the doctor to give you beforehand, to make sure.'

She nodded. She could believe anything of Frank now. 'And he never told me that you came.'

'Of course not. It suited him to have you think I'd callously abandoned you. I went away half-crazy with guilt at the harm I thought I'd done you.'

'It wasn't you, Luca, it wasn't you.'

He regarded her sadly.

'You can tell me that now, but how can you tell the boy I was then? His agony is beyond comfort. Do you remember how it was between us at the very start, how I tried to resist you, for your sake?'

She nodded. 'And I wouldn't let you.'

'My conscience had always troubled me about taking you away from the life you were used to, making you live in poverty.'

'You didn't make me. I chose it when I chose you. And I never felt poor. I felt rich because we loved each other.'

'But I knew I ought to have been stronger. And in the end your father convinced me that the best thing I could do for you was to free you. He said that if I kept trying to "force myself on you", you might never recover.'

'He was a bad man,' she said. 'I never fully understood that before.'

Luca nodded.

'I took his money to make myself rich and powerful enough to revenge myself on him. I promised myself we would meet again, but we never did. My business flourished, so I made it my life. Now it's all I know. Becky—'

'I'm Rebecca now,' she said quickly. 'Nobody calls me Becky any more.'

'I'm glad. I want it to be just my name for you. It was special, that time.'

'Yes,' she agreed. 'It was special. But it was another life.'

'But I don't like my life now. Do you?'

'Don't,' she begged, 'don't ask me that kind of question.'

'Why not? If you're happy, you have only to say so. Danvers Jordan is the man of your dreams, right?'

She almost laughed at that. 'Oh, please! Poor Danvers. He's not the man of anyone's dreams.'

'No, he's a dead fish.'

This time she did laugh. 'Your English is still shaky. You mean a cold fish.'

'Whatever. I prefer my version. So life with him isn't blissful. Are you going to marry him?'

'If I decide to, yes! Leave it, Luca. I'm glad to have found out the truth. I've misjudged you, and perhaps we can be friends now. But it doesn't give you the right to question me about my life.'

'Friends? You think we can be friends?'

'It's the best there is.'

He sighed and she thought his shoulders sagged.

'Then let us celebrate our friendship with a drink,' he said.

'All right.' She followed him to the drinks cabinet. 'What do you drink now?' she asked. 'Surely not—?' She named a Tuscan wine, valued for its rough edge.

'No, these days I don't move among people who could appreciate it. You have to be Tuscan.'

'True,' she said. 'Dry sherry, please.'

She watched him pour, watched the deft movements of the big hands that were so powerful, and so tender. They were a rich man's hands now, but no amount of manicuring could hide their suggestion of force. When she looked up she found him looking at her with a softened look on his face.

'Am I very changed?' she asked quietly.

'Your hair's different. It used to be light brown, not as fair as it is now.'

'That isn't what I meant.'

He nodded. 'I know what you meant.'

He stepped closer so that he could look directly into her eyes, not moving for a long moment. Rebecca tried to turn away, but his gaze held her with its fierce intensity, and its sadness. She hadn't expected his sadness, and she couldn't cope with it.

'No,' he said at last. 'You haven't changed.'

She gave him a melancholy smile. 'That's not true.'

'I say it is. No, don't move.'

He had laid a hand on her shoulder to keep her there. She stopped and raised her head again, unwilling to meet his eyes but unable to do anything else. At last she could see the connection that spanned the years. The old force and power streamed from him, the confident authority that had been there even when he was penniless. This was Luca as he had been, and as she recognised him now.

Slowly he moved his hand upward so that it brushed against her neck, then her cheek. He seemed almost in a trance, held there by something stronger than himself. She saw his face soften, his expression become almost bewildered, as though something had taken him by surprise.

'Becky,' he murmured, raising his other hand and letting the fingers drift down her face.

The effect was devastating. His touch was so light that she barely felt it, yet it sent through her sensations that she had not known for years. They threatened her, filled her with alarm, yet she could not move.

'Do you remember?' he whispered.

'Yes,' she said sadly. 'I remember.'

If only he would let her go. If only he would never let her go. The feather-light movement of his fingers against her cheek was filling her with a bitter-sweet turmoil, too intense to bear.

As if in a dream she found herself putting up a hand to touch his face. Then she took a sharp breath as she realised how close to danger she had allowed herself to drift.

'Goodbye, Luca,' she said.

His face became set. 'You can't say goodbye to me now.'

'I must. There can't be anything else. It's too late.'

She tried to draw back her hand from his face, but he seized it and turned his head so that his lips lay against the palm.

'Don't,' she whispered. 'It's too late—too late—'

He didn't answer in words, only in the soft scorching of his breath against her palm. She braced herself against it, refusing to yield. He thought he could overcome her, and she would not allow it.

But it was harder than she thought because his touch affected her on two levels. She could cope with the physical excitement that scurried along her nerves, but not the memories of that other, sweeter life.

She was assailed by sensations, not only of pleasure but also of sunshine and happiness. She had forgotten about happiness, what it felt like, even what it was. But now it was there again in visions of a love that had been too intense to last.

The gentle caressing movements of his lips brought back unbearable joy, the nights when she had lain in his arms, revelling in the passion and tenderness of his love.

It had been almost frightening to feel such bliss, but his presence in the bed beside her had been reassuring, and she had fallen asleep against his shoulder, knowing that the next day would bring the same.

Now he was recalling the echoes of that time, and she wanted to avoid them and stay in the safe, chilly cocoon she had built for herself. It was painful to risk leaving that safety, but he was demanding it more insistently with every moment.

'Do you remember?' he murmured. 'Do you remember—?'

'No,' she said urgently. 'I don't want to remember.'

'Don't shut me out, Becky.'

'I must.'

He didn't fight her. He simply withdrew his lips and laid her palm against his cheek again, looking so sad and despairing that she couldn't bear it.

'My darling—' she used the words without knowing '—my darling, please—try to understand—'

'I do,' he said heavily. 'It was a stupid idea, wasn't it?'

'No, it was a beautiful idea, but I guess I have no courage any more.'

'My Becky had courage enough for anything.'

'Long, long ago.'

He looked down, and suddenly she couldn't bear for him to look at her face with the glow of youth gone from it. She pulled his head down to her, so that his lips covered hers.

She knew at once that her body had slept all this time. It wasn't sleeping any more, because he was summoning it to vibrant new life, urgent in its need, carrying her with it despite her sensible self.

His mouth had the same power to coax and demand, but now there was an extra excitement. The boy had gone. The man had a hard edge that coloured all his actions, making her crave to know more of him. She found herself doing what she had sworn not to do, kissing him in a way that urged him on.

He needed no more encouragement to make him extend the kiss into an exploration of her jaw-line, down the length of her neck to the soft place at the base of her throat. Her heart was beating wildly with anticipation, excitement scurrying down from her throat, between her breasts—

'Luca,' she whispered, 'Luca—don't...'

Something in her voice pierced the cloud of desire that pervaded him, and he looked at her intently. There were tears in her eyes.

'Don't cry,' he begged.

'I'm not really. I'm glad it happened. I'll never, never be sorry we met again, and put things right. But I can't go on.'

'Don't give up so soon,' he urged. 'I'm here. You can hold on to me. Becky, take what we have. I don't believe in "too late".'

'I wish I didn't. Let me go, let me go.'

He didn't try to restrain her as she slipped out of his arms, but he watched her all the way to the door.

'You'll come back to me, Becky.'

'No,' she said. 'No, please believe me.'

She slipped out before he could speak again, and she knew that she was fleeing danger. She called herself a coward, but she couldn't help it.

She reached her apartment like a refuge and secured the door behind her, leaning against it, as though fearing an invasion.

She tried to pull herself together. A heavy day faced her, and now she should be sensible and go to bed. But her body was too full of tension and excitement to relax.

She closed her eyes, trying to banish the feel of being held against his hard body, but the more she fought it the more she became aware of it. She'd started something that she had to finish.

All she had to do was go to him now. He might be

asleep, but she knew he wasn't. Her heart told her that he was waiting, listening for the ring of the telephone or the knock on the door. Because he knew, just as she did, that they had not reached the end.

She seized the phone and dialled the penthouse suite. He answered at once, just the one word. 'Yes?' spoken in a voice that was tense and urgent. He knew who it was.

She hung up. She was trembling.

Half an hour passed. He did not ring back.

She slipped quietly out of her apartment, and to the elevator, which drifted up almost soundlessly through the darkened building. At his door she paused only briefly before knocking, and it was opened immediately. He had been waiting for her.

He looked at her for a moment before pulling her fiercely inside and clasping her in his arms so that she was lifted clear off her feet. She could feel the relief that shook him as she put her own arms about him and laid her lips on his.

This was her kiss, with nothing held back. She was too honest to play coy. This had been inevitable from the moment she touched him, because after that she had to touch him again and again. She had to find out if his body was as strong and thrilling as she remembered.

'What do you want?' he whispered.

'I want you,' she murmured back against his mouth. Her hands were at work, pulling open the rest of his buttons, feeling the light sprinkling of hair beneath.

He took over, ripping off the rest of his clothes before ripping off hers. They fell on the bed together, both equally lost in a delirious need to be satiated with each other's bodies.

Rebecca was awake now, every inch of her, vibrant, passionate and hungry, giving him everything she had or was, making feverish demands from the one man who had it in his power to fulfil her.

Luca had always had vigour, but time and experience had added subtlety. He explored her with hands and lips, using both with consummate skill to inflame her senses until she was drawing long, heated, half-moaning breaths.

How could so many years vanish without a trace? How could they still know each other so intimately? She was ready for every move he made, answering with caresses that were skilled in the ways he had always loved, caresses she had offered to no other man, because in her heart she had known they belonged only to him.

As he moved over her she had one last wild moment of doubt. This man was essentially a stranger. But it was no stranger who entered her with the slow, relentless power that had once thrilled her and now thrilled her a thousandfold. Her flesh had slept too long. The awakening was fierce, devastating and total.

She was in his rhythm at once, claiming and releasing him, demanding while she gave, until the mounting pleasure seemed to explode deep within her. Now there was light everywhere, blinding, dazzling, breathtaking. It filled the world, the universe, and it was what she'd been waiting for during all the dead, meaningless years.

CHAPTER SIX

SHE came down from the heights to find herself held tightly in Luca's arms. Perhaps a little too tightly, but she missed the threat of possessiveness because the shattering feeling of sexual release was so powerful, so welcome.

She knew now what she had always suspected, that the reason she was so unresponsive to any other man was that there had always been one man for her. And this was the man.

Luca, blunt, harsh, vengeful, unforgiving: everything she found hard to like. Yet he was the one, because he always had been, and part of her had never changed.

Then he said the wrong thing.

'That was good.'

The hint of calculation chilled her.

'Wasn't it?' he demanded.

Inwardly she withdrew a little, feeling bullied.

'Yes,' she said politely.

'What's the matter?' he asked, just clever enough to know that he'd lost ground, not subtle enough to know why.

'Nothing. I'd like to get up, please.'

'Tell me, first.'

'I want to get up.'

'Tell me!'

'Luca, if you don't release me right now you'll never see me again.'

He released her at once. She was surprised. She hadn't expected the threat to work on this hard man, let alone instantly.

'What is it?' he demanded as she rose and quickly covered her nakedness with a robe. 'What changed?'

'I guess we shouldn't expect too much all at once. Let it go for now.'

Her tone contained a warning and, again to her surprise, he heeded it. After a few moments the silence made her look at him and what she saw melted her heart.

His face showed confusion, and the hurt bewilderment of a child who didn't know what he'd done wrong. It sent her back into his arms.

'Yes, it was good,' she reassured him.

'I still know how to please you?'

'Yes, like nobody else.'

It was the wrong thing to say. His face darkened.

'I don't want to hear about other men.'

'And I'm not going to tell you, but my husband existed. I haven't lived on the shelf all these years, any more than you have. I've been married, so have you.'

'That's enough!' he shouted. 'I don't want to hear it.'

'Fine, you don't have to. You don't have to hear anything you don't want to.' She pulled away from him, looking around for her clothes. Instantly he was beside her.

'Don't go, Becky. I don't want you to go.'

'I think I should,' she said, starting to pull on garments.

'No, you mustn't.' He put his hands out to restrain her, then snatched them back again.

'Don't tell me what I must and mustn't do,' she told him.

'No, I didn't mean that,' he said hurriedly. 'Look, I'm not touching you, but please don't go. Please, Becky. I'll make it right, just tell me what to do, but stay, I beg you.'

His words softened her again. Suddenly they were back in the old days, when this fierce man was putty in her hands, but only hers.

She stopped what she was doing, went over and put her arms around him in consolation. He hugged her back, but gingerly, as though afraid of offending again.

'If you go away, I'm afraid you won't come back,' he said gruffly.

'I will come back. I want to see you again. But take it slowly.'

'I can't,' he admitted. 'I want all of you at once. Stay with me. Come back to bed.'

'No, the hotel will be getting up soon and I don't want to risk being seen.'

'Spend today with me.'

She mentally reviewed the day she'd planned. There were important appointments that she simply couldn't cancel.

'All right,' she said. 'I'll have to make a few calls but—I can do it.'

'We'll go somewhere that we won't be seen by anyone who knows either of us. But you'll have to say where that is. I don't know London.'

'Have you never been here before?' she asked.

'Oh, yes, brief visits, business deals, hotel rooms, travelling in the back of a car to conferences, never seeing anything through the car windows because I was always on the phone. I couldn't tell you how London is different from New York or Milan. If it *is* different.'

'That sounds really dreadful.'

'It's your world too, Becky.'

'Yes, but I get away sometimes.'

'On long country weekends with Jordan?'

'Jordan's a forbidden subject.'

'Suppose I say he isn't?'

'Only a minute ago you told me you didn't want to hear about anyone else.'

'I'll make an exception for Danvers Jordan.'

'But I won't,' she said quietly.

His lips tightened with anger. 'So it has to be on your terms, does it?'

'You said we weren't to talk about the past. They were your terms. I agreed to them. Do you think you can just change them when it suits you? Think again. I'm not dancing on the end of your string.'

'All right, all right,' he said quickly. 'I give in. Your terms.'

She touched his cheek, smiling with rueful tenderness. 'You don't have to give in. That's not what it's all about. But let's not spoil it.'

He took her hand and kissed the palm. 'Anything you say.'

It was like driving at speed around a sharp corner, and only just avoiding the wall. You were left with a desperate sense of relief and a need to rediscover the road you were supposed to be taking.

'So,' she said, determinedly bright, 'you were saying about cities looking the same. Didn't you ever long for the hills of Tuscany?'

He nodded. 'Or any greenery at all. In New York I always tell myself I'll go to Central Park, but I've never been yet. Once I saw some trees as I was driving through

London, and told the driver to stop the car. But then the phone rang. I was late for a meeting, so I told him to start it again.'

'Where were you when this happened?'

He thought for a moment. 'We'd just passed a huge round red building. I think the driver said they gave concerts there.'

'The Albert Hall. The trees you saw were in Hyde Park. Let's go there, then.'

'Fine.' He reached for the telephone.

'What are you doing?'

'Calling my driver.'

She placed her hand firmly over his. 'We're not calling your driver, or mine.'

'Aren't we?'

'Nope. We're going to go out and hunt for a taxi, and then nobody will know where we've gone.'

That turned it into a conspiracy, and suddenly everything was fun. They took the elevator down almost all the way, and Luca got out one floor from the last. Anyone who happened to be in the lobby saw him walk out of the hotel alone. None of them saw him turn the corner and meet up with Rebecca, who'd gone down the back stairs, left by the kitchen entrance, and was already hailing a taxi.

It was little more than a mile to Hyde Park, but the congestion had already started, and it was three-quarters of an hour before they arrived.

'Green,' Luca said, looking around him with joy. 'Grass. Trees.'

He took her hand and began to walk, across the grass, and she hurried with him. It touched her that Luca, reared amidst savagely beautiful scenery, could still find pleasure in this place with its manicured lawns. It told a whole story about how cut off he'd become from his roots.

'What's that?' He had stopped abruptly at the sight of a large stretch of water, snaking out of sight in both directions. 'A river?'

'No, it's a long, thin lake,' she laughed. 'It's called the Serpentine.'

'And we can take a boat. I see them over there.'

'Come on, then. I haven't been on a boat on the Serpentine for years.'

They hired a rowing boat, big enough for her to sit facing him in a cushioned seat. Luca took the oars and began to pull on them strongly, while Rebecca leaned back, enjoying the chance to relax and simply watch him. After the turmoil of the last few days it was good to think of nothing but the beautiful day, and the pleasure of being on the water. She fixed her eyes on him and let her thoughts drift.

But this was a mistake because in a haze of drowsy contentment she found herself looking at his hands, remembering last night. He had touched her in so many ways, sometimes gently, intimately, sometimes fiercely, and she had responded ecstatically to all of them.

And the way she'd touched him back—she found it hard to recall details now. She had explored and celebrated him with reckless joy, revelling in his instant response, demanding more. She had not known herself capable of such vigorous possessiveness.

Her mind drifted back to her ex-husband, the man she thought of as 'poor Saul'. He'd been entitled to pity because she'd had less than half a heart to give him, and almost no passion. He'd been infatuated and she'd yielded to his eagerness from hope of finding a purpose in her life.

But she had disappointed him, and in his bitterness he'd called her 'the iceberg'. The kindest thing she had ever done for him was to leave him.

She returned from her reverie to find that Luca's eyes were on her, and he was smiling faintly.

'What is it?' she asked. 'Why are you looking at me like that?'

'I'm trying to behave like a gentleman, and not succeeding. The truth is that all I can think of is how badly I want to make love to you.'

The words 'make love' were like a signal, starting a slow-burning fuse inside her. It was only a few hours since she'd risen, satiated, from his bed, yet with just two words she'd become ready for him again. It was shameless, and slightly shocking. It was also thrilling, and deeply, searingly enjoyable.

'You'd better start rowing back, then,' she said. 'Careful! Don't upset the boat.'

They rocked violently all the way back to the shore and climbed out with such urgency that they nearly ended up in the water.

'Where's the nearest exit?' he demanded.

'Over there.'

They made it in double-quick time, but when they reached the street an obstacle met them.

'Oh, no!' Rebecca groaned. 'Isn't the morning rush over yet?'

'Your traffic jams are as bad as Rome,' Luca complained. 'Nothing's moving.'

'It'll take hours to get back to the Allingham,' Rebecca said.

He gripped her hand tighter. 'We don't have hours,' he said firmly. 'Where is the nearest hotel?'

She began to laugh. 'Luca, we can't—'

'Becky, I swear to you that if you don't direct me to an hotel I shall make love to you here and now, on the grass.'

There was a note in his voice that told her he might actually mean it. There was simply no knowing what this determined man might do. It made him thrilling.

'I'm warning you,' he said, slipping his arms around her.

'Stop it! Behave!'

'Find us a hotel, then, quickly.'

'If we cross the road and take that turning there are quite a few in that street up there.'

Crossing the road was easy, since none of the traffic was moving. They found themselves in a street of small private hotels, some of which had notices bearing the word 'Vacancies' in the window. Luca dashed into the first one they came to.

This was a different world from the whispering luxury of the Allingham. There was a small hall, with a cubbyhole for the receptionist, who was absent. Luca had to ring the bell twice, and the second time he did so with such force that a harassed-looking woman emerged from the rear, looking indignant.

'I'd like a room, please,' Luca said. 'Immediately.'

'It isn't noon,' the woman said, with a glance at the clock on the wall that showed half-past eleven.

'Is that important?'

'If you take possession before twelve I'm afraid I have to charge you for two days.'

'How much is the room per night?' Luca asked, breathing hard.

'Seventy pounds, per person, per night. You would be requiring a double room, I take it?'

'Yes,' said Luca, almost beside himself. 'We would like a double room.'

'Then that would be a hundred and forty pounds for one night, so perhaps you would care to wait half an hour, and only pay for one night, which will be cheaper.'

'That's not a good idea,' Rebecca said hastily. 'We'll take it now, thank you.'

'Very well. Name?'

'Mr and Mrs Smith,' Rebecca said promptly.

The receptionist showed, by raised eyebrows, exactly what she thought of that.

'I see. Well, we operate a liberal regime here, although it did seem to me that this was a foreign gentleman—'

'He's a foreign gentleman called Smith,' said Rebecca, poker-faced.

'Well, if one of you would sign here...'

Rebecca hastily seized the pen. Luca was in no mood to remember what name he was supposed to be signing.

The room, when they finally took possession of it, was basic but adequate. Luca shut the door firmly, locked it and turned to her swiftly.

But she was ahead of him, tossing her clothes aside, her eyes gleaming with anticipation.

'Come on,' she said. 'Slow coach.'

He needed no further encouragement, matching her for speed, until they were both ready to fall onto the bed and claim each other with feverish intensity. No subtlety.

No pretence that this was anything but frantic, exuberant lust, relished for its own sake, with no holds barred.

She wanted him inside her. She'd wanted that since he'd left her only a few hours ago, and when she had what she wanted she kept tight hold of him, arching against him insistently and looking up into his face with a smile that made him smile back.

It was she who decided that the moment had come, moving faster, and then faster.

'Wait,' he told her.

'No,' she said simply.

He tried to hold her back but his own desire was uncontrollable, and they finished triumphantly together, laughing and crowing with triumph.

When he had the strength to move, Luca sat up, and blew out his cheeks. 'I've been thinking of this ever since—since I got up this morning.'

'So have I,' she said, relieved at being able to admit it. 'Luca, I don't know who I am any more. I have never been like this in all my life.'

He raised himself from his back, rolled over and looked down at her nakedness with appreciative eyes.

'Shall I tell you who you are?' he asked, sliding his hand over her breasts again.

She chuckled. 'Does it involve vigorous exercise?'

'It might. Unless you're tired.'

'Who's tired? It's early yet.' She reached for him, letting him know with gestures what she wanted of him, and the pleasure was all given back to her, again and again.

As they lay together afterwards she said dreamily, 'I'll bet it's past noon by now.'

'It's three in the afternoon,' he said.

'Ah, well, it can't be helped,' she said drowsily, not knowing what she meant by this.

'Why did you tell them that we were Mr and Mrs Smith?'

'I had to tell them something.'

'But what did she mean about a liberal regime?'

'In the old days, when people weren't as free as they are now, people who wanted to be together used to book into a hotel under the name of Mr and Mrs Smith. So whenever you told a hotel that your name was Smith—well—'

'They knew you were unmarried lovers,' he finished.

'Something like that.'

'And that's why she gave us such a funny look?'

'Yes. She knew exactly why we couldn't wait until noon.'

Luca began to laugh, burying his face against her neck and shaking. And she too laughed, because it was really incredibly funny. For years there had been no laughter in the world. Now there was nothing else but laughter and joy, pleasure and fulfilment, the one leading to the other, then back again, and round in an endless circle of delight.

All strain and tension seemed to fall away, leaving her relaxed and gloriously content. When Luca raised his head she saw that it was the same with him.

'I could go to sleep now,' he said, laying his head back on her shoulder.

'Mmm, lovely.'

But the shrill of his cellphone brought them back to reality. With a grimace he swung himself off the bed.

'I should have switched it off,' he said. 'Hello,

Sonia—no, I'm not at the hotel for the moment—nothing wrong, just a change of plan. Anything urgent?'

He yawned as he listened. Rebecca too yawned. It felt pleasant to lie here, drifting into a light doze. Luca's voice reached her faintly.

'All right, there's no problem, but he's got to come down on the price, or no deal. Sure, I know what he was hoping for, but he's not going to get it. I can go elsewhere, but he can't.'

For half an hour she floated happily in and out of consciousness.

'There's no point in talking any more, Sonia. He and I have done business before. He knows I mean what I say. Now, about the future—I won't be at the Allingham for a few days. You can reach me on this phone, but not too often, OK?'

He hung up. Rebecca slowly sat up in the bed.

'Where are you planning to be for the next few days, Luca?'

'Here. With you.'

'And what about my appointments? My job?'

'Becky, I can imagine how your appointments read. Lunch with this one, drinks with that one, supervising some hotel function, attending a conference. How am I doing?'

'Pretty good.'

'And how vital is any of it? Nobody needs that lunch, that social occasion. Conferences are hot air. The deals depend on cold cash, nothing else, and they're all sewn up before anyone arrives.'

'You're saying that I'm just playing at doing a job,' she said indignantly.

'No, I'm not. My own job is just as full of froth. It's

the way of the world these days. I escape it whenever I can, and the skies don't fall. Will they fall if *you* take a few days off?'

She was about to say that it was impossible when she realised that he was only voicing her own recent thoughts. Golden, glittering and hollow; that was how she'd seen her life as she arrived at Philip Steyne's house that fateful night.

'I could have a word with my assistant,' she said. 'She's very good.'

She didn't mention that she would have to break a date with Danvers, but that would have happened anyway. After what had occurred between her and Luca there was no way she could maintain the pretence that she and Danvers were an item.

All the way back to the hotel she thought about what she would say to him. Entering the Allingham alone, she went to her office and made the necessary arrangements with her assistant, an efficient young woman who could hardly contain her delight at being left in charge.

'By the way, there's a message from Mr Jordan,' she said. 'He has to be away for a few days, maybe a week, he wasn't sure. He says he'll call you when he gets back.'

'Fine,' Rebecca said, torn between relief that she could defer the problem, and dismay that it was going to drag on.

But perhaps this was best, she thought as she slipped out into the street with a suitcase. Now she could forget everything but enjoying a holiday.

The next few days felt like the first true holiday of her life. Hidden away with Luca in the shabby little hotel, she felt as though she were living in the sun.

He was a tireless lover, who could bring her to the heights again and again, and still want her. And she, who had long ago decided that the traumas of her youth had left her cold and unresponsive, could be ready for him at any moment of the night or day, except that night and day were indistinguishable.

The hotel had no Room Service so they ate burgers at a café around the corner, always hurrying back to fall into bed. For four days they loved and slept, slept and loved. In fact, they did everything except talk. But at the time that didn't seem very important.

One morning Rebecca came out of the shower to find Luca just hanging up the phone, looking exasperated.

'I've got to go back to Rome,' he said. 'One of my deals is unravelling, and I need to be there.'

She tried to smile, but the turmoil inside her was alarming. He was going away, and she couldn't stand it.

'Oh, well,' she said lightly. 'It's been great, but we knew it couldn't last forever.'

'We have to give up this room,' he agreed, 'but I'll be back in a few days.'

She'd got her second wind now and could smile.

'Hey, I won't count on it. You may need to stay.'

He was still sitting on the bed, and as she passed him he caught both her hands in his, looking up into her face.

'I'll be back in a few days,' he said. 'I don't think I could stand it for longer.'

'I suppose I should be glad you're going,' she said with a faint smile. 'It'll give me a chance to catch up with real life.'

'Real?' He regarded her with raised eyebrows. 'This hasn't been real?'

She caressed his hair. 'You know what I mean.'

He grinned. Laughing, she leaned down and kissed him.

'I must try to get my mind back on my job,' she said a few moments later. 'And I suppose I ought to speak to Danvers, just to tell him that what little there was between us is all over. Don't worry about him.'

'I won't,' he said simply. Then he gave a broad grin. 'Danvers Jordan doesn't worry me at all.'

She thought he meant that after the last few days he was riding high on pride and sexual confidence.

Afterwards she was to wonder how she could have been so stupid.

CHAPTER SEVEN

LUCA was away nearly a week, during which he called her ten times. She lived for those calls. It grew harder to pretend that she didn't, and after a while she wasn't pretending at all.

She didn't know what to call this feeling. Somehow love did not seem the right word. The bond between them had mysteriously survived years and distance. Now she could think of nothing else but him. Her whole life seemed concentrated around the thought of him, his next call, the likely date of his return.

And yet, for reasons she did not understand, she resisted calling it love.

Two days before he was due home she was on duty at a hotel reception. It lasted only two hours, yet the time seemed interminable, because these days she could no longer take such occasions seriously. She wondered if she would ever do so again.

Smiling mechanically at someone who had claimed her attention and seemed determined to keep her forever, she managed to look around the room and, to her surprise, noticed Danvers on the far side. She hadn't known that he was back, and that was strange because he was normally so punctilious.

The sight of him made her realise how little she'd thought of him while he was away, so absorbed had she been in Luca. If Danvers had not contacted her, neither had she contacted him. Soon she must see him and explain why their relationship, such as it had ever been, was over.

At last she managed to bring the present conversation to an end and made her way through the crowd, noticing that Danvers was deep in conversation with a young woman. When he became aware of Rebecca a sudden alert look came over his face, and she could almost believe that he met her with reluctance.

'Rebecca,' he said with a forced smile. 'How nice to see you.' As if she were a casual acquaintance.

'Good evening, Danvers.' She smiled at the young woman. A strange feeling was growing in her.

'Ann, this is Mrs Hanley, the Allingham's public-relations officer. Ann is my secretary at the bank.'

The two women greeted each other politely. Danvers looked around in the crowd.

'Is Montese with you?' he asked.

'No. Why should he be?'

'I just wondered. Ann, would you mind...?'

The other woman slipped away, leaving Rebecca looking at Danvers in a puzzled way.

'Did you have a good trip?' she asked.

'Yes, it went very well.'

'Have you been back long?'

'Three days.'

Three days. And he hadn't called her. That was more baffling than painful.

'You normally don't wait that long to call me,' she said, trying to sound light.

'Oh, please, Rebecca, don't pretend. You know perfectly why I haven't been in touch. Don't tell me that you mind.'

She frowned. 'Danvers, I—'

'It would have been quite enough for you to tell me yourself, you know. You didn't have to send in the heavy squad.'

'I don't know what you mean.'

'I mean Luca Montese claiming ownership like some tribal warlord.'

'Ownership of what?'

'You, of course. What else? He left me in no doubt that unpleasant things would happen if I didn't back off.'

'What? Danvers, I don't believe that. It can't be true. You must have misunderstood.'

'Believe me, when Montese sets out to make his point there is no misunderstanding. You belong to him. Keep off. That was the message.'

'I most certainly do not belong to him.'

'Tell him. He thinks you do.'

'Danvers, are you saying he actually threatened you with physical violence?'

'Nothing so obvious. He didn't need to. He's a man who knows everything.'

'About what?'

'About everything and everyone. He knew all about me, things I thought dead and buried.'

'Things the bank wouldn't like?' Rebecca asked. It was a shot in the dark but she knew it had gone home when she saw his face tighten.

'It was just a piece of foolishness and it was long ago. There was no harm done. Nobody lost out. The rules were laxer in those days anyway. But if it came to light now—well, anyway, I'm not taking chances.'

She regarded him curiously. 'I suppose it didn't occur to you to defend your right to me?'

'Get real, darling. I've got a career to make. He'd

never take his claws out of me. He had a complete dossier. Probably got one on you as well.'

'Don't talk nonsense,' she said, but her voice was uncertain.

'Rebecca, don't be naïve. You don't have the first idea what this man is really like. He's hard, dangerous, ruthless. And whatever there is between you, he'll be as ruthless to you as anyone else. Ann, darling! Over here.'

'Yes, you've talked to me longer than is safe, haven't you?' Rebecca said with a touch of contempt, and walked away without a backward glance.

She had to wait two days for Luca to return, and they were the longest two days of her life. Sometimes she told herself that what she was thinking could not possibly be true.

Her recent time with him had been glorious, a brilliant light in the grey that was her normal life. But she knew that the bliss was due entirely to their blazing sexual compatibility.

There was always one more loving to come, one more fierce, shattering pleasure to fill her world and drive out thoughts she didn't want to think.

Lost in a haze of physical delight, she'd had little time to consider the personality of the man. Or perhaps she had chosen to look away, secretly aware that she would find too many things that she would not like.

She had heard him on the phone, giving Sonia his instructions, talking of his associates or his rivals with a blunt disregard of anything except coming out on top. She had brushed the knowledge aside, telling herself that he swam in shark-infested waters, and must survive by using tough weapons.

She had refused to see what kind of man Luca had

turned into, but the knowledge had always been there like an echo at the back of her mind.

Now, she knew instinctively that what Danvers had said was true. She waited only to hear it from Luca's own lips.

She arranged with the desk to inform her as soon as he returned to the hotel, and the call came late in the evening. Two minutes later she was knocking at the door of his suite.

His face broke into a smile at the sight of her.

'I was just calling you,' he said. 'This is wonderful.'

He drew her into the room, shutting the door behind her and taking her into his arms.

As always, the sheer physical explosiveness of his kiss changed the world, driving out everything that was not him. With his lips caressing hers purposefully it was hard to believe that anything else mattered. Why stir up trouble? Why not just give in to her body's need?

She tried not to yield to such thoughts.

'Luca...'

But he was already removing her clothes and she lacked the will to stop him. He could ignite her excitement with a gesture, a kiss, a touch of his finger on her face. After that it was like a chain reaction, flowing like liquid fire, unstoppable until it had reached the inevitable end.

When she was naked she saw a look in his eyes that melted her, as though he was seeing her nakedness for the first time, and was astounded by it. That was one thing about Luca, she realised hazily. He was never blasé. His delight in her now was the same as long ago. After nearly a week his urgency was almost uncontainable, and so was her own, she discovered, secretly shocked.

What she knew of him made no difference to her desire to have him, and that was the scariest thing of all. She gave him back pleasure for pleasure, delight for delight, knowing that her body was responding without her mind's consent. It was like losing herself and being unable to prevent it. Then the thought was lost in the sexual release he could give her.

Luca, holding on to her quivering body, sensed something different about her. It confused him even while it obscurely pleased him. He had done the right thing in seeking her out, for she was like no other woman. What a life they would have!

When it was over he propped himself up on one elbow and looked down at her with frank pleasure. Rebecca had always enjoyed that expression in his eyes, but now the thoughts and fears that she had pushed aside came crowding back to her. And with them came the troubled knowledge that he had overcome her resistance without even trying. He had too much power over her, and if she didn't resist now it would be too late.

'I like you best when you're like this,' he said, smiling and running a hand over her nakedness.

'No.' She seized his hand and held it. 'I want to talk.'

'Can't it wait?'

'It's waited too long. I meant to talk as soon as I arrived but—well—'

'But we want each other too much for talking,' he finished for her. 'Does anything else matter?'

'Yes, I think it does. Something's happened that we have to discuss.'

'All right. Tell me.'

'I was at a hotel reception a couple of days ago, and I saw Danvers. He tried to avoid me.'

Looking into his eyes, she saw a look of wariness, and her heart sank.

'Is it true what he told me? That you warned him off?'

He shrugged. 'OK, OK. Yes, I did.'

With a violent movement she rose from the bed and began dressing quickly. Suddenly it seemed indecent for him to see her naked.

She had expected the answer, but somehow that didn't prepare her for the brutal reality. Now she needed to set a distance between them. He too rose and dressed, glancing at her with a dark expression.

When she was finished she turned on him, her eyes kindling. 'You dared to dictate who I could see or not see?'

'I needed a clear field to get near you, so I drove off the competition. Don't be so tragic about it. Men do it every day.'

'But how many men are like you, Luca? Danvers said you threatened him with something in his past. You'd compiled a dossier. That must have taken some time. You knew about him before you ever came here, didn't you? And not just him.'

He was watching her carefully, like a man trying to guess which way a cat would spring. How strange, she thought, that she had blinded herself to that calculating look in his eyes. How often had it been there, and she would not let herself see it?

'The clue was there on the evening we met,' she said quietly, 'but I ignored it.'

'What clue?'

'You immediately called me "*Mrs* Hanley". Of

course, you might have worked out that that was my married name, or someone might have told you, but actually you already knew, didn't you?'

He didn't answer.

'Tell me, Luca, was that meeting really a surprise to you?'

'No,' he admitted.

'You knew who I was. You knew I'd been married, and my married name. You knew everything before I arrived at the house, didn't you?'

'Yes.'

'In other words, you had a dossier on me too.'

He shrugged. 'Does it matter?'

'Does it—? Of course it matters. All this time I thought we just chanced to bump into each other, and you let me think it. But you'd planned everything. Calculated everything. You deceived me.'

'I never deceived you,' he shouted. 'Not you.'

'Just everybody else?'

He shrugged.

'What does anyone else matter? I wanted to find you, and I found you.'

'But how? You had me hunted down like a block of shares, didn't you? Luca Montese, financier and predator, gets the prey in his sights and moves in for the kill.'

'If you want to find someone you put it in the hands of an expert. What's wrong with that?'

'Nothing, if you'd told me. But you let me think it was just life working out naturally.'

'Life never works out. You have to tell it where you want it to go, and then make sure it does. Your father would have said the same.'

'Don't. It makes you sound like him, and I don't want that.'

'Then tell me what you do want,' he said.

'I want to turn back the clock to before this happened,' she said desperately. 'You were never this kind of man before.'

'You're wrong,' he said harshly. 'I was always this kind of man. You just never saw it.'

'Then I'm glad I never saw it,' she cried. 'Because I couldn't have loved you as a bully and a schemer, twisting people, twisting facts, anything as long as you get your own way. That's what my father used to do, and I can't bear it. If you've turned into him, it spoils what we had then and I wanted to keep it.'

'We can't keep it,' he shouted. 'It was destroyed long ago. We've created something else, and that's what we have to hold on to. Don't endanger it by brooding about things that don't matter.'

'Don't matter?' she echoed. 'You don't know what matters and what doesn't. You say we've created something else, but what have we created? What *can* it be when it's based on lies?'

'I had to find you, Becky. I *had* to. I couldn't let anything stand in my way.'

'No, nothing stands in your way, does it, Luca? Not honour or fair dealing or decent behaviour, or other people's feelings. Nothing. I'm seeing a lot of things now.'

'I had to find you,' he repeated stubbornly. 'It was more important than you'll ever know.'

'So why not be honest? All those pretty delusions you fed me, about fate! And it was a lie because you set it all up.'

She looked at him curiously.

'Luca, just how much did you know about me, that night at Philip Steyne's house?'

'A good deal,' he admitted unwillingly.

'Did you know I was going to be there?'

'I was pretty sure. I knew Jordan was going to be there, and you were seeing him, so it figured. I also knew you worked for the Allingham, so I was bound to find you sooner or later.'

'You knew I worked for the Allingham?' she echoed. 'Is that why you bought shares?'

'Yes.'

She gave a wild laugh. 'All that, just to find me again?'

'Does it matter how it happened, as long as we found each other again?'

'But we haven't found each other, can't you see that? No, you can't, can you? And that means we're further apart than we ever were. At one time you would never have deceived me.'

He flinched, and she knew she'd struck home.

'I would have told you the truth eventually,' he growled. 'But this was important. I couldn't take chances. It has to be you, it can't be anyone else.'

'Don't tell me you've been pining with love for me all these years. You married, remember.'

'Yes, and it was no good.'

'It must have been good for part of the time.'

'She had a son by a damned hairdresser,' he snapped.

'So she was unfaithful, but that doesn't mean—'

'Six years and never a hint of a baby. Barren for me, fertile for him. *Dear God!*'

He said the last words violently, his face distorted. Rebecca stared at him, aghast. She had partly known this from Nigel Haleworth, but now a dreadful suspicion had come into her mind. It was impossible. She was imagining crazy things. In a moment he would say something that proved it couldn't be true.

He was still talking, but more to himself than her.

'I had a child once. She died, but she need not have done. She would have been fifteen.'

'I know,' she said, stony-faced.

'Fifteen! Think of it.'

'I think of it all the time,' she cried. 'I think of it every year on what would have been her birthday, and I never stop grieving. But we can't bring her back to life.'

'But we can create new life. You and I. What we've done once we can do again.'

'Luca, what are you saying?'

He turned on her, eyes blazing with intensity.

'I want a child, Becky. Your child.'

'And that was in your mind when you searched for me?' she asked slowly.

'Yes. It's important.'

'I can imagine it would be. And now, of course, I realise why you didn't tell me at once.'

'I could hardly do that,' he said, misled by her reasonable tone.

'Of course not,' she agreed. 'It wouldn't be easy to say, would it? "Good evening Rebecca, nice to see you after fifteen years, and will you be my brood mare?"'

'It's not like that—'

'It's exactly like that, you cold-blooded, insensitive, calculating machine. Luca, I'll never forgive you for this, and if you can't see why, then you've moved further down the wrong path than any man I've ever known.'

'All right, all right, I haven't handled it well, but—'

'Listen to yourself!' she cried, tormented beyond endurance. 'Handled it! Do you know how often you use that phrase? That's how life is to you, something to be "handled". Do this, and everything will work out according to the Luca Montese book of sharp practice. Do that, and it'll all go wrong, because you weren't ruthless enough. Well, nobody could accuse you of not being ruthless enough, but I promise you it's gone wrong. And it'll never be right again.'

'You're determined to misunderstand everything I say.'

'On the contrary, I've understood only too well. You want a son—'

'I want *your* son. Yours. Nobody else's. No other woman's child would mean the same to me.'

But her face was unforgiving.

'You mean,' she said bitterly, 'that I've already proved myself with you, so I'm a safer bet than a stranger?'

He paled. 'That's a hard way of putting it.'

'Tell me another way that comes anywhere near the truth.'

She turned away and began to stride the room.

'I can't believe myself. To think I actually let you touch me after what I heard from Danvers.'

'But you did,' he said harshly. 'Doesn't that prove how strong the bond between us still is?'

'No, it only proves we're good in bed together. There's no true bond between us now, Luca. Just sex, sex and more sex. And then more sex. You're the most sexually exciting man I've ever known, or ever will know, and it makes quite a bond, I admit. In fact it's such a wonderful bond that I've told myself fairy tales about it ever since we met again. I've tried so hard to believe that it was enough, and I suppose that for your purposes it *is* enough.'

'Becky, don't—'

'Why not? It's the truth. If you want to impregnate a woman so that you can flaunt her fertility to the world, then you don't need love or emotional connection. Cold, heartless lust will do the job just as well, won't it, Luca?'

'Stop it, Becky,' he said savagely.

'Sure, I'll stop it. I've made my point. Sex isn't enough, even when it's as good as ours. But it's all we have. Perhaps it's all we ever had.'

'*No!*' It was a cry of agony. 'No, that isn't true. Never say it, do you hear?'

'Still giving me orders. Still trying to arrange everyone like pawns on your chess board. Don't worry. You'll never have to hear me say anything again.

'Go away, Luca. Leave the Allingham, sell your shares, go back to Italy, and tell yourself that you're well rid of that awkward woman who wouldn't fall into line. Find a woman you can be honest with—if you can take the risk.'

She was gone while he was still too stunned to speak. The slam of the door was a deliberate act of contempt.

The phone rang. It was Sonia, with a mountain of problems that had sprung up the moment he left Italy. He suppressed the impulse to slam down the telephone and pursue Rebecca, and was glad, afterwards. In her present mood it would have been the worst thing he could have done.

Despite her words his mind persisted on the old fixed track. He had handled it badly. The best thing was to give her time to cool down, then they would talk. She would see things his way. It was all a question of how you handled it.

He worked until late in the evening, talking to Sonia, sending emails. By the time he logged off the internet he was about half a million richer than he had been at the start.

He was wondering if enough time had passed for him to call her when he heard a knock on his door. He opened it, only half believing that it could be her. But it was.

She gave him a half-smile, as though considering whether to tell him a secret.

'May I come in?'

'Of course.' He stood back, trying to decipher her mood. 'Does this mean you're going to let me explain?'

'No, let's not bother. We both know the score.' She shrugged and turned to him, laughing. 'We were keeping score in different ways, that's all.'

He grinned. 'We can put that right.'

The phone rang. He muttered something under his breath as he snatched it up. 'Sonia, not now—'

'Finish what you have to do,' Rebecca said lightly. 'There's no hurry.'

But he did hurry, because there was a note in her voice that was unfamiliar to him and he wanted to know more. He had no idea what she was up to, but he was willing to find out.

He disposed of the call fast, and turned to find that Rebecca had closed all the curtains. She was standing there, arms folded across the buttoned jacket of her trouser suit, smiling at him in a way that could have only one meaning.

He took her into his arms, feeling her lean towards him. As her arms went around his neck he began to unbutton her jacket and immediately realised that she wore nothing underneath.

He had never before known her so bold and daring, and accepted the implied invitation with eagerness.

When she was naked she took his hand and led him to bed, falling onto it and opening her arms. As soon as he went into them she closed them around him with a movement that was almost as predatory as his own.

Their times together had given her a new confidence, and now she could guide and even direct him, urging him on to what pleased her. Her own caresses were almost casual in their skill, arrogant in their assumption that power lay with her, and she could please him at will. She succeeded beyond his wildest expectations.

Rebecca had an eerie sensation of being two people. One of them was floating above all this, looking down at the woman who seemed so immersed in making passionate love with this man, and who was actually detached from him, from everything that was happening, and—terrifyingly—from herself.

And she was cold, so cold that it was a wonder that the man didn't turn to ice in her arms.

Luca caught a glimpse of her eyes and thought he detected a look of desperation. Then it was gone and all he knew was that she was surging against him, crying incoherently with pleasure.

His own pleasure was shattering, driven to new heights by her responsiveness, and by the skills that had lain, hitherto unsuspected, in her slim body. He guessed that she was not making love, but making sex, and it left him gasping and close to exhaustion.

The end came when she decided. When she pushed him gently away from her he lay, his head turned on the pillow, unwilling to take his eyes from her.

She drew herself up in bed and sat there like a shameless nymph, letting him appreciate her glorious nakedness. She was laughing.

'That was good,' she said.

Failing to pick up the echo, he said, 'Yes, it was.'

His cellphone rang. He grabbed for it, switched it off and tossed it away onto the floor. That made her laugh even more.

'What is it?' he asked, laughing with her but not knowing why.

'Nothing, just a private joke.'

'So tell me.'

'Leave me my secrets.'

'When will you tell me?'

She put her hands behind her head and lay back on the pillow. 'You'll know in time,' she said. 'Go to sleep.'

He did so, letting himself drift away in a blissful haze, until he fell into the deep sleep of total physical contentment.

Rebecca watched him, the laughter gone from her face. Now the look of desperation he'd briefly glimpsed was back in her eyes, and when her tears began to fall she did not wipe them away.

CHAPTER EIGHT

LUCA awoke with only one thought. He had won. Again. As always.

She had tried to leave him and couldn't. She belonged to him again, just as he'd planned, and now there was nothing standing in the way of their future together.

He turned over, reaching for her, wanting to share warmth with her, to see in her eyes his own knowledge that they belonged together.

She wasn't there.

He listened for the sound of the shower, but there was only silence from the bathroom. Her clothes were gone. She was gone.

He dialled her room, but the ringing went unanswered.

No matter. She'd gone out for a walk, to contemplate what had happened between them. She was planning for their future. He told himself this while his mind frantically tried to shut out his fears.

He called her cellphone, but it was switched off. Next he tried Nigel Haleworth, the hotel manager, attempting to make his voice sound casual.

'Nigel, sorry to call so early, but I need to contact Mrs Hanley. She doesn't seem to be in her room. Do you know when she'll be back?'

'Funny you should ask that,' came Nigel's bluff voice. 'I've just had her on the line, saying she won't be back.'

'Of course she will, she...' Luca checked himself on the verge of an indiscretion. Since he couldn't say... 'She just gave me the night of my life', he substituted, 'She has her job here.'

'Not any more, apparently. She's given in her notice and simply walked out, which is a bit inconvenient, actually. She should have let me have some notice, instead of just clearing out her things and going.'

'Where is she now?' His throat was tight. His voice sounded strange to his own ears.

'Didn't say.'

'But suppose mail should come for her?'

'She said she'd be in touch about that. Look, why don't you call Danvers Jordan? They were practically engaged, so he's bound to know. In fact, he's probably the one who wanted her to leave. Young love, eh?'

Luca ground his teeth, but this was no moment to tell the manager that his information was out of date. He tried Rebecca's cellphone again, but it was no real surprise to find it still switched off. He knew now that she meant business.

A knock at his door revealed a hotel messenger with mail that had been delivered for him at Reception. He sorted through the envelopes quickly, automatically setting aside those that looked important, although none of them felt important at this moment.

Then he stopped as he came to one with Rebecca's handwriting. He suddenly seemed paralysed. He did not want to read it, in case it said what he knew it would.

Then he tore it open and read,

Luca, my dear,
   Last night was a goodbye. I couldn't bear to leave you finally without one last reminder of the best there was between us. I know now I can't love you again.

Please don't blame me for that, but treasure the sweetest memories, as I shall.
Goodbye,

Becky

His first reaction was denial. It was impossible that he had found her and lost her, and that she had simply vanished without giving him the chance to bar her way.

He kept pain at bay by fixing on details. It chilled him to think of the smirks in Reception as she handed this in at the desk when she'd left. They would guess.

But then he studied the envelope, and saw that it had a cancelled stamp and a postmark. It had come in the mail, which meant it must have been posted yesterday.

Suddenly all the strength seemed to drain out of him as he realised that she had made love to him last night in the knowledge of that letter already written, and beyond recall.

With strength gone, he had no defence against pain, and he found himself caught up in it like a man caught in heavy waves, being smashed against rocks. There was no way out, no protection, just suffering to be endured.

At last anger came to his rescue. It was the talisman by which he silenced all other feeling and he invoked it now against his enemy.

He was waiting at Danvers Jordan's office before the working day began.

'Just tell me if you know where she is,' he said dangerously as soon as he'd closed the door.

'I don't know what you're talking about,' Danvers said coolly.

'I hope, for your sake, that's true. I'll ask you one more time. Where is Rebecca?'

'Look, if I knew, I'd tell you. She's nothing to me any more. You're welcome to her. But she seems to have finished with the pair of us.'

He barely controlled a sneer as he surveyed Luca.

'I did what you demanded, and left you a clear field. It doesn't seem to have done you much good, but what did you expect? Rebecca is a lady. Of course she didn't hang around once she'd enjoyed her "bit of rough".'

At one time Luca would have knocked him down for that, without a second thought. But now he couldn't move. When he finally managed to get some strength into his limbs it was only enough to walk away.

He didn't look where he was going, for his attention was fixed on the grinning clown in his head. It hooted with derisive laughter, mocking him for his weakness in swallowing an insult, and saying that it was all her fault. The habit of not doing what she wouldn't like had returned at a fatal moment. And he was the clown.

Travelling was the best way to escape, because a woman could convince herself she was headed somewhere, instead of going around in circles.

Just who that woman was Rebecca couldn't have said. She no longer knew herself since the day she'd discovered the worst of Luca, and then spent the night in his arms, driving him on to excess after excess, knowing that she was leaving in the dawn. She had taunted him with cold, heartless lust, and then something had driven her to pay him back in his own coin.

The woman she had once been could never have done it. The woman she had become could have done nothing else. She had told him, in his own terms, that she would not let herself be his victim. After that there was nothing to say.

She supposed he hated her now, which was probably a good thing. At last they could really be free of each other.

She discovered that anger was the best defence against grief, and now that she was alone her anger flared fiercely. He had deceived her in the worst way, creating an illusion for his own purposes. And all the time he'd sat above the scene like some infernal creator, pulling strings. The calculating look she had seen in his eyes had been the true one.

She could not forgive him, not merely because he'd manipulated her, but because he had destroyed her memories.

She knew now why she had never used the word love about their new relationship. It had been hard, shiny, superficial, and, for all its pleasure, unsatisfying. It had ended as it had deserved to end.

Once they had had so much more, and now she blamed herself for being content with so little from a man who had nothing else to give.

And nor did I, she thought. It's too late for me too.

She headed for Europe—France, Switzerland, Italy— visiting out-of-the-way places, while the weeks passed and the days ran into each other. And all the time she knew that if she was to make a final break with the past there was one place that she must go.

She travelled everywhere by train and bus, refusing to hire a car for fear of leaving traces that Luca might pick up if he was pursuing her. She had taken some precautions to prevent herself being found, but she was still being careful. When she went to Carenna it was on an ancient bus that choked and grumbled over the roads.

The sight of the hospital evoked no memories, although it looked as though it had been standing for a hundred years, save for some building work at the rear.

There was the police station, also old, and presumably the same one where Luca had been held to keep him from her. And there was the little church where they were to have been married. Probably the priest was the same man.

But when she wandered in she discovered a young man who had been there only a year. After the first impulse to leave she found herself talking to him. He was easy to talk to, and the whole story came out.

It was two hours before she left, and then she wandered around the town for an hour, trying to come to terms with what she had just learned, and what she had seen. It changed everything. Nothing in the world looked the same in the light of the discovery she had made. But she had nobody with whom to share it.

When her inner haze cleared she found she was standing in front of the little house where she had once lived, for a brief, happy time. It was occupied now by a large family, some of whom she could see through the open door.

She walked closer, noticing automatically that the wallpaper was the same that Luca had put up fifteen years ago. There were rows of leaves of yellow and green.

Suddenly the rows began to swim together. She leaned against the wall, telling herself it would pass soon, but she knew better.

A large woman came out of the house, volubly expressing sympathy, and almost hauling her indoors.

'I was the same with every one of mine,' she said. 'Have you known long?'

'Suspected,' Rebecca said, sipping a hot lemon drink thankfully. 'I haven't been sure until now.'

'And your man? What does he want?'

'A son,' she murmured. 'His heart is set on it.'

'Best you tell him soon.'

She insisted on coming with Rebecca to the bus stop and seeing her safely on board.

'You tell him quick,' she called, waving her off. 'Make him happy.'

Oh, yes, she thought. He would be happy, but she would simply have fallen into his trap. She would not let that happen.

But what else could happen instead, she had no idea.

It was like standing in the centre of a compass, with the needle flickering in all directions, with nowhere to go because everywhere was equally confusing.

At last she recognised that there was only one place where she could do what was necessary. Anger might stifle misery, but it could not deny it altogether. She needed somewhere to grieve for her dead love, and finally bury it. So she set off in that direction.

Luca had said that when you wanted to find somebody you put it in the hands of professionals, but this time the professionals failed him.

Four separate firms, working for three months, had learned only that Rebecca Hanley had travelled to France by ferry. After that she had vanished, and no amount of searching French files produced results. At last he understood that if she had managed to elude such skilled pursuers it meant that her decision to leave him was irrevocable.

When he'd faced that fact, he called them off.

He was back in Rome now, throwing all of himself into maximising Raditore's potential.

'You mean making more money?' Sonia said when he used the phrase. She would never let him get away with corporate-speak.

'Yes, I mean making money,' he said. 'Let's get on with it.'

But he spoke with none of the old bite and that alarmed her more than anything. She could cope with Luca when he was wild, furious, ruthless and rude. But Luca, subdued, was alarming because so unheard-of.

'Go away,' she said to him at last. 'Go right away, not like when you were in London and we talked about business on the phone every night. You're useless to yourself and everyone else while you're here.'

He took her advice and headed his car north, through Assisi, Siena, San Marino. The weather was turning cooler, and driving was pleasant, but everywhere looked the same to him.

Reaching Tuscany, he called in at the construction firm that he'd set up with Frank Solway's money, and from which everything else had grown. It was still flourishing under the command of a good manager that he'd put in charge long ago. Luca examined the accounts, checked the healthy order book, commended his manager on an excellent job, and departed, realising that nobody there needed him.

After that he headed for the place he guessed he'd always meant to go eventually.

There was the long track, stretching up the gentle

slope of the hill. There were the trees from behind which he'd heard angry voices, and had burst through to find a young girl being confronted by three men. The ground was bumpy here, threatening the suspension of his expensive car, but he didn't even notice. His head was too full of visions that blurred and sharpened, taunting him with his sudden reluctance to go further.

He forced himself on until the cottage came into view. He came to a halt near the front door, got out and stood for a moment, surveying the wreckage of what had once been a liveable home. Much of the roof had been burned until it had fallen in, and beams showed against the sky.

A wall was half gone, revealing an interior that had been a bedroom, although there was nothing left to show that now. What remained was black with smoke. Once it had all looked worse. Now the devastation was partly hidden by an overgrowth of weeds. They covered the blackened walls and crowded around the door.

But then Luca saw something that made him stop. The weeds had been partly pruned back, the sharp cuts showing that it had been recently done. And now he could hear faint noises coming from the inside.

Anger possessed him that anyone should dare invade the place that was private to himself. He walked slowly around the cottage, and at the back he saw a tricycle with a makeshift trailer attached to the rear that was little more than a box on wheels. Close inspection revealed that this was indeed how it had started life. It also bore signs of having once fallen to pieces and been inexpertly mended.

Returning to the front, he shouted, 'Come out! What are you doing in there? Come out at once, do you hear me?'

Nothing happened at first. The noise within ceased, as though whoever was there was considering what best to do.

'Come out!' he yelled again. 'Or I'll come in and get you.'

He heard footsteps, then a shadow fell across the door, and a figure emerged into the light.

At first he stared, not believing that she was really there.

He had feared never to see her again, had dreamed of her and found her gone with the first waking moment.

Their last meeting had been three months ago when she had dazzled him with the night of his life, before abandoning him in a gesture of contempt. Now it was like encountering a ghost.

She was dressed in trousers and a tweed jacket, with one hand at her throat to close it against the autumn chill. Her glamorous long hair was gone, cut boyishly short, and returned to its natural light brown colour. Her face was pale, thinner, and there were shadows under her eyes, but she was composed.

She stood only just outside the door as though reluctant to come further out into a world she didn't trust. He approached her slowly. For once he was unsure of himself.

'Are you all right?' he asked.

She nodded.

'What are you doing here, in this rough place?'

'It's peaceful,' she answered. 'Nobody comes calling.'

'How long have you been here?'

'Um—I'm not sure. A week or two, maybe.'

'But—why?'

'Why did *you* come?' she countered.

'Because it's peaceful,' he echoed. 'At least, it is if there are no intruders.'

She nodded. 'Yes,' she said with a faint smile. 'Yes.'

'How are you managing to live here? It's not habitable.'

'It is if you're careful. The stove still works.'

He followed her inside and looked around the kitchen in surprise at how she had made the place liveable.

Everything had been thoroughly cleaned, not an easy task with no electricity. How long, he wondered, had it taken her to sweep up the dust, then scrub the floor and the walls? The range looked as though it had been recently black-leaded.

Warmth was pouring from it now, and a kettle on the top was just beginning to sing. She indicated for him to sit down, and made the tea.

'I know you like sugar,' she said politely, 'but I'm afraid I don't have any. I wasn't expecting visitors.'

'Do you never see anyone?'

'Nobody knows I'm here, not for certain. I ride the bike into the village, put supplies in the trailer, then get back here as quickly as I can, and park it out of sight. Nobody bothers me.'

'You're very determined to hide away. Why? What are you afraid of?'

She seemed surprised by the question.

'Nothing, except being disturbed. I like being alone.'

'Here?'

A faint smile touched her face. 'Do you know of a better place to be alone?'

After a moment he shook his head.

They drank their tea in silence. Luca wanted to say more, but he was nervous and uncertain how to speak to her. This woman, living a hand-to-mouth existence in a ruined shack, had somehow gained the upper hand. He wasn't sure how it had happened, except that she seemed to have discovered a peace that eluded him.

'Do you mind if I look around?' he asked.

'Of course. It's your property.'

'I'm not using that as an excuse to pry. I'm just interested in what you've done.'

There wasn't much to see. Apart from the kitchen only the bedroom was habitable, and that only because the weather was dry. She had pulled the bed away from the hole in the roof and hung a blanket across a rope to make a kind of wall between herself and the exposed part of the room.

One corner of the bed had been badly burned, so that the wooden leg was weakened, and was now boosted by a wooden box. The bed itself sported a patchwork quilt that he remembered from his childhood, although not so bright.

'I hope you don't mind,' she said. 'I found it in a cupboard and when I'd washed the smoke out it looked good.'

'No, I don't mind. My mother made it. But it seems to be all you have on the bed.'

'I've got a cushion for the pillow, and I just huddle up. It's cosy, and I'm warm enough.'

'You are now, but the weather's turning.'

'I like it,' she said stubbornly.

He opened his mouth to protest, but then it struck him that she was right. The place was homely and snug, and although it wasn't actually warm it gave the impression of warmth. He thought of the Allingham with its perfect temperature control, and he could remember only desolation.

'Well, if you like it, that's what counts,' he said, and went back into the kitchen.

'Is this all the food you have?' he asked, opening a cupboard. 'Instant coffee?'

His scandalised tone made her smile briefly.

'Yes, I'm afraid it is instant,' she said. 'I realise that to an Italian that's a kind of blasphemy.'

'You're a quarter-Italian,' he said severely. 'Your grandmother's spirit should rise up and reproach you.'

'She does, but she gets drowned out by the rest of me. I don't keep all my food in here. Fresh vegetables are stored outside, where it's cooler.'

He remembered that outside, attached to the wall, was a small cupboard, made of brick, except for the wooden door. This too had been scrubbed out, and fresh newspaper laid on the shelves, where there was an array of vegetables.

'No meat?' he asked.

'I'd have to keep going into the village to buy it fresh.'

He grunted something, and went back inside.

She poured him another cup of tea, which he drank appreciatively.

'This is good,' he said. 'And it doesn't taste of soot. Whenever I've been here and made coffee, I've always ended up regretting it.'

'Have you returned very often?' she asked.

'Now and then. I come back and cut the weeds, but they've always grown again by the next time.'

'I wonder why you haven't rebuilt it.'

He made a vague gesture. 'I kept meaning to.'

'Why did you come here today?'

He shrugged. 'I was in the area. I didn't know you were here, if that's what you mean.'

It would have been natural, then, to ask her why she'd taken refuge in this spot, when there were so many more comfortable places, but for some reason he was overcome with awkwardness, and concentrated on his tea.

'You've done wonders here,' he said at last, 'but it's still very rough. If anything happened, who could help you?'

She shrugged. 'I'm content.'

'Just the same, I don't like you being here alone. It's better if you...'

He stopped. She was looking at him, and he had the dismaying sense that her face had closed against him. It was like moving through a nightmare. He had been here before.

'I'm only concerned for you,' he said abruptly.

'Thank you, but there's no need,' she said politely. 'Luca, do you want me to leave? I realise that it's your house.'

He shot her a look of reproach.

'You know you don't have to ask me that,' he said. 'It's yours for as long as you want.'

'Thank you.'

He walked outside and strode around to where the bike and trailer were parked.

'Is that thing of real use?' he demanded.

'Oh, yes, if I persevere.' She smiled unexpectedly. 'And I couldn't bring the wood for the range up in a car.'

'You'll be needing some more soon,' he observed, looking at the small pile by the wall. Then he said hastily, 'I'll be going now. Goodbye.'

He walked away and got into his car without another word. A brief gesture of farewell, and he was gone. Rebecca stood watching him until the car had vanished.

CHAPTER NINE

SHE tried to sort out her feelings. It had been a shock to see Luca, even though the sound of his voice, calling from outside the cottage, had half prepared her. He had looked nothing like she'd expected. He was thinner, and instead of anger there had been confusion in his eyes. It had been hard, at that moment, to remember that they were enemies.

And, after all, what was there to say? They were civilised people. She could not have said 'You used me, deceived me, and tried to trick me into having your child'. And he could not have said 'You made a fool of me with a pretence of love that was really a display of power'.

They could not have said these things, but the words had been there between them, in the stunned silence.

Their meeting had been less of a strain than it might have been. He had asked no awkward or intrusive questions, and, except for one moment, had not disturbed her tranquillity.

She told herself that she was glad to see him go, but the cottage looked lonely without him. It was his personality, of course, so big that it filled the place and left an emptiness when he departed. When he had been gone for a while the sensation would cease.

She shivered a little and pulled her jacket around her. The weather had cooled rapidly and the place was rather less snug than she had claimed. The last few evenings she had stayed up late because the kitchen, with the range, was the only warm room in the house. She had tried leaving the door to the bedroom open, but the heat went straight through the open roof.

She began to prepare some vegetables for her evening meal. When she'd finished she realised that she was running low on water, and took a jug out into the yard, to the pump. She hated this part because the pump was old and stiff, and needed all her strength. But the water it gave was sweet and pure.

She was just about to press down on the handle when she saw that a car was approaching in the distance. After a moment she realised that it was Luca, returning.

Setting down the jug, she watched as the car came up the track until it reached the cottage. Luca got out, nodded to her briefly, and began hauling something from the back seat that he then carried into the cottage. Following, Rebecca saw him go right through to the bedroom, and dump a load of parcels on the bed.

He seemed to have raided the village for sheets, blankets and pillows.

'I shall only be here a moment and then I'm going,' he said brusquely before she could speak.

He headed back to the car at once, delving inside again and emerging with a cardboard box, which he brought in and set on the table. This time the contents were food, fresh vegetables but also tins.

'Luca—'

'That's it,' he said, and hurried through the front door.

But instead of getting into the car he went to the pump and began to work it vigorously, making the water pour out into the jug.

'One jug won't last long,' he said tersely. 'Better fetch any other container you've got.'

She fetched two more jugs and when he had filled those too he carried them inside.

'Luca—'

'I just don't want you on my conscience,' he said hurriedly. Then, as she opened her mouth, with a touch of desperation, 'Be quiet!'

Silence.

'Can I say thank you?' she asked at last.

'No need,' he snapped and walked out before she had time to say more.

Through the car window he grunted something that might have been a goodbye, and in another moment she could see his tail lights growing smaller. Then he was gone altogether.

In the bedroom she began to go through the pile of bed linen and realised that there was enough here to ward off the night chills. None of it was very expensive, nothing to overwhelm her, just the gift of a thoughtful friend, if she wanted to take it that way.

But then she remembered the box of food, and something made her hurry back to the kitchen to begin turning it out and examining the contents.

When she did not find what she was looking for her search became feverish, though whether she was trying to prove him better or worse than her suspicions she could not have said.

There were several cartons of fresh milk, for which she was genuinely thankful, tea, a box of shortbread biscuits, fresh bread, butter, ham, eggs and several tins of fruit. And two large, juicy steaks.

But no sugar.

No real, fresh coffee.

Either of those things would have told her that he intended to return. Their absence left her not knowing what to think.

She cooked one of the steaks that evening, and ate it with bread and butter, washed down with a large mug of tea.

She made up the bed, not sorry to exchange the rough sheets for the smooth new ones and pile on the blankets, although she replaced the brightly coloured quilt on top.

Before retiring she treated herself to fresh tea and shortbread, then slipped blissfully between the sheets. She had expected to lie awake for a long time, puzzling about Luca's sudden appearance, but she fell asleep almost at once, and slept soundly for eight hours.

In the morning she felt more refreshed than she had for months. She had been planning to go into the village to stock up, but Luca's gift had made this unnecessary. She could keep her privacy a little longer, and spend today enjoying her favourite occupation, reading one of the books she had brought with her.

She wondered if she ought to do some thorough housework first, in case he returned. She didn't want him to feel that she was neglecting his property.

So she cleared everything away, swept the floor and did a thorough dusting. But still she did not hear his car approaching, and the house began to feel very quiet.

There was a patch of grass in the garden that caught the sun well, and where she could place her chair and read to her heart's content. It also had the advantage that she could not see the track up which he would come, if he came.

It was as well to be free of that kind of temptation, so she chose this spot. After a while, she moved.

When she did finally see a vehicle it was not Luca's expensive car, but an old van that lurched drunkenly along the rough track, until it came to a standstill just outside the gap in the fence that served as a gate. Luca's head appeared through the cab window.

'Have I got room?' he yelled to her.

She studied the gap. 'I don't think so.'

He jumped down and came to see for himself.

'No, it's too narrow by six inches. OK, I'll put that right.'

He went to the back of the van and returned with a large hammer, which he swung at the wood until it gave way. He was dressed in jeans and a shirt, and looked like a different man from the one she had known recently.

One hefty kick completed the demolition of the wood, enabling him to bring the van further in and halt near the front door. He jumped down and looked up into the sky, then at his watch.

'I've got time to make a start, anyway,' he said.

'A start on what?'

But he'd already gone to the back, opening the doors. Inside was a mountain of long planks, and a ladder, which he pulled out and carried around the side of the house, setting it against the wall, just below the hole in the roof.

With Rebecca watching, he climbed up and inspected the damage with the eye of a professional. She saw him tap some beams and try to shake them. What he found seemed to satisfy him, for he shinned back down the ladder.

'A cup of tea would be nice,' he said.

He spoke hopefully but he wasn't looking at her, and she knew that what she said next was crucial. It would take only a word to wither him with the snub she sensed that he dreaded, or to set their relationship on a new, less stressful footing. The future would be decided in this moment.

'Tea already?' she said, smiling slightly. 'You've only just arrived.'

'But the British always give their workmen tea,' he pointed out. 'Otherwise no work ever gets done.'

'In that case, I'll put the kettle on,' she said lightly.

It was done. For good or ill, she had made it possible for him to stay.

While she made the tea she heard him crawling about on the roof, until he descended, went to the van, and came back with a smaller ladder that he took through to the bedroom.

She knew he would check to see if she'd used the sheets and blankets he had brought her, and was glad, now, that she had. A few moments later she found him in there, examining the roof from the inside.

'Those beams won't stand any weight,' he said. 'I'm going to have to take them down, so for a while you'll have less roof than you have now.'

'It hardly makes any difference,' she pointed out cheerfully. 'A large hole or a very large hole, the effect is the same.'

'True. I'm glad to see that you have the right pioneering spirit.'

'Meaning that I'm going to need it? All right, I'm prepared for the worst.'

'You're lucky something hasn't fallen on you already. Look just there.' He was pointing upwards.

'Let me get closer.'

'All right.' He held the ladder while she climbed up, and she could see at once what he meant. The beams were less sturdy than they looked from below, and would not have survived much longer.

'Come down,' he said, 'and I'll get rid of them.'

'Will they land on the bed?' she asked.

'Some of them, yes.'

'Then give me a moment to cover it.'

He helped her protect the bed with the old blankets, then said, 'Right. Stand well clear.'

He was giving orders again, but it did not irk her as it had done before, because here his expertise justified him, and there was reason in everything he did.

Nor did she feel like getting too close when he started swinging the hammer and sending wood crashing down. Some fell outside the house, but some landed inside. Having made an appalling noise, he studied the result with satisfaction and began clearing up the wood.

He performed this task with brisk efficiency, without seeming to notice that this was her bedroom. His only comment came when she tried to lift a heavy plank.

'If you do that, what am I for?' he asked, sounding pained.

She stood back, and waited until all the wood was gone. But then she insisted on helping him gather up the blankets with their burden of dirt and splinters. Together they carried them outside and shook them thoroughly, resulting in a double coughing fit.

'Now we both look a mess,' he said, trying to brush dust out of his hair and from his clothes. 'I need to go into the village, and I think I'll go now before I get any dirtier. Do you want anything?'

She hesitated only a moment before saying, 'Yes, please. I'd like some sugar, and some good coffee.'

It was acceptance, the sign that she was making a small space for him. She wondered how he would react.

'Fine,' he said briefly. 'Nothing else?'

'No, thank you. Nothing else.'

He jumped into the van and made a noisy departure. He was gone an hour and when he returned he had more provisions. There was food, milk, meat and pasta, and the back was piled high with logs, each about twelve inches long.

'For the range,' he said. 'You're going to run out of them soon.'

She had been planning to go to the village for more logs, but it was a heavy job, and her bouts of queasiness had left her not feeling up to it.

She wondered if he suspected, but it was too soon for her to show. And Luca was not perceptive enough to guess.

But when she tried to pick up some logs he stopped her instantly.

'Why don't you take that?' he said, pointing to the box of food. 'I could do with some pasta. You'll find vegetables, tomato purée, and Parmesan cheese.'

It meant nothing. Of course he wanted to do all the heavy work because his pride was tied up in this. And he had always been chivalrous, she recalled. How he had loved to wait on her and tend her, as though she was almost too precious to touch. How gently he had spoken to her, never raising his voice, trying to stand protectively between her and the world.

It was old-fashioned and definitely not 'liberated'. She was a modern, independent woman, who needed no such cosseting. But her eyes softened as she recalled how wonderful it had been.

'Hey!' yelled Luca.

She came out of her happy dream. 'Did you speak to me?'

'Yes. I said, are you going to make that pasta, or are you going to stand there dreaming all day? There's one very hungry man here. Get moving!'

To his bafflement she began to laugh. She tried to stop but something had overtaken her and it quickly became uncontrollable.

'Becky—'

'I'm sorry, I'm trying to—to—'

'What's so funny?' he demanded, aggrieved.

'It's just the contrast—never mind. It's not important.'

'If it's not important, what's stopping you feeding me before I die of hunger?'

'Nothing. I'm on to it now.'

She grabbed the box and hurried inside, still laughing. It took a moment to bring herself under control, but she felt better afterwards. Somehow the little incident had restored her sense of proportion, and she had a feeling it had needed restoring.

Her pasta skills had been rusty when she'd first arrived here, but she'd been polishing them up, and now made a respectable job of it, including the tomato sauce.

'Ready in ten minutes,' she called.

He looked in through the window.

'Fine, I'll just clean up a bit. The logs have made me dirty again.'

She gave the pasta another stir before going outside,

where he was at the pump. He'd stripped off his shirt and was trying to pump water over himself with one hand and wash himself with the other. Since the pump belched water only jerkily, he wasn't managing very well.

Fetching a few useful items from the kitchen, she went to help him.

'I'll do the pump,' she said, handing him the soap.

He soaped himself thankfully while she poured water over him. The sun glinted gloriously off every drop streaming from the spout, over his long back and powerful arms.

'Now your hair,' she said, spraying something over the dust that seemed embedded in his scalp, and massaging hard to work up a lather.

'It's in my eyes,' he bellowed.

'Oh, stop being such a baby!'

'You're a heartless woman.'

'OK, here comes the rinse,' she cried, pumping again.

When the suds had gone she handed him the towel she'd brought out and he dried himself thankfully.

'That's better. Hey, what's this?' He snatched up a plastic cylinder from the bench where she'd set it. *Washing-up liquid?*'

'It's as good as anything for the purpose.'

'You washed my hair with washing-up liquid?' he repeated, aghast. 'Do you realise you've made me smell of lemon?'

'Well, I had to use something before your hair set solid, and the only shampoo I have smells of perfume.'

'Lemon's just fine,' he said hastily.

Now that the ice had been broken they bickered amiably over the meal, inching their way carefully towards a place where this new relationship would be possible.

After lunch he went around the house, testing locks, and was shocked by what he found.

'The front door doesn't lock properly, and the back door doesn't lock at all. Lucky I brought some more.'

As he fixed the new locks into place he said crossly, 'You've been sleeping here like this? No locks? Anyone could have walked in.'

'Since nobody comes here, it didn't seem important. Still, I'm glad you've done that.'

He went back to work on the roof, hauling wood up and hammering mightily, until he had put in place a rough frame.

'With any luck, this will be your last night under that hole,' he said, looking up from directly beneath it. 'By tomorrow night I should have rigged up some covering.'

'It's going to be very cosy in here,' she said appreciatively. 'Thank you, Luca.'

But he was yawning and didn't seem to hear her.

'I feel as though I'm falling apart,' he said, rubbing his shoulders as he wandered out into the kitchen.

'Let's eat.'

He collected logs to refill the range while she lit candles, for the light was fading fast.

A candlelit meal might have been romantic, but he seemed determined to rob the atmosphere of any semblance of romance, watching her cooking like a hawk and making a stream of interfering suggestions until at last she said crossly, 'All right, do it yourself.'

'I will. I will.'

'Fine!'

'Fine!'

She went into the bedroom and sat on the bed, in a huff, for about ten minutes. Then she returned to the kitchen, having recovered her sense of humour.

'You'll turn the food sour,' he objected.

'No, I'm all right now. Shall I take over?'

'No, thank you,' he said with more haste than politeness. 'I have everything under control. This will take a while, so why don't we have mushrooms and rice first? You can prepare the mushrooms and I'll put the water on for the rice.'

She worked on the mushrooms for the next few minutes, until forced to stop by a queasy stomach.

'Are you all right?' Luca asked.

'There's just something about the smell of raw mushrooms,' she said.

'You've never said that before.'

'I'm saying it now,' she said fretfully.

'It'll be all right when they're cooked.'

'Now you're talking.'

She went out for some fresh air, wanting to escape his notice. The nausea was there again but a few deep breaths took care of it. If last time was anything to go by, she should be coming to the end of her sickness. If only Luca did not suspect the truth before then.

As for what she would tell him, she was so confused that even thinking about it would be a waste of time. Before he came here she'd had no intention of informing Luca that she was carrying his child. Now? She didn't know. But, for the moment, she intended to keep the decision in her own hands.

She knew, though, that time was running out. If she did not tell him, she would have to leave soon and decide where to have her baby.

When she went back inside she was smiling. He was busy cooking the mushrooms and rice, and somehow after that he ended up cooking the whole meal.

'You're a great cook,' she said as they ate.

'That's not what you used to say. You used to criticise my cooking.'

'Only because I was jealous. You were better than me. It made me so mad.'

He stared. 'And I thought I'd never get you to admit that.'

'You knew all the time, huh?'

'Of course. There was never anything wrong with my cooking.'

'You arrogant so-and-so.'

'Well, there wasn't. I'm a great cook. Why not be honest about it?'

'Not only arrogant, but conceited.'

'Always was,' he said briefly. 'Do you want those extra mushrooms?'

She gave him her last mushroom, and the subject was allowed to die.

The candles were burning down as he helped her with the washing-up. Then he said, 'That's it for today. I'm ready to turn in. Goodnight, Becky.'

He gave her a brief nod and walked outside. She went to the door, expecting to see him get into the cab and drive away, but instead he went to the back and climbed in. When he did not reappear she went to look for him, and found him unwrapping a bed roll by the light of a torch.

'What are you doing?' she asked.

'Going to bed.'

'Out here?'

'Where else?'

'Haven't you got a nice, comfortable hotel room?'

'Yes, but it's several miles away, and I'm not leaving you here alone. It's too isolated.'

'Luca—'

'Goodnight. And, Becky—'

'Yes?'

'Lock the front door.'

'I thought you were going to fend off invaders for me.'

'I meant, lock it against me.'

'Do you plan to come into the house?'

'No.'

'Then I don't need to lock it. Anyway, there's a big hole in the roof, in case you hadn't noticed.'

'Becky, will you quit arguing and just lock the door?'

'All right, all right.' She went away, muttering, 'But it seems silly to me.'

As she snuggled down in her own bed she reflected how odd it was that she should feel so able to trust his word. He had said he would not intrude on her, and she knew that he would not.

She was up early next morning, but he was already moving about outside. She opened the door, calling, 'Coffee!' and he hurried in, moving stiffly, like a man who'd spent a cold night on a hard floor.

As he drank his coffee she heated up some washing water for him, then cooked bacon and eggs while he washed. He said little over breakfast, being absorbed in the food, and as soon as he'd finished he went straight to work.

Halfway through the morning she took him a snack, and they drank tea together.

'You're doing a lovely job,' she said, indicating the roof, which was taking shape.

'I got my start this way: hammering my own nails in and hiring as little help as I could manage with. I could turn my hand to anything in those days, but it's years since I did any honest work.'

He grinned suddenly. 'It's also years since I got as filthy as this.' He spread out his hands with their finely manicured nails, looking incongruous with the grazes they had acquired in the last two days.

'I bet you weren't hammering your own nails in for long,' she said.

'I employed a few men and it went to my head; I took on more than we could cope with and ended up having to work my head off at night, on my own. I snatched one job right out from under the nose of the biggest builder in the district. He thought the really profitable jobs were his by rights, and he didn't like it. That's how I got this.' He rubbed his scar.

'You had a fight?'

'No, but for a while I was pretty sure he was going to send his gang for me. I took to spending my nights in the yard, staying awake, waiting for them.'

'And they came for you?'

'No, they never did. But I got so tired that I fell off a ladder.' He grinned in rueful self-mockery.

'You're kidding me.'

'No, really. Mind you, I always let people believe it was done in a fight. My stock went up no end.'

'How did you get from being a builder to being where you are now?'

'I bought some land to build on. It increased in value and suddenly I was a speculator. It's more profitable to buy and sell houses than to build them, so I concentrated on that. Once I started making money I couldn't stop. In fact, it's not difficult to make more money than you could ever need if you devote yourself to it twenty-four hours a day, and never think of anything else.'

'You must have thought about something else at some time,' she said. 'What about your wife?'

'Drusilla married me for my money.'

'What did you marry for?'

He was silent awhile before he said, 'She was a status symbol. Her family have a very old title, and only a few years earlier she wouldn't have looked at me. That made me feel good.'

He grimaced. 'Not nice, is it? But I'm not a nice man, Becky. I never really was. You made me better, but without your influence I reverted to being what I am.'

'No!' she said violently. 'That's too easy, too glib.'

'It's the truth about me. And it's not so long ago that you'd have been the first to say so. If I can face it now, why can't you?'

'Because I don't believe it *is* the truth. Nobody can be explained that simply. Luca, are you trying to make me feel that it's my fault, that I let you down in some way?'

'No, I'm not. I'm saying that you can't buck nature.'

'What nature? Who knows what anybody's nature is? It isn't fixed, it develops through what happens to you.'

'It's sweet of you to defend me—'

'I'm not defending you,' she said crossly, 'I'm calling you a lame-brained idiot.'

'I'm just saying that I know myself—'

'Rubbish. Nobody knows themselves that well.'

'That time in Carenna, when all I could think of was

taking care of you—I never acted meek and mild with anyone else before, and I've never done it since.'

'You never had a baby with anyone else.'

'That's true,' he said quietly.

Carried away by her arguments, she'd failed to see the pit opening at her feet until she fell into it. She had forgotten about the cause of their quarrel. Now it came back to her, and she fell silent.

'Do you want to talk about that?' he asked.

'Not really,' she said hastily. 'There's nothing to say.'

'No.' He seemed deflated. 'No, I guess there isn't.'

CHAPTER TEN

SHE was gathering up the remains of the snack and preparing to go indoors when she heard the faint sound of a voice behind her.

'I'm sorry, Becky, for everything.'

'What?'

She turned sharply, not sure if she'd really heard the words, but Luca was already rising.

'Time I was getting back to work,' he said, stretching his limbs. 'Let's see how far we can get with this roof today.'

He fixed several beams, but then the light was too poor for him to go any further, so he fetched some roofing felt from the van.

'I'll just nail this over the gap for tonight, so that you'll have some cover,' he said. 'Tomorrow, with any luck, the roof should be finished.'

When he'd fixed the felt into place he ate the meal she'd prepared as quickly as possible. She had hoped they might talk some more, but he said goodnight and left.

He had made the repairs just in time. That night the heavens opened. Summer was finally over and the first storm of autumn was impressive, especially to the woman looking up at the felt, and wondering how strong it was. But no water was dripping down into the bedroom. As a builder, Luca knew his stuff.

Just as she was beginning to relax she heard a crash

from outside, and sat up sharply, listening for any further worrying noises. But the pounding of the rain blotted out all else.

At last she got out of bed, threw on a dressing gown and made her way outside. The wind hit her like a hammer, hard enough to blow her back inside if she hadn't clung to the doorpost. Breathing hard, she steadied herself and tried to look around through the rain that was coming down in sheets.

She could see no sign of trouble, but another noise came from around the corner of the cottage and she headed that way, arriving just as a fork of lightning illuminated the lean-to where the logs were stored, revealing that the roof had come down.

'Oh, great!' she muttered. 'Now the wood will get wet and it won't burn, and the kitchen will fill with smoke, and probably fifty other things will happen. Great! Great! Great!'

There was only one thing to do. Gathering up a pile of logs, she began to stagger back to the front door. On the way the dressing gown fell open and she tripped over the belt, falling into the mud and taking the logs with her.

Cursing furiously, she got to her feet and surveyed the soaking logs, aided by the lightning that obligingly flashed at that moment.

'Damn!' she told the heavens. A blast of thunder drowned her out. 'And the same to you!'

Suddenly Luca's voice came from near by. *'Becky, what are you doing out here?'*

'What does it look as if I'm doing?' she demanded at the top of her voice. 'Dancing the fandango? The lean-to came down and the wood's getting even wetter than I am, which is saying a good deal.'

'OK, I'll fetch it in,' he yelled back. 'Go inside and get dry.'

'Not while there's wood to be moved.'

'I'll do it.'

'It'll take too long for one person. It'll be drenched.'

'I said I'll do it.'

'Luca, I swear if you say that once more I'll brain you.'

He ground his teeth. 'I am only trying to take care of you.'

'*Then don't!* I haven't asked you to. I'll do the wood on my own.'

'You will *not* do it on your own!' He tore his hair. 'While we're arguing, it's getting wet.'

'Then let's get on,' she said through gritted teeth, and went back to the pile of logs before he could argue again.

They got about a quarter of the wood inside before he said, 'That's it. There's enough there for a few days, and during that time we can bring some of the rest in and dry it out.'

'All right,' she said, glad to leave off now her point was made. 'Come in and get yourself dry.'

They squelched back indoors, Luca slamming the van's open door in passing with a force that showed his feelings.

Once inside, Rebecca lit some candles, then rooted inside a cupboard, glad that the one luxury she had allowed herself was a set of top-quality towels and two vast bathrobes. They were chosen to be too big, so that the occupant could snuggle deep inside, which was fortunate, or Luca could never have got into one.

'Why didn't you call me?' he asked, sitting down and pulling the robe as far around him as he could.

'Because I'm not a helpless little woman.'

'Just a thoroughly awkward one,' he grumbled.

'Oh, hush up!' She silenced him by tossing a hand towel over his head and beginning to rub, ignoring the noises that came from underneath.

'What was that?'

He emerged from the towel, tousled and damp, and looking oddly young.

'I said you should have knocked on the van door and woken me.'

'I'm surprised you didn't hear the lean-to go down, the noise it made.'

But then she remembered that he had always slept heavily, sometimes with his head on her breast.

'Well, I didn't. It was mere chance that I woke up when I did. Otherwise, I suppose you'd have taken the whole lot indoors.'

'No, I'd have been sensible and stopped after a few, like we did.'

He grunted.

'And don't grunt like that as though you couldn't believe a word I say.'

'I know you. You'd say anything to win an argument.'

She grinned. 'Yes, I would. So don't take me on.'

'No, I've got the bruises from that, haven't I?' he asked wryly.

'We've both got bruises,' she reminded him. 'Old and recent.'

He looked at her cautiously. 'But you're still speaking to me?'

'No, I'm speaking to this man who turned up to mend

the roof,' she said lightly. 'Good builders are hard to find.'

He gave a brief laugh. 'My only honest skill.'

'Don't be so hard on yourself,' she said quietly.

She thought he might say something, but he only grabbed the towel and began rubbing his head again.

She made some tea and sandwiches and they ate in near silence. He seemed tired and abstracted, and she wondered if he was regretting that he had ever started this.

'What happened to you?' he asked suddenly, while he was drying his feet.

'How do you mean?'

'Where did you vanish to?'

'Didn't your enquiry agents tell you that?'

He grimaced an acknowledgement. 'They traced you to Switzerland, then the trail went cold. I guess you meant it to.'

'Sure. I knew you'd hire the best, and they'd check the airlines and the ferries, and anywhere where there was passport control. So I slipped across the Swiss-Italian border "unofficially".'

He stared. 'How?'

She smiled. 'Never mind.'

'As simple as that?'

'As simple as that. Then I made all my journeys by train or bus, because if I'd hired a car I'd have left a trail.'

'Is that why you have that incredible bike around the back?'

'That's right. I bought it for cash. No questions asked.'

'I should think so. They must have been glad to get

rid of it before it fell apart. What's that thing at the back made of?'

'You mean my trailer?'

'Is that what you call it?'

'Certainly,' she said with dignity. 'I'm very proud of it. I just got some boxes and hammered them together. There was an old pram in the little barn behind the house and I took the wheels off. I'm sorry, I know they belong to you.'

'Don't worry, I won't ask for them back. If it's the pram I think it is, it was collapsing anyway. In fact, it was collapsing when my parents got it. My father won it in a card game when my mother was expecting me, and I gather she made him sorry he was born. I can't believe that you actually use it.'

'I only go short distances to the village for supplies, food, logs, that sort of thing.'

'You've brought logs back in that little box?'

'I did once, but I put in too many and it fell apart. I had to come back here for a hammer and nails, then go back, put it together and finish the job. The logs were just where I'd left them.'

'Of course. People around here are honest. But why didn't you have the logs delivered?'

'Because then people would have known for sure where I lived.'

'What about hotels when you were travelling? Didn't they ask to see your passport?'

She shrugged. 'I pass as Italian. I've been all over the country, never staying anywhere for very long.'

He drew a long breath. 'Of all the wily, conniving...! I thought I was a schemer, but I've got nothing on you.'

'Pretty good, huh?' she said with a touch of smiling cockiness.

'You could teach me a thing or two,' he said, grinning back at her.

But their smiles were forced, and faded almost at once.

'I kept meaning to stop awhile in this place or that,' Rebecca continued, 'but I never felt I belonged in any of them. So I always moved on to the next place.'

'Until you came here.' He left the implication hanging in the air, but she did not pick it up.

At last he said quietly, 'You were very determined to escape me, weren't you?'

'Yes,' she said simply.

He didn't answer, and she looked up to see his face in the flickering candlelight. It might have been the distorting effect of the little flames, but she thought she had never seen such a look of unbearable sadness.

He didn't turn away or try to hide it, just sat regarding her with a look so naked and defenceless that it was as much as she could do not to reach out to him.

'Luca...' She didn't mean to say his name, but it slipped out.

Then emotion overcame her and she covered her eyes, letting her head drop onto her arm on the table. She didn't know what else to do. What she was feeling now was beyond tears: despair for the lost years, the chances that could never be recovered, the love that seemed to have died, leaving behind only desolation.

And if there was a hint of hope, it was of a muted kind. She might yet have his child, but it was too late for them.

She thought she felt a light touch on her hair, and

perhaps her name was murmured very softly, but it was hard to be sure, and she did not look up. She didn't want him to see her tears.

She heard him go to the stove and put in some more logs, then sit down again.

'That will keep it going until morning,' he said. 'Go back to bed and keep warm.'

She looked up to see him near the door.

'Where are you going?'

'Back to the van. I'll put some dry clothes on in there, and let you have the towels back tomorrow.'

'No, wait!'

She hadn't asked herself where he would sleep, but it seemed monstrous for him to have to return to his bleak conditions while she had all the comfort.

'You can't go back to the van,' she said.

'Of course I can. I'm quite happy there.'

She jumped up, arm outstretched to detain him, but stopped abruptly at the weakness that came over her. For a moment her head was fuzzy and the kitchen danced about her. Then the giddiness cleared.

She wasn't sure whether he'd taken hold of her, or whether she was clinging to him, but they were gripping each other tightly and she was furious with herself. Now he would know.

She waited for his exclamation, the questions: why hadn't she told him? And at the end of it all she would feel cornered and trapped.

'Maybe you didn't have enough for supper,' he said. 'Hauling logs about on an empty stomach. Shall I get you something?'

'No, thank you,' she said slowly.

'Then you should go straight back to bed. Come on.'

He kept a firm but impersonal hold on her all the way into the bedroom, held her while she sat down on the bed, then tucked her in.

'All right?'

'Yes. Thank you, Luca.'

'Let's get some sleep for what's left of the night. There's another heavy day tomorrow.'

He closed the door quietly behind him, and after a moment she heard the front door also close.

The darkness held no answers. She tried to conjure up his eyes in that brief moment when he'd steadied her, and to read what she had seen there.

But she had seen only what he'd chosen to reveal. Nothing. His eyes had been blank, their depths barred to her. It was as though he'd stepped back, giving her space, even space enough for a denial, if she wished.

She had thought she knew him through and through. Now she wondered if she had ever known the first thing about him.

She discovered in the following days that the space she'd sensed him offering her was no illusion. In a way it was what he'd done since the moment he appeared, sleeping outside in all weathers, never intruding or saying a word that could have come from a lover.

But now something was different, as though he too needed that space. Perhaps, she thought, he was doing this for himself. He would finish the house to keep her safe, but then he would drive away and never ask about the child. Because now he did not want to know. It was rather like living with a ghost. But above all it was peaceful, and peace was what she most valued.

Bit by bit the house was coming alive again. The completion of the roof would mean that another room, which had been completely open to the skies, would become inhabitable. Rebecca set herself to clean it out, sweeping soot from the floor and the walls.

Luca's response was to vanish for nearly a day. When he returned he had a small portable generator and a vacuum cleaner.

'I had to go to Florence to get these,' he said. 'The generator was the last they had. It's not really big enough, but the bigger one had just been bought by someone else, and all my pleading wouldn't make him part with it. Still, it's big enough to scoop up the soot, and prevent you looking like a chimney sweep.'

She blew a stray lock of hair away from her forehead, but it settled back again. He grinned and brushed it back.

'Is supper ready?'

'Nope. I didn't know if you were coming back, so I didn't prepare anything.'

'OK. That's cool.'

'Oh, stop being nice!' she growled. 'It's steak. I'll start it now.'

From then on the job was easier and they had some light in the evenings, although they still relied on the range for warmth and cooking.

'You could move in there,' Rebecca said cautiously one day, when the room was finished. 'To sleep, I mean. Better than the van.'

He considered for a moment. 'OK,' he said at last briefly.

He took the van into the village and returned with an iron bedstead, bought second-hand, as he explained to her with great pride.

'It's very narrow,' she said doubtfully. 'It can't be more than two feet six.'

'People live in small houses around these parts. The furniture has to be narrow.'

But the mattress was unusable, and he was forced to buy another. This time he splashed out on a brand-new mattress that was a foot wider than the bed.

'You see, it won't matter that the bed is narrow,' he said triumphantly. 'All I'll feel is the mattress beneath me.'

'But it'll hang over six inches each side. Every time you turn over you'll roll off.'

'Nonsense. I've worked it out scientifically.'

He explained the science of it to her in detail, and Rebecca made a noise indicating scorn. That night he went scientifically to bed and fell out scientifically three times. After that he put the mattress on the floor and used the bed as a dumping ground for anything he couldn't find a place for.

Humour was a lifeline, making the journey possible until they knew where the road led. But even while they were laughing over his mishaps they knew that the fragile atmosphere could not last forever.

The thing that shattered it crept up on them without warning. They were sitting in the kitchen, listening to a concert on Rebecca's battery radio, and laughing over Luca's attempts to repair the 'trailer'.

'Well, I've got it together,' he said at last, 'but is it worth it? Do you have a use for it?'

She shook her head.

'Good.' He tossed it into a corner, where a wheel fell off.

'My father insisted on keeping that thing,' he said

after a moment, 'just in case they had another child. But it never happened. Then Mama died when I was ten.'

'Yes, I remember you telling me once,' she said, thinking back. 'It must have been lonely without brothers or sisters.'

'I had my father to look after. He was lost without her.' He gave a brief laugh. 'Bernardo Montese, the local giant, big man, made everyone afraid of him. But he was a softie inside, so first she looked after him, then I did. It was like looking after a child.'

'You loved him very much, didn't you?' she asked softly.

'Yes, I did. We were on the same wavelength. I realise now that it was partly because he was like a child that never grew up. You wouldn't have thought it to look at him shouting the odds, but under all that mountainous strength there was a hidden weakness, and if you touched it he crumbled.'

She watched him, holding her breath, knowing that something was happening. Beneath the calm of that little cottage things were whirling out of control. If she wanted to stop it happening she must do it now.

'Go on,' she whispered.

'And he still wouldn't get rid of the pram. He said my wife would be glad of it one day. I didn't have the heart to tell him it was only fit for the scrap heap. The thought seemed to mean a lot to him. Then he got drunk and fell into a stone quarry, and died the next day. I was sixteen.'

He had talked about his parents when they knew each other before, but never like this. She tried to find the right words to encourage him to say more, but before she could speak he said,

'When we met in London...' He stopped as though his courage had failed him.

'Go on,' she said.

'I never asked you about the birth. I kept meaning to, but—'

'The time was never right.'

'No, it wasn't. But I'd like to know, if you can bear to speak of it. Was it very hard?'

'It was over fairly quickly. She was small, being premature. It was what came after that was hard. I longed for you so much. I didn't know that you were being kept from me by the police.'

'Your father must have called them while I was calling the ambulance. They arrived fast and arrested me, on his say-so, for "violent behaviour". I pleaded to be allowed to go with you, but they wouldn't let me. I remember the ambulance doors shutting, and it driving away with you inside, while I was being pulled in the other direction by the police.

'I went mad, and then I did become violent. It took four of them to haul me away, and I know I gave one of them a bloody nose, so then they had something to charge me with.

'I was in the cells for days, unable to get any news of you. Then your father came to see me. He said the baby had been born dead, so I could "forget any ideas I had".'

'He said what?' She was staring at him.

'He said our child was born dead. Becky, what is it?' She was staring at him with a livid look that alarmed him.

'She wasn't born dead,' she whispered. 'She lived just a few hours in an incubator. I saw her. She was so tiny, and attached to machines in all directions. It looked terrible, but I knew the doctors and nurses were fighting for her. They tried so hard, but it was no use. She just slipped away.'

'But she was alive?' he asked hoarsely. 'She actually lived, even if just for a little while?'

'Yes.'

'Were you able to hold her?'

'Not while she was alive. She needed to be in the incubator. It was her only chance. But when she'd died they wrapped her in a shawl and put her in my arms. I kissed her, and told her that her mother and father loved her. And then I said goodbye.'

'You can remember that?'

'Yes, at that stage I was still functioning. The depression didn't hit me until a few hours later.'

'Didn't you wonder where I was?'

'Yes, I kept asking Dad, and he said, "They're still trying to find him."'

'He said *that*, knowing I was trapped in a cell, where he'd put me?' Luca asked with quiet rage.

'He kept saying you'd gone. And then she was dead, and after that—' she faltered '—after that things became dark. A black cloud enveloped me without warning. I felt crushed, suffocated, and absolutely terrified. The whole world seemed to be full of horror, and it went on and on without hope.'

She passed a hand over her eyes. 'Maybe it would have happened anyway, with losing the baby. But maybe if we could have been together it wouldn't have happened. Or I might have got over it sooner. I'll never know.'

'There was nothing your father wouldn't do to separate us,' Luca said. 'No matter how wicked or deceitful, it didn't matter as long as he got his own way.'

She nodded. 'I think he believed it would be easy at the start. Only then things spiralled out of control, and he had to do worse and worse things so as not to have to admit he'd been wrong. He kept trying to rewrite the facts to prove he'd been right, and of course he couldn't do it.'

He looked at her quickly. 'You defend him?'

'No, but I don't think he started out as a bad man. He became one because he didn't know how to say sorry. He destroyed us but he also destroyed himself. He knew what he'd done. He couldn't admit it but he knew, and he couldn't face it.'

'Did you ever confront him with what he'd done?'

'Yes, just once. We had a terrible fight and I told him that he'd killed my baby.'

'What did he say?'

'Nothing. Just stared at me and turned white. Then he walked away. Later I found him staring into space. About a year after that he had a massive heart attack. He was only fifty-four, but he died almost instantly.'

'I am not sorry for him,' Luca said with bitter emphasis. 'I do not forgive him, and I will not pretend that I do.'

'I know. I can pity him a little because I saw what he'd done to himself as well as to us. But forgiveness is more than I can manage too. Besides...'

She was silent for a long moment, getting up and pacing the room as though tormented by indecision.

'What is it?' he asked, looking up at her quickly. 'Is there more?'

'Yes, there's something I've been waiting to tell you,

but it had to be when the moment was right. Now, I think...'

She stopped, torn by indecision, even though she knew there was no turning back. Luca took her hands between his.

'Tell me, Becky,' he said. 'Whatever it is, it's time I knew.'

CHAPTER ELEVEN

'Yes,' she said. 'You ought to know. Luca, have you ever been back to Carenna?'

'No,' he said after a moment.

'Me neither, until recently. I went a few weeks ago, and I found out something else my father lied about.'

She stopped again. Suddenly the next part seemed momentous, and she wondered if she had been wise to start.

'Go on,' he said.

'I'd always thought she died without being baptised, without a name. Dad never told me otherwise.'

'You mean—?'

'She's there, in the churchyard. She was baptised by the hospital chaplain.'

'But how could you not have known?'

'They took her away to the incubator as soon as she was born, while I stayed behind for the nurses to finish tending to me. The chaplain was already in the baby unit, seeing another child. They thought our little girl might only have a few minutes, so he baptised her there and then, in case he wasn't in time.'

'And they never told anybody?'

'Yes, they told Dad. I suppose they assumed he'd tell me, but he never did. But she was buried in consecrated ground.

'The priest died last year, but I spoke to the new one, and it's all there in the records. Apparently the priest held a little funeral, and told Dad when it was going to be. He couldn't tell me, because my father kept him away, and he didn't know where you were. So when our daughter was buried—' a tremor shook her '—none of her family were there.'

'Not even your father?'

'He wanted to pretend that she never existed, and he wanted *me* to forget about her. So he tried to blot her out, and blot you out. He even told the priest her name was Solway.'

'You mean—?'

'That's the name on her grave,' she said with rising anger. 'Rebecca Solway. But she's there, Luca. She didn't vanish into the void. He didn't manage to obliterate her, not completely.'

Luca rose violently and paced the room as though sitting still was suddenly intolerable. He began to shake his head like a beast in pain, and she thought she had never seen a man's face look so ravaged.

At last he came to a halt, and without warning swung his fist into the wall. It landed with a thunderous shock, and immediately he did it again, and then again. It was as well that the old cottage was made of solid stone or it could never have withstood the impact of his rage and agony.

'Oh, God!' he kept saying. 'Dear God! Dear God!'

Torn with pity for him, she put her arms around his body. He didn't stop thumping the wall, but his free hand grasped her so tightly that he almost crushed her.

'Luca—Luca, please...'

She wasn't sure that he heard her. He seemed lost in a haze of misery, where only the rhythmic thumping made sense.

At last he was too tired to go on, and leaned his head

against the stone, shaking with distress. Rebecca rested her own head against his back, weeping for him. She could endure her own pain, but his pain tore her apart.

He turned far enough to draw her against his chest in a convulsive grip.

'Hold on to me,' he said hoarsely, 'or I shall go mad. Hold me, Becky, hold me.'

He almost fell against her. All his massive physical strength seemed to have drained out of him, and there was only hers left to save him.

She did as he asked and held him. The path he was travelling was one she herself had walked only a short time before, and she resolved that he would not walk it alone, as she had done.

Leaning on her, he got back to the chair and almost fell into it. His eyes were vacant, as though fixed on some inner landscape where there was only desolation.

His right hand was red and raw where the wall had torn it, and she gently took hold of it, sensing how even the lightest touch made him wince. She began to dab it with water, her eyes blurred with tears at what he had done to himself in his torment.

She dropped to one knee beside him so that she could clean the bleeding wound. He stared at it, as though wondering how it had happened.

'What did it look like?' he asked at last.

'What, darling?' The word slipped out naturally.

'Her grave, what was it like?'

'Just a little grave, very plain and small, with the name and the date she was born and died.'

'And nobody of her own was there at her funeral,' Luca murmured. This fact in particular seemed to trouble him. 'Poor little thing. Laid away in darkness, all alone.'

He shook his head as though trying to get free of something.

'I was glad when I found out,' Rebecca said. 'It's better than her having no baptism and no proper burial. I thought you'd be glad too.'

'I am glad about that,' he said quickly. 'But we should have been told. If I'd known, I would have gone back there to see her, often. She wouldn't have been alone.'

It was as if a light had shone through her mind, illuminating him as never before. Luca was an Italian, with the Italian's attitude to death. Like almost everything else in Italy, it was a family matter. A child's grave was visited regularly, with flowers and tokens on birthdays, because even in death that child was a member of the family. To him it was an outrage that his daughter had lain unvisited for fifteen years.

'She's still there, waiting for us,' she said. 'Perhaps it's time her parents visited her together.'

He couldn't speak. Dumbly he nodded.

'But you should see a doctor about your hand first.'

He made an impatient movement. 'It's nothing.'

'I've only got water to clean it with, and I'm afraid it will get infected. Or you may have broken something.'

'Nonsense, I'm never hurt.'

'Oh, yes, you are,' she said softly. 'Now, come and lie down.'

After a moment he nodded and let her lead him to his bed. His hand was clearly painful and he had to accept her help to undress down to vest and shorts, but when she mentioned it he said gruffly, 'It'll be all right tomorrow.'

By the next day it was swollen and still hurting him, but he wouldn't consider 'wasting time' with a doctor.

His manner was feverish, as though nothing mattered but getting to Carenna as fast as possible.

'We can't go in that van,' Rebecca observed. 'Where's your car?'

'Garaged in the village, with the man who hired me the van.'

'You'll have to show me how to drive it.'

'I'll drive it.'

But he had to give up after the first mile, and she drove the clanking vehicle the rest of the way.

'Turn left, down there,' he said almost as soon as they were in the village. 'Becky, I said down there.'

'Later,' she said, bringing the van to a noisy halt outside the doctor's surgery. 'First we go in here.'

'I told you I'm all right,' he groaned.

'And I'm telling you that you're not.'

'Becky, I don't want—'

She lost her temper.

'Did I ask you what you want? Luca, it's very simple. I'm the only person who can drive at the moment, and I'm going nowhere until you've been to the doctor.'

'That's blackmail.'

'Yes, it is. So what?'

'You're just being stupid.'

'Fine, then the doctor can tell me so.'

But the doctor said no such thing. He was an old man with modern ideas, who'd equipped his surgery with a lot of good equipment, including a small X-ray machine. It took only a short time to establish that Luca had cracked two bones and smashed a third.

'It's good that you came straight to me, *signore*,' said the doctor as he set the hand in plaster. 'Otherwise your hand would have been crippled. You were very wise.'

He regarded them knowingly. 'Or maybe you are just fortunate in your wife?'

'Yes,' Luca said.

'Here are some painkillers, and two of these other pills will give you a good night. I hope you weren't planning anything strenuous for the rest of today.'

'No,' Rebecca said quickly. 'We were thinking of a journey, but now we've put it off until tomorrow.'

Luca simply nodded. He was looking worn and ill, and she sensed that this was only partly due to his injured hand. It was as though all the fight had gone out of him. He even agreed to stay quietly in the doctor's waiting room while she returned the van and collected the car.

It was dusk as she drew up at the cottage, and she immediately set about getting the place warm and making him comfortable. His appetite was poor but he managed to eat some pasta with his left hand.

'Go to bed now,' she said gently. 'And I think you should take the proper bed, and I'll have the mattress.'

But he shook his head firmly and she made no further protest. He accepted her help undressing, then let her usher him into the rough bed like a mother with an exhausted child. He touched her hand briefly.

'Thank you,' he said. 'For everything.'

She squeezed his hand, kissed him briefly and hurried out.

They were on the road early next morning, eating up the miles to Carenna in the silkily gliding car.

For this journey they had abandoned the jeans and sweaters in which they had been living, becoming sober and conventional again. In a severe, well-cut suit, Luca might have been the man she'd met again months ago, but he was not that man. His face had changed. It was thinner and almost haggard, as though he'd aged overnight.

At the start of the journey she touched his hand, and he briefly smiled at her, but then seemed to withdraw into a place inside himself. She could only guess at the suffering that was there.

They reached Carenna in the early afternoon and drove straight to the church. The town had grown since they were last there together, the streets were more crowded, and once they were caught in a traffic jam.

'Do you remember the hospital?' she asked, indicating the building through the window.

'Yes, I remember.'

They were moving again, turning a corner so that he could see the builders working at the rear. He followed it with his eyes until the building was out of sight.

In another few minutes they had reached the little church, where they had once planned to be married. As she parked the car Rebecca glanced at Luca, wondering what he was thinking and feeling. But his set face showed no reaction and she was slightly disappointed. Until then she had felt that this was something they were doing together. Now she began to feel that he was further away than she had suspected, in a place where she was not invited to follow.

'Is she here?' Luca asked as they entered the churchyard. 'Can you show me where she lies?'

'Yes, come with me.'

The little grave was in a far corner and they had to pick their way carefully because the graveyard was densely crowded. At last they reached the little enclosed section where several children lay together.

'Why are they here and not with their families?' Luca wanted to know.

But then his eyes fell on the sign, *Gli Orfani*. Orphans. She saw him flinch.

At the end of the line they found the tiny grave bearing the legend 'Rebecca Solway', and the date of her birth and death. The stone was no longer quite straight, and although the grass had been cut back neatly the grave still looked as though it was struggling not to vanish among the others.

Luca dropped to one knee, leaning forward and peering at the words. Rebecca knelt beside him and saw how he reached out one big hand and laid it flat on the grass.

'She must have been so tiny,' he said in a choking voice.

'Yes, she was. You could have held her in that hand.'

He closed his eyes. She could feel him trembling and her heart ached for him. She waited for him to turn to her.

The moment stretched on and on. He did not move and his eyes stayed fixed on the stone. At last she got up and walked away.

The little church was empty as she pushed the door open. Everything was quiet and her footsteps sounded very loud. It was disappointing that Father Valetti wasn't here. She had liked the young priest with his round, friendly face and understanding eyes.

She strolled out again and saw Luca coming towards her.

'Thank you for leaving me alone with her,' he said briefly. 'Shall I wait here while you go back?'

'Yes, I...'

She stopped, realising that someone was hailing her from near the gate.

'It's him,' she said, pleased. 'It's Father Valetti.'

The father advanced, a big smile on his plump, youthful face, recognising her.

'I'm sorry I wasn't here,' he said. 'I've been at the bank. I'm afraid I'm not very good at finance.' He shook Rebecca's hand. 'I'm so glad you came back.'

'I always meant to, when the time was right. Father Valetti, this is Luca Montese.'

'The little girl's *papa*,' said the priest immediately, shaking Luca's hand. 'Have you been to see her?'

Luca nodded.

'And she does not seem quite real,' the father said. 'You think, what does this patch of earth have to do with my child? Especially after so long.'

Luca looked at him with sudden interest.

'Yes,' he said. 'That was exactly how it felt. It has been so long—I didn't know she was here.'

'But one day you were bound to come,' said Father Valetti gently. 'And she has waited for you.'

'I'm grateful to you for taking care of her. May I look round your church?'

'Of course. It will be my pleasure to show you.'

Rebecca slipped away to have a few moments alone with her daughter. When she returned the two men were deep in conversation, and she knew that Luca had discovered what she had discovered herself, that this was a good man, and easy to talk to.

He can talk to him, she thought sadly. *But not me.*

Luca smiled as he saw her, but he seemed abstracted, as though some thought was occupying him.

'What did you mean about the bank?' he asked the priest. 'Is the church in financial trouble?'

'We will be if I can't pay off the two-million loan I've just arranged,' Father Valetti said, with a weak attempt at humour.

'Two million euro?' Luca echoed. 'Is the church falling down?'

'Not the church. The money is for the new baby unit that we're building at the hospital. Costs are spiralling out of control, and without the loan we might have had to give up the work. It was my decision to sponsor that unit but, as I say, I have no gift for finance.' He grimaced. 'The archbishop is not pleased with me.'

'But you managed it?' Luca asked.

'On conditions. The bank wants guarantors, so now I must go around local businessmen asking each of them to guarantee part of the loan. And they all know what I want, and will run when I approach.'

'Then don't approach them,' Luca said.

'I don't understand.'

'I'll take care of it.'

'You mean you will guarantee the loan?'

'No, I mean you don't need a loan. I'll give you the money.'

Father Valetti looked doubtful, and Luca gave him a wry smile. 'It's all right, I have the money. I won't let you down. Will it be enough, or will the unit need more?'

'You can afford more?' the priest asked, wide-eyed.

Luca took out his cellphone and dialled Sonia.

'How long will it take to transfer three million euros?' he asked. 'Can you do it in twenty-four hours? Good. Then send it to this destination.'

He read out from a piece of paper that the priest hast-ily scribbled for him. When he hung up he spoke in a hard voice.

'I'd like the baby unit named after my daughter.'

'Of course.'

'Rebecca Montese. Not Solway.'

'It shall be done. It is most generous—'

Luca shook his head to silence his thanks. 'Let me know if you need more,' he said. He handed the priest a card. 'This is my headquarters in Rome. That number will get you through to my assistant, and she will call me, any time. Are you ready to go?' This was to Rebecca.

On the way home she struggled with her thoughts. She wanted to thank him, but was checked by the feeling that she had no right to. In a strange way his action had had nothing to do with her. Luca had reclaimed his daughter, but he'd done so alone, in a way that excluded her.

Now she understood how much hope she had invested in this moment. She had never realised that it could strand her in limbo.

Why? she asked herself as they headed home in the gathering dusk. Why had it happened like this? She had thought they were travelling a road that would bring them together, but she'd been deluding herself. Luca had turned off abruptly onto another road where all could be made well with money. He was, after all, a businessman, and she had been foolish to forget it.

What price one daughter? Three million euros. Signed, sealed and sorted.

You couldn't criticise a man who'd just endowed a baby unit and potentially saved many lives. Not even if you knew he'd bolted and barred his own heart in the process.

The cottage was still mercifully warm as they hurried in and settled determinedly into the domestic details, as though in them lay safety.

He did not speak during the meal, except to thank her. When she stole a look at his face she found it set like stone. Never once did she find him looking at her, or seeking in any way to reach out to her.

Darkness was falling as she went outside to collect more logs for the range. As she worked her mind was turning, making plans. She knew now that her future must be without Luca. He had dealt with this in his own way, and it could not be her way. He could not have made it plainer that he did not need her, and from now on their roads lay apart.

It was good that her love for him had died, and none of this hurt as much as it might once have done. She told herself this, and tried hard to believe it.

She had just finished piling logs in her arms, when she heard the first scream.

At first she couldn't imagine what it was, and stood listening. After a moment the scream came again, and then again. There was no doubt now that they were coming from inside the cottage. Dropping the logs, she began to run.

Luca was sitting where she'd left him, his hands on the table. His fists were clenched, but he wasn't punching this time, just leaning on them, his head down, while the sounds that came from him were those of a tormented animal. A bear, caught in an agonising steel trap, might have made those sounds.

On and on they went while she watched in horror. He seemed unable to stop.

'Luca—'

He straightened up and raised his fists to his head, covering his eyes, while the terrible howls went on.

It was ghastly, and worst of all was her realisation of her own stupidity. She had thought him unfeeling because he didn't speak of his emotions, but what he felt went too deep for that. He was telling her now, without words, that he suffered to the point of madness.

'Darling...' she whispered, putting her arms about him.

At once his own arms went around her, and he buried his face against her, clinging to her, as though there was nothing else in the world that could make him feel safe.

It had been bad enough when she first told him, and he'd punched the wall, but that was nothing. Today had come near to destroying him, and he was begging for her help in the only way he could.

'All these years,' he gasped, 'she's been alone—we never knew—'

'No, we never knew. But we won't let her be alone any more. Luca, Luca...'

She wanted to say a million things but now it was she who could not find words. She could only murmur his name over and over while she held him close, feeling his shoulders shake with the sobs that had been held in for fifteen years.

When, at last, the storm abated he leaned wearily against her, still trembling, but growing quieter.

'It just happened suddenly,' he said huskily. 'One moment I was coping, and the next I was engulfed in hell.'

'Yes, that's what happened to me. There's no defence against it. You have to feel it until it passes.'

'Does it pass?' he asked in a voice that tore her heart with its despair.

'In the end, yes. But you have to feel it first.'

'I can't do it alone.'

'You don't have to. I'm here. You're not alone.'

He looked up at her, his face ravaged and stained with tears.

'I'll be alone when you leave.'

She took his face between her hands and kissed him gently.

'Then I won't leave.'

At first he didn't react, as though she had said something too momentous to be true. Then he said,

'You don't mean that.'

'I can't leave you, Luca. I love you. I've always loved you, and I always will. We belong together.'

Very slowly he drew back a few inches, and laid his hand over her stomach, looking up with a question in his eyes.

'Yes,' she said. 'It's true.'

Silently he laid his face against her again, not trembling now, but finally at peace. When she took his hand he followed her into her room without protest.

CHAPTER TWELVE

As the first light came through the window Luca said softly,

'I thought you were never going to tell me that you were carrying our child.'

'How long have you known?'

'Almost at once. There was something about you— just like last time.'

'You can remember that?' she asked in a wondering voice.

'I remember everything about you, from the first moment we met.'

They had lain in each other's arms all night, sometimes talking, but mostly silent, seeking and finding consolation in each other's presence. As the minutes passed into hours she felt the shell about her heart crack and fall apart, releasing her from the imprisonment of years, and had known that it was the same with him.

'I guessed about the baby almost as soon as I saw you,' he said, 'but I couldn't see any hope for us then. I knew I'd made a mess of everything. You used to say I went at things like a bull at a gate, and it was true. I've gone on doing things that way all these years, because I could make it work for me. By the time we met again, I'd forgotten that there was any other way.'

'Yes,' she said tenderly. 'I gathered that.'

'When we were young I knew how to talk to you. It was easy to tell you that I loved you. There was nothing in the world but love, nothing that mattered. When we met again, there were so many other things that seemed important. Chiefly my pride.

'I sought you out because I'd convinced myself that you were the one woman in the world who could give me a child. It was nonsense, of course.

'Sonia saw it. She said at the start that I only believed it because I wanted it to be true, and she was right. So I came looking for you, convinced that I had a sensible, logical reason, because I couldn't admit the truth to myself.'

'And what was the truth?' Rebecca asked softly.

'That I'd never stopped loving you in all those years; that life without you was desolate and empty. All that time there was a barrier about my heart. I built it up year after year, thinking if it was thick enough it would protect me, but in the end it didn't, thank God.

'Then I found you, and I bought shares at the Allingham to give myself an excuse to meet you. I thought I'd planned it all so well.'

He gave a faint smile, aimed at himself. 'If you could have seen me on the night we met. I was almost sure you'd be at Steyne's house, and I was in a state of nerves. I heard your voice in the hall and I nearly panicked and ran. Then you came in with Jordan, and you were so beautiful, but so different, I didn't know what to say to you.

'I don't know what I expected—that'd you'd greet me by name, run into my arms? But you didn't seem to know me. You were so cool and poised and suddenly I was the country bumpkin again, fumbling for words.

'I tried to rush you—well, you remember that. But all I knew how to do was give orders, and you seemed to get further away with everything I said or did. I nearly blew it with those diamonds, but I couldn't think what else to do.'

'So you went at it bull-headed,' she said, smiling.

'As always. When I came here I'd given up all hope. I just wanted to look at the place where we'd been so happy. And when I saw you, I didn't dare believe that we might have another chance.'

He raised himself on his elbow, anxiously searching her face in the faint dawn light.

'We do have another chance, don't we?' he asked.

'We do if we want it.'

'I want nothing in the world but you.'

'And the baby,' she reminded him.

'Just you. The baby is a bonus. But the point of everything is you.'

He was asleep before she could answer, as though simply saying the words had brought him peace. All strain seemed to have drained away from him, as it had from her, and now she understood why.

For fifteen years they had been denied the right to grieve together for their child. That denial had been a disaster, freezing something in their hearts, preventing them both from moving on.

It was not too late, she thought, holding him close and watching the dawn grow. They were free now, free to feel the pain of their loss, and then free to grow beyond it, to find each other again.

She heard a faint pattering of rain on the roof. It became louder until she knew they were in the middle of a downpour.

It went on for several days, and during that time they never left the house. Some of the time they spent in talking, but mostly they just lay in each other's arms, beyond the need for words.

At last they made love, gently and tenderly. There was pleasure still, but it mattered less than the love they had found again, and at last he held her in his arms, whispering, 'Rebecca.'

'You called me Rebecca,' she said in wonder. 'Not Becky.'

'I've been doing so for some time. Have you not noticed?'

'Yes, I think I have,' she said, and fell asleep in his arms.

She had the strange, comforting fantasy that the water pouring down on the little house in a torrent was washing away all pain and bitterness. When the last of the storm had passed they went out together to look down the valley at the clean washed world.

'Breakfast,' she said.

Soon there were other things that would have to be said, but for the moment she wanted to think only of the small prosaic matters, and make this enchanted time last as long as possible.

'Breakfast,' he said, understanding her perfectly.

He helped her, fumbling slightly because of the plaster on his hand.

'I guess you won't get mad the next time I try to take care of you,' he said, waggling his fingers. 'I've never bullied you like you bullied me that day.'

'Some men need bullying,' she told him.

'Now, where did I hear that before? Oh, yes, it was what Mama used to say to Papa.'

'And what did he say?'

'Nothing. Just stood to attention.'

He suited the action to the words and she laughed. He grinned back, regarding her tenderly. There was a different quality to their laughter. It was no longer tense and brittle now that it was not being used to keep reality at bay.

One morning she opened her eyes slowly to find that, as always, the cottage was warm because Luca had risen earlier and built up the range. Pulling on her robe, she went out to find him bringing in a final load of logs; he dumped them in the basket, and blew on his hands.

Smiling, she went to him and took his hands between her own, trying to rub some warmth into them.

'That's lovely,' he said. Then, mischievously, he put his chilly fingers against her neck, and she shrieked.

'Sorry.' He grinned. 'It's just that your neck is so deliciously warm, and it's freezing out there.'

'Well, it's lovely in here.'

'And, as you will have observed, the kettle is boiling.' He indicated it with a flourish. 'If you'd care to sit down, it'll be ready for you in a moment.'

She let him enjoy himself cosseting her, but she was thoughtful, and he seemed to understand, because he was quiet until they were both eating.

'How are you feeling this morning?' he asked. 'Any sickness?'

'No, that's gone now, thank goodness.'

'But there is something on your mind, isn't there?'

'Yours too,' she agreed. 'I've felt it for the last few days.'

'I feel it every time I go in that cold yard. Winter's coming, and soon it'll be a lot colder.'

She nodded. 'It's been wonderful, being here like this, but I guess it's coming to an end.'

'It has to,' he agreed regretfully. 'Both for your sake and the baby's.'

'So what have you planned?'

'Nothing,' he said quickly. 'I was waiting for you to make suggestions.'

'You haven't arranged anything? You?'

'I may have had a few ideas—'

'I somehow thought you might have done,' she said, smiling.

'But they're only ideas. You may not like them, and then we could think of something else.'

Her lips twitched. 'You're making an awfully good stab at being "reticent man", Luca, but I can tell it's a struggle.'

'I'm doing my best, but I admit it doesn't come naturally.'

'Why not just abandon it and tell me what arrangements you've made?'

'They're not arrangements—not exactly. I only called my housekeeper in Rome, and told her to have the house ready—just in case.'

'Very sensible. You never know when you might decide to up sticks and go home.'

'But only if you want to. Would you rather go back to England?'

'Would you come with me?'

'Anywhere that's warm, as long as it isn't the Allingham.'

'No, I haven't got a home in England,' she said. 'There's nothing to go back to.'

'Then let's go forward. My house—it's never been a home, but you could make it one—'

'Let's take it one step at a time,' she said gently.

They started preparing for departure immediately after breakfast. It didn't take long. Luca doused the fire in the range while Rebecca gathered up food and took it outside to scatter for the birds. When she returned to the house he was waiting for her in the doorway, with her coat.

'Are we ready to leave?' he asked, helping her on with it.

'Just a moment. I want to...'

She didn't finish the sentence, but he seemed to understand because he stood back to let her pass inside.

There wasn't much to look around, just the bedroom where they had lain together truly united at last, and the kitchen where they had cooked and talked, and bickered, and rediscovered their lost treasure.

He came with her, not intruding but simply there, holding her hand, letting her know that their feelings were in harmony.

'We were happy here,' she whispered.

'Yes, we were—both times.'

'We will come back, won't we?'

'Whenever you want.'

'Then we can go now.'

With their few things packed into the car they drove back into the village, then he swung onto the road that would take them to Florence, and the *autostrada* that led to Rome. In Florence they stopped for lunch.

'You're not having regrets, are you?' she asked.

'No, of course not.'

'It's just that you're very quiet.'

'I was only thinking—'

'Yes,' she said. 'I've been thinking too. We're only

about twenty miles from Carenna. It wouldn't take very long.'

'Let's do it, then.'

Instead of heading straight for Rome he turned off onto a different road, and they were in Carenna in half an hour. At the church they found Father Valetti in the graveyard, heavily wrapped in scarves, deep in discussion with two men, with whom he seemed to be consulting plans. He hailed them with delight.

'Wonderful to see you. I didn't think you could have had my letter yet.'

'Letter?' Luca echoed. 'We've had no letter.'

'Then it's providence that sent you here just when I needed to talk to you.'

'Is something wrong?' Rebecca asked.

'Oh, no, not at all. It's just that in a tiny churchyard like this we always have trouble finding space, and graves don't last forever. Some of them receive few visitors after ten years, so it's normal practice to rebury those together in a smaller space, to make room for new occupants. But of course the families are always given the option of keeping the original grave for a fee. And I wrote to you to ask your wishes in this regard.'

'Do you mean,' asked Rebecca, 'that our baby is going to be raised?'

'She can be, but of course the coffin will be reinterred elsewhere with all respect.'

'Yes, but where?' Rebecca asked with a rising excitement.

'Well—'

'I mean, couldn't she come to Rome, with us?'

Luca turned on her quickly, his eyes alight.

'It might be possible,' Father Valetti said thoughtfully.

'Of course, it would have to be done in the proper form—lots of paperwork, I'm afraid. Come inside and let's look into it.'

In his office he sorted through forms while Rebecca and Luca sat holding hands, hardly daring to breathe in case their hopes had been raised only to be dashed.

'I'd need to know to which church she will be going,' he said at last, pushing papers across the desk at them, 'and the name of the priest who will conduct the ceremony.'

'I thought of having part of my own grounds consecrated,' Luca said, tense with hope, 'and keeping her with us.'

'Get the priest to send me official notification of the consecration, and I'll arrange the proper transport.'

'Then—it can be done?' Luca asked.

'Oh, yes, it can be done.'

Father Valetti was a tactful man, for he left them quickly. As soon as he was gone they turned to each other, speechless with emotions for which there were no words.

When at last Luca managed to speak, it was to say huskily, 'Thank you for thinking of this, my dearest.'

Rebecca rested her head on his shoulder and at once his hand came up to stroke her hair.

After a while they went out again into the churchyard and made their way quietly to the place where the little grave lay. Luca dropped to one knee, and laid his hand on the ground, looking intently at the spot.

Rebecca stayed back a little, guessing that what Luca wanted to say to his child was for themselves alone. Nor did she need to hear the words, for they echoed in her own heart.

'Be patient awhile longer, little one. Your mother and father are taking you home at last. And you will never be lonely again.'

When Luca had mentioned the grounds of his house Rebecca had somehow formed the impression of a very large garden. What she found was an extensive estate, partly covered with woodland.

It stood just outside Rome, on the Appian Way, a mansion, with more rooms than one man could possibly need. She didn't need his confirmation to know that it had been bought as a status symbol and chosen by Drusilla.

Despite this, there was no hint of Drusilla's presence, partly because she had stripped the place of all she could carry, and partly because, as Luca explained,

'We called it our home for lack of anything else to call it. But it was never a true home. We did not love each other, and there are no regrets.'

She knew instinctively that this was true, believing that a house where there had been love always carried traces of that love. Here there were no such traces. She and Luca could make of this home whatever they pleased.

He chose the brightest, sunniest room for the nursery, and decorated it himself in white and yellow.

'I'll paint pictures on the wall after the baby's born,' he said. 'When we know if it's a boy or a girl.'

'Have you thought about names?' she asked.

'Not really. At one time, if it was a girl I'd have wanted to call her Rebecca, after her mother. But now...'

'Now?' she urged. She wanted to hear him say it.

'We already have one daughter of that name. To have

two would be like saying the first one didn't count, and I don't want to do that.'

She nodded, smiling at him tenderly. If there was one thing above all others that made her heart reach out to Luca it was his way of recognising their child as a real person, who had lived, even if only for a short time, and died with an identity.

'What was your mother's name?' she asked.

'Louisa.'

'Louisa if it's a girl, Bernardo if it's a boy.'

He did not reply in words, but his look showed his gratitude.

'I think Bernardo Montese sounds good,' she mused.

But he shook his head. 'Bernardo Hanley.'

'What?'

He hesitated slightly before saying, 'Where the mother is unmarried, the child takes her surname.'

'I don't like that idea.'

Luca took her hand and spoke gently. 'Neither do I, Rebecca. But the decision is yours.'

They were married quietly, in the tiny local church. Luca held her hand as though unwilling to risk letting her go for a moment, and there was a calm intensity in his manner that told her, better than any words, what this day meant to him.

When the birth began he refused to leave her. It was harder and longer than last time, but at last their son lay in her arms, and she and her husband were closer than they had ever been.

'You have your heir,' she told him, smiling.

But he shook his head.

'Labourers don't have heirs,' he said, as he had said once before. 'It was a child that I wanted. Your child, and nobody else's.' He touched her face. 'Now I have everything I want—well, except perhaps for one thing more.'

He had his wish in the spring when their daughter came home at last, and was laid in the spot he had chosen.

'I thought it would be nice here, surrounded by the trees,' he said to Rebecca when the service was over and they were alone. 'And there's plenty of room, do you see?'

She nodded, understanding.

'You don't mind?' he asked, a little anxiously.

'No, I'm glad you thought of it. But I want many years together first. We were apart for too long, and we have so much to make up.'

He kissed her hands and spoke with the same calm fervour as at their wedding.

'Years ago,' he said, 'two nights before we were to be married, I promised you that my heart, my love and my whole life belonged to you, and always would.

'Now I say it again. I will spend all my days making up to you for the suffering I couldn't prevent. And when life is over, nothing will change. Do you understand that? Nothing. For then I shall be with you forever, and that is all the world can hold for me.'

ASSIGNMENT: BABY

by

Jessica Hart

Jessica Hart was born in West Africa, and has suffered from itchy feet ever since, travelling and working around the world in a wide variety of interesting but very lowly jobs, all of which have provided inspiration on which to draw when it comes to the settings and plots of her stories. Now she lives a rather more settled existence in York, where she has been able to pursue her interest in history, although she still yearns sometimes for wider horizons. If you'd like to know more about Jessica, visit her website www.jessicahart.co.uk.

CHAPTER ONE

Fresh from her success in last Friday's award ceremony, Britain's favourite redhead, TV presenter Fionnula Jenkins, arrives at London's hottest restaurant, Cupiditas, with Gabriel Stearne, founder of US construction giant Contraxa (above). The couple met in New York, where Fionnula attended a charity ball sponsored by Contraxa. Entrepreneur Gabriel's activities are more usually reported in the financial pages, but since arriving in London he has been seen out several times with Fionnula, who refused to confirm speculation that he had moved to England to be with her. 'We just enjoy each other's company,' she said.

TESS had barely finished reading the caption when the door to the inner office opened, and she shoved the paper hurriedly out of sight in the wastepaper bin beneath her desk.

By the time Gabriel appeared, shrugging himself into an overcoat, she was innocently absorbed in typing up the letters he had dictated earlier.

'I'm going to a meeting with our insurers,' he said, brusquely buttoning his coat. 'Have those letters ready by the time I get back. I want a copy of the design report and the architects' files on my desk. All of them. In date order.'

'Yes, Mr Stearne,' said Tess.

Her voice was cool, with just a hint of a Scottish accent. Gabriel eyed her sardonically. She was watching him over the spectacles she wore when she was working, pen poised to note his instructions, the very model of a perfect PA.

In the four weeks she had worked for him he had learned

only three things about Tess Gordon. She was exceptionally efficient. She was always immaculately groomed.

And she didn't like him one little bit.

Too bad, thought Gabriel indifferently. He wasn't here to be liked. He was here to drag this company into the twenty-first century and give himself the toe-hold he needed into Europe, and worrying about what the icy Ms Gordon thought about him was very low down his priority list.

'When you've done that, you can send an e-mail reminding all staff that the phones are not for their personal use,' he went on in a hard voice. 'That goes for e-mail as well. A monitoring system is going to be introduced shortly, so they'd better start getting used to it now.'

An order like that would no doubt cause a furore, but Tess didn't react. She just made a note on her pad and kept her inevitable reflections to herself.

'Any messages?' Gabriel asked curtly.

'Your brother rang. He asked if you could ring him back.'

Gabriel grunted, and privately Tess marvelled that he could be related to the irreverent American with the voice like warm treacle who had rung while his brother was closeted in his office. 'No calls,' Gabriel had said, and after a month Tess knew better than to try and interrupt him, no matter how important the caller might be.

Greg, as he had introduced himself, was evidently an incorrigible flirt. Tess, braced to dislike anyone even remotely associated with Gabriel, had found him charming. He had been warm, funny, sympathetic…everything his brother was not!

Unaware—or, more likely, uncaring—of the unflattering comparisons she had drawn, Gabriel was checking that he had all the relevant papers for his meeting in his attaché case. 'Anything else?'

'No,' said Tess, but she hesitated and Gabriel looked up

from the case. He had very light, very keen grey eyes that were a startling contrast to his strong, black brows, and she still hadn't got used to the way they seemed to look right through her.

'What?' he demanded.

'I wondered what time you would be back, that was all.'

'About six-thirty. Why?'

'I was hoping to have a word with you.' Tess's calm expression gave no hint of her inner trepidation.

Gabriel frowned. 'What about?'

Nobody could ever accuse him of beating about the bush, thought Tess with an inward sigh. She had to ask him for a rise, but it wasn't the kind of thing you could blurt out just like that.

'I'd rather explain when you're in less of a hurry,' she said.

'Can't it wait until tomorrow?'

'We'll be busy putting the Emery bid together tomorrow,' Tess pointed out. And then it would be the weekend, which would mean two more days to worry about Andrew. She set her teeth. It went against the grain to beg, but she had to try. 'If you could spare me five minutes when you get back, I would appreciate it.'

Gabriel looked at her. She had one of those faces that made it almost impossible to tell what she was thinking. It wasn't that she was unattractive. She had a fine-boned face with clear skin and beautiful eyebrows, and her hair, always pulled neatly back, was an unusual golden-brown colour. She might even be pretty, he thought dispassionately—if she ever lightened up and got rid of that snooty expression of hers.

It occurred to him suddenly that she might be going to hand in her notice, and his black brows drew together. He didn't have the time to find a new PA with this crucial contract coming up. He had inherited Tess when he'd taken over SpaceWorks, and her knowledge of the company was invaluable. He couldn't afford to lose her just yet. It was worth putting up with the frosty atmosphere until he got things under control.

'Very well,' he said, irritable at the thought of wasting precious time trying to cajole her into staying. 'If you wait until I get back, I'll see you then.'

'Thank you.'

That was typical Tess. No gush or fuss, just a cool thank you. Gabriel had never seen her anything but crisp, composed, competent. In many ways she was the ultimate personal assistant. She never flapped. When he shouted, she didn't get upset or muddled. She was intelligent and discreet. Gabriel knew that she was ideal.

It was just that he would like her more if she made the occasional mistake.

Or smiled.

Annoyed to realise that he'd allowed himself to be diverted, Gabriel shut his attaché case with snap and headed for the door. 'Oh, and book a table at Cupiditas,' he remembered at the last moment. 'Tonight, nine o'clock.'

Why could he never use the word 'please'? Tess wondered. It wasn't that hard to say. 'For two?'

'Yes, for two,' he barked, irritated anew by her composure. Most people either fawned or trembled in his presence, but not Tess. No, she just sat there in her sensible grey suit and looked down her nose at him.

'Certainly, Mr Stearne,' she said.

Gabriel scowled. 'I'll be back later,' he said, and strode out.

The moment he had gone, Tess retrieved the paper from the bin and smoothed out the crumpled page as she read the caption again, shaking her head in disbelief. Gabriel Stearne and Fionnula Jenkins! Who would have thought it?

All day, e-mails had been flying around the office about their unpopular new boss's appearance in the gossip columns. Tess had seen them, and had assumed that it was all some kind of joke until one of the other secretaries had brought along a copy of yesterday's paper to show her.

Now she studied the photograph, half expecting to spot that it was all a mistake, but no, it was definitely Gabriel. No one else had brows like that! Some of the girls in the office claimed to find him attractive, and were always dropping by in the hope of catching a glimpse of him, but Tess couldn't see what the fuss was about. To her, Gabriel wasn't broodingly handsome. He was just surly.

And there he was in the paper, looking as grimly formidable as ever, with Fionnula Jenkins clinging girlishly to his arm and smiling that famous Fionnula smile. Tess had never seen a more mismatched pair. Fionnula had all the gloss and glitz of a star. Gabriel was a workaholic, abrupt, impatient and, in Tess's opinion at least, downright rude.

What did a celebrity like Fionnula see in him? Tess wondered as she tossed the paper back in the bin and dialled the restaurant's number. Fionnula was beautiful and successful. She could have anybody she wanted, so why pick on Gabriel? It couldn't be money, as Fionnula had plenty of her own, and it certainly wasn't charm.

Perhaps, mused Tess, Fionnula was the kind of girl who liked a challenge. Gabriel's reputation had preceded him from the States. He was known to be utterly ruthless and unsentimental. If Fionnula thought she could find a heart beating somewhere beneath that steely exterior, good luck to her, thought Tess wryly. She was welcome to him.

By six, she had everything ready for Gabriel's return. His table was booked, and the letters, files and reports lay neatly arranged on his desk. Tess checked them automatically. She knew Gabriel was waiting to catch her out, but so far she hadn't made so much as a typing error for him to complain about. It had become an unacknowledged battle of wills between them and, in a perverse kind of way, Tess almost enjoyed the challenge of keeping up with the punishing pace he set.

Now, she squared up the last paper and mentally congratulated herself. Gabriel would have to try a bit harder if he wanted her to be unable to cope.

Back at her desk, she sent Andrew a quick e-mail to tell him a cheque was on its way, and that she hoped to be able to send him more next week, and was just rehearsing the arguments she would make to Gabriel for a rise when the phone rang.

'I've got a visitor here for Mr Stearne,' said the receptionist. 'She won't give her name, but she says it's personal.'

Tess looked at her watch. Gabriel hadn't said anything about a visitor. She hoped this didn't mean he wouldn't have time to listen to her request for a rise after all. 'You'd better send her up,' she said, suppressing a sigh.

She wasn't quite sure what she had expected Gabriel's visitor to be like, but it certainly wasn't the woman of about sixty who pushed a pram into the office a few minutes later.

Trying not to show her surprise, Tess took off her glasses and stood up with a polite smile. 'Can I help you?'

The woman looked around her as if she couldn't decide whether to be daunted or impressed. 'I'm looking for Gabriel Stearne,' she told Tess with a belligerent air.

'I'm afraid he's not here at the moment. I'm his assistant,' Tess explained. 'Perhaps I can help you?'

'I don't know if you can.' Digging around under the pram, the visitor pulled out a copy of yesterday evening's paper. It was folded open at the picture of Gabriel and Fionnula, and she tapped the photo. 'This *is* your Gabriel Stearne?' she asked doubtfully.

Tess looked down at the stern mouth, the dark, striking

brows and the unsmiling face next to the sparkling
Fionnula. 'Yes, that's Mr Stearne,' she said.

'He's not what I expected,' the woman confessed,
frowning down at the picture with Tess. 'Leanne said he
was gorgeous. The most handsome man she'd ever met,
she said.' Her mouth turned down disparagingly. 'I
wouldn't call him handsome, myself, would you?'

'Not personally, no,' said Tess. It wasn't a very loyal
answer, but it was hard enough putting up with his bad
temper without having to rave about his looks as well.

'Ah, well, that's love for you.'

There was a tiny pause. 'Love?' she echoed cautiously.

'That's what Leanne called it. Leanne's my daughter,'
the woman explained, seeing that Tess was still looking
mystified. 'She met Gabriel on a cruise last year. She's a
croupier,' she added proudly, 'and he was one of the first-
class passengers. She said he was a lot of fun.'

A puzzled look came over her face as she looked around
the plush office. 'Somehow I didn't imagine him somewhere like this. Leanne always said he was a free spirit.'

She wasn't the only one who was puzzled. Tess was
still trying to come to terms with the idea of Gabriel hanging around in a casino and being a lot of fun, let alone a
free spirit! She would love to know what the unknown
Leanne was like.

'Well, I'm sorry he's not here,' she said after a moment.
'He won't be back until later. Can I give him a message?'

'You can do better than that,' said the woman, appearing
to make up her mind abruptly. 'You can give him his son.'

For once Tess was shaken out of her composure. 'His
son?' she repeated stupidly.

'That's right.' She nodded towards the pram. 'Harry, his
name is.'

Tess stared at the pram as well. Gabriel, a father? It
seemed very unlikely. 'Um…does he *know* about Harry?'
she asked delicately.

'No.' The woman's mouth closed like a trap. 'Leanne would have it that he wasn't the kind of man you could tie down. I wanted her to tell him about Harry when he was born, but she wouldn't. She was determined to look after him herself. That's all very well, I said, but what about the money side of things? She was going to get a job at home, but then they offered her another contract on the ship. It was just for six weeks, and such good money that she couldn't turn it down.'

Tess was getting confused. She didn't quite understand what her unexpected visitor was trying to say, but one thing she was sure of: the last thing Gabriel would want was to come back to the office and find himself presented with a baby. She would have to stick to essentials.

'I think it's up to your daughter to discuss any paternity issues with him,' she said firmly. 'Mr Stearne keeps his private life quite separate from the office.'

'Leanne's not here to discuss anything,' the woman pointed out. 'That's just the point. The thing is,' she confided, 'I said I'd look after Harry for her while she was away, but a few days ago I heard that I'd won a trip to California. Me! It's the first time I've won anything!

'I've always wanted to go to the States,' she went on wistfully, 'but it means flying out straight away, and I thought I was going to have to turn it down until I saw in the paper last night that Gabriel Stearne was over here. I don't see why I should give up my holiday when Harry's father can look after him just as well.'

'I don't know about that,' said Tess, alarmed. 'He's extremely busy.'

'Not so busy he can't swank around with that Fionnula Jenkins,' said Harry's grandmother, brandishing the paper as proof. 'If he's got time to do that, I reckon he's got time to look after his own son. If you ask me, it's high time he took some responsibility for him. Why should

Leanne have to cope all by herself? She didn't get pregnant by herself, did she?'

'Well, no, obviously not, but—'

'It's not as if I'm leaving him for ever. I'm only going for a fortnight. He's a good baby—he won't be any trouble.'

Tess came hurriedly round the desk as she realised just what the other woman was saying. 'You're not seriously thinking of leaving the baby here?' she said, appalled.

'Why not? From everything Leanne ever said, your precious Gabriel isn't short of a bob or two. I'm sure he'll manage.'

'But you can't just abandon him!'

The woman's chin set stubbornly. 'I'm not abandoning him. I'm leaving him with his father.' She leant over the pram and kissed the baby. 'You be a good boy, love. Your gran'll be back for you in a couple of weeks.'

She glanced at Tess and pointed at the rack underneath the pram. 'He's got everything he needs for a couple of days, but you'll need to buy some more formula and nappies after that.'

'*Nappies?*' Tess was aghast. 'You can't just *go*,' she cried, but the baby's grandmother was already heading for the lifts. 'Look, wait!' she called, hurrying after her. 'Wait!'

But her cry had woken the baby, who promptly began to yell. Distracted, Tess hesitated in the doorway. She couldn't believe his grandmother wouldn't come back to the crying child, but when she ran out into the corridor she was in time to see the lift doors closing and the other woman had gone.

Frantically, Tess pressed the button to call the lift back, only to see its lights descending inexorably. She looked around for help, but the entire floor seemed to be deserted. Everyone else had obviously gone home at five-thirty, like sensible people. Tess wished fervently that she had done the same.

Behind her, Harry had redoubled his cries, and she took her finger off the button. There was no way she was going to catch his grandmother. By the time the lift came back she would be long gone.

Now what was she going to do?

In the office, she could hear the baby at full throttle. Hurrying back, she was alarmed to see that his face was red and contorted. What if he was having some kind of fit? She joggled the pram ineffectually for a while and, when that didn't work, picked him up and cuddled him gingerly against her shoulder the way she had seen her friend, Bella, do with her new baby.

'Shh, it's all right,' she told him, wishing that she believed it herself. Wryly, she remembered the smug way she had laid out the papers on Gabriel's desk and congratulated herself on being able to cope with whatever he threw at her! Her famous unflappability didn't extend to babies, which she found alarming at the best of times.

Tess threw a harassed look at the clock on the wall. If only Gabriel would come back!

It felt like two hours, but according to the clock it was only twenty minutes before Gabriel appeared. He walked into the office to be greeted by an unmistakable sigh of relief.

'Thank God you're back!' said Tess, who would have scorned the very idea of being pleased to see him when he had left only a matter of hours ago.

Gabriel stopped dead at the sight of her. He had left an icily efficient, immaculately groomed PA. He returned to find her clutching a snivelling baby, her pristine blouse crumpled by tears and tiny, clutching hands, and the honey-coloured hair escaping in wisps from its usually demure style.

The black brows contracted. 'What's going on?'

He might enjoy the sight of Tess less than her normal, coolly composed self, but the meeting with the insurers hadn't gone well. There was a good deal of work to be done to get the bid ready for the next day, and the very last thing he needed right now was a bawling infant cluttering up the office.

Gabriel eyed it askance. 'Whose is that baby?' he demanded, without even giving her a chance to reply to his first question.

By this stage Tess was too harassed to think of a way to break the news diplomatically. 'It's yours.'

'What?' he roared so loudly that Harry flinched and began to cry again.

'Don't shout! Now look what you've done!' she accused him. 'I'd just got him to stop, too.' She joggled the baby in her arms until his sobs subsided. 'There, that's better,' she murmured. 'The nasty man's not going to shout any more.'

Gabriel controlled his temper with an effort. 'Tess, will you please explain to me what you are doing with that baby?' he said ominously, laying his attaché case on her desk.

Over the sound of Harry's snuffling cries, Tess told him what she could remember. 'But it all happened so quickly,' she finished. 'One minute I was putting the letters on your desk, the next I was left holding the baby!'

'Let me get this right,' said Gabriel, a muscle beating dangerously in his jaw. 'A woman turns up out of the blue, tells you she's going on holiday and deposits a baby with you...and you let her walk away without even finding out her name?'

When he put it like that, it didn't sound as if she had handled the situation very well, Tess had to admit. 'She said you were Harry's father,' she said lamely.

'And you believed her?'

'I didn't know *what* to believe,' she said, forced onto

the defensive. 'You haven't exactly been forthcoming
about your private life. For all I know, you've got a dozen
sons!'

Gabriel glared at her. 'I can assure you,' he said in gla-
cial tones, 'that I not only have no son, I've never even
been on a cruise, and I certainly haven't seduced any stray
croupiers without being aware of it.'

Biting her lip, Tess looked worriedly down at the baby
in her arms. 'What are we going to do?' she asked.

'*We?*' He lifted his brows in a way that made her long
to haul out and hit him.

'It's not my baby,' she pointed out tightly.

'It's not mine either,' he retorted, ignoring the danger
signals snapping in Tess's brown eyes. 'You're the one
who took responsibility for him. You deal with it.'

The dismissive note in his voice caught Tess on the raw.
For a moment, she could only gape at him, torn between
astonishment at the colossal nerve of the man and inarticulate fury at his callous lack of support.

'Now, just a minute—' she began furiously, but before
she could tell Gabriel exactly what she thought of him, the
phone on her desk began to ring, a loud, jarring sound that
ripped through the tense atmosphere in the office.
Involuntarily, they both turned to look at it.

Gabriel cursed under his breath at the interruption.
'You'd better answer it,' he said snidely. 'It might be
someone else who wants a place to dump a child or a dog
while they go on holiday! Why not tell them all to come
along? Tell them we'll take care of their pot plants too!'

Tess glared at his sarcasm. 'How do you suggest I answer it?' she said through her teeth. 'In case it's escaped
your notice, I've only got two hands and both are full at
the moment! Or am I expected to pick up the phone with
my teeth?'

The phone continued to ring insistently, impossible to
ignore. 'Oh, all right, *I'll* get it,' snapped Gabriel.

He leant over the desk and picked up the phone. 'Yes?' he snarled. 'Oh…Greg…yes, I did get your message…no, there's nothing you can do,' he said brusquely, adding as an afterthought, 'unless you happen to know where I can find a croupier called Leanne?'

Tess couldn't hear what Greg was saying, but it was obviously not what Gabriel was expecting. She saw his face change, and he shot her a quick glance. 'Hold on a second,' he interrupted his brother, 'I think I'd better call you back. Give me two minutes.'

'That was my brother,' he said unnecessarily as he put down the phone. For once he seemed at a loss.

'Your brother? What's *he* got to do with Harry's mother?' asked Tess, bewildered by the unexpected turn of events.

'That's what I'm going to find out.' Gabriel sounded terse. Shrugging off his coat, he headed for his office.

There was something going on, thought Tess, aggrieved, and he clearly had no intention of telling her what it was! 'What am I supposed to do in the meantime?' she said crossly.

'Just…' he gestured vaguely '…keep the baby quiet.'

'Great, thanks a lot!' she muttered as the door shut firmly behind him.

She shifted Harry onto her other arm. He might be small, but he was surprisingly heavy, and she flexed the arm that had been supporting him with a grimace. He was grizzling into her neck, small, sniffling little sobs as if he wanted to cry but was too tired to make the effort.

Tess knew just how he felt. She looked at the clock again, and was amazed to find that it was less than an hour since she had looked up to see the pram being pushed into the office.

Not knowing what else to do with him, Tess walked around the office, patting Harry awkwardly on the back, the way she had seen her friends do with their babies. She wished Gabriel would hurry up. It was all very well for him to tell her to keep Harry quiet, but she couldn't walk up and down like this all night.

The sound of the door opening made her swing round, and Gabriel emerged in his shirt sleeves, looking grimmer than ever.

'Well?' she demanded.

Gabriel loosened his tie as if it felt too tight. 'Greg was on a Caribbean cruise last year,' he told her after a moment. 'He told me that he met a croupier called Leanne, and they had an affair while he was on the ship but, typically of Greg, he can't remember her surname, so we can't track down her mother that way. That doesn't mean that Greg is Harry's father,' he added quickly, 'but at least we know why your visitor picked on me.'

'She definitely said *Gabriel* Stearne,' objected Tess. 'It's not that easy to muddle up Gabriel and Greg.'

The suspicion in her voice made Gabriel grit his teeth. 'Look, you wanted to know what the situation was, and I'm telling you,' he said tautly. He didn't really want to tell Tess about Greg, and give her yet another reason to look down her snooty little nose at him, but she was obviously going to go on asking questions until she had some satisfactory answers. Briefly, Gabriel let himself think longingly of Janette, his PA back in the States, who accepted everything he said unquestioningly.

But Janette wasn't here, and Tess was.

'It turns out that Greg sometimes uses my name when it suits him to let people believe that the G in his name stands for Gabriel and not Gregory,' he told her, resigned. 'He says it gets him better tables in restaurants and seats on overbooked planes and, in the case of the cruise, he upgraded his cabin on the strength of my reputation. Having booked as Gabriel Stearne, he carried on using my name, and it was too late to change it when he met Leanne. Anyway, Greg didn't think it would matter. He knew I would never go on a cruise and it was very unlikely that Leanne would ever read the business pages and see my picture.'

'So it might not just be Leanne who thinks that she has had an affair with you? There could be girls all round the world who believe that you're incredibly handsome, a fantastic lover and great fun to be with?'

Gabriel shot Tess a suspicious look. Her face was quite straight, but there was glint in her eyes and a distinct undercurrent of sarcasm in her voice. Why didn't she come right out and say that the idea of anyone associating him with fun or believing him to be a wonderful lover was absolutely hilarious?

He scowled. 'Right now, we're only concerned with Leanne,' he said quellingly. Not that Tess seemed very quelled.

'And Leanne thinks that Greg is Harry's father?'

'Yes.'

'That would make Harry your nephew,' she said slowly, looking from one to the other as if looking for a resemblance.

'It's a possibility,' Gabriel admitted grudgingly, evidently less than thrilled at the prospect of a new addition to the family.

'Did Greg think that he might be Harry's father?'

Gabriel sat on the edge of her desk and rubbed the back of his neck a little wearily. 'I didn't tell him about Harry,' he said after a moment.

Tess was taken aback. Surely that had been the point of ringing Greg? 'Why not?'

'Because for once in his life, Greg is where he ought to be,' said Gabriel flatly. 'He's in Florida, with my mother. His father—my stepfather—is having open-heart surgery and my mother can't cope on her own. She's not strong at the best of times, and I'd rather he stayed and supported her than came haring over here. It's not as if he knows anything about babies.'

'Oh, unlike us?' said Tess, not even bothering to hide her sarcasm this time.

Gabriel ignored her. Straightening from the desk, he began to pace around the office. 'This is the last thing we need tonight,' he said, muttering under his breath. 'All the figures in our proposal are going to have to be checked, and I want to rewrite the section on our design policy. I haven't got time to run around London looking for an un-named grandmother who's just dumped a baby here.'

'Why don't you ring the police?'

'I can't risk the story getting into the papers. If Greg does turn out to be the father, and my mother got to hear of it, she'd be devastated. She dotes on Greg and she's got enough to deal with at the moment with Ray so ill.'

Tess's arm was aching and she decided to try putting Harry back in his pram. How odd, she thought, as she rocked the pram tentatively, terrified that the baby would start crying again. She wouldn't have had Gabriel Stearne down as a devoted son, but he seemed to be making a lot of effort to spare his mother any trouble. Perhaps deep down he was human, after all? He certainly did a good job of hiding it most of the time!

Oblivious to her thoughts, Gabriel was contemplating his options. Thrusting his hands into his pockets, he hunched his shoulders and continued his pacing, up and down, up and down, until Tess longed to stick out a foot and trip him up.

'I could hire private investigators to track down the baby's mother,' he decided after a little while, frowning at the floor. 'There can't be that many croupiers called Leanne. Make a note to get onto them first thing tomorrow morning,' he added in an aside.

Tess refrained from leaping for her notebook. 'Even if they can find Leanne, she's still got to get back to this country,' she pointed out unhelpfully. 'What are you going to do with him until then?'

'That's what nannies are for.' Having made up his mind what needed to be done, Gabriel was already moving onto thinking about the proposal they had to submit the next day. His shoulders straightened. 'You'd better get hold of an agency now. Say I'll need a nanny for a week initially. With any luck, we'll have been able to track down his mother by then.'

Ready to dismiss the matter from his mind, he turned back towards his office. Tess looked at him in disbelief. 'It's almost seven o'clock,' she said, speaking very slowly and clearly so that he would be sure to understand. 'All the agencies will be closed. I won't be able to contact anyone until tomorrow morning at the earliest.'

Exasperated, Gabriel glowered at her, his jaw working in frustration. Logically, he knew that it wasn't Tess's fault, but her objections seemed designed to prevent him from getting on with more important things. He simply didn't have the time to deal with all this.

'What do you suggest, in that case?' he asked her through gritted teeth.

Tess smiled sweetly at him. 'You'll have to look after him yourself.'

'*Me?*'

'Yes, *you*!' she said, savouring the expression on his face. He looked so aghast that she nearly laughed. 'It seems that Harry is your responsibility, after all.'

'But I don't know one end of a baby from another!'

'It's only for a night,' she told him briskly. 'I'm sure it's just a matter of common sense.'

Gabriel eyed her with acute dislike. A matter of common sense, was it? *She* hadn't looked quite so confident when she'd been holding the baby, had she? He set his jaw.

'I can't do it on my own,' he said. 'You'll have to help me.'

'Sorry,' said Tess, not sounding the slightest bit apologetic. 'I'm going out tonight.'

'On a date?'

He stared at her with unflattering surprise. It had obviously never occurred to him before that she might actually have a life outside the office, let alone be attractive enough to have a date.

'Yes, a date,' she said, peeved, although it wasn't strictly true. She was only meeting some friends, but she didn't feel like telling him that. She was tired of being treated like a cardboard cut-out who got propped in the corner of the office every night!

'Couldn't you break it?'

Silently, Gabriel cursed his absent brother. It went against the grain to beg a favour from anyone, let alone from Tess Gordon with her frosty Scottish voice and her disapproving expression, but he was desperate. There was no way he was going to be left alone with that baby.

'Look, I know it's a lot to ask,' he went on, forcing the words out, 'but I need help. I can't manage Harry on my own. I've never even *held* a baby before.'

The edge of desperation in his voice couldn't help but strike a chord with Tess, but she hardened her heart, remembering how quick he had been to disclaim any responsibility for Harry at first. He hadn't exactly been supportive then, had he?

'You must have friends who could help you,' she said.

'I don't know anyone else in London,' said Gabriel. 'I've only been here a month.'

'Oh?' Tess thought of the newspaper in the bin under her desk. 'I did hear somewhere that you knew Fionnula Jenkins,' she said pointedly.

'Not well enough to ask her to give up her evening and a whole night to take care of a strange baby.'

'You don't know *me* very well, but you're asking me to do it.'

'That's different.' Gabriel glowered at her lack of logic. 'You work for me.'

'I'm your personal assistant, not a nanny!'

'Yes, and it would assist me personally if you helped me look after this baby tonight.'

Tess put up her chin. She wasn't going to be bullied into this! 'I'm sorry,' she said firmly, 'but I—'

'I'll pay you overtime, of course,' Gabriel interrupted her, switching tactics. 'Double the usual rate,' he added cunningly.

It was a masterly stroke. Fatally, Tess hesitated. She had been wondering how she was going to find the money to help Andrew out of his difficulties, and now here was an opportunity to earn some extra cash, without the need to grovel to Gabriel for a pay rise that he would almost certainly refuse.

Could she really afford to turn it down?

'I don't know any more about babies than you do,' she said, but Gabriel could tell she was weakening and he pressed home his advantage.

'You can't know less,' he said. 'Come on, Tess, you can't leave me on my own with him.'

When she thought about how prepared he had been to leave her on her own with Harry, Tess longed to be able to tell him that she most certainly could, but then she made the mistake of looking down at the baby. His face was puckering with misery, and she bent instinctively to pick him up. The poor wee mite had already been abandoned once today. She couldn't walk away and abandon him again.

CHAPTER TWO

SHE sighed. 'All right,' she said, 'I'll help you—but *help* is the operative word.' Lifting her chin, she met Gabriel's gaze with a challenging expression in her clear brown eyes. 'I'm not looking after him all by myself. You're going to have to do your share.'

'Fair enough,' said Gabriel, too relieved to object to any conditions. Anything was better than being left on his own with the baby. 'We'll take him to my apartment,' he went on quickly, before she had a chance to change her mind. 'I can drive you home to get whatever you need for the night, and then we can go straight on.'

He was all set to hustle her off there and then, but things were happening a bit too quickly for Tess's liking. 'We could do with some advice first,' she prevaricated, not sure she was ready to be swept off to Gabriel's apartment just yet. She might have agreed to help him, but there seemed to be a lot of things they hadn't discussed yet, and she wanted to be clear just what it was she had agreed to do.

'I thought you said all the agencies would be closed?' said Gabriel, frowning.

'I'm not talking about ringing an agency. I've got a friend who had a baby earlier this year. Since neither of us know what we're doing, I think it would be worth giving her a ring—if that's OK with you, of course,' she couldn't resist adding with an innocent look that didn't fool Gabriel for a moment. 'I know you don't like us making personal phone calls,' she reminded him virtuously.

'Yes, yes, get on with it!' snapped Gabriel, thinking that staff phone calls were the least of his problems right now.

To his horror, he found the baby thrust into his arms as

24

Tess reached across the desk to twist the phone round to face her. She had Bella's number on the phone's memory, but since she had just reminded Gabriel about his threatened crack-down on personal calls, she decided it would be wiser not to draw attention to it. That meant looking it up in her diary, which was something she rarely had to do with all the technology at her fingertips, and laboriously dialling the number in full.

Not that Gabriel was likely to have noticed. He had followed her to the desk, clearly in case he had to hand Harry quickly back, and was holding him awkwardly at arm's length, eyeing him with a mixture of trepidation and appalled fascination. Tess wouldn't have believed that anyone could look more uncomfortable with a baby than her, but Gabriel managed it easily.

The ruthless arrogance had been wiped from his face now he'd been presented with a baby, she noticed with some amusement. In his shirt sleeves, with his tie askew where he had been tugging at it in frustration, he seemed younger and much more approachable all of a sudden.

That had to be an illusion, thought Tess sourly. She had never met anyone *less* approachable than Gabriel Stearne. He was cold, unscrupulous, and completely out of touch with the people who worked for him, whom he treated with a blend of indifference and contempt.

And this was the man she was going to spend the evening with, she reminded herself with a sinking heart.

Oh, well, she thought, she would just have to keep thinking of the money.

Perching on the front of her desk, she listened to the busy beeping in her ear as the phone connected and watched Gabriel jiggle the baby nervously up and down. For a moment, Harry looked unsure whether he liked it or not and, as his face screwed up, Tess held her breath, waiting for the outraged wail that she was sure would follow.

But Harry didn't cry. He dissolved without warning into

a gummy and quite irresistible smile which left Gabriel
completely nonplussed. Tess saw astonishment, relief and
perplexity chasing themselves across his face, swiftly succeeded by a kind of baffled pride at the baby's unexpected
reaction to his handling, before he smiled instinctively
back at Harry.

Tess nearly fell off the desk. It was like running up to
someone you thought you knew and finding yourself face
to face with a perfect stranger. She had never seen Gabriel
smile before—she had never even *imagined* him smiling—
and she was caught off guard by the way the cold eyes lit
with humour and the stern mouth relaxed, creasing his
cheeks and revealing teeth that were strong and very white
against his dark features.

Her heart jerked suddenly in her chest. If Gabriel had
been taken aback by Harry's smile, it was nothing to her
own reaction to his, and she hoped her own expression
wasn't as easy to read. She felt jarred and breathless, and
it was some moments before she realised that a puzzled
voice was speaking in her ear.

'Hello…? Hello? Who is this?'

'Bella!' Tess jerked her gaze away from Gabriel and
recollected herself with an effort. 'It's Tess.'

'Tess!' cried Bella in carrying tones. 'I haven't heard
from you for ages! How's the boss from hell?'

'Standing right beside me,' said Tess thinly. She didn't
dare look at Gabriel. Had he heard Bella or not?

As succinctly as she could, she explained the situation
to her friend, but it wasn't easy with Bella exclaiming and
interposing irrelevant questions, and it took Tess some
time to get her to the point. Once, she risked a glance at
Gabriel, who raised a sardonic eyebrow. He had heard all
right.

'Just tell us what to do, Bella,' she said hastily. 'Harry's
grandmother said that we would have everything we
needed under the pram, but I might as well be looking

under the bonnet of a car. There's a whole lot of stuff there, but I've got no idea how any of it works.'

Responding to her frantic gesture, Gabriel pushed the pram nearer, so Tess could describe the various packets and bits of equipment that had been packed onto the lower rack.

'Hmm.' Bella considered. 'How old is this baby?'

Tess covered the receiver with her hand, although since Gabriel had clearly already heard both sides of the conversation it seemed a little late for discretion. 'How old is Harry?' she asked him.

'How do I know?' he replied unhelpfully.

The 'boss from hell' jibe was still rankling, and he was annoyed to find that he had been distracted by the way Tess was leaning against her desk. She was wearing the same discreetly elegant grey suit she always wore, the same sensible court shoes, but she looked somehow different. Had she always had legs like that? Gabriel wondered. And, if so, how was it that he had never noticed them before?

'A baby is a baby, isn't it?' he added crossly, hoping that Tess hadn't noticed him staring.

'Apparently not,' she said, holding onto her own temper with an effort. It wasn't easy to concentrate on what Bella was saying when she could feel him frowning at her. Obviously Bella's comment hadn't gone down well.

Tough. Tess tried to convince herself that she didn't care. It wouldn't do Gabriel any harm to realise what they all thought of him, although the timing was less than ideal, she had to admit. If he had to learn how much she disliked him, it might have been better if it hadn't been *just* before they had to spend the entire night together!

Pushing the prospect to the back of her mind, Tess turned back to the problem of Harry's age. 'Did your brother mention when he was on this famous cruise?' she tried again.

'Some time last summer... August, I think he said.' Gabriel calculated quickly. 'That would make Harry about five months now.'

Tess, still trying to add nine months onto August, abandoned her attempts at mental arithmetic and uncovered the receiver once more. 'Five months, we think,' she told Bella.

'Hmm... And where exactly are you proposing to take this baby?'

'To Mr Stearne's apartment.'

'Oh?' Bella managed to invest two letters with at least sixteen syllables. 'You mean you're going to spend the *night* with him?'

Tess hadn't wanted to think about that aspect of the situation. Of course, she and Gabriel weren't going to be spending the night together in the way Bella meant, but still, there was something uncomfortably intimate about the thought of being alone with him in his flat.

Involuntarily, she glanced at Gabriel, who had heard both the words and the intonation. He didn't say anything, but he didn't need to. The faint lift of his brows spoke volumes. A man who went out with the likes of Fionnula Jenkins was hardly likely to have any problems keeping his hands off *her*.

Suddenly acutely aware of the wet patch on her blouse where Harry had pressed his face miserably into her shoulder, and of the wisps of hair escaping around her face, Tess turned her back on him and told Bella crisply not to be silly. 'It's simply a matter of looking after the baby until we can get hold of a nanny tomorrow. If you could just explain what we give him to eat, Bella...'

It took some time, but eventually Tess managed to extract instructions about sterilising bottles, heating milk, washing, winding and sleeping positions, all of which she scribbled down frantically, wishing that Bella wouldn't be quite so vague about exactly what to do and when.

When Bella had finished, Tess cast an eye over her notes and discovered that there was one thing missing.

'What about changing his nappy?' she asked at last, bracing herself.

'What about it?'

'Well, you know…how do we know when to do it?'

Bella laughed. 'Have you tried smelling him?'

Without being told, Gabriel lifted Harry nearer and sniffed cautiously. He wrinkled his nose and the downward turn of his mouth told Tess all she needed to know.

'Ah,' she said, her heart sinking. 'It looks as if we might have to tackle that now. What should we do?'

'Tess, I cannot believe that you've got to thirty-four without changing a nappy!' Bella scolded. 'If you took a more hands-on interest in your goddaughter, you'd know all this by now. And what's all this ''we'' business?' she went on before Tess had a chance to object. 'Since when did you get quite so cosy with Gabriel Stearne?'

Tess avoided looking at Gabriel, although she could feel him listening. *'Bella,'* she said through gritted teeth, 'could we just stick to the nappy changing?'

'Oh, all right, but you'd better ring me tomorrow and tell me *everything*!'

Noting down Bella's sarcastically simplistic instructions, Tess had the feeling she wasn't going to enjoy the next few minutes very much. 'Thanks, Bella,' she said dryly. 'I can't wait.'

'Good luck,' said Bella, and then raised her voice wickedly to make sure that Gabriel would hear her. 'And tell that boss of yours that I've always thought he sounded very sexy, whatever you say!'

Tess put the phone down hastily. She would kill Bella next time she saw her! Faint colour tinged her cheeks as she pretended to read over the instructions that Bella had given her.

What exactly *did* she say? Gabriel wondered darkly. Nothing very flattering, that was for sure!

'I didn't realise that you were in the habit of discussing me with your friends,' he said with a cold look.

'I didn't realise that *you* were in the habit of listening in to private conversations!' Tess snapped back, provoked, and they glared at each other.

Tired of being dangled from outstretched arms, Harry had begun to grizzle. Remembering just in time that he needed Tess's help that evening, Gabriel swallowed the savage retort on the tip of his tongue with an effort.

'Look, let's get this nappy changing over and done with,' he growled. 'We'll do it together, since it's obviously not going to be a very pleasant job.'

'All right.' Tess took the opportunity to back down too. The presence of Harry seemed to have a dangerously disinhibiting effect on both of them, and if she wasn't careful she would find herself out of a job altogether.

The extra money she would earn on overtime tonight might be useful, but her salary was essential, Tess reminded herself guiltily. She had been looking for another job ever since Gabriel had arrived at SpaceWorks, but all those she could have applied for would have meant taking a drop in salary that she simply couldn't afford at the moment. Standing up to Gabriel was one thing, provoking him into sacking her was another. It might be an idea to keep her mouth shut and keep her job, she reflected ruefully.

Still holding Harry at arm's length, Gabriel carried him through to the sleekly modern bathroom that was attached to his private office. There, after some discussion, they spread out a towel on the black marble surface by the basin and laid Harry on top of it.

'Well, here goes!' Tess took a deep breath and resolutely unbuttoned Harry's little body suit.

By now, Harry was crying in earnest and wriggling

alarmingly, and it took two of them to stop him squirming off the marble onto the floor while they worked out how to unfasten the nappy.

Both grimaced when it finally fell apart, and they looked at each other for a pregnant moment. Gabriel found himself staring into Tess's eyes and noticing with an odd, detached part of his mind that they were a beautiful shade of brown, the colour of clear honey, shot through with gold. He had never really seen her eyes before, he realised. Usually they were hidden behind the spectacles she wore when she was working at the computer or taking dictation, and looking into them now for the first time he felt as if he had received a tiny electric shock.

It was an odd feeling. Even odder was the strange tightening of the air between them as they looked at each other. Afterwards, Gabriel would think it could only have lasted a second or two, but at the time it seemed as if their eyes held for an eternity, and when Tess turned back to the protesting baby he felt unaccountably jarred, even dislocated.

Brushing the sensation from his mind, Gabriel set his jaw and forced his attention back to the messy business of changing Harry's nappy.

To Tess, it all seemed unbelievably complicated. She couldn't understand how the mothers she had seen deftly changing babies in washrooms managed on their own. She and Gabriel had to keep stopping to refer to Bella's instructions, and running backwards and forwards to the pram to find the various wipes and creams and spare nappies that seemed to be required.

Although she would have died rather than admit it, Tess was glad that Gabriel was there. It was a relief to discover that he was even more squeamish than she was, and by the time they had finished he was looking positively green about the gills, but his hands were very steady as he held Harry still. There was something oddly reassuring about them, Tess thought inconsequentially. They were big and square and competent, with very clean nails, and for some reason she was very conscious whenever her fingers brushed against his.

At last it was over. Harry, buttoned up again, was obviously more comfortable, and he stopped grizzling when Tess picked him up and cuddled him carefully against her shoulder. She must be getting the hang of it, she congratulated herself.

'Thank God that's over!' said Gabriel, disposing of the dirty nappy with distaste, and Tess found herself nodding in sympathy as their eyes met again. There was that same puzzling charge to the air, the same sense that a smile was lurking, waiting for the slightest excuse to shimmer between them, before Tess looked quickly away, more disturbed than she wanted to admit. It wouldn't do to start thinking that she and Gabriel had anything in common, even if it was only a squeamishness about nappies!

Fortunately, that uncomfortable sense of complicity didn't survive the trip down to the underground car park to Gabriel's car. Tess had frequently wondered why it took so *long* for friends with babies to do anything, but that evening she discovered that with a baby in tow you couldn't simply put on your coat, pick up your bag and go.

Harry refused to be put down in his pram, so they had to take it in turns to hold him while they repacked all his stuff, switched off lights and computers, and gathered up their own things. It all took forever, and then they had to negotiate the lift with the pram. They were halfway down before Gabriel remembered the papers he needed to check that night, so they had to go back up again.

His temper was not improved when they got to the car at last and had to work out how to collapse the pram. Cursing fluently under his breath, Gabriel wrestled with knobs and levers.

'It can't be that difficult,' said Tess unwisely. 'You see mothers with these prams the whole time. They can't all have degrees in mechanical engineering.'

'No, and they don't all have people hanging around making pointless remarks, either!' Gabriel snarled, and Tess bridled.

'There's no need to bite my head off just because you can't do it,' she said coldly, forgetting her earlier resolution to keep her tongue between her teeth. 'It's not my fault you're in a bad mood.'

Gabriel thought that was a matter of opinion. If she had dealt properly with Harry's grandmother, the evening wouldn't have turned into the unmitigated disaster it was already shaping up to be. As it was, he had been forced to beg for her help, had endured a revolting session with the baby's nappy, and was now making an idiot of himself struggling with this cursed pram.

And all he had to look forward to was an evening spent in the company of his PA, who had made no secret of the fact that she disliked him intensely. Gabriel reckoned that Tess had plenty to do with his bad mood, but he had to content himself with casting her a filthy look as he turned back to the pram. He vented his temper instead on a lever that he had already tried more than once, jerking it savagely towards him, and the pram collapsed in one smooth motion that smacked uncannily of reproach for his excessive use of brute force.

At last they were on the way, but almost immediately found themselves in heavy traffic heading south of the river to where Tess lived. Gabriel drummed his fingers impatiently on the steering wheel as they edged forward, annoyed to find himself very aware of Tess sitting beside him.

He wished he hadn't noticed her eyes. He wished he hadn't noticed her legs. He wished he hadn't noticed *any-*

thing different about her, because now that he had started noticing, it was somehow difficult to stop.

There was no reason to notice her. She hadn't done anything to attract him—quite the opposite, in fact—but Gabriel couldn't stop his gaze sliding sideways to where she sat staring haughtily out of the window. That exasperatingly crisp competence had deserted her for once, he noted with a kind of perverse satisfaction. If nothing else, this evening so far had demonstrated that she had a healthy temper of her own beneath the poised and unflappable mask she usually wore.

It was dark outside, and in the dull light of the dashboard Gabriel could just see the fine curve of her jaw, and the corner of her mouth, compressed into a cross line. By rights, she should have had frosty blue eyes to match her manner, he thought, but Tess's eyes hadn't looked like that at all. They were clear and brown and dappled with gold, the eyes of someone warm and alluring, and not those of the PA who treated him with such icy civility. Gabriel was unnerved by how vividly he could picture them still.

Irritably, he flexed his shoulders. He had only looked into Tess's eyes for a matter of seconds. Nothing had changed. She was just sitting there with her nose stuck in the air, so why should he suddenly find her so distracting?

He didn't have time to be distracted, he reminded himself roughly. Taking over SpaceWorks had been a risky strategy, and if they didn't get the Emery contract, he would have lost his gamble, not to mention a lot of money. Gabriel didn't like losing. He wasn't going to jeopardise the whole bid by letting himself get diverted by a baby, and certainly not because his secretary had taken her glasses off!

Harry was asleep by the time they drew up outside Tess's house almost an hour later, so Gabriel waited in the car with him while she ran inside and threw a few things for the night into a bag. Then they had to turn round and crawl back through the traffic to the City where Gabriel lived in a recently converted warehouse near the river.

Tess was fed up of sitting in the car by the time they got there and, when she saw his flat, she wished that she had suggested they simply stay at her house, which might be shabby but which at least had the advantage of being comfortable. She had thought about making the offer when she'd been packing her bag, but her home was her haven, and she wasn't sure she wanted Gabriel there.

His apartment was aggressively modern, all gleaming steel and glass and neutral fabrics. Cosy, it was not. Open-plan throughout, the various living areas were cleverly suggested by the arrangement of furniture or lighting. It was chic, stylish and completely soulless. Tess couldn't imagine anyone actually *living* in it. As it was, Harry's pram with its bright, plastic colours struck a jarring note amongst all that restrained taste.

Perhaps it was just as well she hadn't invited Gabriel to stay with her, she decided. If this was his style, he would have hated her house.

'It's very…new,' she said.

'You don't like it.' Too late, Gabriel heard the accusing note in his voice, which made him sound almost as if he cared what she thought.

'It's not that. It's just doesn't have much character, I suppose.'

'I don't want character,' he said tersely. 'I want convenience. These apartments have been snapped up. They all come fully equipped with sheets, towels, crockery, even a selection of wine in the wine rack. They're ideal for successful people who don't have time to waste finding somewhere to buy a corkscrew.'

Tess was unimpressed. 'I don't think I'd want to be successful if it meant I didn't have time to make a home,' she said.

'Home is just somewhere to sleep.'

Nettled by her lack of enthusiasm, Gabriel went to draw the vertical blinds over the expanse of glass that stretched almost the entire length of the apartment. He hadn't noticed it until now, but when it was dark outside and the rain was splattering against the window like now, the apartment didn't look very welcoming. Perhaps she would appreciate it more if he shut out the blackness.

'I only moved in two days ago,' he said, looking for some way to pull the blinds. He liked the view at night, so he hadn't had to work out how to close them before. 'I was living in a hotel until then,' he went on as his hand moved up and down the edge of the blind in search of a cord or some kind of mechanism, 'but this is much better. It's serviced in the same way as a hotel, but it's private and, because it's new, everything works.'

'Not quite everything,' said Tess, observing his increasingly frustrated efforts to deal with the blinds. He was muttering under his breath, and looked ready to rip the blinds bodily from the window as she moved him aside. 'Here, let me try.'

To Gabriel's intense irritation, she located the high-tech controls straight away that had been cleverly concealed in the wall, and with one touch of a button the blinds swished smoothly across the vast window.

'Very convenient,' she murmured.

Gabriel glared at the irony in her voice, but Harry was making little mewling noises from the pram.

'He's waking up,' said Tess nervously.

Drawn together insensibly by their shared apprehension, they peered into the pram, where the baby was squirming and knuckling his eyes.

'Now what do we do?' asked Gabriel, keeping a cautious distance.

Tess pulled Bella's instructions out of her bag. 'I think we need to feed him,' she said, squinting in an attempt to decipher a squiggle in the margin. 'We've got to make up some formula,' she added, hoping that she sounded more confident than she felt. Crouching down, she searched through the equipment that Gabriel had carried up from the car. 'There should be a tin…ah, that must be it.'

'Are you sure you know what you're doing?' said Gabriel suspiciously as he followed her into the kitchen area.

'No.' She held out her scribbled notes with a challenging look. 'If you can read my shorthand, you're welcome to try and work it out for yourself.'

'No, no,' he said, recoiling. 'You'd better do it.'

Tess was reading the instructions on the back of the tin. 'Can you find me a saucepan?'

'I expect I could manage that,' said Gabriel with dignity, still smarting over his defeat with the blinds. He began opening cupboards, having ignored the kitchen, like the windows, until now. Eventually he found a pan and gave it to Tess, who sent him back to keep an eye on Harry.

'This is complicated,' she told him frankly. 'I can't concentrate with you standing over me.'

Harry grew increasingly restless as Gabriel hovered by the pram, watching anxiously as the little face contorted itself into a variety of plaintive expressions, each of which looked alarmingly as if he was on the point of wailing miserably.

When he did finally utter a spluttering cry, Gabriel threw a glance of appeal at Tess, who was carefully measuring powder into a jug. 'Is his milk ready yet?'

'No, I've still got to warm it,' she said, throwing Harry a harassed glance. 'You'll have to distract him.'

'How?'

'I don't know…give him a cuddle or something.'

With a sigh, Gabriel hoisted Harry awkwardly against his shoulder and joggled him about a bit. 'It's not working,' he complained when the baby's cries only increased in volume.

'I'm not surprised.' Tess looked up from the hob where she was puzzling over a control panel that wouldn't have looked out of place at NASA. 'Is that your idea of a cuddle?'

'What's wrong with it?' he said stiffly.

'Nothing, if you think cuddling means holding someone at arm's length and shaking them up and down.'

'I didn't realise you were such an expert,' he said with a snide look.

'I'm not,' she said, 'but I know how I like to be held.'

She didn't have to say that it wouldn't be the way *he* would hold her. 'Perhaps you should give lessons,' snapped Gabriel, unaccountably provoked. He could imagine her doing it, too, with the same cold efficiency she did everything else. No doubt she would allot special cuddling windows in her diary and keep one eye firmly on the clock to make sure they didn't run over schedule.

'Lessons would be extra,' Tess snapped back, 'and I'm already on double overtime this evening.'

'Don't worry, I hadn't forgotten,' said Gabriel sourly.

Grudgingly, he held Harry a little closer and walked up and down in what he hoped was a soothing manner. Not that it made the slightest difference to the volume of the baby's crying. So much for Tess and her advice on cuddling.

'What's taking so long?' he demanded at last, breaking the hostile silence. 'It's only milk, isn't it? Anyone would think you were preparing a five-course meal.'

Tess gritted her teeth. 'I'm being as quick as I can. I've got to check the temperature before I can give it to him.'

Craning her neck to refer to her scribbled notes, she shook the bottle and upended it to squeeze a few drops of milk onto the inside of her wrist. It felt just warm, but not hot, just as Bella had said it should.

Relieved, Tess looked around for somewhere to sit, but it wasn't the kind of kitchen designed to be cluttered up with tables where you could read the paper, drink coffee, let things pile up and generally gather mess. The chairs set perfectly around the glass dining table looked downright uncomfortable, and in the end she sat down a little dubiously on one of the cream sofas.

'OK, let's try him with this.'

Gabriel handed a bawling Harry over with relief. Tess pretended not to notice when their hands brushed, and concentrated on presenting the baby with the bottle. Fortunately, Harry knew more about bottle-feeding than she did and, once he recognised the teat, he soon settled into sucking.

Their sniping momentarily forgotten, Tess and Gabriel watched warily, and were just allowing themselves to relax when he coughed and choked milk down the front of his Babygro. Too late, Tess remembered the bibs that had been tucked in a bag with the nappies.

'What's happening?' said Gabriel.

'*I* don't know, do I?' Tess sat Harry upright and patted his back, which seemed to be the right thing to do, for he stopped spluttering. Cautiously, she let him have the bottle again. 'I'd no idea what a tense business it was looking after a baby.' She sighed.

'Me neither,' Gabriel agreed with feeling. He had taken off his jacket and was standing at the glass table, loosening his tie with one hand and pulling papers from his briefcase with the other. 'Give me executive stress any day!'

'I wouldn't have thought that was something *you* suffered from,' said Tess and Gabriel glanced up at her with a frown.

'What do you mean?'

'No one could call your management style relaxed,' she pointed out, thinking of the last frantic weeks putting the Emery bid together. 'You only seem to operate under high pressure.' She bent her head back over the peacefully suckling baby. 'I'm surprised you even know what executive stress *is*!'

'Of course I know what it is,' said Gabriel irritably. 'I hear my executives whining about it often enough! It's not something I've got a lot of time for, I admit.'

'Not everyone thrives under pressure the way you do,' said Tess. 'You have no idea what it's like to work in an office where the pace is relentless, where the boss storms around making unreasonable demands of his staff and everything always has to be done yesterday.'

Gabriel's fearsome brows twitched together. Looking up from his papers again, he found his gaze resting on her bent head, the brown hair caught the light and gleaming with gold, reminding him of her eyes. He could see the pure line of her cheek, the downward sweep of lashes, that small but stubborn chin.

He wrenched his eyes away. 'It doesn't seem to bother *you*.'

Tess glanced up briefly and then away. 'I cope with it,' she said. 'That doesn't mean I like it.'

'You don't have to like it,' said Gabriel, reverting to his brusque manner to disguise the sensation that had stirred so strangely inside him as he watched her cradling the baby in her arms. 'You just have to do the job you're paid to do, and that's helping me put the Emery bid together. Once we get that in, you can start worrying about stress! Until then, we've got better things to do.'

He glanced at his watch. 'We ought to be able to get quite a bit done tonight. I've got to redraft the introduction, and I want you to cross-check every single figure we put forward. There's going to be some stiff competition for this contract, and we can't afford to look sloppy.'

'You want me to check figures tonight?' said Tess incredulously.

'I am paying you overtime,' Gabriel reminded her.

'For helping you with Harry!'

He brushed that aside. 'Since you're here, you might as well help me with the bid, too. There's no TV, no books. There's just you, me, and a whole heap of paperwork. What else is there for us to do this evening, after all?'

The sardonic note in his voice brought a flush to Tess's cheeks. Most men and women could find something better to do with an evening alone together, but she and Gabriel didn't have that kind of relationship, did they? They might be alone in his apartment with the whole night ahead of them, but he was still her boss and she was still his PA.

'In the circumstances, nothing,' she agreed stiffly.

'You don't have to help,' said Gabriel with an indifferent shrug. 'It's up to you if you want to lose your job.'

Tess's head jerked up and she stared icily at him. 'Is that a threat?'

'No, it's not a threat.' Gabriel's voice was flat and hard and as cold as her own. 'It's reality. We need this contract. If we don't get it, I'm going to have to reconsider my investment in SpaceWorks. In that case, the company will fold, and your job with it. It's as simple as that. Contraxa is a leader in its field, and our reputation depends on consistent quality and success. We can't afford to be associated with failures, even in a minor division.'

Tess knew that what he said was true, but she couldn't help bridling at his casual dismissal of the company where she had worked so loyally for over ten years. SpaceWorks was more than a *minor division*! 'I wonder you bothered with us at all if we're that unimportant!' she said tightly.

'Because I believe in taking risks to get what you want,' said Gabriel. He dropped the last of the papers from his briefcase onto the table where they landed with a dull slap. 'SpaceWorks isn't important now, but it's got the potential to be very important indeed. If my gamble pays off, it will give me the toe-hold I need to expand into Europe. It's a global market now, Tess. You've got to stay ahead of the game, and you don't do that by playing safe.'

'Sometimes playing safe is the only option.' Tess sighed a little, thinking of Andrew with still another year to go before he finished his education. 'Some of us have got commitments. We can't all afford to take risks.'

'That's why I avoid making commitments,' said Gabriel dismissively. 'You can't succeed if you're always looking over your shoulder, worrying about your responsibilities.'

It was all very well for him, thought Tess crossly, removing the empty bottle from Harry's tenacious grasp. Some commitments were there whether chosen or not.

She put the bottle on the floor and stood up with Harry. 'Well, here's one responsibility you can worry about right now,' she said, deliberately brisk. 'You can take your nephew for a while.'

CHAPTER THREE

GABRIEL eyed the baby Tess was holding out to him. 'What shall I do with him?' he asked uneasily, his high-handed indifference abruptly deserting him.

'According to Bella, he needs to be winded. I've seen her husband do this,' Tess said, relenting in the face of his panic-stricken expression. 'It's easy. All you have to do is walk up and down, patting his back until he burps.'

Gabriel felt that he had already done quite enough walking up and down with Harry but, since Tess had fed him, he couldn't really refuse. Stretching out his arms reluctantly, he let her put the baby into them.

'Got him?' she asked sharply to disguise the inexplicable frisson of awareness as her hands brushed against his again.

'Yes,' he admitted, although without much enthusiasm.

'Now, hold him against your shoulder, and pat his back—gently.'

Gabriel patted gingerly. 'Like this?'

'Well, Roger sings while he's at it,' said Tess as she went into the kitchen to rinse the bottle, 'but I think that's optional.'

She watched Gabriel under her lashes as she dragged the steriliser out from under the pram and unpacked it from its box. Face intent, he was walking dutifully around the apartment with Harry. If only the others at SpaceWorks could see him now, the ruthless arrogance and uncompromising confidence demolished by one small baby.

Sometimes, thought Tess, life could be sweet.

Completing another circuit, Gabriel arrived back in the kitchen. 'I think I'm beginning to get the hang of it,' he confided, and ventured a hum to demonstrate his new-found confidence.

Harry was promptly sick over his extremely expensive shirt.

Yes, definitely sweet, decided Tess, hiding a smile. Even perfect.

'You *were* a bit out of tune,' she reproached him.

Gabriel shot her a look as he craned his neck over his shoulder to assess the damage. 'That's all I need,' he said sourly. 'A critic.'

Tess hunted through the pristine cupboards for a cloth, eventually locating an unopened packet which she ripped open. 'That must be why Roger always wears a cloth over his shoulder when he winds Rosy,' she said, extracting one and wetting it under the tap.

'I'm so pleased you remembered that now,' he grumbled.

Ignoring him, Tess wrung out the cloth and put a hand on his arm. 'Stand still,' she instructed. She wiped away the mess on his shoulder, but she had barely finished before Harry obligingly gugged up a little more milk.

Gabriel screwed up his nose. 'Yeuch!'

'Oh, don't make such a fuss.' she said, half-exasperated, half-indulgent. 'It's only a bit of milk.' She rubbed his shirt vigorously. 'There…all gone.'

He peered suspiciously at the unpleasantly damp patch behind his shoulder before raising his gaze to meet Tess's. The honey-coloured eyes were dancing with amusement, and Gabriel felt as if his stomach had disappeared without warning, leaving him with a strange, hollow feeling inside. All at once he was acutely conscious of Tess standing close beside him, of her hand burning through the fine material of his shirt, of her hair, glimmering in the glare of the overhead light, of her perfume, elusive, beguiling, faintly spicy.

At almost exactly the same moment, Tess became aware

of the solid strength of the shoulder she was dabbing in such a casual manner. The arm she had taken hold of so intimately was *warm*, and she had a sudden, shocking sense of him as a man. A man with steely muscles and sleek, bare flesh beneath his clothes. Unaccountably flustered, she jerked her hand away and stepped back.

'I'll…er…I'll see what we have to do next,' she muttered.

Her fingers were not quite steady as she smoothed out Bella's instructions on the kitchen worktop. Really, she had to get a grip. She had never found Gabriel remotely attractive before, and she wasn't about to start now.

Tess concentrated on the notes. 'There's something here about a bath,' she said after a moment, glad to hear that her voice sounded almost normal again. 'I wonder if we should have done that before feeding him? It's a bit hard to tell from this.'

In the end, they decided that it wouldn't hurt Harry to miss a bath for one night. The nanny would be able to wash him the next day and in the meantime wiping him with a flannel, changing his nappy and buttoning him into a clean Babygro presented enough of a challenge for them.

'Let's put him in here.' Gabriel snapped on a light by a low, wide bed set against the far wall of the apartment. To one side, a wall of glass gave a spectacular view over the city lights, while a range of wardrobes curved round like a protective arm, providing privacy from the rest of the apartment.

Tess looked around her, noting the gleaming bathroom to one side. It, at least, had a door. Apart from the front door, it appeared to be the only one in the apartment.

'Is this where you sleep?'

'Yes.' Now that he knew how they worked, Gabriel went over to pull the blinds over the window, but something in the quality of Tess's silence made him turn. 'Not tonight, however. You needn't worry,' he went on in a dry voice. 'You'll have the bed to yourself. I'll sleep on the couch.'

Tess flushed a little. 'I wasn't worrying,' she said, lifting her chin in a familiar gesture. 'I was simply thinking that you wouldn't be very comfortable.' The sofas were luxuriously wide, but he was well over six foot with a massive strength that she couldn't imagine fitting very easily onto the cream cushions.

He shrugged. 'It's not a problem.'

'I don't mind sleeping on the sofa,' she offered hesitantly. 'I'm shorter than you.'

Gabriel had been opening and closing wardrobe doors, but he paused at that and looked over his shoulder at her. 'I realise you have a very low opinion of me, Tess,' he said with some asperity, 'but I didn't know it was quite that low. Do you really think I would let you sleep on the couch while I was warm and comfortable in bed?'

Tess bit her lip as he turned back to continue rifling through the wardrobes. She would have been surprised if he had accepted her offer, it was true, but there had been no need for him to make her feel ridiculous for even suggesting it.

'What are you looking for?' she asked awkwardly instead of answering him.

'Clean bedding,' said Gabriel briefly. He shut the last door with a frown. 'I can't find anything. I guess the bed gets changed as part of the service here, but that won't be for a couple of days.'

'It doesn't matter,' she said, trying not to think about sleeping in his bed, in his sheets.

'The sheets are quite clean,' he said stiffly, certain that she was notching up another black mark against the convenience of his new apartment. Everything had worked perfectly until she had arrived. 'I've only spent one night here.'

Where had he spent the other night? wondered Tess involuntarily. *Two* days ago, he had said he'd moved in. Then she remembered Fionnula Jenkins. No doubt he had been with her, and not sleeping on her sofa either!

'I'll be fine,' she said, rocking Harry with a fine show of nonchalance. She certainly wasn't about to let Gabriel Stearne know that the very idea of sleeping in his bed, in his sheets, left her feeling curiously ruffled.

Harry wasn't keen on being left alone in a strange room, and made his feelings known in no uncertain terms. Every time Tess and Gabriel made to creep out, he would set up a desolate wail that brought them hastily back to his side. They were just beginning to wonder if they were going to have to spend the entire evening hanging over his pram when exhaustion got the better of him, in spite of his valiant struggles to keep his eyes open.

Holding their breaths, they watched as his long, baby lashes flickered, drooped and lifted manfully twice, three times, four and then rested against the downy cheeks. Tess saw his tiny fists relax as his breathing grew slow and steady at last, and she nodded when Gabriel turned up his thumbs with a hopeful look.

Together, they tiptoed out into the living area.

'What an evening!' muttered Gabriel, raking his fingers tiredly through his dark hair.

Tess collapsed onto one of the cream sofas. 'I know.' She sighed with feeling. 'How do you think parents do that every night?'

'God knows!' he said bitterly as he lay back opposite her and closed his eyes. 'All I know is that if I had ever wanted children, this little experience would have changed my mind.'

Easing off her shoes, Tess massaged her feet and wondered if it would be OK if she took her tights off later. Without thinking, she pulled the clips from her hair and shook it loose with a stifled yawn, the way she did every night as soon as she got home.

'I don't think I'll be giving up my job to train as a nanny either,' she said, obscurely comforted to realise that Gabriel was as tired as she was.

'I'm glad to hear—' Gabriel began dryly, only to stop short as he opened his eyes to see Tess curled up on his sofa, massaging her feet, luxuriant brown hair tumbling to her shoulders. He blinked, stunned by the transformation. Where had all that hair come from? It made her look like a different girl altogether, no longer cool and remote, but warm, vibrant and sexy.

Sexy? *Tess?*

The thought made him jerk upright.

Startled by his sudden movement, Tess pushed back her hair and looked at him in concern. 'What is it?'

Gabriel opened his mouth and closed it again. 'What about a drink?' he said, getting abruptly to his feet and hoping that Tess wouldn't notice the hoarseness of his voice. 'I don't know about you, but I could sure use one tonight.'

Escaping to the kitchen, he took longer than strictly necessary to find the corkscrew and open a bottle of wine. The sight of Tess with her hair loose and her long legs curled comfortably up beneath her had caught him unawares. He hadn't realised she could look like that, and he just needed a few minutes to adjust, that was all.

He had himself well under control by the time he carried the bottle and two glasses back to the sofa. 'There's nothing to eat in the apartment,' he told Tess, 'so I've ordered in a pizza. Is that OK?'

'A *pizza*?'

Gabriel raised his eyebrows at her expression as he poured the wine into the glasses. 'What's the matter? Don't you like pizza?'

'Pizza's fine,' said Tess. 'I'm just surprised at the idea of you ordering a take-away,' she tried to explain. 'I suppose I think of you always eating in smart restaurants like

Cupiditas.' She broke off as Gabriel swore and slapped his palm to his forehead. 'What have I said?' she asked, puzzled.

'You've just reminded me that I'm supposed to be having dinner there tonight.'

'I thought you would have cancelled,' said Tess. She had taken the opportunity to ring her friends when she'd been packing her bag at home, and assumed that Gabriel would have done the same while he'd been waiting in the car.

'I had other things on my mind.' Gabriel felt for his mobile before remembering that he had left it in the kitchen. He got up. 'I'd better ring Fionnula.'

Leaning back against the cushions, Tess sipped her wine and wondered just what kind of relationship he had with Fionnula Jenkins. It couldn't be that close if Gabriel had forgotten her so completely.

From the kitchen she could hear the murmur of Gabriel's voice. Grovelling apologies wouldn't come easily to him, and it sounded as if Fionnula was giving him a hard time. Tess couldn't imagine the beautiful redhead would get stood up very often. She had better get used to it if she was planning on spending much time with a workaholic like Gabriel, thought Tess cynically. He wasn't the type to change his habits for anyone.

Sure enough, Gabriel was looking boot-faced when he came back from the kitchen a few minutes later, snapping his mobile closed. Fionnula had been furious to learn that she had been stood up in favour of a baby, and aghast when Gabriel had told her that he'd had to take responsibility for Harry on behalf of his brother.

'You realise that everyone's going to think that it's your baby?' she had said angrily.

'Nobody's going to know, and if they did know, they're not going to be interested,' he'd told her impatiently.

'Easy for you to say. You're not a celebrity over here.

I don't suppose you gave a thought to what it might do to my reputation if it leaked out that you had a secret love child?'

Since Gabriel hadn't, it had been hard for him to deny it. Fionnula had not been impressed, and he'd been hard put to it to control his temper. Now, his jaw worked angrily as he took a slug of his wine.

'Come on, we might as well start work while we're waiting for the pizza to arrive,' he said.

At least she wasn't the one who had put him in a bad mood for once, thought Tess, reaching resignedly for the first set of papers.

They sat down together at the dining table, but the chairs had clearly been designed for show rather than for sitting on, and it wasn't long before they decamped back to the sofas by mutual agreement. Gabriel sat on the edge, leaning forward to study the report on the coffee table, while Tess found a comfortable position on the floor.

For a while they worked in a silence that felt almost companionable. Tess worked her way methodically through the figures, checking each set against the originals. Every now and then she stopped to take a sip of wine or push her hair behind her ears so that she could adjust the glasses on her nose, but as the minutes ticked past for some reason she became increasingly aware of Gabriel.

He was sitting opposite her, leaning his elbows on his knees, sleeves rolled up to reveal strong forearms, and brows drawn together in concentration. Without that acute grey gaze boring into her, Tess could study him under her lashes. The dark, stern face with its intimidating brows was familiar to her, but she had never noticed the scattering of grey hairs at his temples before, nor the lines fanning out from the corner of his eyes.

He was rubbing a finger thoughtfully along his upper lip and Tess found herself remembering how he had looked when he'd smiled at Harry. Worse, she found herself wondering what it would be like if he smiled at *her*.

The realisation made her shift uncomfortably, breaking Gabriel's concentration. He glanced across at her. 'How's it going?'

'OK.' Tess was alarmed to hear the squeak in her voice, and she cleared her throat hastily. 'I've done last year's figures.'

'Good.'

Gabriel's eyes flickered towards her, then away. He wondered if Tess had any idea how disconcerting it was to see her sitting casually on the floor with her hair falling to her shoulders. She had taken off her jacket and was wearing a short-sleeved top in a silky ivory material with a string of pearls at her neck. It was exactly the kind of classic outfit she wore every day, so why did she suddenly look so *different*?

He tried to go back to his report, but it was impossible to concentrate. An indefinable tension had trickled into the atmosphere, making the print jiggle before his eyes, and it was a relief when the pizza finally arrived and gave them an excuse to push the papers to one side.

Tess opened up the box on the coffee table, while Gabriel poured her another glass of wine. She was so hungry by then that she was beginning to feel light-headed, and it didn't even seem strange any more to be sitting on the floor in Gabriel's trendy apartment, eating pizza out of cardboard box.

Afterwards, Gabriel made coffee. 'There's no milk, I'm afraid,' he said as he handed her a mug, but I found these in the fridge.' He indicated the box of luxurious Belgian chocolates tucked under his arm. 'I think they must have been left as a welcoming gift. 'Do you eat chocolates?'

'Occasionally,' said Tess, who was a closet chocaholic. She eyed the box longingly as Gabriel set it down on the coffee table.

'Be my guest,' he said.

'Thanks.' Tess wasn't about to give him the chance to change his mind. Reaching for the box, she tried not to look too eager as she unwrapped the Cellophane and lifted the lid with reverence.

She pored over the chocolates, her fingers hovering with anticipation before finally making her selection, and popping it into her mouth with a sigh of pleasure. 'My favourites,' she confessed through a mouthful of chocolate.

Gabriel lifted an eyebrow. 'Have another,' he offered. 'Have the whole box!'

For once, the irony went over Tess's head. She was too busy choosing another chocolate. Oblivious to the curious expression in Gabriel's eyes, she settled her glasses comfortably back on her nose and went back to her figures, absently eating her way through the entire box.

'What's wrong with that one?' asked Gabriel some time later when they paused to stretch stiff muscles.

Tess had taken off her glasses and was running her fingers through her hair, pulling it back from her face. 'Which one?' she asked blankly.

For answer, Gabriel upended the box to reveal a solitary chocolate nestling in an expanse of packaging.

'It's got nougat in it,' she explained. 'I don't like nougat.'

'Nor do I.'

'You did say I could have the whole box,' she reminded him, faintly defensive.

'I didn't think you'd take me literally.' said Gabriel, but the corner of his mouth twitched.

'You shouldn't have said it if you didn't mean it.'

'Obviously not,' he said dryly, regarding her with such a peculiar expression that Tess began to feel uncomfortable.

'Why are you looking at me like that?'

'I was just thinking that you're quite…' He searched for

the right word. 'Quite unexpected,' was the best that he could do.

It was hardly a lavish compliment—it might not even have been meant as a compliment at all—but Tess felt her heart tighten. It wasn't what Gabriel had said. It was something to do with a new charge in the air, with the jittery, uncertain feeling that was stealing over her, as if she had strayed unknowingly onto dangerous ground.

She moistened her lips. 'Most people like chocolates. What's unexpected about that?'

'It's not the fact that you like chocolate. It's the fact that you just ate a whole box,' said Gabriel. 'Normally you're so restrained, so controlled.'

Tess put up her chin, not really liking the image that he had conjured up, but knowing that was how she came across. 'I am, in the office.' She allowed that much.

'And out of it?'

Gabriel's voice was light, laced with mockery, but when Tess glanced involuntarily at him she found her eyes trapped by his, and she was paralysed by a sudden, absurd shyness. There was something in his expression that held her still while her senses sharpened to an acuteness that made her catch her breath, and she was startlingly aware of the lingering taste of chocolate in her mouth, of the faint stickiness on her fingers, of the sound of her own heartbeat.

And of Gabriel.

Of the dent at the corner of his stern mouth. Of the crease in his cheeks. Of the pulse beating slowly in his throat.

Shaken, Tess dragged her gaze away. What on earth was the matter with her?

'I'm just the same out of the office,' she managed to say. 'I just eat more chocolate.'

She'd hoped to sound suitably crisp, but there was a treacherously breathless note to her voice, and when she picked up her coffee the cup rattled so much in the saucer that she had to put it down again.

Pushing her hair behind her ears in an unconsciously nervous gesture, Tess drew a breath and fumbled for her glasses. 'We…we'd better get on.'

She felt better with her glasses on. They made her once more the cool, capable PA Gabriel believed her to be, and not the kind of girl whose heart lurched alarmingly at his smile. Not the kind of girl who couldn't tear her eyes away from his.

Certainly not the kind of girl who stared at his mouth and wondered what it would take to convince him that her crisp efficiency was just a façade and that underneath she was warm and sensual and passionate.

Not that she *was* that kind of girl, of course.

Not with her glasses on, anyway.

After that it was even harder to concentrate. There was a new constraint to the silence between them and Tess was excruciatingly aware of Gabriel's every move, tensing each time he turned a page or leant forward to make a neat note in the margin. The figures kept dancing in front of her eyes and blurring into the image of his face.

Tiredness, Tess told herself firmly.

Struggling to the end of the file, she dropped it onto the coffee table and leant back with a sigh that turned into a yawn as she linked her hands above her head and stretched her arms.

Gabriel looked at his watch. It was nearly midnight. 'Go to bed,' he said brusquely.

'I've still got two more files to check.'

'You've done enough for tonight. Go on, go.'

'What about the bid?'

'We'll do the rest tomorrow,' he said.

'But—'

'Stop arguing,' said Gabriel crossly to disguise an unfamiliar feeling of guilt. Apart from a few minutes break to eat the pizza, Tess had been working all evening, and she looked very tired. 'You'll be no good to me tomorrow if you're half asleep.'

Putting his hand under her arm, he lifted her bodily to her feet and propelled her towards the bedroom. Tess was too stiff and weary by then to resist the warm strength of the hand gripping her arm. Swaying tiredly, she checked that Harry was still sleeping while Gabriel grabbed some shorts and a T-shirt out of a drawer.

He turned to see her sitting on the edge of the bed, looking blankly ahead of her as if too exhausted to get undressed. 'Will you be all right?' he asked, rough concern in his voice.

'I'll be fine.'

'I'll say goodnight, then.' Gabriel hesitated, as if he were about to say more but, whatever it was, he evidently changed his mind, contenting himself with a curt nod of farewell instead.

Tess slid beneath the duvet and lay with her eyes closed. It was dark and quiet and she was very tired, but she couldn't sleep. Her body was strumming, the nerves fluttering beneath her skin. It was something to do with being in Gabriel's bed, something to do with remembering the lean, powerful body and the way his face had changed when he smiled at Harry.

Something to do with the feel of his hand on her arm.

Unthinkingly, she rubbed the inside of her arm where he had gripped her, and where her skin was tingling as if his fingers were imprinted on her like a burn. She hadn't realised how strong he was, nor how warm his hands would be.

The thought made Tess shift uneasily. She loved expensive lingerie and only ever wore silk or satin to bed, but now for some reason its sensuous softness made her uncomfortable and all too aware of her own nakedness. If only she possessed one of those Victorian nightgowns that enveloped her from neck to toe, instead of this slithery satin number which left her arms and shoulders bare. It made it too easy to imagine that she could feel the warmth of his body on the sheet beneath her.

Restlessly, Tess turned over and buried her face in the pillow, but that didn't help at all. The cool linen held the scent of his skin, of his hair. How had she come to recognise it so unmistakably? It was almost like having him in bed with her.

And *that* thought didn't help her relax either.

Tess pummelled the pillow and rolled onto her back once more with an irritable sigh. This was ridiculous. She didn't even *like* Gabriel. He was rude, surly, selfish, and an impossibly demanding boss—the last person she was prepared to lose any sleep over, in fact. If she had to lie awake, she should be calculating the overtime she had already earned this evening.

Somewhere in the middle of working out her hourly rate and trying to multiply it by two, Tess fell asleep.

She didn't know how long she slept, but it felt like mere moments before she was jerked awake by a piercing wail. Disorientated, she lay with her heart pumping in alarm before she remembered where she was.

Gabriel's apartment.

A baby. Crying.

Get up and do something about it.

Fumbling for the bedside light, she screwed up her eyes as she clicked it on and stumbled over to the pram.

What had Bella said about sleeping patterns? Tess couldn't remember. She tried rocking the pram, and when that didn't work, bent to pick Harry up. He was tense and miserable, his small body arching away from hers and his arms flailing wildly in distress.

A light snapped on in the living area, and the next minute Gabriel appeared, rubbing a hand wearily over his face. He looked cross and rumpled, but the sight of him was enough to snap Tess back to full consciousness in a way that Harry's screams hadn't done.

Averting her eyes from his long, straight, strong legs and the breadth of his chest beneath the T-shirt he wore, she cuddled Harry against her, patting his back and attempting the kind of croon she had heard Bella use. He resisted at first, before the taut little body relaxed slightly, but the heart-rending sobs continued.

'Can I do anything?'

Gabriel's voice sounded a bit odd, but perhaps he was feeling as befuddled as she was. Tess forced herself to think about what Bella had said. 'Could you get his bottle?' she asked. 'I got it ready earlier. Maybe he just wants something to drink.' She knew she was clutching at straws, but it was the only useful thing she could think of to do.

Gabriel nodded briefly and turned towards the kitchen. The sight of Tess, warm from the bed, with her hair dishevelled, and that seductive nightdress skimming lovingly over the curve of breast and hip had hit him with the force of a blow. He was glad to escape and give himself time to recover and remember how to breathe.

He had himself under control by the time he returned with the bottle. Harry's cries had subsided as Tess cradled him and, although he drank a little, he didn't seem very interested. When his eyes started to droop once more, Tess lowered him gently back into the pram.

Her eyes met Gabriel's as she straightened. The bedside lamp cast a soft puddle of light, and she was very glad of the shadows, but they didn't stop her feeling very conscious once more of how little she had on. She hugged her arms together nervously.

'Perhaps he'll go back to sleep now,' she said hopefully, holding up crossed fingers.

He did, but only for a few minutes. Barely had Tess dropped back into sleep than Harry woke again.

And again. And again. And again.

It set the pattern for a night that rapidly turned into a nightmare for Tess. They tried everything they could think of to get Harry back to sleep. They made up some milk. They walked him up and down patting his back. They sang to him. They even changed his nappy, and none of it made any difference. No sooner had they plummeted into an exhausted sleep than the screams would start again.

After the third time, they agreed that they would take it in turns to get up to him. By that stage, they were beyond caring or even noticing how little the other was wearing. Tess had lost track of time altogether. It was as if she and Gabriel were subjects in some awful trial on the effects of torture, and Harry had been specifically programmed to deny them the sleep they craved.

She surfaced groggily at one point to see Gabriel cautiously laying Harry in his pram, and turning back towards his sofa.

'You might as well stay here,' she mumbled, her voice blurred by sleep, and her arm gestured vaguely to the other side of the bed. 'There's plenty of room.'

Gabriel hesitated. He was rather more awake than Tess at that point and, although it was a very tempting idea, he wasn't sure that it was a good one. 'Are you sure you don't mind?' he whispered so as not to wake the baby.

'Mmm… Stupid going back to sofa when you're only going to have to come back again.' She was slurring her words, barely conscious. ''s nice and warm…'

Nice and warm. Gabriel swallowed. He could believe it.

He watched Tess roll over and burrow her face in her pillow, and grimaced. She was already asleep, and too tired to care where he slept. He knew perfectly well that she hadn't known what she was saying, but it did make sense. He was sick of going backwards and forwards. The couch was cold and uncomfortable, and the bed looked very inviting.

Carefully, he lifted the duvet and slid in beside Tess. In

spite of his own exhaustion, he was dangerously aware of her, slumbering, oblivious to his presence only inches away. He could feel the soft warmth of her body, and hear her slow breathing.

Moving right to the edge of the bed, he turned his back to her and prayed for sleep.

Gabriel surfaced slowly to the feel of a warm, female body nestled into the hard curve of his. She was utterly relaxed. His arm lay half over her, moving gently up and down in time with her quiet breathing. There was some soft, slithery material beneath his hand where it rested on her thigh and his face was pressed into a mass of silky hair that smelt clean and sweet and familiar.

He was warm and comfortable. Still half asleep, Gabriel was conscious only that it felt right to be lying there, and he tightened his arm around her. When the slinky material slipped tantalisingly over her skin, pulling her into him was a purely instinctive response.

She stirred, and rolled sleepily within his arm to nuzzle against him. Gabriel twisted his hands in the thick hair and kissed her throat, smiling as he shifted her beneath him and let his lips drift deliciously up to her jaw. The sleep had cleared from his brain, but he wasn't thinking. He was simply reacting to her softness and her warmth, to the enticing feel of her body and the beguiling scent of her skin.

Murmuring inarticulate pleasure, she wound her arms around his neck. Still smiling, Gabriel lifted his head to look down into her face.

And froze.

CHAPTER FOUR

DRAWN blissfully up from the fathoms of slumber, Tess smiled languorously and opened her eyes. Still clouded with sleep, it took a little while for her to realise that the bewitching drift of his lips had ceased, and that the man leaning over her was looking down at her with an expression of horror.

Gabriel could see the exact second at which the puzzlement in her eyes was blinked away by the sudden, appalling recognition of where they were, and what they were doing. There was a long, paralysing silence while they stared at each other, aghast, and then, at the identical moment, they jerked themselves apart as if a gun had gone off.

'What…what…?' Tess's hammering heart kept missing a stroke, and she struggled upright, frantically trying to clear her head.

What had happened? What was she doing in bed with Gabriel? What was she doing *kissing* Gabriel?

She hadn't actually kissed him, she told herself, grasping desperately at any straw that might somehow make the situation less than excruciatingly, horribly, appallingly embarrassing. Technically, he had been kissing *her*, and even then it hadn't been a real kiss. It wasn't as if their lips had met. When she had slid her arms around his neck, when she had smiled and arched in blissful anticipation as his mouth had drifted towards hers, she hadn't known what she was doing. She hadn't wanted him to kiss her, not really.

She had just been dreaming.

Perhaps she was still dreaming. Perhaps this was just

some terrible nightmare. Tess put her head in her hands and clutched her hair. Please, let it not be real, she prayed.

But it felt real. Her body was booming and twitching as if she could still feel his hand sliding insistently over her hip, his hard, strong body pressing her down into the mattress, the bewitching drift of his lips over her skin. She couldn't have imagined that they would feel that good.

'I'm sorry about that.' Fighting for control, Gabriel had been sitting on the edge of the bed with his back to her, but he turned slightly at last and made himself look at her. 'I don't know what happened there,' he said with an effort.

Tess lifted her head. 'I don't know either,' she said huskily. 'One minute I was dreaming, and the next...' She trailed off as the memory of just what had happened next flamed between them.

'Yes.' Gabriel grimaced. 'I think we must have both been half asleep. I didn't realise I was with you, obviously,' he tried to reassure her.

Obviously? Perversely, Tess stiffened. Why *obviously*? Obviously you're not Fionnula—was that what he was trying to say?

'I'd forgotten what happened last night,' he went on.

Clutching the duvet to her chest, Tess eyed him uneasily. 'What *did* happen?' she asked.

'It was your idea. You invited me to share the bed, and at the time it seemed like a good idea.'

'*I* invited...?' Tess stared at him, appalled. 'When did I do that?'

'About half past five this morning. Don't worry,' Gabriel added ironically, 'it was easily the least flattering invitation I've ever received but, at the time, I had a choice between sleeping with you and sleeping on the couch, and I chose you.'

Tess bit her lip. 'Then, I didn't...?'

'No, you didn't,' said Gabriel in a dry voice. 'You just told me to get in, then rolled over and went back to sleep.

I guess we must have gravitated towards each other in the night—or what was left of it.'

He tried to sound casual, as if it was no big deal and every boss and secretary spent the night together at some stage. He tried not to look at Tess, but somehow his eyes caught hers and held. She was sitting bolt upright in the bed, hugging the duvet to her, and he was very aware of her tumbled hair, of her bare shoulders, of the hollow at the base of her throat where he had kissed her...

With an effort, Gabriel dragged his eyes away and cleared his throat.

'It was just one of those things,' he said gruffly. 'Embarrassing for both of us, but it didn't mean anything.'

Why was it that didn't make her feel any better? Tess wondered.

'No,' she agreed bravely. 'Of course not. Let's forget it.'

Easier said than done, she thought. Being kissed awake by your boss wasn't the kind of thing you could just wipe from your memory, especially not when your skin was still pulsing from the touch of his hands.

Well, she would just have to try and, if she couldn't quite forget, she could at least pretend that she did. She would simply carry on as normal. 'What time is it?'

Good question. Gabriel frowned, noticing the light outside for the first time. He looked at his wrist, but he had left his watch on the coffee table. With the alarm that he had set for six o'clock that morning. There was a sinking feeling in the pit of his stomach as he went through to check.

Groping for her own watch on the bedside table, Tess picked it up just as a muffled curse came from the living area. Half past eight! No wonder Gabriel was furious. He had planned to be in the office an hour ago.

She scrambled out of bed and had a quick shower. When she came out of the bathroom, Gabriel was shoving papers into his attaché case and trying to tighten his tie at the same time.

'No time for breakfast,' he said, after one quick glance at Tess, who was fastening the pearls around her neck. She was wearing the same grey skirt as the day before, with a clean white top. She had gone into the bathroom looking warm and dishevelled, and emerged crisp and businesslike and very much a PA.

How did she do it? Gabriel wondered, momentarily diverted. No one seeing her now would guess that she had been up half the night with a screaming baby.

Nor that she wore satin to bed.

'Are you ready to go?' he asked curtly.

'I am,' said Tess, shrugging on her jacket, 'but what about Harry? He's still asleep.'

'We'll just have to take him with us,' said Gabriel. 'We can't afford to hang around here waiting for him to wake up, and I need you at the office.'

The receptionist's eyebrows crawled into her hairline as she saw Tess and Gabriel coming into the office together, and they nearly disappeared altogether when she spotted the baby. Oblivious to her pantomimed questions behind his back, Gabriel was already working out how to catch up on lost time.

'Get onto an agency and tell them we need a nanny here as soon as possible,' he told Tess as the lift carried them upwards. 'If they can't send someone straight away, see if you can find one of the junior secretaries to look after him until then. I want you to go through the files and make sure all the alterations we checked last night are made on the computer. I'll chase up the legal side.'

He was doing fine, thought Gabriel. Tess was just his PA again. If it hadn't been for the baby she was carrying, he could almost have believed that last night had never happened. And as for this morning, and the softness of her skin and the silkiness of her hair...well, he had practically forgotten it already, he tried to convince himself.

By the time he strode into Tess's office, Gabriel had the day planned out with military precision, plans that were thrown into instant disarray by Harry, who woke up and demanded attention in no uncertain terms the moment Tess sat down at the computer.

The agency Tess rang couldn't get anyone there until lunch-time. Precious time had to be spent changing Harry and then feeding him, and when they tried handing him over to one of the girls from personnel he screamed with such fury that in the end it seemed less trouble to keep him with them.

Having got his own way, and having caught up on all the sleep he had missed the night before, Harry was wide awake and ready to be entertained. Refusing point blank to go back in the pram, he was all smiles when Tess set him on her lap. She did her best, but it was difficult to concentrate on the alterations she was trying to make on the screen when Harry wanted to play with the keyboard too. He thumped at the keys with his dimpled hands and, when Tess moved them away, made a grab instead for the papers she was working from.

Gabriel removed the files and suggested that he read out the alterations, so that Tess didn't have to keep checking between the paper and the screen, and for a while this seemed to work. Harry was distracted by the collection of rulers and pens she'd laid out for him to play with, but it didn't take long for him to put them in his mouth and throw them on the floor, and he was soon reaching enthusiastically for the keyboard once more.

'This is hopeless!' said Gabriel impatiently. 'I'll take him.'

He bent to lift Harry from Tess's lap and, as he did so, he caught the drift of her fragrance, the same scent he had breathed in from her hair when he'd lain in bed beside her.

Straightening abruptly, he stepped away as if from the memory. There were enough distractions to cope with to-day without him getting diverted by thoughts of last night. *Tess* wasn't distracted. She was wearing the same grey suit she always wore; her hair was neatly tied up; her glasses were on; her fingers, unimpeded by Harry, were flying over the keyboard. She was getting on with the job in hand, not wasting time thinking about last night.

He ought to be pleased to find that she was as efficient as usual, Gabriel knew that, but it didn't stop him feeling vaguely disgruntled. Why should she be able to forget last night, when he couldn't get the feel of her out of his mind? He wanted to be able to concentrate on the bid the way she was doing instead of remembering the warmth of her body beneath his hand, the smooth slither of satin over her skin as she rolled against him, the silky tumble of her hair.

Tess was looking enquiringly at him over the top of her spectacles. Gabriel met her eyes for a moment before be-latedly realising that she was waiting for him to continue, and he shifted Harry onto his other arm to cover his dis-comfiture at having lost his place.

'Read back that last figure,' he barked, avoiding her gaze.

'Ninety-seven thousand,' said Tess without inflection, but Gabriel was certain that she knew that he had been thinking about her.

'Right, ninety-seven thousand.' Gabriel had it now. Feeling an idiot, he began reading his way down the next column of figures. If Tess could pretend that last night had never happened, then so could he. He wasn't even going to mention it.

When they reached the end of the section, Tess began printing out the corrected version and got to her feet. 'Shall I see if Harry's ready for a sleep yet?' she offered.

Taking the baby from Gabriel, she lay him in the pram.

Harry made a few half-hearted protests but, to their relief, it wasn't long before his eyes were drooping.

Perhaps now they would be able to get on, thought Gabriel, exasperated by their slow progress. They still had the rest of the report to print out, and he hadn't checked the appendices yet. He should be working out how best to use the time while Harry was asleep.

'Tess?' he said instead.

She looked up from the pram where she was tucking a blanket around Harry. 'Yes?'

'Am I really the boss from hell?'

What kind of damn fool question was that? Gabriel wondered savagely. The words had slipped out before he had realised what he was saying, and now he was going to look like the kind of employer who actually cared what she thought of him!

Tess's eyes had flown up to meet his for a jarring second before they dropped back to the pram. Carefully, she smoothed the blanket. 'That was just Bella trying to be funny,' she said after a moment, amazed that Gabriel had even remembered.

'She wouldn't have said it if you hadn't told her about me,' he said, even as he told himself the sensible thing would be to let the matter drop right now. But somehow he couldn't.

'Everyone complains about their boss,' Tess prevaricated.

'Did you complain about Steve Robinson?'

Steve had been her boss until Gabriel's arrival. From an upstairs room in Kennington, he had built SpaceWorks into a small but prestigious company that had eventually attracted the attention of Gabriel Stearne. SpaceWorks had been no match for the might of Contraxa. Gabriel had circled like a vulture for eighteen months, swooping down the moment the company had hit a low point, and had annexed SpaceWorks to his empire.

The staff had been stunned by the speed of the takeover, none more so than Tess who had found herself working for the very man who had evicted Steve from the company he loved. No one had expected Gabriel to take charge personally and, with a radical restructuring programme in place, no one wanted him to succeed where Steve had failed. The trouble was that there were an awful lot of people like Tess who weren't in a position to walk out the way they might have wanted. Gabriel's one positive action had been to increase the salaries of those who remained after the drastic downsizing operation. When you had dependants, it was difficult to opt for a cut in pay, no matter how much you might dislike your boss.

'Did you?' Gabriel persisted.

Tess put up her chin. If he was so determined to know the truth, he could have it! 'Not very often, no,' she said. 'We all liked Steve,' she added deliberately. 'He's a very nice man.'

'He may have been nice, but he wasn't effective.' Gabriel was annoyed with himself for starting this conversation. What the hell did it matter to him what Tess thought of him? 'If left to Steve Robinson, SpaceWorks would have been bankrupt within the year, and then you would all have been looking for a new boss anyway.'

'I know Steve wasn't very good at the financial side of things, but he was effective in other ways,' said Tess loyally. 'He could motivate people in a way you would never understand. He knew everybody's name, and made everyone feel important. It didn't matter whether your job was coming up with an original design or just photocopying, Steve would always congratulate you if you'd put a lot of effort into what you were doing.'

'I expect my staff to make an effort as a matter of course,' said Gabriel distantly. 'Why should I congratulate them for doing the jobs they're paid to do?'

'Because they'll work even harder the next time if you

do. It wouldn't kill you to show a little appreciation now and then. You haven't made the slightest effort to get to know the people who work for you.'

He hunched an irritable shoulder. 'I know you.'

'No, you don't.'

'I know you better than I did yesterday,' Gabriel said unfairly, and the air between them reverberated suddenly with the memory of waking up in each other's arms.

Tess flushed and bit back a sharp retort. She didn't want to think about the way they had kissed. Gabriel had no business bringing it up here in the office.

'The point is that the staff here are all loyal to the company,' she said grittily. 'They all want SpaceWorks to succeed, and that's a huge asset to any business. But if you're not careful, you're going to lose it. You could learn a lot from Steve's management style.'

Gabriel's black brows snapped together. 'Oh, you think so, do you?' he said dangerously, but Tess refused to be intimidated.

'Yes, I do.'

'I didn't realise you were a management consultant as well as a PA.'

Tess set her teeth at his sarcasm. 'You asked,' she reminded him with a defiant look. It wouldn't do Gabriel any harm at all to realise how much everyone at SpaceWorks disliked him.

And after waking up in his arms this morning, it wouldn't do her any harm to remember, either.

'Well, if you've quite finished your analysis, perhaps we can get on,' said Gabriel tightly, ignoring the fact that he had started the conversation. Stalking over to the printer, he picked up the finished pages and headed for his office.

'Finish those alterations and then you can start making up the final report. I'll be in my office. I don't want to be disturbed!'

He slammed the door shut behind him, leaving Tess staring after him in impotent rage.

'I see our boss is being his usual charming self this morning,' said an amused voice behind her, and she turned to see Niles who worked in the marketing department, and who was an inveterate flirt and an even worse gossip. Few people took him seriously, but it was impossible not to like him.

Unlike some, thought Tess darkly, thinking of Gabriel.

'What can I do for you, Niles?' she asked, and he strolled into the office, clasping a hand dramatically to his chest.

'Stop breaking my heart, Tess, and say you'll marry me.'

'I'm afraid I can't help you with that one,' said Tess, who was used to this routine. She sat back at her computer and reached for the next file. 'Anything else?'

'You can tell me what's going on between you and Gabriel Stearne,' Niles suggested, perching on the edge of her desk. 'There are all sorts of rumours going around the office about you two coming in together this morning with a baby.'

Amused at the idea of Tess having a secret affair with Gabriel, he started to laugh, only to break off as he caught sight of Harry's pram, and he turned to stare at her. 'Don't tell me it's true!'

Tess sighed. 'It's a long story, Niles, but it's not what you're thinking.'

'You're not sleeping with the boss?'

Only the faintest tinge of colour betrayed Tess's confusion. 'Of course not.' she said sharply. 'Niles, I'm very busy. Did you want something or are you just here to gossip?'

'No, I'm here in my capacity as social secretary,' he said grandly. 'We've decided to do something different this year for our charity bash. The idea is to have a promises auction, in aid of the children's hospital. It's a great night, so we're hoping everyone will come.'

'How does it work?'

'Haven't you ever been to one before?' Niles settled more comfortably onto her desk. 'You promise to do something—say, babysit for an evening—and anyone who wants a babysitter will bid for you, and the money goes to charity instead. This time, we're going to have a raffle as well,' he added.

'Frankly, some of the things people have offered aren't likely to attract that many bids, so we thought we'd run it as a kind of lucky dip. You buy a ticket, and win whatever has been promised for that number. It was the only way we could think of to get rid of some of them, but it should be laugh.'

He paused and looked expectantly at Tess. 'So what are you going to promise?'

'Me?'

'Come on, Tess, you've got to set a good example. Lynette in accounts is promising to wash your car wearing only a bikini!'

Tess laughed. 'I'm sure there'll be some heavy bidding for that one!'

'That's what we're hoping. But I bet you could match it if you tried. It's all in a good cause, remember.'

'Well, I'm certainly not putting my bikini on in October, but I'll try and think of something,' she promised.

'Tess, where is—?' Gabriel came out of his room and stopped dead at the sight of Tess laughing with Niles, who was perched far too familiarly on her desk.

Niles slid off at the expression on his face. 'Good morning, sir,' he said.

'I wondered what all the noise was about.' Gabriel was looking boot-faced. 'Haven't you both got something better to do than sit there gossiping?'

Tess opened her mouth to protest, but Niles got in first.

'I'm here about the staff party in November,' he said. 'We're running a promises auction to raise money for charity, and Tess was just agreeing to take part.'

'Really?' said Gabriel discouragingly.

'We're hoping we can count on your support too, sir. It would be a boost for staff morale if you'd come along.'

Gabriel had opened his mouth to refuse when he caught Tess's eye, and shut it again. He didn't want another lecture on treating employees like her precious Steve had. 'I'll do my best,' he said grudgingly.

'That's great.' Niles decided to push his luck. 'And you'll make a promise for the auction?'

'Yes, yes,' said Gabriel testily, waving Niles aside. 'Put me down for anything. Tess, I can't find the Liechenstein file.'

'Thank you, sir.' Niles grinned at Tess and made a thumbs-up sign behind Gabriel's back as he slid out of the office.

A briskly competent nanny appeared at twelve. Gabriel gave her the key to his apartment and directions as to how to get there, and she took Harry away. She assured them that she knew exactly how to deal with him, but his wails of protest as she pushed him in his pram out to the lift seemed to linger accusingly in the office long after he had gone.

After less than three hours' sleep, Tess knew that she ought to have been grateful not to have to think about the baby any more, but the office seemed strangely empty without him, and she kept turning to look for him.

It was a very long day. The proposal was completed at five o'clock and couriered round to meet the five-thirty deadline. As soon as it had gone, Tess was overwhelmed with exhaustion, and she collapsed into her chair. Her eyes felt gritty and there was a tight band inside her head. She wanted nothing more than to go home, soak in a deep bath and go to bed. At least the next day was Saturday. She could have a lie in and catch up on her lost sleep.

Yawning, she filed all the papers they had been using, checked her e-mail for any urgent messages, and decided that as the clock now stood at five forty-five she could legitimately leave the office.

Gabriel came in from his office as she was switching off her computer. 'Are you going home?'

'There's nothing else, is there?'

'No,' he said, but he hesitated.

'Are you sure?'

'Of course I'm sure,' he said irritably. How could he tell her that he didn't want her to leave? That he didn't want to go back to his impersonal apartment alone, with only that terrifyingly competent nanny for company?

There was a pause. Tess fumbled with her coat, suddenly unable to find the sleeve opening, and in the end Gabriel held the coat for her so that she could slip her arm inside.

'Thank you for all your help today,' he said as if the words had been forced out of him.

A thank you from Gabriel Stearne! Tess knew that she ought to feel triumphant, but all she could think was that he was standing very close. When Steve had complimented her, it had been easy to respond, but she wasn't used to Gabriel being nice, and she didn't know what to say. It was easier when he was being unpleasant, in a way.

'That's all right,' she said awkwardly. 'I was just doing my job. It's what you pay me for.'

Conscious that she had sounded rather ungracious, she made a big deal of fastening the buttons of her coat as he stepped away from her. Fixing a bright smile to her face, she bent to pick up her bag. 'I'll see you on Monday, then.'

'Have a good weekend,' said Gabriel in a strangely colourless voice. 'Goodnight, Tess.'

'Goodnight, Mr Stearne.'

'For God's sake, Tess!' he burst out, suddenly furious with her.

How dared she be so cool and formal with him when he had kissed her skin, when he had buried his face in her hair, when his hand had traced the soft contours of her body? 'We slept together last night,' he said savagely. 'In the circumstances, I think you could call me Gabriel, don't you?'

He was pleased to see a faint hint of colour along her cheekbones at his reminder. So she hadn't forgotten completely.

'If that's what you'd prefer,' she said stiltedly after a moment.

'It is,' Gabriel snapped. There was no need for her to make it sound as if he was forcing her into an unwanted intimacy. She hadn't called Steve Mr Robinson, had she? No, it had been Steve this, Steve that, Steve's a very nice man!

'I'll see you on Monday,' he said curtly, turning on his heel.

Letting herself into her house after an even slower bus ride than usual, Tess was conscious of a feeling of anticlimax. It was inevitable after coping with an unexpected baby and a crucial deadline, she told herself. Nothing whatsoever to do with not seeing Gabriel until Monday.

She wished he hadn't reminded her about sleeping together. She had tried so hard to dismiss their awakening as unimportant, and there had been times during the day when Gabriel had been so difficult that it had been easy to tell herself that she had put the entire incident out of her mind.

And then he had helped her into her coat, and his hands had brushed against her shoulders and memories had come back in a rush of sensation. It was all very well to tell herself that she had been practically asleep, but she could still feel his lips moving over her skin, still feel his hands hard against her with disturbing clarity.

Tess shivered anew at the memory and shut the front door behind her with unnecessary emphasis.

The red light was blinking on the answer machine in the kitchen. Glad of the distraction, she listened to the two messages while she took off her coat.

'Tess, it's Bella. Why haven't you rung me? I'm dying to know how you got on with the baby and—more importantly—how you got on with Gabriel Stearne. You promised you'd tell me everything, remember?'

Tess grimaced at Bella's words. She might have promised, but she wouldn't be telling her friend *quite* everything, that was for sure. She could tell her about Harry and changing his nappy, but not about ending up in bed with Gabriel, and certainly not about waking up with him! She would ring Bella back tomorrow and give her some very edited highlights when she was feeling better able to cope with her friend's probing questions. Sometimes Bella knew her a little too well for comfort.

The second message was from Andrew.

'Hi, sis, it's me. Thanks for your e-mail. I hate to ask, but I was wondering when you'd be able to send the cheque you mentioned? The landlord's hassling us about the deposit, and I'm really short of cash at the moment. I had a quote to repair the car after those joyriders pranged it too, and it's going to cost a packet.'

Tess hung up her coat with a sigh. She had been so proud when Andrew had got into university, but she'd had no idea how expensive his studies would prove to be. Not that he seemed to do much studying. From all she could gather, he spent most of his time playing sport or going out with friends.

He had got himself a part-time job in a pub to earn some extra cash so that he didn't have to rely on her too much, but she didn't want him working any more hours than he already did. He spent little enough time at his books as it was. She would just have to find the money from somewhere. Double or not, the overtime she had earned last night obviously wasn't going to be enough.

Too tired to think about it then, Tess wearily climbed the stairs to the bathroom and ran a hot bath. She felt better after a long, luxurious soak by candlelight. Her tense muscles had relaxed and her skin was pink and glowing by the time she got out. Wrapping herself in a towelling robe, she wandered downstairs to the kitchen in search of something to eat. She was rubbing her wet hair absently and contemplating the contents of her fridge without enthusiasm when the doorbell rang.

Tess frowned as she looked at her watch. Nine-thirty. Who would be calling now? One of her neighbours? She hoped it wasn't the man from number seventeen, who was the local Neighbourhood Watch contact and took his duties very seriously. He was always popping round at odd times, extolling the benefits of security lights and double locks.

Barefoot, she padded along the narrow hallway and peered cautiously through the peephole in the front door.

Her heart jolted when she saw who was standing on her step, and her hands weren't quite steady as she opened the door.

'Can we come in? Gabriel asked. He was holding a sleeping Harry in his arms, and he sounded oddly hesitant.

Without a word, Tess stood back to let him past into the narrow hall. 'What's the matter?' she said, oddly breathless as she closed the door behind them. 'Where's the nanny?'

'Gone.'

'Gone? Gone where?' Tess began, only to break off. Gabriel was looking so frayed that it seemed unfair to subject him to a cross-examination in the cramped and uncomfortable confines of her hall. 'You'd better come and sit down,' she said instead, pointing him towards the sitting room.

Gabriel lowered himself gratefully onto a small sofa facing the fireplace, and dropped his car keys onto the low wooden table in front of it. Harry was sound asleep. He shifted the baby carefully in his arms and wondered how he was going to explain to Tess why he had invaded her house and her private time once more.

His massive presence seemed to fill the room. Very conscious of her wet, tangled hair and pink face, Tess sat on the edge of an armchair and folded the towelling robe primly around her bare legs.

'I think you should tell me exactly what's happened,' she said, trying to sound as crisp as she could when she was half naked and her hair was dripping down her neck. She squeezed the ends with the towel. 'Couldn't the nanny find your apartment?'

'Oh, she found it all right, but apparently it's not what she's used to.' In spite of his uncharacteristically tired appearance, there was plenty of the old bite in Gabriel's voice as he recalled his reception when he had walked into the apartment. 'She insists on her own room and her own bathroom,' he went on, mimicking the girl's demands. 'She expects the use of a car, and regular time off. Oh, and meals provided. Sending her off to an apartment with an empty fridge was completely unacceptable!'

'Oh, dear,' said Tess weakly. 'Perhaps we should have taken the time to tell her what to expect.'

She hadn't been told what to expect last night, but she had coped, thought Gabriel. She hadn't made a fuss or irritated him with truculent demands. She hadn't complained about having to sleep in his bed or make do with take-away pizza.

He looked across at where she was perched on an armchair, and realised for the first time that she must have just stepped out of the bath. Her skin was glowing, and her hair hung damply around her face, and he had a sudden, sharp awareness that beneath the towelling robe she must be naked.

He forced his gaze back to the fire. 'When I got back to the apartment, it was to find Harry bawling and the so-called nanny more concerned about clarifying the terms of her contract than looking after the baby.'

Tess grimaced, imagining the scene. Gabriel's temper was short at the best of times, and after a broken night and a long, stressful day in the office he would have been in no mood to deal with hectoring demands.

'The final straw was when she refused to allow me to spend the night in my own apartment,' Gabriel went on grimly. 'She didn't like the fact that there was no bedroom door, and she clearly didn't trust me to stay on the couch.' He snorted at the memory. 'I told her I didn't anticipate any problems in keeping my hands off her, but that just caused more offence!

'I lost my temper in the end,' he confessed, and Tess was only surprised that he had kept it as long as he had. 'I told her that if she didn't like it she could go,' he said, deciding to omit the fact that he had put it in much stronger terms than that. 'I said I could look after Harry by myself.'

'And she took you at your word?'

'Yes.' Gabriel avoided her clear brown gaze. 'I know I shouldn't have snapped at her,' he said grudgingly, 'but I was tired and Harry was crying, and she wouldn't shut up. I thought I'd be able to manage without her...'

'But?' said Tess, resigned, when he trailed off.

'But I couldn't,' he admitted.

CHAPTER FIVE

'I DID try,' he said defensively. 'I changed his nappy and walked him around, the way we did last night, but he wouldn't stop crying, and when I gave him something to eat, he went purple and started choking. I was desperate in the end. I didn't know what to do.' He looked at Tess. 'All I could think of was you.'

There was a slight frown in his eyes as he remembered that humiliating sense of inadequacy and how instinctively he had thought of Tess: Tess with her cool voice and her cool air, Tess with her warm eyes and her warm body; Tess who was calm and competent and who wouldn't let him down.

'I couldn't ask Fionnula,' he went on, as if he needed to justify why he had turned to her. 'She's working tonight, some programme that's going out live, and anyway, she's still angry with me about standing her up last night. I couldn't think of anything else to do. I put Harry in the car and came over and...well, here we are.'

He looked down at the sleeping baby in his arms with an expression of baffled frustration. There was no trace now of the screaming bundle of furious energy he had been only half an hour ago. What could be so difficult about looking after a peacefully slumbering baby like this?

'He fell asleep in the car,' he told Tess, remembered relief at the sudden silence mingling with annoyance that Harry was making it so difficult to convince Tess of what he had been like. 'But I can't drive around all night.'

Tess was rubbing her hair with the towel, as if she needed something to do with her hands to disguise her uncertainty about the whole situation. She looked wary, thought Gabriel. She knew what he was going to ask her.

'Please, Tess,' he said, reflecting that he seemed to spend most of his time begging her to help him these days. 'I know it's a lot to ask. I know you didn't get much sleep last night, and how hard you've worked all day, but I really need you.'

He stopped, hearing too late what he had said. Tess had paused, one hand clutching the towel against her head, and it seemed to Gabriel that his words echoed mockingly in the sudden silence. *I really need you…need you…need you…*

'Well, you know,' he amended awkwardly.

Tess smiled a little crookedly as she lowered the towel. 'I know,' she said without meeting his eyes.

It was chastening to have to admit how useless he felt, but Gabriel set his teeth and floundered on. 'You must remember what it was like last night. Harry won't stay sleeping like this. He'll wake up and he'll cry and I won't know what to do with him. If you would just come back with me again tonight, I promise I'll make other arrangements tomorrow.'

He paused and looked at Tess, who was dabbing absently at the drips down her neck and avoiding his eyes. She was trying to think of a way to refuse, thought Gabriel with a sinking feeling.

'I'll give you anything you want if you'll come with me.' he said rashly.

She looked up at that. 'Anything?'

'Money…time off in lieu…a plane ticket to wherever you want…anything.'

'How about you promising to be nice to your staff for a change?'

Tess's voice was very dry. She hadn't meant it seriously, but Gabriel had said 'OK' almost before she had finished speaking, and she put her head on one side, considering how she might turn his dilemma into a general advantage.

'You'll acknowledge greetings instead of ignoring people the way you usually do?'

'Yes.'

'You'll say please and thank you?'

'Yes.'

'You'll come to the office party?'

Gabriel set his jaw. 'Yes.'

She lifted her brows in exaggerated surprise. 'You must be desperate.' she said.

'I am.'

The grey eyes looked directly into hers, and Tess saw with a trace of compunction that there were dark circles beneath them. His face was drawn and he needed a shave. She had been working hard in the run up to submitting the bid today, but Gabriel had worked even harder and longer. He had had no more sleep than she'd had last night, and after a frantic day in the office he hadn't even had the luxury of a long, hot bath nor any time to himself at all before being faced with a stroppy nanny and a screaming baby. No wonder he looked tired.

'All right,' she said abruptly.

She got to her feet before she had a chance to change her mind, inadvertently revealing a length of thigh as her robe slipped apart. Pulling it hastily together, she tightened the belt with unnecessary emphasis. 'You'll have to wait while I dry my hair and get dressed.'

'Of course,' said Gabriel with a smile.

His smile held nothing but a kind of weary relief, but Tess felt her heart stumble. He might not be smiling the way he had smiled at Harry, but he was smiling at *her*. She could hear the clock on the mantelpiece ticking into the silence, and she was suddenly, disturbingly aware of him, of his dark hair and his pale eyes, of the lines bracketing his mouth and the stubble on his jaw, of his hand cupping Harry against his chest.

She swallowed. 'Well…make yourself comfortable,' she said, and was horrified to hear that it came out as a croak rather than the gracious and composed invitation she had intended. 'I won't be long.'

'Tess?' said Gabriel abruptly as she turned to leave.

She paused with one hand on the door, and looked over her shoulder. 'Yes?'

'Thanks,' he said simply.

Upstairs, Tess tipped her head down and turned the hairdryer on full blast. She felt ridiculously thrown by Gabriel's smile. Really, she thought, she must be getting soft! She should have said no. She could have made up some excuse. Why hadn't she said that she was going out, or expecting an important phone call? Now Gabriel would expect her to give up all her free time whenever he needed her to help him out of his personal mess.

It wasn't as if he had ever done anything for her. She didn't even *like* the man! There was no reason for her to face another sleepless night when her body was already buzzing with exhaustion.

Except that he had thanked her.

Except that he had smiled.

Except that he had looked straight into her eyes and had said that he needed her.

Left alone in the sitting room, Gabriel let out a long sigh and settled himself back on the couch. As if sensing the tension draining out of him, Harry snuffled and snuggled closer.

'Make yourself comfortable,' Tess had said. Gabriel eased off his shoes and stretched out until he lay diagonally across the couch with his feet propped up on the coffee table, and Harry sprawled face down on his chest.

He could hear Tess moving around upstairs. It was a comforting sort of noise, and gradually Gabriel let himself relax. His gaze travelled around the room, taking it in for the first time. It was decorated in warm, rich colours, and the haphazard piles of books and objects that covered every surface gave the room a feel of cosy chaos.

Remembering how organised Tess was in the office, and the uncluttered efficiency of her desk, Gabriel lifted his brows in surprise. This wasn't the kind of room he had imagined her to come home to every night. It was somehow unexpected.

Like Tess.

The warmth and tranquillity of the room were having their effect. Gabriel tried to keep himself awake by studying the collection of unusual objects Tess had displayed in the alcoves on either side of the pretty Victorian fireplace. There was an old spice box and an ornate, oriental birdcage next to a photograph of a smiling couple in a heavy silver frame. Gabriel couldn't see it clearly from where he was, and it would have disturbed Harry if he had got up to inspect the picture. He had better stay right where he was.

From upstairs came the sound of a hair-dryer. She would be down in a minute, and he could have a closer look at the photo then. In the meantime, there would be no harm in closing his eyes for a minute…

Tess's hair had dried into a wayward cloud. Unable to control it any other way, she tied it back with a scrunchie and surveyed her reflection critically. In jeans and a sweatshirt, she looked practical rather than pretty, she decided. Safe rather than seductive. Not like a girl who would invite her boss to bed, or open the door to him wearing only a towelling robe.

And what exactly do you need to feel safe about? Tess asked herself, but couldn't come up with a satisfactory answer. She concentrated on packing her bag instead, scrabbling through her drawers to find a more demure nightdress this time, just in case she ended up sharing a bed with Gabriel again.

A slow shiver snaked down her spine at the memory of waking that morning with his arms around her, and his body hard against her own. No, it would be safer if she dealt with Harry herself tonight, and let Gabriel sleep on the sofa.

Safer. There was that word again.

Zipping up her bag with unnecessary emphasis, Tess carried it downstairs and dropped it by the front door.

She hesitated outside the sitting room. It was ridiculous to be nervous at the thought of spending another night with him. It wasn't as if it were a date. It was just a practical arrangement. Gabriel was her boss and, if it wasn't for Harry, there was no way he would be sitting on her sofa, waiting to drive her back to his apartment. He would be out with the likes of Fionnula Jenkins and his PA would be the very last person on his mind.

So why was her heart thudding at the thought of the night ahead?

Taking a deep breath, Tess pushed open the door. 'I'm rea—' she began, only to break off as she saw Gabriel sprawled across the sofa, Harry spread-eagled on his chest.

Both were sound asleep.

She stood and looked down at them for a moment, a curious expression in her eyes. In sleep, the harsh lines of Gabriel's face had softened, and he had lost that grim, guarded look that was so typical of him. His head had fallen to one side, and the dark hair flopped over his forehead in a way that he would hate if he were awake. Tess's fingers twitched with an involuntary impulse to smooth it back into place.

Abruptly, she stepped back out of reach.

If she had any sense, she told herself severely, she would shake Gabriel awake and make him drive her back to his cold, characterless apartment. This was her home. He had no business falling asleep here.

But he had looked so tired, and she didn't have the heart to wake either of them.

Gabriel's car keys were sitting on the coffee table. Tess picked them up and weighed them in her hand for a moment's indecision before making up her mind. She let herself quietly out of the house and found the car parked almost right outside. Trust Gabriel to get the best spot.

As she had hoped, he had brought Harry in the carrycot which he had detached from the pram. A bottle and a spare nappy were on the seat beside it. He had obviously set out prepared for the worst. Tess put them in the cot and carried them all back inside.

Neither Gabriel nor Harry had stirred. Very gently, Tess lifted the baby off Gabriel's chest. He squirmed and mouthed in instinctive protest at being moved from his comfortable position, but he didn't wake, and she was able to carry him upstairs and lay him in his cot beside her bed.

There was a duvet on Andrew's bed. Bundling it up, she took it downstairs and covered Gabriel as best she could. The wayward lock of hair was still straggling over his forehead. Succumbing to temptation, Tess pushed it gently away from his face. Her fingers lingered for a moment against his temple before she realised what she was doing and snatched her hand away. A faint flush stained her cheeks as she left him, switching off the light with a sharp click as she went.

Gabriel woke with a stiff neck and an even stiffer back. He was lying half on, half off a couch that was several feet too short for him, and his face was pressed uncomfortably into a cushion.

He sat up with a groan, disentangling himself with difficulty from a mass of bedding. Where had all that come from? he wondered blearily.

Dropping his head into his hands, he raked his fingers through his hair. He remembered arriving at Tess's house, and how she had looked when she'd opened the door with her face pink and glowing and her hair all damp and tangled. He remembered the sense of relief when she'd agreed to come with him, leaning back on the couch as the iron bands of tension that had held him in their grip had loosened and unlocked one by one.

And then...nothing. He must have fallen asleep.

Gabriel looked at his watch and grimaced as he got stiffly to his feet. He had slept the night through!

Cautiously, he opened the sitting room door. A radio was playing somewhere, and he followed the sound down the narrow hallway, past the wooden stairs, and into a surprisingly large kitchen. Autumn sun poured through the French windows, which opened onto a tiny patio garden, and made him blink after the dimness of the hall.

Tess was sitting at a scrubbed pine table, giving Harry a bottle of milk. She looked up as Gabriel appeared in the doorway. 'Good morning,' she said.

'Sorry,' he said, rubbing a hand over his face. 'I didn't mean to fall asleep.'

'You were tired.'

She did her best to sound casual, as if she hadn't even noticed the intimacy of his rumpled clothes and dark, dishevelled hair. There was a red mark across his cheek where his face had been pressed into the braid of one of the cushions.

'I must have been to have slept like that.' Gabriel sat down at the table, wincing at the stiffness of his muscles. 'Thanks for tucking me up,' he added.

There was an odd note in his voice, and a hint of colour stole into Tess's cheeks. What if he had been aware of her tenderly smoothing the hair from his forehead? Her fingertips prickled with the remembered feel of stubble on his warm skin. 'I didn't want you to get cold,' she said, avoiding his eyes.

A pause.

'How was Harry last night?' asked Gabriel after a moment.

'He woke up a couple of times, but the second time I took him into bed with me, and after that he was fine.'

As well he might have been, Gabriel thought involuntarily. He remembered what it was like being in bed with Tess himself.

'You should have woken me,' he said stiffly, uncomfortably aware of the awkwardness of the situation. How the hell were you supposed to behave to your PA when you had fallen asleep on her? 'I didn't mean you to cope with him by yourself.'

'It was no problem.'

Typical Tess, thought Gabriel with an edge of resentment. Nothing was ever a problem for her.

He studied her as she sat Harry up and rubbed his back. There was a confidence about the way she dealt with the baby now. It was hard to believe that she had once been as nervous about Harry as he still was. There must be some kind of mysterious feminine gene that gave her the assurance he lacked.

She was wearing a blue sweatshirt, the sleeves pushed casually above her delicate wrists, and the sunlight through the window brought out the gold in her hair. This morning, she had tied it back in a loose plait, which made her look younger and much more relaxed than she did in the office, but there was still a coolness and a freshness about her that was characteristic.

Her neatness was a reproach. Conscious suddenly of his own crumpled state, Gabriel rubbed a palm over his jaw with a grimace.

'Why don't you have a shower?' Tess suggested. 'You'd feel better. There's a razor in the bathroom, too, if you wanted to shave. You can't miss the bathroom—it's right at the top of the stairs.'

Whose razor was it? Gabriel wondered as he climbed the wooden stairs with their ridiculously narrow steps.

As Tess had predicted, he found the bathroom without difficulty, but she hadn't warned him about the array of frivolous, luxurious silk lingerie drying on a cord strung over the bathtub. Raising his eyebrows, Gabriel moved it cautiously out of the way. He wished he hadn't seen it. It was proving hard enough to keep his image of Tess as a cool, professional secretary intact as it was without knowing that beneath those prim grey suits of hers she was wearing *that*.

The razor proved to be of an old-fashioned variety, but he managed a shave, only cutting himself twice, and by the time he had showered he realised that Tess had been right: he did feel better.

The smell of freshly brewed coffee wafted up the stairs. Gabriel sniffed appreciatively as he went back into the kitchen. 'That smells good.'

Tess turned quickly from where she was trying to plunge the cafetière one-handed, with Harry on her hip.

'Here, let me,' said Gabriel.

She stepped away, very aware of his strong hands, and the dark hair still wet from the shower and sleeked close to his head.

'Um…I'm sorry about all the washing,' she said, embarrassed. 'I forgot all about it.'

'No problem,' said Gabriel briefly, his eyes on the cafetière. 'I moved it so it didn't get wet, but I've put it back.'

A queer feeling stirred inside Tess at the thought of his hands on her underwear. 'Thanks.' She cleared her throat. 'Well…how about a coffee?' Shifting Harry onto her other hip, she got two mugs out of the cupboard above.

'You're getting good at this,' commented Gabriel, nodding at Harry, who was drooling placidly onto her sweatshirt, and looking quite at home on her hip.

'I know.' Relieved at the change of subject, Tess ran her fingers through Harry's downy curls. 'I was terrified of him when he first arrived, but I'm getting quite fond of him now,' she confessed.

'I need to do something about tracking down his mother.' Gabriel poured coffee into the mugs and carried them over to the table. 'There wasn't time yesterday but finding her is a priority now. I'll get private investigators onto it.'

He sat down and frowned into his coffee as he pondered who best to approach. He presumed that there would be people in London who could do the job, but if Leanne had indeed gone back to the Caribbean, it might be better to go through a firm in the States. 'It can't take that long to find her, surely,' he said.

'I would have thought it would be a few days at least,' said Tess, who was also considering the matter. 'And once you've found her, you've still got to get her back here. I think we should plan on having him for a week.'

'A week!' Gabriel knew that she was right, but it didn't make him like the situation any better. He sighed. 'I'll have to try and get hold of another nanny, but there's still the problem of my apartment. I don't fancy another whole week of sleeping on the couch! Perhaps I should book into a hotel?' he added as the thought occurred to him. 'I could get a separate room for the nanny and Harry.'

'That seems a bit extravagant,' commented Tess, blowing on her coffee to cool it.

'Have you got any better ideas?'

This was the opening she had been waiting for. 'Yes,' she said with a level look. 'I could carry on helping you to look after him.'

'*You*? I thought you didn't know anything about babies?'

'I'm learning fast.' Tess hesitated. 'Look, Harry's just settling down. Why disrupt him again just when he's getting used to us? He's been passed around enough recently as it is.'

There were definite advantages to the idea, Gabriel had to admit. Not the least of which was the time it would save in trying to find a nanny who would stay in his apartment. Even if he found one prepared to put up with the lack of doors, the chances were that she wouldn't last long. As Tess had pointed out so succinctly, his management style wasn't the easiest.

But it didn't add up. Gabriel regarded her suspiciously, his dark brows drawn together in a frown and the pale grey eyes uncomfortably keen. 'Why would you want to give up your weekend, not to mention an entire week, looking after a baby who has nothing to do with you and is, if anybody's, my responsibility?'

Tess fidgeted with her mug. 'I'm not suggesting I do it for free,' she said, and made herself look straight at him. 'I'd expect to be paid on top of my salary.'

Ah, so that was it. Money. He might have guessed, thought Gabriel cynically. 'You want money?'

Tess flushed slightly at his tone. 'I don't think it's unreasonable,' she said, putting up her chin. 'I'd be giving up all my free time for a weekend and, as we've discovered, looking after a baby is hard work.'

'I don't deny it.'

Gabriel wasn't sure why he felt disillusioned. He had always known that money was the greatest motivator of them all. He just hadn't had Tess down as a materialist. He should have known better. In his experience, women talked a lot about emotions but, when it came down to it, he had yet to meet one whose motives weren't entirely mercenary at heart, no matter how hard she tried to dress them up in woolly sentiment. Why had he expected Tess to be any different?

'I'm sure we could come to some arrangement,' he said

distantly. 'But what about your job? I need someone to look after Harry, but I also need you in the office.'

'I could take him in with me,' said Tess, trying not to sound too eager. 'Things should be quieter next week and, if it does get busy, I could always ask one of the other secretaries to help me out. I think it could work.'

Why was she so keen to take on the job? Gabriel wondered, and then took himself to task. What was it to him if Tess was prepared to do anything for money? She was saving him the trouble of finding someone else to help him look after Harry, and that was all that mattered.

'All right,' he said briskly. 'If you think that you can manage, we'll carry on as we are.'

Tess was relieved. She had worked out on the back of an envelope earlier that morning how much overtime she could earn, and if she included nights—and she didn't see why she shouldn't—it came to a surprisingly large sum. It would be hard work, of course, but it was only for a week, and at the end of it she would be able to send Andrew enough to pay off most of his outstanding debts.

She saw Gabriel pushing back his chair as if making ready to leave and she bit her lip. 'There is just one thing,' she said. 'Would you mind staying here?'

Gabriel sank slowly back into his chair. 'Wouldn't *you* mind?' he countered. 'You've always struck me as someone who keeps her private and her professional life quite separate.'

'I do usually,' she said, 'but I don't really want to spend the next week in your apartment. It's not very suitable for a baby,' she excused herself. 'And at least here I've got a spare room. You wouldn't have to sleep on the sofa again.'

'That would make a nice change,' he conceded dryly. He looked directly at Tess. 'Are you sure?'

Tess took a sharp breath. 'Yes, I'm sure.'

'In that case, I'll go home and get some clean clothes. I can bring the rest of Harry's stuff back with me. And then,' said Gabriel, getting to his feet, 'I think we're going to have to go shopping.'

Inevitably, it was awkward at first. There was something uncomfortably intimate about going to the supermarket with Gabriel, finding out what vegetables he liked, puzzling over the array of different nappies on sale, standing next to him in the checkout queue.

Did they look as out of place as they felt? Tess wondered. Or would anyone walking past them as they regarded the baby goods assume that they were an ordinary couple, with their first baby gurgling happily in the trolley beside them?

Her eyes slid sideways to Gabriel who was reading the instructions on the back of a packet of rusks with a sceptical expression. No, he might be a lot of things, but ordinary would never be one of them. In spite of his unexceptional jeans and dark blue guernsey, there was a toughness about him that marked him out in this prosaic setting.

Tess had to keep reminding herself that this was just a job, and that Gabriel was just her boss—and a difficult, exacting boss at that! But it was hard to keep up the formality when Gabriel, evidently deciding that the only thing to do was to throw money at the problem, swept her off to a store and insisted on buying an entire range of equipment for Harry.

'We can't keep using that old pram,' he said roughly. 'I'm sick of taking it to pieces and putting it together again. I'm going to buy him a proper cot, and his mother can have it—if she ever reappears!'

He got hold of an assistant who could hardly believe her luck when she realised that they needed help and that money was no object. It wasn't long before they found themselves loading Gabriel's car with a high chair, a cot with bedding, a special mat for Harry, an assortment of bibs, bowls and bottles, and a bouncy chair that the assistant had assured them that he would enjoy. Tess had found some little outfits, too, that had gone in with it all, along with some educational toys that the assistant had recommended, although they'd had more fun choosing a glove puppet and arguing over the merits of a mischievous fox and a dopey-looking rabbit.

Fun. It seemed an odd word to associate with the dour Gabriel, thought Tess as they drove back to her house but, once the initial constraint had evaporated, he had been surprisingly easy to get on with.

She slid a puzzled glance at him, her gaze lingering on the forceful planes and angles of his face and coming to rest at last on his stern mouth. It looked cool and firm, but those lips had been warm against her throat…

Tess jerked her eyes away. Her heart was drumming with unwanted memories and she had to take a steadying breath. She was supposed to have forgotten how he had kissed her.

She *had* forgotten, Tess tried to convince herself. It was just that every now and then the memory would catch her unawares, and she would have to forget it all over again.

Harry was hungry by the time they got home. Gabriel took a turn at feeding him while Tess heated some soup for lunch, and he studied her covertly as she stood with her back to him at the stove, stirring. Funny how he had never realised before what a good figure she had. Nor how her face lit when she smiled.

Gabriel forced himself to look away. He stared instead at the photographs, postcards and cartoons pinned to a board by the table. In pride of place was an enlargement of a good-looking young man leaning proudly against the bonnet of a car. His arms were folded, and his face was split by a broad grin.

A boyfriend? Gabriel frowned. The boy in the photograph looked much younger than Tess, but that didn't mean very much.

'Who's that?' The question came out more abruptly than he intended.

Tess turned to see what he was looking at. Cupping her hand beneath the wooden spoon to catch any drips, she came over to follow his gaze. 'Oh, that's Andrew,' she said.

'Andrew?' Even to his own ears, Gabriel sounded hostile, and Tess glanced at him curiously.

'My brother,' she explained. 'I took that picture of him on his twenty-first earlier this year.' She shook her head at the photograph, but she was smiling. 'He loves that old car.'

She didn't add that she had given him most of the money to buy it. It had been little more than a heap of metal then, so heaven knew what kind of state it was in now that the joyriders had finished with it.

Standing beside Gabriel's chair, she was close enough for him to smell her perfume. Looking up at her, he could see how her expression softened as she thought about her brother. The corner of her mouth curved upwards in a fond smile, and Gabriel was conscious of a pang of something that he might have suspected was jealousy if he hadn't known better.

Because how could he possibly be jealous?

He looked back down at Harry. 'I didn't know you had a brother,' he said, and it occurred to him that there were an awful lot of things about Tess that he didn't know.

Tess went back to her soup. 'There's just the two of us,' she told him. 'My parents were killed in an accident, twelve years ago now. Andrew was only nine, and I've looked after him ever since.' She stirred, remembering. 'He was just a little boy. It was terrible for him.'

Gabriel thought that it must have been terrible for her too, losing both her parents and finding herself responsible for a small boy. He frowned. 'You can't have been very old yourself,' he said.

'I was twenty-two. My parents moved down from Edinburgh for Dad's job not long before the accident. They'd bought this house, so at least Andrew and I had somewhere to live, but Dad was never very good with money, and there was hardly anything else. I'd just finished a secretarial course and I'd wanted to travel, but Andrew was still at primary school, so I took the first job I was offered.'

'With Steve Robinson?'

'No, I had another job before that.' There was a certain reserve in Tess's voice and she frowned down at the soup she was mindlessly stirring. She tried not to think too much about that job and how it had ended. More than ten years ago now, but the memory of her humiliation still hurt.

'When I left there, I temped for a while, but it was difficult with Andrew at school. Then I went to SpaceWorks for a two week assignment, and I've been there ever since.

'Steve was fantastic,' she remembered gratefully. 'He believes that businesses should be flexible, and make allowances for the fact that their employees have to juggle their commitments at work and at home. So it was never a problem if I had to go home early to pick Andrew up from school or stay with him if he was sick.'

Gabriel set the empty bottle carefully on the table and sat Harry up to pat his back. 'No wonder you're so loyal to Steve Robinson,' he said, conscious of the same pinch of jealousy he had felt when she'd talked about her brother. Except that it *wasn't* jealousy, of course.

'It's not just me,' said Tess, on the defensive for some reason. 'Steve was like that with everybody. Working for him wasn't like a job. It was like being part of a family, until—'

'Until I came along?'

There was a pause, while they both remembered belatedly that they weren't two friends talking. He was her boss, and she was his PA.

'Yes,' she said. 'Until then.'

Only the day before yesterday they had disliked each other intensely, she remembered. And today?

Today, Tess wasn't sure. The realisation left her edgy and unsettled. It wasn't that she had changed her mind, nor that she suddenly liked Gabriel.

But perhaps she didn't dislike him quite as much as she had thought.

CHAPTER SIX

'THINGS are easier now, of course,' she said, making an effort to steer the conversation away from what felt like dangerous ground. 'Andrew's away at university, so I don't need to make time for him any more, just money.'

Tess smiled wryly as she poured the soup into two bowls. 'He's just started his final year. Sometimes I wonder how he's got as far as he has.' She sighed. 'He never seems to do any work. He just has a good time.

'I was so pleased when he got into university,' she confided, setting the bowls on the table and turning to find some spoons, 'but I had no idea how expensive it was going to be.

'I know it's hard for students nowadays, but Andrew always seems to be in debt. He still owes money from last year, and now he and some friends are trying to rent a house, but the landlord is demanding a huge deposit which none of them can afford. He's lost his car, too. Some boys took it for a joyride, and according to Andrew they've practically written it off. It's going to cost a fortune to repair.'

Sighing, Tess sat down at the table, only to get up again as she remembered the bread. 'That's why I was so keen to earn some extra money looking after Harry,' she told Gabriel, who was struggling to slot the baby into his new bouncy chair.

He looked up, the light grey eyes suddenly alert. 'Oh?' he said.

'I'd thought about asking you for a raise,' she confessed, 'but I know it's a generous salary as it is, and, anyway, it would soon get swallowed up just by the expense of living in London. I worked out that overtime for a week would give me a lump sum which I could send to Andrew so that he could sort out his accommodation and get his car fixed. I'd like him to give up his pub job, too. He needs to spend more time studying—it's not that long until his finals.'

She trailed off as she noticed that Gabriel was looking at her with a most peculiar expression. Tess couldn't decipher it at all, but she had a nasty feeling that she had just convinced him that she was obsessed by money.

Why had she told him all that about Andrew? Tess agonised. It wasn't like her to pour out her problems to anyone, least of all Gabriel Stearne. He wasn't interested in her petty little worries.

'Well, anyway, that's why I'm happy to spend this week looking after Harry,' she said awkwardly. 'I'm afraid my motives are entirely mercenary,' she went on in a flip voice to disguise her embarrassment. 'But, then, you probably guessed that.'

'Yes, I did,' said Gabriel slowly, 'but I didn't know why you needed the money.' He was disconcerted by the lightening of his heart. There shouldn't be any reason why it made a difference knowing that Tess hadn't wanted the money for herself, but somehow it did.

'I understand that you want to help your brother,' he said almost roughly, 'but you can't keep paying his debts for him. You said that he's twenty-one? Isn't it about time he learned that he has to stand on his own two feet?'

'I know,' said Tess, to whom this was a familiar dilemma. 'I feel responsible for him, though. I'm sure my parents would have helped him out. And anyway,' she went on, plucking up spirit, 'you're one to talk! You've taken on responsibility for your brother's baby.'

'Only temporarily,' Gabriel began to object, before acknowledging her point with a rather twisted smile. 'I guess I do feel responsible for Greg,' he admitted. 'I grew up in London, did you know that?'

'No, no, I didn't,' said Tess, thrown by the apparent change of subject, but intrigued by the idea of Gabriel as a boy. A British background explained some of the things that had puzzled her about him, the way he spoke that didn't quite fit with his American accent, that air he had of not quite belonging on one side of the Atlantic nor the other.

'My father left when I was fourteen,' Gabriel told her. 'Traded in his old family for a new one—it happens all the time.'

He shrugged. 'My mother is American, and she took me back to the States. Ray Stearne had been the boy next door when she was growing up, and they picked up right where they'd left off. Going home was the best thing that ever happened to my mother.

'It can't have been very easy having a sullen adolescent around the whole time, but Ray was very good to me, and when they married, I took his name. He was certainly more of a father to me than mine ever was,' he added with a trace of bitterness. 'It was Ray who spent time with me when my mother was wrapped up with Greg, Ray who encouraged me to set up on my own and lent me money to start my first business. I feel I owe it to him to bail Greg out of trouble. Greg's the centre of their lives, and they would only be upset if they heard the half of what he gets up to.'

'He sounds so charming on the phone,' commented Tess, remembering Greg's warm, treacly voice.

'Sure, he's charming,' said Gabriel. 'That's part of the trouble. Everybody loves him, everybody makes allowances for him, everybody falls over themselves to help him out. It would probably do Greg good to do some work for a change but, between Ray and me, he's never needed to. Ray gives him a generous allowance and, when he's spent that, he gives me a call. He says one of us might as well enjoy my money.' Gabriel gave another shrug. 'Perhaps he's right.'

Tess eyed him covertly as she drank her soup. For such a demanding and intolerant man, he seemed oddly resigned to his feckless brother's activities.

She had been strangely moved by Gabriel's terse account of his background. It wasn't, as he had said, that unusual a story, and in many ways he had been lucky in finding such a supportive stepfather, but still she had found herself aching for the boy he had been: abandoned by his father, uprooted from everything familiar and taken to a new country. No wonder he wore that guarded expression sometimes. Fourteen wasn't an easy age at the best of times.

Remembering how difficult Andrew had been then, Tess was half tempted to offer Gabriel sympathy, but something in his face told her it wouldn't be welcome. 'Have you had any news of your stepfather?' she asked him instead.

'I rang yesterday evening, after you'd gone home.' Gabriel seemed to welcome the change of subject. 'He'd had the operation, but was still in intensive care.' He glanced at his watch. 'I'll ring after lunch and see how he is today.'

'Are you going to go over and see him?'

'I'd planned to, but I can't leave Harry now.' There was a crease between Gabriel's dark brows as he looked down at the baby happily pulling at his feet in the bouncy chair. 'I'll have to track down his mother first and, as you pointed out earlier, that could take some time. If I can't, I guess we'll have to hope his grandmother reclaims him sooner or later, but there's no guarantee that she'll come back at all.'

He looked so concerned that Tess had an unaccountable impulse to reassure him. 'You'll find her,' she said. 'And, if your stepfather takes a turn for the worse, you can fly over in a few hours, and leave Harry with me. In fact, why not go anyway? I'm sure I could manage on my own if I had to.'

Tess could probably manage anything, thought Gabriel. 'I'm sure you could, but I hope that won't be necessary,' he said, unable to explain, even to himself, his reluctance to book a flight straight away. It wasn't as if he was any good at dealing with the baby. Why not go and see Ray as he had planned? Surely he didn't really want to stay with her and the baby in this small, cluttered, oddly comfortable house any longer than he had to?

Did he?

Of course he didn't.

After lunch, they put Harry to sleep in Tess's bedroom in his new cot. While Tess covered the mattress with a sheet and took the blanket out of its wrapping, Gabriel held the baby and looked around him, trying not to appear too obviously interested.

Yes, he could imagine Tess in here. It was a cool, light room with stripped floorboards and ethnic fabrics. The morning sun would stream through the windows and splash across the bed. He could imagine her all too clearly, in fact. He could practically see her lying there, stirring, stretching, opening her eyes with a sleepy smile, the way she had smiled when she had woken in his bed.

Throat very dry, Gabriel handed Harry over and took refuge in irritation. 'Why do none of your doors have any handles?' he demanded as they backed out of the room, leaving the door ajar. 'Every time I went to open one this morning, all I found was a hole.'

'They work all right,' said Tess defensively. 'Anyway, you can't complain. Your apartment hasn't even got any doors.'

'There's no point in having them at all if you can't shut them.'

'I don't need to shut them when I'm here on my own,' she pointed out as they made their way back down to the kitchen. 'Besides, they'll work fine when I've finished with them. Andrew stripped all the doors for me when he was home in the summer, and I bought some wonderful Victorian doorknobs in an antiques market. Look.' She took one down from the pile that had been gathering dust on top of the fridge to show him. 'Aren't they lovely?'

Gabriel inspected the mechanism. 'Very pretty,' he said with an ironic look, 'but not much use sitting on top of the fridge.'

'Andrew had to go back to university before he had a chance to put them on,' she explained. 'He promised he'd do them at Christmas.'

'But all you need is a screwdriver,' Gabriel objected, putting the doorknob back with the others. 'It would only take a few minutes.'

'I know, but I hate doing things like that,' she confessed in a burst of confidence. 'I'd rather do without doorknobs than tackle any kind of DIY.'

'You surprise me,' he said, regarding her thoughtfully. I'd have said you were a very practical person.'

'I'm organised. That's not the same as being practical. I'm hopeless when it comes to using my hands.'

She held them out with a rueful smile, as if to demonstrate their incompetence, and, quite without thinking, Gabriel took them and inspected them. They were beautifully shaped, with long, slender fingers and very clean, immaculately manicured nails.

Tess was right, he thought absently as he turned them over to rub his thumbs over her palms. They weren't practical hands at all. They were soft and smooth; they were warm. They were the same hands that had slid around his neck when they had woken up together in his apartment.

Gabriel dropped them abruptly.

'Have you got a screwdriver?'

'Wh-what?' Tess stared at him, dry-mouthed. She had been mesmerised by the feel of his fingers, the gentle stroke of his thumbs across her palms. He had hardly been touching her, probably hadn't even realised what he was doing, so why did it feel as if the graze of his skin against hers had been charged with an electricity that was still sparking and shorting along bones.

Swallowing, her eyes fell to her hands. She half expected to see scorches across her palms where they burned from his touch, but they just hung there at the ends of her arms, looking perfectly normal but feeling extremely odd, as if they didn't quite belong to her.

What did she normally do with her hands when she wasn't using them? Tess couldn't remember. She ended up folding her arms and tucking her hands away out of sight in an unconsciously defensive gesture.

'A what?' she said again, moistening her lips as she realised that Gabriel was still waiting for an answer.

'A screwdriver,' he repeated. 'If you've got one, I could put the door handles on for you.'

Tess's jaw dropped. The Gabriel Stearnes of this world weren't domesticated animals. They were like big cats, padding through the urban jungle, where home was just a place to sleep and survival of the fittest was all that mattered. They didn't do DIY.

'Why are you looking like that?' he said. 'How do you think I started out in construction business? I used to get my hands dirty the same as anyone else. I might spend all my time in the office now, but I can still tell a spanner from a screwdriver.'

'You mean you could really fit all these doorknobs for me?' said Tess doubtfully, still struggling to assimilate this new idea of Gabriel as man about the house.

'If you'd like me to.'

'Well, if you're sure it's no trouble…'

'It'll only take me five minutes.'

In the end he not only put handles on all the doors, but mended the dripping tap in the bathroom, changed an awkward light bulb on the landing that Tess had never been able to reach, oiled the hinges on a creaking cupboard door and fixed a mirror to the wall in her bedroom, a job which she had been meaning to do for over two years.

'What about that?' he said, coming into the kitchen where Tess was pottering around, and pointing at the shelf unit which was propped forlornly against the wall. 'Where do you want it to go?'

'There's no need for you to bother,' Tess began feebly, but Gabriel was already measuring the length of the shelf.

His movements were quick and economical, and she studied him under her lashes as she began preparing the meal for that night. She couldn't get used to him like this, with dust from the drill in his dark hair, and a dirty mark on his cheek, but at the same time it felt strangely comfortable to have him moving around her house.

It felt almost *right*.

'About here?'

Gabriel's voice broke into her thoughts and made her start. He was looking at her oddly, and a little colour stole into her cheeks. Had he noticed her staring at him?

'Yes, about there is fine, thanks,' she muttered, turning back to the onions she was chopping, but she could feel his eyes on her with a puzzled expression, and when the phone rang suddenly in the silence, she seized it quickly, grateful for the diversion.

She soon wished that she hadn't. It was Bella, wanting to know why Tess hadn't returned her call the evening before. 'Didn't you get my message?' she demanded.

'Yes, I did.' Tess turned her back on Gabriel and carried the cordless phone over to the French windows, as far away from him as she could get. 'I would have called you back but something came up,' she said awkwardly.

'What? Don't tell me you're still looking after that baby!'

'Well, sort of.'

'Tess, what's going on?'

Beginning to feel harassed, Tess lowered her voice. 'Nothing,' she said.

'Then why are you being so cagey? Have you got someone with you?' Bella's voice sharpened. 'Is it Gabriel Stearne?'

As Gabriel chose that moment to start drilling, it was difficult for Tess to claim, as she had intended, that she was on her own. Hastily, she opened the French windows and stepped into the garden, where she hoped she would be out of earshot.

'Look, it's perfectly simple,' she said, and gave Bella the bare outlines of the previous forty-eight hours, prudently keeping details like sharing Gabriel's bed to herself. She would never hear the end of it if Bella got wind of *that*.

'So, let me get this right,' said Bella when she had finished. 'You're spending the weekend with your boss, a man you said you hated. You're looking after his baby—'

'His brother's baby,' Tess put in feebly, but was ignored.

'For him; he spent all last night with you—'

'On my sofa—'

'And now he's putting up *shelves* for you?'

'It's not how it sounds,' said Tess, uncomfortably aware of how it *did* sound.

There was a pregnant pause.

'Tess,' said Bella sternly, 'you're not going to do anything stupid like fall in love with your boss, are you?'

'Fall in love with—?' Tess spluttered furiously. 'Of course I'm not! Don't be so ridiculous, Bella!'

Gabriel looked up as Tess stalked back into the kitchen, cutting the connection on the phone with unnecessary emphasis. Her cheeks were flaming and the golden-brown eyes were dangerously bright.

'You look very cross,' he commented. 'What's up?'

Tess slammed the phone back into its cradle. 'I am not in the least cross,' she said through gritted teeth, 'and nothing is *up*!'

But Bella's warning had done its work. The easy atmosphere of the afternoon had evaporated, leaving Tess excruciatingly aware of Gabriel. Had she really thought it was comfortable to have him in the house? Now his presence made her twitchy and unsettled, and she found herself avoiding his eyes and edging warily around him as they put Harry to bed, as if even an accidental contact would send an electric charge jolting through her.

She half hoped that the baby would prove difficult about going to sleep in his new cot, so that she would have something to do all evening but, perversely, Harry settled immediately. Tess looked at her watch in something like despair as she tiptoed out of the bedroom. Only quarter past seven. Still the whole evening to get through!

'I—er—I think I'll have a bath before supper,' she told Gabriel stiltedly.

Lying up to her neck in bubbles, Tess sipped her drink and tried to relax by focusing on the flickering flames of the candles she had placed at the end of the bath, but Bella's words kept sneaking into her mind.

You're not going to do anything stupid like fall in love with your boss, are you?

Of course, the suggestion was absolutely ridiculous. There was no question of her falling in love with Gabriel. Once before, she had got involved with someone at work, and it had ended in disaster. There was no way she was going to repeat that particular mistake.

And anyway, she didn't even like Gabriel—at least, not much. The very idea was laughable.

By the time she had dried herself and dressed in the dowdiest and least seductive clothes she could find, Tess had talked herself into a mood of brittle bravery. She was not—repeat *not*—going to let Bella's stupid suggestion un-

settle her. Surely two adults could spend a weekend together looking after a baby without everyone thinking that
there had to be something else between them.

There was no reason to suppose that Gabriel found her
attractive in the slightest, Tess pointed out to herself. If
Fionnula Jenkins was anything to go by, his taste was for
glamorous redheads—disappointingly predictable, perhaps, but fine by *her*. She preferred her own men less dark
and difficult.

Less disturbing.

Still, it was a relief when the evening was over at last.
In spite of her best efforts to behave normally and keep
up a flow of polite, inconsequential chat, every now and
then the conversation would shrivel and die without warning, marooning them in a pool of awkward silence. Tess
would find herself watching Gabriel's hands or his mouth
or the pulse in his throat and the air would evaporate from
her lungs and her heartbeat would boom in her ears, so
loud that she'd been afraid he would hear it. And then she
would gulp and plunge back into speech, not knowing or
caring what she said, just desperate to break that strumming silence.

'Sorry about the mess,' she said with forced brightness
when the interminable meal had ended, and she was able
to show him into Andrew's room. 'It should be more comfortable than the sofa, though.'

'I'm sure it will be fine,' said Gabriel, equally constrained. 'Thank you for the meal,' he added after a moment.

'Thank *you* for all the work you did around the house
this afternoon.'

Another agonizing pause.

'Well…goodnight,' she said uncomfortably, feeling that
she should be saying something else, but unsure what it
should be. She clasped her hands nervously in front of her.

If he had been anyone other than Gabriel, she would have hugged him with a smile and told him to sleep well.

But he *was* Gabriel, and what would have seemed so easy and so natural with a friend was somehow fraught with danger. The sensible thing was to turn and go, but something held her there, her eyes skittering around the room until drawn irresistibly back to his and she could only stand staring helplessly at him while the silence tightened around them.

She stood by the door, as if poised for flight, but the room was so small that she was still close enough for Gabriel to smell the scented bath oil that lingered on her skin, a heady fragrance of flowers and spices.

Close enough for him to kiss.

Not a real kiss, of course, Gabriel told himself. Just a friendly peck to thank her for all she had done today. Wasn't that the obvious, the appropriate, thing to do in the circumstances? He could bend his head, touch his mouth to the warm curve of her face, and that would be that. Easy.

But not as easy as reaching out and drawing her towards him, so that he could twine his fingers in her hair. Not as easy as letting his lips drift from her cheek to find her mouth. Not as easy as kissing her properly, the way he had been trying not to think about doing all evening.

Gabriel swallowed. Perhaps that brief, impersonal kiss on the cheek wouldn't be that easy after all. He made himself step deliberately back so that she was out of reach.

'Good night, Tess,' was all he said.

Things were better the next day. Tess felt as if she had somehow passed through a danger zone, and had emerged unscathed on the other side. She woke feeling calmer, the jittery feeling of the night before having vanished as if it had never been.

She had just been rattled by Bella's suggestion, she realised, remembering how she had backed carefully out of Andrew's room when Gabriel had said goodnight, unsure whether to be disappointed or relieved that he had made no move to get any closer to her. He had clearly remembered that their relationship was entirely professional, and that the intimate situation they had been forced into by Harry was only ever going to be temporary.

And that was good, of course.

Uncomfortably aware of just how close she herself had come to forgetting it, Tess could only be glad that she hadn't made a fool of herself by kissing him. But now that they both knew where they were, she told herself, everything would be fine.

And to her secret relief, she was right. It turned out to be an ordinary, lazy Sunday. Gabriel was already up and had made coffee by the time Tess went downstairs with Harry. They read the Sunday papers in companionable silence, and after lunch took him for a walk on the common nearby.

It was a raw, blustery day and the autumn leaves swirled in golden eddies along the paths. Tess turned her collar up against the wind as she walked beside Gabriel, who pushed the pram with the same decisive control that he drove the car or logged onto his computer. Studying his profile surreptitiously under her lashes, Tess couldn't help thinking how strong and definite his features were, and how everyone else they passed looked pale and insubstantial in comparison, and something that was not quite pride and not quite pleasure stirred faintly inside her.

It started to rain as they turned for home. By the time they reached Tess's street, it was pouring, and they ran the last few yards, falling breathless and laughing through the door into the warmth of the house. The hallway was so narrow that the pram almost filled it, and the two of them were wedged close together in the space between it and the front door. Gabriel shook himself, wiping the rain from his face, and turned to say something to Tess, but the words died on his lips.

Her face was glowing, her hair blown around by the wind and spangled with raindrops. The clear brown eyes were alight with laughter as she tried to catch her breath, but her smile faltered as she met his arrested gaze and for a moment the air between them shimmered with the tension they had both hoped was forgotten.

Tess turned away first. 'I'll make some tea,' she said brightly—too brightly—squeezing past the pram to the relative safety of the kitchen.

She had herself well under control by the time she carried a tray into the sitting room. Gabriel and Harry watched her as she drew the curtains to shut out the rain and the gathering darkness, and then knelt to switch on the fire. The line of her back was somehow soothing, Gabriel found himself thinking.

She had toasted crumpets to have with the tea. Gabriel hardly tasted his. He kept noticing how she licked the melted butter from her fingers, how she cupped her hands around her mug, how the firelight burnished her hair as she sat cross-legged on the rug with Harry. She had the glove puppet they had bought yesterday, and was making him chuckle by playing peekaboo with the fox, making it wave at him and then duck back into hiding behind her arm.

Gabriel's throat was absurdly dry. 'Better not get too attached to him,' he managed. 'I hope his mother will be home soon, and you'll have to give him back.'

'I know.' Tess looked at Harry, who was reaching chubby hands out for the fox. 'I wonder how she could have left him?' she said, almost to herself. 'I wouldn't if he was mine.'

Gabriel quirked an eyebrow at her. 'Getting broody?'

'No,' she said quickly, perhaps a little too quickly. 'Harry's adorable when he's like this,' she admitted, watching the baby stuff the glove puppet thoughtfully into his mouth, 'but it's not so much fun when you're changing nappies or getting up in the middle of the night. It's hard work on your own. I should know,' she said. 'I brought Andrew up by myself.'

'If you had a baby you wouldn't be on your own,' said Gabriel.

'Wouldn't I?' He had never heard her so cynical before. 'It happens all the time,' she quoted his own words back at him. 'You think you're in love and that everything's going to be wonderful—and for a while it *is* wonderful. And then you find yourself alone. You cope because you haven't got a choice.'

Tess stroked Harry's head. 'Maybe that's what Leanne had to do. Maybe that's why she left him.'

'It was her choice not to tell Greg about the baby,' Gabriel pointed out in his brother's defence.

'True.' She glanced at him. 'Will you tell him?'

'I think it's up to Harry's mother to do that.'

'Wouldn't you want to know if it was you?'

Gabriel's mouth turned down at the corners as he considered the question. 'I don't know. Probably not. I've never thought about children. The whole family business is too much of a commitment. I don't like compromise, and that's what families are all about.'

'They're about more than that,' Tess protested.

'Like what?'

'Security? Comfort? Trust? Love?'

'Oh, love…' Gabriel made a dismissive gesture. 'You can have love without being married and having children.'

'Yes, but how long does it last?' she countered sadly.

'Long enough.'

Her face closed. 'Long enough for what? For you to get bored? That's not love.'

He eyed her curiously. 'You sound as if you're speaking from experience.'

Turning her head away, Tess cradled the mug between her hands and stared into the leaping flames. 'I fell in love once,' she told him, her voice carefully expressionless. 'Oliver worked in the same office. It was my first job and he was much older, more assured. I trusted him completely, and when he told me he loved me but we had to be discreet because of his position in the company, I believed him.'

Gabriel listened, but his eyes were on the fine arch of her brows and the way her hair fell in a soft caress against her cheek and, without wanting to, he found himself wondering what it would be like to be able to reach out and smooth it gently behind her ear. It was alarming to discover just how clearly he could imagine doing just that, and he had to catch himself up sharply when he realised what he was doing.

'I was very young,' Tess was saying. 'Very young and very naïve. I never thought that the reason he was so anxious to keep our relationship quiet was the fact that he had a wife who was related to the managing director.

'It turned out that everyone knew anyway,' she went on with a bitter smile. 'You can't keep that kind of thing secret in an office. They all knew long before I did that Oliver was going to dump me and, when the director got wind of the affair and called me, they knew exactly what was going to happen.'

Her cheeks burned at the memory of that final interview. 'That was the first I'd heard about Oliver's wife. I had to leave, of course. I was expendable, and Oliver wasn't. I vowed there and then that I would never get involved with anyone at work again, and I haven't. I never mix work with my private life.'

'What about now?'

Startled by the strange note in his voice, Tess lifted her head to look at him. 'What do you mean?'

'I'm your boss, I'm here in your home. You could say I'm intruding on your private life.'

'That's different,' said Tess. 'Our relationship is professional, not personal, and that hasn't changed. I work for you during the week, and I'm working for you now. You're here because of Harry, not because you want to be here, and you're not here because I want you here. This weekend is about business, not pleasure.'

CHAPTER SEVEN

GABRIEL glared at the red light, his fingers tapping morosely on the steering wheel. It would be afternoon before they got to the office at this rate. It had taken long enough to load Harry and all his stuff into the car, and now they were stuck in the Monday morning traffic.

He blew out an irritable breath, nettled by the way Tess sat beside him, infuriatingly self-possessed. She had come downstairs that morning in one of her demure suits, with her hair swept into a neat chignon at the back of her head, looking dauntingly cool and unapproachable. Without saying a word, she had made it crystal clear that the situation was back to normal, and that relations between them were strictly business.

Gabriel knew that he ought to be relieved. The last thing he needed or wanted was to complicate matters by getting involved with his PA, and he should have been glad that she clearly had no intention of presuming on the enforced intimacy of the weekend, but somehow her composure rankled. *He* was the one who liked to keep people at arm's length.

The light turned green ahead. Muttering under his breath at the slowness of the traffic, Gabriel edged the car forward, but only managed a few yards before it changed back to red. He felt grouchy and unsettled, the way he had been feeling ever since that conversation in front of the fire. 'You're not here because I want you here,' that was what she had said. 'This weekend is about business, not pleasure.'

Gabriel's lips tightened whenever he thought about it. He had been misled by the warmth and the firelight and

113

the smile in her eyes, had forgotten that he was only there because of Harry, had forgotten the office, had forgotten that Tess was his PA. Her cool reminder that their relationship was a purely professional one had been like a slap in the face, and had left him humiliated and feeling a fool.

It wasn't a feeling Gabriel liked, and it did nothing to improve his temper. When they finally reached the office, he stiff-armed his way through the glass door and strode through reception, deaf to the receptionist's timid greeting and blind to the wary looks of those who automatically cleared a passage for him, aware only of Tess following calmly behind him with Harry.

Tess sucked in through her teeth. She had seen at once what kind of mood he was in that morning, and had intended to ignore it. She had obviously done something to upset him, but that was no reason for him to take it out on everyone else.

'Haven't you forgotten something?' she asked coldly as she caught up with him at the lifts with Harry.

'What?' Gabriel was carrying Harry's bouncy chair in one hand, and jabbing at the button to call the lift with the other.

'You made a promise on Friday night.'

Thrown off his stride, he took his finger off the button and scowled at her. 'What do you mean? What promise?'

'I'll be nice, you said. I'm desperate, you said. I'll do anything. Remember?'

Gabriel's jaw tightened. 'What am I supposed to do? Skip around dispensing sunshine and days off?'

'A simple good morning would be a step in the right direction,' said Tess in a frigid voice. 'You didn't even acknowledge Elaine's existence.'

'Since I've no idea who Elaine is, that's hardly surprising.'

'She's been the receptionist here for the last six years.

You must have seen her every day since you arrived. The least you could do is learn her name.'

Gabriel drew an exasperated breath and turned with a muttered comment that Tess chose to ignore. 'Good morning, Elaine,' he called across to where she sat behind the reception desk.

Elaine's jaw dropped. 'G-good morning, Mr S-stearne,' she stuttered.

'How are you this morning?'

'Er—fine, thank you,' she managed, looking thoroughly alarmed by his bizarre behaviour.

'Satisfied?' Gabriel demanded of Tess, who shifted Harry into her other arm and looked coolly back at him.

'It's a start.'

The lift doors slid open, revealing a number of Tess's colleagues, who all looked apprehensive at finding themselves face to face with the fearsome Gabriel Stearne, and, like Elaine, were positively unnerved when he bared his teeth in a savage smile.

'Good morning,' he said pointedly to each in turn.

There was a chorus of subdued and frankly baffled greetings in return. Tess stood next to Gabriel at the front, staring woodenly ahead, but uncomfortably aware of the knowing looks being exchanged behind her back, along with nods and winks at the significance of her arrival at the same time as Gabriel, still with the baby in tow.

There was no need to tell anyone that they had spent the weekend together, she thought with a sinking heart. Conclusions were obviously being drawn already. The news would be all round the office in no time, and the grapevine would arrive at its usual calculation that two plus two inevitably made at least sixty-seven!

It was a relief to escape the speculative eyes boring into her back and into the comparative sanctuary of her office. Gabriel stomped off into his own room, leaving Tess to settle Harry in his bouncy chair while she organised herself. He seemed happy to sit there, pulling at his socks, and watching her as she moved around her desk, but his uncle was clearly in a less amenable mood. Tess could hear him banging around in his office, slamming files onto his desk as if they were somehow responsible for his bad humour.

Gabriel, in fact, was finding it hard to concentrate and, when Tess came in with her notebook and the diary a little while later, he glared at her from behind his desk, irritated even more than usual by that air of crisp efficiency.

'Yes?' he barked.

Ignoring him, Tess consulted the diary. 'You've got a meeting at eleven-fifteen, and another at three,' she reminded him. 'John Dobbs would like to see you some time today about insurance.'

'Tell him three forty-five.'

'You're expected in the design department at four.'

'Cancel that.'

Calmly, Tess made a note.

Gabriel eyed her with a kind of baffled resentment. She was unperturbed by his black humour, just as she had been unperturbed by the weekend they had spent together. He had seen her sitting in front of the fire with her hair tumbling over her shoulders. He had seen her bathrobe slip open, seen her smiling and laughing. How could she put on a suit and some glasses and act as if he didn't know what she was really like?

She was looking at him over the top of her glasses. 'Will there be anything else for now?'

Yes, he wanted to shout. Be the way you were this weekend. Be the Tess who hummed as she stirred the soup. Be the Tess who ran through the rain. The one who made Harry laugh with that stupid fox, and took long, scented baths by candlelight.

'No, nothing,' he said curtly.

'Would you like a cup of coffee?'

'Yes.'

Tess raised an eyebrow. That was all it took. Gabriel sighed irritably.

'Yes, *please*,' he ground out. 'If you wouldn't mind.'

He had made *her* coffee yesterday morning, he remembered, glowering out of the window. They had had coffee and croissants and had chatted companionably as they'd read the Sunday papers. Not that Tess would remember that now. She was too busy being an efficient PA to waste her time actually talking to her own boss.

It annoyed Gabriel that he couldn't stop thinking about her. She was only his PA, for God's sake! There was nothing special about her, if he discounted that ability to freeze him with a look. She wasn't particularly beautiful, nor particularly stylish, nor particularly clever.

So why was he wasting his valuable time thinking of excuses to go out into the office and talk to her? Anyone would think he needed to hear her voice.

Which was ridiculous.

Knowing how ridiculous it was didn't stop him from snatching up the phone when it rang.

'Yes?'

'I've got Fionnula Jenkins on the line for you.'

Something about the utter lack of inflection in Tess's voice made Gabriel furious. She might at least sound as if she cared whether he spoke to another woman or not! The truth was that he hadn't given Fionnula a thought all weekend, but Tess wasn't to know that, was she?

'Put her through,' he ordered. 'Oh—if it's not too much trouble, of course,' he added sarcastically.

Tess refused to give him the satisfaction of rising to the bait. She connected him to Fionnula without comment, and relieved her feelings by slamming down the phone with such violence that she made Harry jump.

'I'm sorry, sweetheart,' she apologised as his little face

puckered alarmingly, and she bent to pick him up for a cuddle. 'It's not your fault your uncle is impossible.'

'Uh-oh!' said a familiar voice from the doorway. 'It looks like I picked a bad time.'

Tess turned with Harry. 'Come in, Niles,' she said, resigned.

'So this is the boss's baby.' Niles's eyes were bright with curiosity. 'He doesn't look much like Dad, does he?'

'That's because Mr Stearne isn't his father,' said Tess repressively.

'But he's looking after him, I hear—with you.'

'It's just a temporary arrangement.'

'Ah.' Niles regarded her speculatively. 'The word is that you and the boss spent the weekend together. Emma said she saw the two of you in the supermarket.'

Tess suppressed a sigh. She might have known someone would have seen them. Everyone thought that London was a big city, but there were times, usually when you most wanted to mind your own business, when it might as well be a village.

'I expect she did,' she said as coolly as she could. 'We had to get some stuff for Harry here. You can tell everyone not to get excited,' she added with an ironic look. 'There's no big secret. Harry is Mr Stearne's nephew, and I'm acting as nanny for a few days to earn some overtime. That's all there is to it.'

'Shame,' said Niles. 'I was hoping to hear you'd cut out Fionnula Jenkins!'

'I don't think that's very likely.'

'I don't know about that,' he said, studying her appreciatively. 'You're a beautiful girl, Tess, in a quiet kind of way. I reckon you could give Fionnula a run for her money if you let your hair down.'

Tess's mind flickered back to the weekend. She had a picture of herself sitting by the fire with her hair loose, and Gabriel on the sofa, leaning forward, his eyes intent,

holding Harry upright between his big hands, smiling...
The memory made her shiver for some reason, and she
pushed it hastily aside.

'Well, as you can see, my hair is firmly up,' she told
Niles briskly as she sat Harry on his mat and found a few
toys for him to play with. 'What did you want, anyway,
Niles?'

'I just stopped by to see if you'd thought any more about
the promises auction. We're relying on you to come up
with something good.'

Tess had forgotten all about the auction. 'I could do a
couple of hours ironing for you, if you like,' she offered,
improvising quickly.

'Ironing?' Niles scoffed. 'Don't be so boring, Tess. You
can do better than that.'

'Like what?' She sighed.

'Rumour has it that you're a good cook.' Niles had obviously been waiting for his opportunity. 'Why don't you
promise to cook a romantic meal for two? Lots of people
would want to bid for that.'

'Oh, all right,' said Tess, just to get rid of him, and he
grinned.

'You're a star!' He gave her an affectionate hug just as
the inner door opened and Gabriel came out.

Gabriel's mouth thinned as he saw the two of them
break apart guiltily, and Tess was furious to find herself
blushing.

'We were—er—just discussing the firm's social event
in November.'

'Really?' said Gabriel with an icy look. 'It seems to me
that quite enough socialising goes on right here in this
office.'

'I'd better get back to work,' said Niles prudently. 'See
you later, Tess—and thanks for your promise.'

The look Gabriel sent after him was distinctly hostile.
'Why is he always hanging around here?' he demanded.

Tess closed her lips firmly. She wasn't about to get into an argument. 'Is there something I can do for you?'

'Yes, you can book me a table at Cupiditas. I'm taking Fionnula out to lunch,' he told her unnecessarily. 'To make up for the meal we missed the other night.'

The other night when *she* had had to give up her evening to help look after his baby nephew, thought Tess furiously. Fionnula hadn't exactly been supportive then, had she? But all she'd had to do was ring Gabriel up with her husky voice and crook her little finger, and he came running. He ought to have more pride, thought Tess austerely.

'What time?' was all she said.

'Twelve-thirty. Fionnula's going to meet me here. I'm sure you'll look after her if I'm late back from the meeting,' he added with what Tess strongly suspected was deliberate provocation.

'Of course, Mr Stearne,' she said, her voice empty of expression.

'*Gabriel*,' he bit out.

'Of course, Gabriel,' she corrected herself after the tiniest of pauses.

Gabriel cast her a fulminating look and slammed back into his room, infuriated to discover that she had succeeded in provoking him far more effectively than he had in irritating her. He had only asked Fionnula to lunch to prove to Tess that he too could behave as if they had never spent the weekend together. Not that she cared one way or another: she couldn't even remember to use his first name.

He was still looking thunderous when he left for his meeting, and Tess told herself that she was glad to see him go. At least now she might be able to get some work done without him prowling around the office. Even Harry had picked up on his black temper, and what with trying to soothe one and placate the other, she had achieved virtually nothing.

But somehow it wasn't any easier when he had gone.

The office felt empty without him, and Tess was annoyed to find herself looking up quickly every time the lift doors pinged out in the corridor in case it was Gabriel returning.

Rather to Tess's surprise, Fionnula turned up bang on time. She paused dramatically in the doorway and shook back her famous red hair. 'Is Gabriel here?' she asked in the equally famous throaty voice. She didn't introduce herself, evidently assuming that Tess would recognise her straight away.

Tess longed to pretend that she didn't, but had to force a polite smile instead. 'I'm sorry, he's still in a meeting, but he is expecting you,' she said. 'He asked me to apologise if he was a little late. Can I get you a coffee or anything in the meantime?'

'No thank you, darling, I'll wait until lunch.' Fionnula shrugged off her expensive-looking jacket and dropped it carelessly over a chair. 'I hope Gabriel's booked somewhere nice?'

'Cupiditas,' Tess admitted grudgingly. She had had to spend some time persuading the manager to find a table for two at such short notice.

'Oh, marvellous!' Fionnula looked smug. 'He knows that's my favourite.'

In the flesh, Fionnula was even more beautiful than in photographs, Tess had to acknowledge. There was a glow about her, a sheen of sheer glamour that went beyond the flawless skin, green, green eyes, and stunning figure. Her hair was a deep, coppery red, without so much as a hint of carrot, and Tess knew that she must look prim and colourless in comparison. No wonder Gabriel had fallen over himself to take her out again.

Unaccountably depressed, Tess forced her attention back to her computer, but the next moment Fionnula had spied Harry, kicking and gurgling quietly in his bouncy chair. 'Oh, what an adorable baby!' she cried, swooping down on him and scooping him up into her arms. 'Gabriel didn't tell me what a gorgeous boy you were,' she told him, tickling his face with her long eyelashes until he squirmed and giggled.

Tess watched, obscurely hurt to see Harry so easily won over by Fionnula's beauty and charm. Men! She sighed to herself. They were all the same!

She stared fixedly at the computer screen, bitterly aware of Fionnula, who was now dandling him on her knee, tickling and flirting until Harry was enslaved like all the others.

The two of them made a perfect picture when Gabriel walked into the office some fifteen minutes later. Fionnula was holding Harry above her, while he gazed adoringly down into her face. Tess had been silently willing him to be sick over Fionnula's cashmere top, but to her disappointment he was behaving beautifully and, at the sight of Gabriel, both of them lit up on cue.

Which was more than Tess did, Gabriel noted sourly. She had barely looked up from her computer screen.

'There you are, darling!' Still holding Harry, the perfect, radiant, mother figure, Fionnula moved towards him with a brilliant smile.

Behind her, Gabriel was almost sure that he had seen Tess's lips tighten fractionally. A reaction at last! It was enough to make him greet Fionnula with extra warmth.

'I'm sorry to have kept you waiting,' he said, kissing her deliberately. 'I hope Tess has been looking after you.'

'She's been *marvellous*,' husked Fionnula, who had pretty much ignored Tess's existence since she had latched onto Harry. 'What a treasure you are,' she added graciously to Tess, who stared woodenly at her screen.

'I see you've met Harry,' said Gabriel, drawing Fionnula's attention back from Tess.

'Oh, I'm utterly, utterly in love with him,' Fionnula declared in her husky voice, and laughed delightedly as

Harry snuggled into her shoulder. 'You're my ideal man, aren't you, precious?'

She laid her free hand on Gabriel's arm and smiled bewitchingly up under those lashes. 'Well, one of them, anyway,' she murmured.

For a fleeting moment, Gabriel met Tess's eyes over the top of her glasses, before both looked away.

'We'd better go,' he said abruptly to Fionnula, who hung back, still playing the role of devoted mother.

'I'm not sure I can bear to leave Harry,' she said, pouting. 'Can we take him with us?'

Gabriel frowned. 'I don't think Cupiditas take children.'

As Fionnula must know full well, thought Tess dourly. If she was that thrilled with Harry, let her feed him between bites of a sandwich, which was obviously what *she* was going to have to do.

A pair of huge green eyes turned on her. 'Then, perhaps Tess…?' She held Harry out with a show of reluctance.

Tess took off her glasses and rose to her feet. 'I'll look after him,' she said, taking the baby back.

'Oh, *thank* you,' Fionnula gushed, as if Harry were her responsibility.

'There's no need to thank me,' said Tess, very cool. 'Mr Stearne is paying me to look after Harry.'

Mr Stearne is paying me. Gabriel mimicked her accent savagely to himself as he waited for the lift with Fionnula. As if he ever got a chance to forget it!

Disgruntled and restless, he was already regretting having invited Fionnula out to lunch. What was wrong with him? Gabriel wondered, the third time he found himself sneaking a surreptitious glance at his watch. Fionnula was beautiful, talented, sexy. Most men would give anything to be in his position, with her hand covering his, and the green eyes gazing seductively into his face. They wouldn't be wasting their time mentally comparing her with their PA, would they?

But Gabriel couldn't help it. Fionnula smouldered, Tess was cool and restrained. Fionnula was flamboyant, Tess precise. Fionnula was stunningly beautiful, and Tess... Tess was just Tess.

And Fionnula wanted him. Tess didn't.

So, when a box of chocolates caught his eye on his way back to the office, why did he waste his time going into the shop and buying them for Tess?

'These are for you,' he said gruffly, practically shoving the box across the desk towards her.

Tess, who had spent the lunch hour trying not to think about Gabriel and Fionnula and feeling out of sorts, stared at the chocolates.

Unthinkingly, she got to her feet, clutching the box to her chest. 'For me?' she asked incredulously.

'You said they were your favourites.' He sounded almost defensive.

'They are...but...why are you giving me chocolates?' asked Tess, completely thrown by the unexpected gesture.

Yes, *why*? Gabriel asked himself savagely. 'They're a thank you for looking after Harry,' he said after an infinitesimal pause.

'You're paying me for doing that,' she pointed out, embarrassed.

'Yes, I know I'm paying you,' he said grouchily. 'This is extra, all right? You don't have to have them! I just saw them and I thought of you—'

He stopped, uncomfortably aware of revealing more than he wanted. There was no reason why a box of chocolates should conjure up such a vivid picture of Tess sitting on the floor of his apartment, her beautiful hair tucked behind her ears and her eyes closed in blissful anticipation as she popped a chocolate in her mouth.

Suddenly self-conscious, he hunched an irritable shoulder. 'It's come to something when you have to justify thanking your secretary,' he grumbled. 'You were the one who told me I ought to show more appreciation.'

It was true. She had said that. She just hadn't known how disconcerting it would be when he took her advice. Tess could feel a treacherous glow spreading inside. Rarely had a gift been presented with less charm, but that didn't matter. He had thought about her. He had remembered which chocolates were her favourite.

And he hadn't spent long over lunch with Fionnula. That meant most of all.

'Thank you,' she said simply.

Gabriel hesitated. 'I know I can be difficult sometimes,' he acknowledged grudgingly.

Sometimes? thought Tess.

'I'm getting used to it,' she said.

And the worst thing was that it was true.

Gabriel's expression relaxed for the first time that day. He smiled at her and, without quite meaning to, Tess found herself smiling back until both became aware of the charge in the air and stopped abruptly at exactly the same time.

There was a pause which felt awkward for some reason. Tess's gaze dropped to her desk and she busied herself tidying some papers that were already neatly laid out.

She cleared her throat. 'Is it all right with you if I leave early this afternoon?' she asked after a moment. 'I'd like to get Harry home before the rush hour.'

'I'll drive you,' Gabriel offered.

'No,' she said quickly. 'I mean…there's no need. We can get a taxi. Harry slept pretty well last night,' she went on carefully, still straightening papers. 'I can manage him by myself now.' She forced a smile but didn't meet his eyes. 'I might as well earn that overtime. There's no point in you being there as well. I'm sure there are other things you'd rather be doing than changing nappies.'

There were, of course, Gabriel insisted to himself as he prowled restlessly around his apartment that night. Tess was right. He hadn't been much use with Harry, and why should he spend his time changing nappies and making up bottles when he was paying her to do it? He had better things to do.

Here he was, at the peak of his profession, he reminded himself. He had taken over an ailing company, and there was every reason to believe that he could turn it into a thriving concern, as a step towards moving into the rest of Europe. He had lots of money, a smart car, a convenient apartment. *Two* convenient apartments, he amended, remembering his home in New York. He was free, in his prime. He went out with beautiful women. What more, Gabriel asked himself, could he possibly want?

Surely it had to be something more exciting than a small warm house and Tess, barefoot and smiling, with her hair tumbling softly around her face?

Gabriel looked around the apartment that seemed suddenly cold and characterless, and he frowned. He had to stop thinking about Tess. Complications of that kind were the last thing he wanted. Building up the business was his priority, and he needed Tess as his PA. He didn't believe in office relationships any more than she did.

Not that there was any question of…whatever. Tess wasn't his type, and he clearly wasn't hers. She had made it plain that she was quite happy on her own.

Just like he was.

And he *was*, Gabriel told himself. Perfectly happy.

On the other side of the river, Tess was reassuring herself that she had done the right thing. Gabriel's lunch date with Fionnula had left her feeling unaccountably disgruntled, and she had been determined to show him that she could manage Harry without any help from him. If he wanted to spend his time going out with Fionnula, that was up to him. She didn't need him. She would be fine on her own. Absolutely fine.

But then Gabriel had come back with the chocolates,

and he had smiled, and her dudgeon had faded, only to be replaced by something much more dangerous, something alarmingly close to liking, and that would never do. With her house to herself again, it would be much easier to remember all the reasons why she didn't really like him at all, and why she didn't care *who* he had lunch with.

Only it wasn't really easier at all. Gabriel's absence was nearly as disturbing as his presence. Tess kept turning round, expecting to see him. Every time she went through a door, she would look at the handle and think about how competently he had fixed it into place with his strong, square hands, the same hands that had curved over her body, and a strange feeling would slither down her spine.

Tess told herself that she was being silly. It was inevitable that she and Gabriel had got to know each other better over the course of the weekend, but nothing had changed. Sitting disconsolately in front of the fire that night, she remembered what she had said about keeping her private and professional lives quite distinct. The longer Gabriel had stayed, the harder that would have been to do. Yes, it was much better this way.

It didn't stop the house feeling very empty that night, though.

Using the meagre information he had from Greg, Gabriel had briefed a firm of private investigators to find Harry's mother as quickly as possible but, as the days passed without any word, they began to fall into a new routine in the office.

Every morning, Tess brought Harry in after his breakfast. For the most part, he was happy to sit in his chair, or play with his toys on the mat, and let himself be fussed over by everyone who came into the office. Tess was just grateful he wasn't yet at the crawling stage and it was easy enough to keep an eye on him.

When he got bored, she took him on her lap and let him

smack his hands onto her keyboard, or inspect the strange objects on her desk. Everything went into Harry's mouth. She was constantly rescuing things from his grasp, and soon learned to remove pens and paperclips out of reach of those curious little hands.

Using the phone wasn't a problem, once she had explained the source of the chatty babbling in the background, but she only really managed to get any work done when Harry was sleeping. The other secretaries helped her out a lot, and sometimes, if she needed to do something urgently, Gabriel would take him and walk him round the office, although actually Tess found it even harder to concentrate when he was there. Harry awake was less of a distraction.

Tess didn't like the fact that she was so aware of Gabriel. It wasn't like her to be unsettled like this. She had done her very best to put the memory of waking up in bed with him to the back of her mind, but it wouldn't go away no matter how hard she tried to convince herself that it had been no more than an embarrassing incident that was better forgotten.

She would think that she *had* forgotten it, only to find that the memories were waiting to ambush her at the least appropriate moment. Gabriel would be dictating or demanding a file or shouting down the phone, and Tess would catch her breath at the thought of his lips and his hands and his hard body.

Gabriel himself seemed to be making an effort to be as difficult and demanding as normal, and he only let down his guard with the baby, and only when he thought no one was looking. Outwardly, he was brusque with Harry, but once or twice Tess caught him playing with him in his inner office, tossing him in the air until he squealed, or tickling his tummy. The moment he realised that she was watching him, he would stop, covering his embarrassment with bluster, and Tess would pretend that she hadn't noticed.

By Thursday, Harry was part of the office. Tess couldn't remember what it was like to settle down to work without having to stop to feed him or change him or let him stand on her knees and explore her face with glee.

When the phone rang that afternoon, Tess had him on her hip as she stood at the filing cabinets, searching one-handed for a document Gabriel wanted. Carrying Harry back over to the desk, she picked up the receiver.

It was Elaine. 'There's a Leanne Morrison in reception,' she told Tess doubtfully. 'She says she has to see Mr Stearne. It's urgent, she says.'

Tess had a weird sense of *déjà vu*. She had been here before, she thought with an odd, detached part of her mind.

'Send her up,' she said slowly.

She knocked on Gabriel's door. 'What is it?' he said, as if having to remind himself to be irritable.

'Harry's mother is on her way up.'

Gabriel stared at her. 'Why didn't the investigators tell us that they had found her?'

'I don't think they did,' said Tess. 'I think Leanne has found us.'

CHAPTER EIGHT

LEANNE wasn't at all Tess's idea of a croupier. She had softly curling blonde hair and a sweet expression overlaid with anxiety. Hesitating in the doorway, her big blue eyes swept around the office until they saw the baby in Tess's arms.

'Harry!' she said in a choked voice, and Tess's throat tightened as his little face lit up at the sight of his mother. Leanne clutched him to her, murmuring his name over and over again, oblivious to anyone else.

It was some time before Leanne could speak. 'I'm so sorry,' she said at last, her eyes still brimming with tears. 'I got a flight home as soon as Mum told me what she'd done. I've come straight from Heathrow. I was terrified he wouldn't be here,' she went on, hugging Harry close. 'I can't tell you what a relief it is to see him.'

'He's been quite safe,' Tess reassured her.

'I can see that.' Leanne managed a wavering smile. 'I shouldn't have left him, I know, but I needed the money, and it was only for six weeks...I can't believe what Mum did. She had no right to go to Gabriel.'

She squared her shoulders. 'I'd better see Gabriel and explain,' she said. 'Is he here?'

Gabriel, who had been watching Harry's reunion with his mother with a distant expression that effectively concealed how moved he felt, glanced at Tess. 'I'm Gabriel,' he said.

Leanne looked confused. 'I'm sorry, I meant Gabriel Stearne.'

'That's my name.' Picking his words with care, Gabriel explained how the misunderstanding had arisen. It was hard to excuse his brother's deception, but Leanne had obviously got to know Greg quite well in a short time, because she didn't seem that surprised. 'Greg still doesn't know about Harry,' he finished. 'I think you should be the one to tell him.'

'I should have told him before,' Leanne said with a sigh. 'But I didn't think he'd want to know. He was so charming and such fun,' she remembered a little wistfully, 'but he never pretended that he was serious. It was my choice to have Harry, not his and I didn't think it was fair to expect him to take any responsibility for him.'

Remorsefully, she looked from Gabriel to Tess. 'It turns out that you've taken responsibility for Harry instead. I'm sorry.'

'We've enjoyed it,' said Tess, realising for the first time that it was true. 'We're going to miss Harry.' She sent Gabriel a look, willing him to help her reassure Leanne. 'Aren't we?' she added pointedly.

He met her look. 'Yes,' he said after a fractional pause. 'We are. You're tired,' he went on, uncomfortable with all the emotional undercurrents. Leanne looked close to tears, and Tess didn't look much more in control. 'I'll drive you to Tess's house,' he said roughly. 'You can pick up Harry's things and I'll take you both home.'

In the end, Tess persuaded Leanne to spend the night, since her mother was still away and she was too jet-lagged and emotional to cope on her own. 'You can sleep in the spare room,' she said. 'Take Harry home tomorrow.'

'I'll send a car for you,' said Gabriel, getting to his feet, glad that it was all sorted out. 'I'd better go,' he added to Tess.

Leanne looked surprised. 'Aren't you staying? I thought you two were...' She made a gesture linking them.

'No,' they both said quickly.

Tess's cheeks were burning as she showed Gabriel out,

and she avoided his eyes. 'See you tomorrow,' she said stiltedly.

Leanne was full of apologies when she went back into the sitting room. 'I just assumed you two were together,' she tried to explain. 'It was the way you looked at each other.'

'There's nothing like that.' Tess forced a bright smile. 'Gabriel is just my boss.'

And that was *all* he was, she had to keep reminding herself over the next few days.

Gabriel was very brisk the next morning. 'I've arranged for your overtime to be added to your salary this month,' he told her, omitting to mention that he had doubled the amount they had agreed. 'I'm going to see my stepfather this weekend, but I'll be back next Wednesday. Perhaps then we can get back to normal.'

Tess couldn't quite remember what normal *was* any more. The office felt very dreary when she went in on Monday. I'm just missing Harry, she told herself. It's got nothing to do with the fact that Gabriel isn't here.

All day long, people trooped into her office and congratulated her on his absence. 'It's so much more relaxed when he's not around, isn't it?' they said, and Tess agreed, although she didn't think that it was true. She certainly didn't feel relaxed. She was edgy and irritable, and she couldn't settle to anything. Gabriel had told her that he would ring from New York and she found herself waiting for his call, jumping whenever the phone went.

As it turned out, he sent her an e-mail instead, telling her that he wouldn't be back until the following Monday after all. 'You know why, don't you?' smirked Niles when he heard the news.

'He said he had a few things to sort out in New York.'

'Right, and one of those things has long red hair and green eyes.'

Tess frowned. 'What do you mean?'

'Don't you ever read the gossip columns, Tess? Fionnula Jenkins is in New York too at the moment. Our Gabriel probably wants to keep an eye on the competition. If you're talking to him, remind him he said he'd come to the promises auction, will you?' Niles went on, oblivious to the sick, hollow feeling inside Tess. 'We're relying on him.'

Tess couldn't care less about the promises auction right then. The news that Fionnula was in New York had made her furious, and not knowing why she felt so angry only made it worse. When Gabriel eventually deigned to come back, she was very cool to him. Not that he noticed nor cared. If anything he was in a worse mood than before he'd left.

Perhaps Fionnula was giving him the run-around, thought Tess unsympathetically. He was certainly working hard to impress her. Tess seemed to spend her whole time sending flowers to Fionnula, booking tables for two, or arranging limousines to ferry them to and from glittering parties. She couldn't imagine how Gabriel got on there. He was too dark and glowering to fit into that sparkling, superficial world, and it was impossible to picture him cruising a room, gossiping and air-kissing and showing off.

He had been much more comfortable tramping across the common in the rain, she was sure. Sometimes Tess thought about the weekend they had spent together and wondered if she had imagined it all. Gabriel gave no sign that he remembered pottering around her house, or playing with Harry, or buying her chocolates. It was as if that brief moment of warmth had never happened. He was curt with her to the point of rudeness, and his face shuttered whenever he looked at her.

Tess told herself she didn't care.

For the first time, she was conscious of a sense of dissatisfaction with her life. She was tired of being efficient, tired of trailing home to an empty house every night. She had kept in touch with Leanne, and was surprised at how much she enjoyed seeing Harry again, but she wanted something more. She wanted to go out and enjoy herself.

She wanted to forget about Gabriel and the way things had been when Harry had been there.

So when her old boss, Steve Robinson, rang one evening and asked her out to dinner, Tess jumped at the chance. 'Put on your glad rags,' said Steve. 'We're dining in style!'

'We are? What's the occasion?'

'I've got a proposition to put to you.'

He wouldn't tell her any more then, but Tess took him at his word, and rifled through her wardrobe in search of something suitably glamorous to wear, settling eventually on a dress that she had bought in the summer sales. It was a softer style than she usually wore, but she loved the deep gold fabric that brought out the colour of her eyes and flattered her figure. She brushed out her hair so that it fell gleaming to her shoulders and slipped her feet into high heels that were impossible to walk more than a few yards in but which made her feel wonderful. She was ready to hit the town.

Steve whistled when he saw her and his obvious appreciation was balm to Tess's sore spirit after a week of being ignored or snapped at by Gabriel. To her relief, Steve had come in a taxi, so they could go door to door.

'On behalf of my feet, I thank you,' said Tess, looking ruefully down at her unsuitable shoes as she settled into the back of the taxi. 'This is all very grand, Steve. Where are we going?'

'Cupiditas,' he told her with a grin.

'Cupiditas?' she echoed in a hollow voice. 'What a great idea!'

It was a horrible idea. Tess had taken a dislike to the very idea of Cupiditas ever since discovering that it was Fionnula's favourite restaurant, and the last thing she wanted tonight was to be reminded of Gabriel, as she inevitably would be. She had booked him so many tables there, she knew the telephone number off by heart.

At least she knew Gabriel and Fionnula wouldn't be there, Tess reassured herself. Gabriel had asked—ordered—her to book another restaurant for tonight.

'I thought you'd be pleased,' said Steve. 'I wanted to give you a real treat.'

Cupiditas had such a starry reputation that Tess half expected them to be turned away at the door for not being beautiful or famous enough, but they were shown to a table on the far side of the crowded room. The whole place reeked of money and glamour, and Tess was sinkingly aware of how much the evening would cost Steve.

'This is wonderful,' she said dutifully as they sat down.

A waiter was hovering to present the menus with a flourish. Tess smiled her thanks up at him as she accepted hers, and she was still smiling when he moved away and she found herself looking over Steve's shoulder at the table which had been blocked from her view, and where a man sat staring back at her.

Gabriel.

Shock wiped the smile from Tess's face, and stopped her heart in mid beat. She was paralysed, skewered by the expression in his eyes which managed to blaze and freeze at the same time, and all she could do was stare helplessly back at him, as if the two of them were quite alone, and the other diners had retreated into the far distance, cut off by an invisible wall of silence.

Steve's hand waving in front of her face jerked Tess back to reality. 'Are you all right?' he said, watching her quizzically.

Tess pulled herself together with an effort and swallowed. 'Yes, yes, I'm fine,' she said, but her hands were unsteady as she bent her head over the menu.

The words swam in front of her eyes. Her heart was

thumping painfully in her chest and she drew a shaky breath, struggling to get a grip of herself. Steve had obviously gone to a lot of trouble and expense to make this a special evening for her. She couldn't get up and run out the way she would like to do.

Forcing a bright smile, she kept her gaze fixed on Steve's face as he talked about the company where he now worked, but all the time she was conscious of Fionnula's coppery hair cascading down her back, of her silvery laugh and extravagant gestures. And of Gabriel sitting opposite her, a dark, intense presence in the middle of the room. It took every ounce of Tess's will not to look directly at him, but his still figure tugged insistently, inexorably at the corner of her eye.

Preoccupied with the effort of not succumbing to its lure, it took Tess a little time to realise that Steve was offering her a job.

'I told you I had a proposition for you,' he said.

'But—haven't you got a PA?' Tess stammered, wishing that she had paid more attention to what he was saying.

Steve looked at her strangely. Obviously he had spent some time explaining all this. 'It's not a PA job,' he repeated patiently. 'It's not that I wouldn't like to work with you again, of course, but you're capable of so much more, Tess. It's time you spread your wings. We need an office manager to oversee the move into a new headquarters, and I think you'd be fantastic.'

'I don't know what to say.' Tess stalled, fiddling with her fork.

'I thought of you as soon as the job came up. I knew you weren't very happy working with Gabriel Stearne and were looking for a chance to move on. This is it!'

Tess bit her lip. She had told everyone she didn't like Gabriel and that she wanted to leave as soon as she found a job that paid as well. She had said it so often, she had thought it was true.

But it wasn't.

Involuntarily, she looked over Steve's shoulder, and her eyes encountered Gabriel's across the room for a charged moment before they fell back to her plate.

He was impossible, demanding, unpredictable, but she didn't dislike him. And she didn't want to leave him.

The truth settled like a stone in Tess's stomach. Why did she have to realise it now? she wondered with something close to resentment. Why couldn't she carry on hating him the way she had before? Everything had been so much easier then.

'Well, what do you say?' Steve was asking eagerly.

'I…I'll have to think about it, Steve.'

She could tell that he was disappointed by her lack of enthusiasm, and exerted herself to make up for it by chatting with feverish gaiety for the rest of the evening and pretending to enjoy the treat he had arranged for her. She exclaimed over every exquisite plate that was set before her and marvelled at how delicious the food was, although it might as well have been made of cardboard.

Gabriel wasn't enjoying his food either. He was shaken off balance by the way Tess looked. He had hardly recognised her when she'd walked in, wearing a dress in some soft, deep gold material that clung to her figure. He had seen her in a suit, seen her in jeans, he had even seen her in her satin nightdress, but he had never seen her dressed up before, and now he couldn't keep his eyes off her.

She looked fabulous, he thought, his throat tightening at the sight of her, warm and glowing with that soft, silky tumble of hair. Gabriel watched her with something close to resentment. He had spent his entire time back in the States trying to forget her, staying longer than he intended in the hope of putting her out of his mind, and when he had run into Fionnula in New York, it had seemed like the perfect opportunity to convince himself that he had.

Tess had been back to her old frigid self when he'd

eventually returned, which had made it easy for Gabriel to let himself believe that the whole business with Harry had never happened, and that he had never glimpsed the warm, vibrant woman who lived behind his PA's cool mask.

And now Tess had spoilt everything by walking into Cupiditas looking like that.

He could see all the other men in the restaurant checking her out, but Tess only had eyes for Steve Robinson. Gabriel remembered *him* all right. Tess's boss, the one she had liked working for so much, before he had come along and broken up their cosy company. *Steve was fantastic.* Wasn't that what she had said? *He's a very nice man.*

Was she in love with him? Gabriel wondered savagely. She certainly thought he was something special, judging by the way she had leant towards him, her chin propped in one hand, smiling that smile of hers, *laughing* with him.

Gabriel wanted to go over and punch him.

Signalling abruptly for the bill, he waited for Fionnula to return from another remorseless round of table-hopping. 'Let's go,' he said.

He was determined not to mention the fact that he had seen her the next day. What Tess did out of the office was entirely her own business. He didn't care where she went or who she was with as long as she did her job properly. So when he called her into his office that morning, he was resolutely businesslike, firing off a ream of memos and letters, while inwardly congratulating himself on his indifference.

Tess's pen raced over the page to keep up as Gabriel paced around the room, apparently filled with a restless energy. It was a relief when he paused at last by the window and stood looking out, shoulders hunched and hands thrust deep into his trouser pockets. She flexed her fingers surreptitiously.

'I didn't realise you were still seeing Steve Robinson.'

The words were out before Gabriel could stop them, and Tess stiffened at the hostility in his tone.

'I don't have to account to you for what I do or who I see in my time off,' she said coldly.

Gabriel swung round. 'Does he often take you to places like Cupiditas?'

'Why? Is there some rule that secretaries aren't allowed?'

'Of course not,' he said irritably. 'I was just surprised to see you there.'

'I was surprised to see *you*. I'd booked you a table at the Dorchester.'

'Fionnula changed her mind.' Gabriel was annoyed to find himself explaining. 'She knows the owner of Cupiditas, so he found us a table.'

Tess's lips tightened. If it was that easy for Fionnula to get in, why did she have to spend so much of her time on the phone booking tables at Cupiditas? 'How convenient for you,' she said between her teeth.

Gabriel took another turn around the room. 'Is he married?' he asked abruptly.

'Who? Steve?'

He sucked in his breath. 'Yes, *Steve*,' he said, controlling his temper with an effort.

'Why do you ask?' Tess was obviously determined not to be helpful.

'He looks married.'

'As a matter of fact, he's divorced,' she told him frostily. 'Not that it's any of your business.'

Gabriel knew that it wasn't, but he was in the grip of some strange compulsion. 'I thought you didn't believe in mixing work and your private life?' he said accusingly.

'I don't.' The eyes that had once reminded him of warm honey were cold and clear. 'But, then, I don't work with Steve any more,' she added deliberately, and Gabriel glowered.

'No, you work for *me*, and please don't forget it. I don't want you passing any confidential information onto Steve Robinson while you're playing footsie under the table. He works for a rival organisation, so don't forget that either!'

Tess stared at him coldly. 'Steve and I have got better things to talk about than work, I can assure you,' she said.

Which wasn't really what Gabriel wanted to hear.

'Going out again?' Gabriel's voice was hard as he watched Tess hang up the dress she had brought into the office that morning.

'It's the promises auction tonight,' she said, taking off her coat. 'We're all supposed to be at the hotel at seven, so it's not worth me going home. I've brought everything I need to change here.'

She eyed him under her lashes, wondering what sort of mood he was in today. She didn't understand Gabriel at the moment. He hadn't mentioned Steve again, but he had been restless and on edge. One minute he would bite her head off, the next she would look up to find him watching her with an expression that made the breath dry in her throat.

Tess sighed inwardly. There wasn't much point in trying to understand Gabriel when she didn't even understand herself. Steve had offered her the perfect opportunity to step up the career ladder, but she kept putting off the moment of decision. They were busy in the office again and, whatever else working with Gabriel might be like, it was never boring. There was an edge to the atmosphere when he was around, a crackle to the air, that compensated for his unpredictable temper.

'Oh, *that*.' Gabriel grunted as he found the report he was looking for on her desk. 'I don't have to go, do I?'

'I think it would be a nice gesture,' said Tess coolly. 'You did promise.'

'What?' His head lifted abruptly. 'I promised? When?'

'You told Niles you would come.'

'I said I'd do my best. That's not a promise.'

'And you promised me.' Tess hadn't really wanted to remind Gabriel of their weekend together, but she knew that Niles was relying on him to turn up. 'You sat on my sofa and promised you would go to the office party if I helped you with Harry—and I did.'

'Oh, very well,' he grumbled, 'but I wish you'd reminded me about this before.'

'It's in the diary,' she pointed out crisply, 'and I sent you an e-mail the day before yesterday.'

Gabriel eyed her with dislike. When she was like this, it was hard to understand why he spent so much time trying not to think about her.

'What do I have to do at this auction?'

'I've no idea,' said Tess, switching on her computer and flicking through the post that had been left on her desk. 'Niles has promised something on your behalf, but I expect it will just be a question of writing a cheque. All you need to do is turn up, and make a generous bid for somebody's promise. And look as if you're pleased to be there. It's a party. This is a chance for staff to get to know you. You're a distant figure at the moment, and most people are scared stiff of you.'

The boss from hell, in fact. Gabriel dropped the report back on her desk where it landed with a resounding slap. 'Well, if I'm going, you'd better buy me a fresh shirt at lunch-time,' he said, getting his own back. 'I'm tied up with meetings all day, and I'm having lunch at the bank. You know my size.'

Gabriel was late back from his afternoon meeting and barely had he walked through the door when an urgent call from the New York office sent them into a whirl of activity. It was half past six by the time the crisis had been sorted out, and the rest of the staff had already set out for the hotel where the auction was due to start at seven.

Very aware that the two of them were to all intents and purposes alone in the empty building, Tess took her dress down from its hook and picked up her bag. 'I'd better go and change,' she said with forced brightness.

Gabriel didn't even look up from the letters he was signing. 'Use my bathroom if you like,' he said.

It was certainly more luxurious than the ladies', thought Tess as she zipped herself into the gold dress once more. She looked at the marble counter where they had changed Harry together. She remembered how startled she had been by Gabriel's smile, how taken aback to find herself noticing his hands. How long ago it seemed now!

For some reason, the memory unsettled her, and she was conscious of a fluttery, stupidly nervous feeling as she made up her face and slipped on her unsuitable shoes. They were getting quite a lot of wear nowadays, she reflected. Brushing out her hair vigorously, she tossed it back and eyed her reflection dubiously. She looked wide-eyed and excited, as if she were getting ready to go out on a date instead of making a dutiful appearance at a work function.

On an impulse, she swept her hair back and pinned it up with clips in her usual style. That was better. She looked more like herself. She looked poised and in control. She felt in control. She *was* in control.

Emerging from the bathroom, she surprised Gabriel in the middle of shrugging himself into the clean shirt she had bought him earlier that day, the packaging scattered over his desk. Tempted as she had been to present him with something pink and frilly to wear, in the end she had chosen a classic deep blue shirt that would go with his tie.

He looked up as she appeared, and his hands stilled at his shirt. There was a taut silence.

'Sorry,' muttered Tess, averting her eyes from his chest.

Gabriel cleared his throat. 'I'll just have a wash. We might as well go together.' He nodded in the direction of the bar in the corner of his office. 'Have a drink while you're waiting.'

Tess helped herself to a glass of wine, not because she wanted it, but for something to do with her hands. She felt jittery, on edge. Her heart was pumping, and a mixture of tension and an unaccountable excitement shivered just beneath her skin. The office was very quiet, and when she looked down on the crowds still thronging the streets far below, they seemed to belong to a different world altogether.

The sound of the bathroom door opening made her heart lurch, and she spilled her wine, only just missing her dress.

'This shirt you bought,' Gabriel was saying, holding out his arms so that she could see the cuffs flapping, 'needs cuff-links.'

'Oh, dear, ' said Tess guiltily. She hadn't even thought to look at the cuffs. 'Haven't you got any?'

'Not with me. I'll have to get some on the way.'

She looked at her watch. 'We haven't got time. We're going to be late as it is.'

'Well, I can't go like this!'

Tess put down her glass. 'We'll just have to improvise.' Glad of something to do, she went out to her own desk and rummaged in her draw until she found some treasury tags she used for filing. 'These might work.'

Gabriel eyed them in disbelief. 'What the…?'

'Look,' she said, demonstrating how the two short metal bars were linked by a green cord. 'They'd be better than nothing, anyway.'

'Well, I'll have a go,' he said, resigned, and held out his hand.

Tess selected two of the tags and passed them to him

but, as their fingers brushed, she felt a jolt that made her jerk her hand back, and the tags dropped to the floor.

Scarlet, she knelt to retrieve them. 'Sorry,' she mumbled, and took care this time to drop them into Gabriel's open palm without touching him at all.

Muttering under his breath, Gabriel managed to fasten the left cuff with one of the tags, but he fumbled with the right until he admitted defeat and asked Tess to help him. 'Otherwise we'll never get to this auction,' he said.

He held out his wrist, and Tess had no option but to stand very close to him. She bent her head over the cuff and tried to concentrate, but her fingers were unwieldy and she was distracted by his nearness, by the crazy inclination to put her arms around his waist and lean into his hard, strong body, to rest her face against his throat and smell his skin.

'It—it's not as easy as it looks, is it?' she stammered.

'No,' Gabriel answered absently. He was looking down at the clips that held the silky hair in place and imagining how it would feel to pull them loose. Her perfume was making his head spin.

This was *Tess*, he kept telling himself. His PA. She was out of bounds. She didn't believe in office relationships, and neither did he.

But he still wanted to kiss her.

Wrenching his eyes from her hair, Gabriel stared resolutely over the top of her head, but now the deep leather sofa was directly in his line of vision, and all he could think about was how easy it would be to sink down on it with her, to persuade her not to go to this stupid auction but stay there with him, just the two of them in the dark office…

'There, I think that's it.'

Tess's words made him look down, just at the moment that she looked up into his face, her fingers still on his cuff, and their eyes met. It was a mistake. The air leaked from his lungs and his throat tightened, while the silence thrummed between them, vibrant with temptation.

Tess's heart was slamming against her ribs. She wanted to move, to let her hands fall from his wrist, to say something bright and normal to banish the terrible tension, but she couldn't. She couldn't do anything but stand like a fool and stare up into his eyes.

He's going to kiss me, she thought, and was afraid. Afraid that he would, afraid that he wouldn't, afraid more than anything of her own response if he did.

Very slowly, Gabriel lifted his hands, and Tess caught her breath with a mixture of exhilaration and something like terror as she waited for him to cup her face and touch his lips to hers. He really was going to kiss her.

But he didn't. His hands hesitated for the merest fraction of a second on either side of her jaw before continuing upwards to find the clips in her hair.

'You looked better in this dress when your hair was down,' he said, a ragged edge to his voice, and he pulled the clips free to let her hair slither and bounce to her shoulders.

The temptation to cast the clips aside and wind the shining strands around his fingers, to hold her head still while he bent to kiss her, was so strong that it took all of Gabriel's will-power to step back.

'Just my opinion, of course.'

He held out the clips. Moistening her lips, Tess took them with unsteady fingers. 'We'd better go,' she said huskily.

She put the clips in her bag. It was too late to put her hair up again and she didn't want to make an issue of it. And quite apart from anything else, her hands were shaking so much that she would only make a mess of it.

Silence simmered as they waited for the lift. Inside it, they stood as far apart from each other as possible but Tess felt as if she was having to lean sideways to resist the magnetic pull that seemed to be tugging her towards Gabriel. She had the bizarre conviction that if she relaxed for an instant she would simply give in to the irresistible force that would propel her across the lift and clamp herself onto him. On her desk she had a magnetic paper clip holder. If you held the clip close enough there was a point at which it simply jumped onto the holder. It had always amused Tess before, but now she knew what the clip felt like, she didn't think she would use it any more.

The party was already in full swing by the time they got to the hotel, and Niles wore a relieved expression as he pushed his way through the crowd to welcome them. 'Now we can start the auction while everyone's still capable of writing cheques!'

A table had been set on the dais at one end of the room. Niles banged it with his gavel to get attention, and explained the rules of the auction to some jovial heckling from those who had been at the bar for some time.

'Right,' shouted Niles at last. 'We're going to begin with the promises that are up for auction. Lot one. John has promised an afternoon working in the garden. How much am I bid?'

Gabriel hardly listened. Tess had moved deliberately away from him and was standing with some of the girls he recognised from the office. He watched her covertly. There had been a moment back there in the office when he had badly wanted to kiss her, when he had known that she wouldn't have resisted if he had.

Thank God that he hadn't! Gabriel told himself. He had always stuck to women like Fionnula who knew the rules of the game and didn't pressurise him with false expectations and messy emotions. You knew where you were with Fionnula, but Tess was different. Tess was the sort of woman who expected you to mean what you said and keep any promises you made. The last thing he wanted was to get involved with a woman like her!

He fingered his mobile phone, wondering if he should confirm his decision by ringing Fionnula right now and arranging to meet her later, but the auction was well under way now, and they would all notice if he tried to slip away. He would call her later.

'Going…going…gone!' Niles brought down his gavel to a burst of applause. 'Lot ten,' he announced, well into his stride by now. 'A truly amazing opportunity! Tess Gordon has promised to cook a romantic meal for two for the highest bidder. She didn't specify whether she was one of the two but, either way, it's an offer not to be missed. So what am I bid for Tess's promise? Starting at twenty-five pounds…'

'Thirty.' someone shouted, and a brisk round of bidding ensued.

Gabriel listened with gathering frown. Most of those bidding were men, he noted darkly. Were they all hoping to have the dinner with Tess herself? He hated the idea of them bidding for her. She might end up anywhere, with anyone.

'A hundred pounds!' yelled Niles, spotting a raised hand. 'Our highest bid so far. Graham has bid a hundred pounds for Tess to cook a romantic dinner for two. Who'll give me a hundred and ten?'

Craning his neck, Gabriel spotted Graham, the director of the supplies division, looking smug. Tess, on the other hand, embarrassed by all the attention, looked as if she wished she was elsewhere.'

'Is a hundred my last offer?' Niles looked round, delighted at having raised such a sum. 'Going…going…'

'A thousand,' Gabriel heard his voice calling out.

There was a gasp. Everyone turned to stare at him in the ensuing dead silence. 'A thousand pounds,' he said again, sounding defensive.

Niles began to grin. 'I'm bid a thousand pounds for Tess's romantic dinner for two. That had better be a good dinner, Tess. Any other bids…? I didn't think so! Going, going, gone. Tess's promise sold to Mr Stearne.'

CHAPTER NINE

A HUGE cheer broke out, along with a lot of whistling and more than a few ribald comments. Mortified, Tess made her way as unobtrusively as possible to Gabriel's side while Niles was announcing that they would take a break and draw the raffle after they'd all had a chance to refill their glasses.

'That was a bit excessive, wasn't it?' she said out of the corner of her mouth.

Gabriel, wondering what madness had seized him, retreated behind a show of arrogant unconcern. 'I thought the object of the exercise was to raise money for charity?' he said, looking down his nose as if daring her to suggest that he could have had any other motive in bidding for her.

'It is, but there was no need for you to make quite such an ostentatious contribution. Everyone was having a good time until you killed the whole thing stone dead. Nobody else could possibly match that kind of money.'

'You were the one who told me to be generous,' said Gabriel, stung by her criticism. 'Obviously I had to make a bid for something, and I'm not interested in having my car washed by an accountant in a bikini.'

'At least bidding for that would have made you seem as if you had a sense of humour,' Tess retorted. 'It's not as if you've got any interest in a romantic meal either.'

'On the contrary,' he said, spotting an opportunity to convince her—or was it himself?—that when he had made that absurd bid he hadn't been thinking about her at all. 'Fionnula was saying just the other day that it would nice to have an evening in. I'm no cook, but if you could pro-

149

duce something special, we could make it a really romantic evening for her.'

He might as well have slapped her. Tess stiffened. Less than an hour ago, he had been thinking about kissing *her*—she had seen it in his eyes—and now she was expected to help promote his romance with Fionnula Jenkins!

'I'll do whatever you want,' she said frigidly, deciding there and then that, whatever the menu, it would be something she could do well in advance so she didn't have to watch him and Fionnula being romantic together.

Gabriel put his hand in his jacket pocket and brought out his cheque book. 'I guess I'd better hand over some money, and then perhaps I can go.'

'I don't think you'll be able to do that,' said Tess with just a trace of malice. 'Your promise hasn't been raffled off yet.'

Cursing under his breath, Gabriel went in search of Niles or one of the other members of the social committee, but when he tried to find out exactly what he had promised Niles would say only that it was coming up as the finale to the raffle. 'You can't go yet, Mr Stearne,' he protested. 'We're all relying on you.'

'What am I going to have to do?'

'We're saving it as a surprise.' Niles winked. 'But I think you'll enjoy it!'

'Is it going to take long?'

'That's up to you, sir. All I can tell you is that it's something you have to do tonight.'

Gabriel sighed and gave up. He obviously wasn't going to get any more out of them. They were all well into the drinks and were no doubt arranging something suitably humiliating for the boss from hell, as Tess called him.

He would just have to put up with it, Gabriel realised. Tess's comment about his lack of humour was rankling still. There was nothing wrong with his sense of humour, and he was quite happy to prove it to her!

The evening seemed endless. Remembering what she had said about getting to know his staff better, Gabriel made laborious conversation with various groups, most of whom seemed to be in awe of him, and tried not to notice how Tess never came near him.

After what seemed an age, with the party getting more raucous, Niles climbed back onto the dais and called for silence for the raffle. 'This is a lucky dip. You've all bought a ticket, so we're going to raffle off the remaining promises.'

There was much hilarity as the promises were solemnly read out and the winners waved their tickets. Gabriel had bought a whole book of tickets, and he was relieved that his numbers hadn't come up. He had no desire for a week's doughnut delivery to his desk, nor to be smiled at by the famously morose accounting clerk.

'And now to our final, very special, promise,' cried Niles at last. 'It's time for Mr Stearne, who's already made such a generous financial contribution this evening, to keep his promise. I know a lot of you ladies have bought tickets hoping that yours will be the one that comes up, so let's see who's going to be the lucky girl!'

Gabriel looked at Tess and raised his eyebrows, but she lifted her shoulders and shook her head to indicate that she had no idea what Niles was talking about either.

'Sir, if you'd like to come up here, please.'

They made a passage for him through to the dais. Resigned to his fate, Gabriel climbed the steps to join Niles with a forced smile.

'Mr Stearne has promised to kiss the first lady whose ticket comes out of the hat.'

There were whistles and cheers. Gabriel's expression took on a decidedly fixed quality, but he kept his smile in place. He had a sense of humour, hadn't he? He hoped Tess was watching.

'OK, girls, are you ready?'

They screamed and laughed excitedly as with a great flourish Niles drew a ticket stub out of the hat. 'Perhaps you'd like to announce the winner,' he said to Gabriel, who took the stub with a constrained smile.

'Number ninety-seven,' he read out, then his eye moved upwards to read the name scribbled above. 'Tess,' he said in a strange voice.

'Rigged!' someone called out in mock outrage, while there was another outburst of cheers and whistles.

Tess stared down at the ticket in her hand in disbelief, and then, very slowly, she lifted her eyes to meet Gabriel's gaze over the crowd.

She had been too preoccupied to pay any attention to the rumours circulating about the promises auction. Why hadn't someone told her that this was the humiliation they'd had in mind for Gabriel? She could have put a stop to it, but it was too late now. If either of them refused to go through with this ridiculous kiss, they would both look foolish, and Tess realised suddenly that she couldn't bear to do that to Gabriel. His reputation was bad enough as it was.

So she let herself be prodded forward, smiling mechanically at the merry calls of encouragement, and before she knew what was happening was climbing the steps onto the dais where Gabriel was waiting for her.

'It seems I have a promise to keep,' he said.

An expectant silence fell on the crowd watching them. Very aware of all those eyes watching his every move, Gabriel took Tess's hands. Her eyes were huge and dark, and her fingers clasped his in mute appeal. Better get this over with quickly, he thought.

Bending his head swiftly, he touched his lips to the corner of her mouth and straightened.

'Call that a kiss?' came a catcall over the whistles and laughter. 'Give her a proper kiss!'

Gabriel looked down into Tess's eyes. Moistening her

lips, she nodded almost imperceptibly. If they didn't do this properly, they would never get off this platform.

Awkwardly, he put his hands to her waist and pulled her closer. Tess's palms rested against his chest. He could feel her trembling slightly. How could he possibly kiss her with a hundred pairs of eyes staring at them?

The silence stretched agonisingly. Gabriel glanced at the crowd, and then back to Tess's golden eyes. And all at once, it was easy. His hands tightened at her waist and, as her lashes closed in sweet anticipation, his mouth came down on hers. He felt her sharp intake of breath at the touch of his lips and for an instant she tensed before something unlocked inside her and she yielded to the warmth and persuasion of his kiss.

The watching crowd was forgotten. Gabriel gathered her closer as he gave in to the temptation to kiss her the way he had so badly wanted to kiss her in office, before he had decided that he hadn't really wanted to kiss her at all. He knew now that he had just been fooling himself. Of course he had wanted to kiss her, and now that he *was* kissing her, it felt absolutely right, as if he had always known how it would be, as if she belonged in his arms.

Equally heedless of the spectators, Tess melted into him, her hands creeping up to his shoulders. Delight span her slowly, irresistibly, around, sweeping her away from reality so that she had to cling to Gabriel, intoxicated and dizzy and oblivious to anything but the warmth of his lips and the taste of his mouth and the hard security of his arms locked around her.

When he let her go, she was shaken and disorientated to find herself back on the dais, and she stared at him, shocked not by the kiss but by the suddenness with which it had ended, and hardly hearing the cheering and whistling from the delighted onlookers who had never in a million years thought that either of them would go through with it.

'Well, Tess, there are a lot of envious girls out there this evening after watching that!' Niles laughed, and a great sweep of colour burned up her cheeks as she realised just how it must have looked. She hadn't even put up a token resistance! They all must have seen how eagerly she had responded to Gabriel's kiss.

Tess didn't know where to look, nor what to do. Her heart was jerking, her nerves jumped and tingled, her mouth throbbed. Part of her wanted the dais to open up and swallow her. The other terrible, treacherous, part longed to bury back into Gabriel and to feel his arms close around her, holding her safe and protecting her from the avid stares of those waiting below.

Somehow, Tess got herself off the dais to find herself welcomed like a returning heroine. Everyone thought it was a great joke. Tess knew that she had to treat it like a joke too, to pretend that it had all been very amusing and that she had simply played along, but it was an enormous effort to steady her trembling mouth, to nod and smile and agree that, yes, Gabriel's expression when he'd heard what he had to do had been very funny.

'We rigged it,' Niles was confiding complacently to Gabriel. 'We thought that since you and Tess had been spending so much time together you would…you know…' He faltered to a stop, unsure how to interpret the look in Gabriel's eyes. 'You didn't mind, did you?' he asked belatedly.

From the dais, Gabriel looked down at Tess. She was surrounded by people who were laughing and congratulating her as if she had passed some terrible ordeal, and he remembered the slender pliancy of her body, her warmth and her softness, the sweetness of her lips.

'No, I didn't mind,' he said slowly.

Tess dressed at her most severe the next morning. After a restless night spent tossing and turning, while her mouth tingled with the imprint of Gabriel's lips and her body thumped and twitched with the memory of his hands and the hard promise they had held, she decided that her only option was to behave exactly as usual and somehow convince Gabriel that she had treated that kiss as light-heartedly as everyone else.

There was no sign of him when she got into work. Belatedly, Tess remembered that he had a meeting first thing, and didn't know whether to be relieved or disappointed that she didn't have to impress him with her dignified lack of concern right away.

The office was very quiet when he wasn't there, and she had too much time to think. Unable to concentrate on anything more complicated, Tess decided that this was the perfect opportunity to catch up on her filing. She was standing by one of the gleaming cabinets with a collection of papers and files in her hands and her back to the door when Gabriel spoke behind her, and the shock of hearing his voice a good hour earlier than she had expected him loosened her grip, sending the entire pile scattering to the floor as she swung round.

'I'm sorry,' he said in a stilted voice. ' I didn't mean to startle you.'

'It's all right. I just wasn't expecting you back yet.'

Crimson and flustered, Tess crouched to gather up the papers. Gabriel put his briefcase on her desk and bent to help her. He handed her two of the files, being very careful not to touch her, and for a moment they were linked by the buff cardboard. Their eyes caught and clung, before he broke the look and straightened abruptly.

He too had spent a restless night, and the meeting that morning had been profoundly unsatisfactory, largely because of his own inability to concentrate on what was being said. By the time he'd reached the office, he had been feeling edgy and irritable, and quite unprepared for the effect the sight of Tess would have on him.

Was still having on him.

She was standing by her desk, making a big deal of tidying the pile of papers they had gathered. Her hair was up, as usual, and he could see the nape of her neck, so soft and vulnerable and alluring. Gabriel had a terrible urge to press his lips to it.

What would she do if he did? Would she recoil in horror? Or would she lean back into him with a slow shiver of response, smiling and tilting her head so that he could kiss his way down her throat?

Appalled at the wayward drift of his imagination, Gabriel swallowed hard and practically snatched his briefcase from the desk. 'When you've finished sorting those out, perhaps you could come into my office?' he said gruffly.

Tess thought she had herself well under control by the time she had found her notebook and knocked on his door. 'You wanted me?' she said without thinking and then blushed like a fool, her precious poise slipping disastrously as she heard the *double entendre* in her words.

Gabriel looked up from his computer, his eyes piercingly light and alert, and he let the silence beat for a second or two, just long enough to let her know that he had heard it too.

'Yes, I did,' he agreed.

He dictated a couple of letters and asked her to make various arrangements which Tess noted, proud of the fact that her hands were absolutely steady. Well, quite steady, anyway.

Then he fell silent, shifting the papers around on his desk. 'About last night,' he said at last, and Tess stiffened. It wasn't fair of him to bring last night up, just when she had let herself believe that he wasn't going to mention it.

'What about it?' she said with a hostile look.

'Do you know who was responsible for setting us up like that?'

Tess had her strong suspicions but she shook her head. 'No, but I don't think you should make an issue of it,' she said as coolly as she could. 'It was meant to be a bit of fun, that's all.'

'I didn't think it was fun,' said Gabriel and held her eyes deliberately. 'Did you?'

The memory of the kiss blazed between them. It had been amazing, overwhelming, terrifying in its intensity, but *fun*? No, not fun.

Her gaze slid away from his. 'I think you'll find that it was a good thing for you to have done,' she said, not answering him directly. 'You showed everyone that you're prepared to have a laugh and let yourself be the butt of a joke. That will have done more for your relations with the staff here than a hundred memos.'

'And that makes it all right, does it?'

She fiddled with her pen. 'I know it was…thought-less…and embarrassing…' she said, choosing her words with care, 'but it's too late to change what happened now. You might as well make the best of it.'

'What about you?' Gabriel was unreasonably annoyed by Tess's calmly sensible attitude. Obviously *she* hadn't spent the night tossing and turning and wondering what it would have been like if they hadn't been kissing in front of a roomful of people, if they'd been on their own, with no one to laugh or to cheer, with no reason to stop…

'It wasn't just me up there making an exhibition of my-self. They set you up, too.'

'Oh, well…' Tess managed a careless shrug. 'Judging by the reaction I got afterwards, it obviously did wonders for my image too. They've always thought of me as a bit prim and proper, I think. That's probably why they chose me.'

Seeing that Gabriel looked unconvinced, she leant for-ward in her chair. 'It was all very silly, I agree,' she said, trying her best to make light of it, 'but it wasn't such a terrible experience, was it?' she added bravely.

Gabriel didn't answer. He just looked at her, remembering the feel of her in his arms. He wished he could dismiss it as casually as she seemed to be able to. 'You're taking it all very well,' he commented in a hard voice.

'I don't see any point in making a fuss,' said Tess lightly. 'It wasn't as if it meant anything. It was just a kiss.'

Yes, all right, he'd got the point that it hadn't meant anything to her, thought Gabriel savagely.

'I think we should forget the whole incident,' she was continuing, ignoring the way his jaw was working. 'It was all for a good cause. They raised a lot of money through the auction.' Tess was very proud of her nonchalant manner. 'Talking of which, when would you like me to keep my promise?'

He frowned. 'What promise?'

'To cook you a romantic dinner for two.'

'Oh,' he said flatly, 'that promise.'

'You paid a lot of money for it,' she reminded him.

He had, Gabriel remembered. Well, it was time to reassure Tess that he wasn't taking that kiss any more seriously than she was.

'I'll see if Fionnula is free this weekend,' he said. 'Shall we say Saturday night?'

Tess flashed a brittle smile as she got to her feet. 'Saturday would be fine,' she said.

'I can't see what I'm doing,' Gabriel complained, looking up from the report he was trying to read. Tess had put off the overhead lights and was setting the blinds to slide across the window with a faint electronic hum.

'You're not supposed to be able to read,' she told him, switching on a table lamp. 'A romantic meal is all about atmosphere.'

That was what he had paid for, and that was what he was going to get, she had vowed to herself.

Returning to the kitchen, she reappeared a few moments later with some flowers and candles, which she set at strategic points around the room. She would light them just before she left, so that they would be flickering romantically when Fionnula arrived. Some perverse instinct had made Tess determined to create the ultimate romantic meal for them both.

'Now all you need is music,' she said, surveying the room with satisfaction when she had finished.

'I haven't got any music,' said Gabriel, who had been watching her as she'd been moving around, graceful in spite of the apron tied over the soft skirt and less than glamorous baggy cardigan she wore. She hadn't really done much to the room, but somehow the whole atmosphere of the apartment had changed. It seemed warmer, softer, more welcoming. Or was it just her presence that had made it that way?

'I've brought a CD with me,' said Tess, organised as ever. 'I'll leave it here for tonight, and collect it when I pick up the rest of my stuff.' She glanced at Gabriel. 'Come into the kitchen. I'll show you what you have to do.'

He followed her reluctantly. 'These are your starters,' she said, gesturing to the plates of fresh asparagus that she had prepared, 'and your puddings are in the fridge.' She opened the door to show him two heart-shaped chocolate desserts. 'There's champagne chilling in there, too. And the chicken just needs to be reheated when you're ready for it.'

'But you'll be here to do that, won't you?' said Gabriel, eyeing the array of dishes apprehensively.

'Me?' Tess was determinedly brisk, the way she had been ever since she had arrived to make the last minute preparations. 'Of course not! I don't think Fionnula would find it very romantic with me lurking around in the background,' she added dryly. 'I'll make sure I go before she arrives. What time did you tell her?'

'Eight o'clock,' he said, conscious of a certain lack of enthusiasm in his voice.

Tess checked her watch. It was twenty past seven. 'That'll just give me time to do the salad.'

Gabriel looked around him, appalled by all the trouble that she had taken to make it a special evening, and even more by the realisation that he was dreading it. How the hell had he got himself into this situation?

'Is there anything I can do?' he asked awkwardly.

'I think you should change, so that you're ready when Fionnula arrives.'

She seemed very keen to promote his relationship with Fionnula, thought Gabriel glumly as he stood under the shower. *He* was the one who ought to be keen. Fionnula was beautiful, uninhibited and too ambitious to be interested in any kind of emotional commitment. She was perfect.

So why was he standing here thinking about Tess in her worn cardigan, about the curve of her jaw and the line of her throat?

'Does your romantic atmosphere call for a tie?' he asked her as he went back into the kitchen, effectively disguising his own confusion beneath an air of ironic resignation. 'Or can I wear this shirt on its own?'

Tess turned from the cooker, where she was tasting the sauce on a wooden spoon. Gabriel had on his most sardonic expression. His hair was still wet from the shower, and he was wearing a pale yellow shirt that intensified his dark features and made the lightness of his eyes even more startling. He looked devastating, Tess thought involuntarily, and her heart, which she had kept so firmly under control until now, spoilt everything by lurching into her throat at the sight of him.

'I think you're all right as you are,' she said, horrified to hear the betraying croak in her voice. She swallowed. 'You look…very nice.'

'Tess,' said Gabriel on an impulse, and then stopped.

'What?'

Yes, *what*? Gabriel asked himself. What had he been going to say? Tess, I can't stop thinking about you? Tess, let me untie your apron and slide that cardigan from your shoulders? Tess, let me kiss you again?

Fionnula would be arriving any minute. 'Oh…nothing,' he said.

There was a constrained silence. It stretched between them, so taut that when Gabriel's mobile phone rang, they both jerked back as if an elastic band pulling them together had snapped.

Gabriel answered it in the living area. Tess couldn't hear what he was saying but, judging by the briefness of his murmured replies, it wasn't a particularly friendly call. And, indeed, when eventually he reappeared his face was grim and his mouth set in a angry line. 'That was Fionnula,' he said baldly. 'She's not coming.'

'Not coming?' Tess echoed in disbelief. 'Why not?'

'Something's come up.'

Fionnula had been invited to fill in on a live panel show at the last minute, she had told him. She'd been sure that he would understand that she couldn't turn down any chance of exposure. If she wanted to stay successful, she had to stay in the public eye. 'It's a bore, darling, I know, but there it is.'

'But I told you that tonight was different,' Gabriel protested. 'Tess has gone to a lot of trouble to cook a special meal for us.'

'Tess?' Fionnula's voice dropped several degrees.

'Yes, you've met her,' he said impatiently. 'She's my assistant.'

'Oh, the one you couldn't keep your eyes off in the restaurant?'

'Yes...no!' He corrected himself hastily.

'She must be a very special assistant if she cooks as well as she does everything else for you,' said Fionnula, dripping sarcasm. 'No wonder you're in love with her. You ought to marry her, darling, and save yourself a salary.'

'Of course I'm not in love with her.' Gritting his teeth, Gabriel tried to explain the promises auction. 'The whole point of her being here is to make it a special evening for you,' he said.

'It wouldn't be very special for me with you spending your whole time trying not to look at your secretary. I had enough of that the other night.'

'Don't be ridiculous!' snapped Gabriel, his temper fraying. 'Look, you've got plenty of work at the moment. You don't have to be on every cheap game show that calls you up at the last minute.'

He drew a breath and made himself sound calm and reasonable. 'Why don't you tell them no for once, and come round here?' he coaxed her, only to spoil everything by adding, 'Otherwise Tess will have gone to all this effort for nothing. The food won't keep until tomorrow, and she's already given up her evening to get everything ready for you.'

'Oh, well, we can't have your precious PA put out, can we?' said Fionnula vindictively. 'If you're that bothered about it, I suggest you share your special meal with her. Frankly, I've got more interesting things to do!' And she slammed the phone down.

Gabriel was furious. He felt a fool telling Tess that Fionnula wasn't coming after all.

'She had to work,' he said uncomfortably. 'I'm sorry.'

Tess looked around the kitchen where everything was set out ready to be served or heated up. 'This will all be vasted,' she said in dismay. 'Is there any one else you can ask to come over?'

Gabriel looked at her with a slight frown. 'You're in love with her,' Fionnula had said. Absurd! He didn't fall in love with anyone, let alone someone like Tess. Still in her apron, she was holding a wooden spoon and looking worried. There was a smudge of flour on her cheek. She looked ordinary, unthreatening, not at all the kind of person who could turn his life upside down.

Gabriel's expression relaxed slightly. Of course he wasn't in love with her. That had just been Fionnula being spiteful. He would prove it.

'Well,' he said slowly, 'there's you.'

'*Me?*'

'Did you have any other plans for this evening?'

'No,' admitted Tess after a moment.

'Then, why not stay and share the meal with me? You said yourself that it won't keep, and I can't eat it all myself. We may as well make the most of it after all the trouble you've taken.'

Tess hesitated. 'I don't know…'

'It's too short notice to ask anyone else.' Gabriel was surprised by how much he suddenly wanted her to stay. 'If you won't keep me company, I'll be stuck here all on my own with the candles and the bottle of champagne, and that won't be very romantic, will it?'

'No, I suppose not, but—'

'I paid for a romantic meal for two,' he reminded her unfairly. 'You were the one who made the promise, so the least you can do is ensure that's what I get.'

Tess could feel herself weakening. 'I've booked a taxi for ten to eight,' she told him.

'Ring and change it to later.'

Helplessly, she looked down at her old cardigan, worn skirt and comfortable shoes. 'I'm not really dressed for a special meal…'

'You look fine to me,' said Gabriel firmly. 'All you need is to take off that apron.'

Going over to her, he took the wooden spoon from her hand. 'It's not like you to dither, Tess,' he told her as he turned her around, untied the apron and pulled it over her head. Casting an eye around, he spotted her handbag and thrust it into her arms. 'You go and freshen up,' he ordered her. 'I'll ring the cab company.'

Tess gave in. Her stomach churned with a mixture of apprehension and anticipation and her hands shook slightly as she washed her face and hands. At least she had her make-up bag with her. By the time she had taken off her cardigan to reveal a close-fitting top with a scoop neck, had brushed out her hair and had put on some lipstick, she was able to face the situation with a bit more confidence.

It didn't stop her feeling ridiculously shy when she came face to face with Gabriel again. He was coming out of the kitchen with the champagne bottle in one hand and two flutes in the other, and they both stopped dead at the same time.

'If you're ready,' said Gabriel lightly after a moment, 'let's start our romantic evening. I've got the champagne and the glasses. What else do we need?'

'Candlelight.' Entering into the spirit of things, Tess found some matches and lit the candles until the room was bathed in a soft, flickering glow. She stood back to admire the effect. 'Perfect,' she said with a smile. There was no need to take this seriously, after all. They were only play-ing at it.

She sat down on the big, squashy sofa and kicked off her shoes so that she could curl her legs beneath her. Gabriel eased the cork expertly out of the bottle and poured champagne into the flutes with a satisfying fizz. Handing one to Tess, he sat down beside her and raised his glass.

'What shall we drink to?'

Tess looked at the bubbles drifting in her glass and tried not to think about how close he was. 'To keeping our promises?' she suggested.

'To promises,' agreed Gabriel, and they chinked glasses solemnly.

There was a silence while both thought about the promise he had kept, about the way they had kissed. Tess could feel memory tightening the air around them and was gripped by sudden panic. This was madness! She should never have agreed to stay. She should have taken her bag and walked away and left Gabriel with his dinner.

Her eyes skittered frantically around the room, desperate for something to hold their attention, but it was no use. They were being dragged irresistibly back to Gabriel, to his hands, to his throat, to his mouth... Oh, God, his *mouth*...

Tess drew in a sharp breath as the memory of how it had felt against her own clawed at the base of her spine, and she wrenched her gaze away, only to find herself looking deep into Gabriel's disquietingly light eyes. They held an expression Tess couldn't identify, but which made her heart shift suddenly in her chest, and she put her glass down on the coffee table with an uncertain click.

'I—I'd better see what's happening in the kitchen,' she said breathlessly.

The lights there were bright and reassuring. To her horror, when she checked the sauce, Tess realised that her hands were shaking. She had been doing so well, too. She had carried off the awkwardness of the situation, had pretended that the idea of being alone with Gabriel didn't bother her in the least, only to spoil everything by talking about the promises they had made and looking deep into his eyes.

She wouldn't do that again, Tess told herself. There was no need for her to be looking at him at all, let alone wondering what that light in his eyes meant or why it should suddenly be so hard to breathe. There was no need for her to be excruciatingly aware of him as a man, of the stern angles of his face and the tantalising texture of his skin and the solid, masculine strength of his body. No need to imagine sliding across the sofa and unbuttoning his shirt.

No need at all.

She would stick to strictly impersonal subjects for rest of evening, Tess decided firmly. She was just here to eat up the food, and she had better not forget it.

So she flashed Gabriel a bright smile when she picked up her glass and rejoined him on the sofa, and steered the conversation into what she hoped were determinedly neutral channels.

Only it didn't quite work like that. They talked about work for a while but, once they got onto personalities, they ended inevitably at the promises auction where they had kissed, so they switched to Harry. A baby ought to be a safe enough subject, thought Tess, and it was fine until they got onto remembering their first ham-fisted attempts to feed him and change him, which made them laugh, at which point Harry didn't seem such a good topic of conversation either.

They tried talking about their respective brothers, about their childhoods, about places they had been and books they had read and movies they had seen. They even tried politics. None of them were runners.

By the time the main course was over, their inspiration was exhausted. They were reduced to bursts of feverish conversation that withered and died after a few exchanges, leaving them racking their brains desperately for some new and inexhaustible subject that would have no connection to anything that they had in common, a subject that they could discuss like two sensible people without looking at each other and realising that they were alone in the candlelight and all it would take was for one of them to reach out a hand and they would be touching.

Tess hardly tasted a mouthful of the food she had spent so long preparing. The more she reminded herself that this should have been Fionnula's evening, the more she noticed how the candlelight threw the hard, exciting lines of Gabriel's face into relief, the more her eyes clung to his hands, to his mouth, to the pulse beating below his ear.

She wanted him to kiss her again.

The breath dried in Tess's throat as she admitted the truth to herself. She wanted him to pull her against him. She wanted him to twist his fingers in her hair and bring his mouth down hard on hers. And she wanted to kiss him back, to tug the shirt from his trousers and run her hands over his chest. She wanted—

Stop it! Stop it!

Tess pushed her plate aside. She had hardly touched the rich chocolate mousse that had taken her so long to make in its pretty heart shape. 'My taxi will be here soon,' she croaked. 'I should think about clearing up.'

'Forget clearing up,' said Gabriel softly. 'This is supposed to be a romantic dinner, and romantic dinners don't usually end with washing up, do they?'

Very slowly, Tess's eyes lifted to meet his, and she knew she was lost.

'No,' she said. 'They don't.'

CHAPTER TEN

GABRIEL'S chair scraped across the polished wooden floor
as he stood up. 'I think it would be a good idea if we
moved somewhere more comfortable, don't you?'

Tess didn't think it was a good idea at all. She thought
it was a very bad idea, even a dangerous idea, but she
could hardly insist on staying where she was. Nursing the
end of her wine, she perched on the edge of the sofa,
turning the glass nervously between her fingers and gazing
with a kind of desperation at the guttering candles in front
of her, to stop her eyes crawling sideways to Gabriel. He
was lounging on the sofa beside her, close, but not touching. Not quite.

'What's happened to the music?' he said, breaking the
strumming silence. He rose and set the CD to play again.
Tess had brought a compilation of love songs from the
fifties and sixties, slow, smoochy numbers that Gabriel
hadn't heard for years but which were instantly familiar.

He turned back to Tess sitting tensely on the sofa.
'Come on,' he said abruptly. 'Let's dance.'

'Oh, no, I—'

'You must,' he said, breaking into her instinctive protest. 'It won't be a romantic evening without dancing.'

'No, really, I'm a hopeless dancer,' said Tess, shrinking
back into the cushions, but Gabriel was already reaching
down to take the wine glass from her nerveless grasp and
setting it on the table.

'I don't believe you,' he said and pulled her to her feet.
'You're good at everything else.'

She wasn't good at keeping her distance, thought Tess.
She wasn't any good at resisting him. She wasn't good at

remembering all the reasons why she shouldn't fall in love with him.

'Not everything,' she said a little unsteadily.

Gabriel clasped her hand against his shoulder, and put a strong arm around her waist to draw her towards him. 'You don't need to be good at dancing, anyway,' he said, glancing down at her averted face. 'You just need to let me hold you.'

Pulling her closer, he trod on her foot as he swung her round. 'See?' he murmured in her ear. 'I can't dance either. We'll have to stand here and sway.'

This is crazy, thought Tess frantically. She would never be able to go back to being his PA after this. How could she take memos and keep his diary and book restaurants for him when she knew how it felt to be held against him like this? But it was too late to think about that now. She should have gone while she'd had the chance. The whole evening had been a terrible mistake.

Except it hadn't felt like a mistake, and it didn't now. It felt like the only place she wanted to be, cocooned in warmth and candlelight with Gabriel, isolated from the rest of the world by this bubble of enchantment. With his arm around her and his hand clasping hers, it was easy to forget that come Monday she would have to walk into the office and pretend that this had never happened. The future didn't exist. There was only now, and the two of them alone together with the words of the old love songs swirling around them.

His fingers were warm around hers, holding her tightly while his other hand smoothed slowly up and down her spine. Boneless and dizzy with desire, Tess was powerless to stop herself leaning into him and closing her eyes.

Gabriel felt her quivering resistance eke away. He gathered her closer, turning his face into her silky hair and breathing in her fragrance. 'Now, this is romantic, isn't it?' he said, his voice very deep and low.

She nodded, unable to speak.

'Of course, if we were going to be really romantic, it wouldn't be enough to dance like this. I'd have to kiss you, wouldn't I?'

A tremor ran through her. 'If this was real,' she managed with difficulty, 'but it's not real. We're just pretending.'

'Are we?' Gabriel bent his head and kissed the lobe of her ear. 'It feels real to me,' he breathed, kissing his way along her jaw and smiling as he felt Tess shudder with pleasure.

'I don't think this is…sensible,' she whispered.

'No, it isn't,' he murmured against her throat. 'It's not sensible at all. But it's romance, it's here and now. It's what you promised and what I paid for. And right now, I don't want to be sensible, do you?'

Releasing Tess's hand, he pushed her hair gently away from her face and cupped her cheek with his palm, tilting her chin so that she was looking up at him.

'Do you?' he asked softly again.

Very slowly, Tess shook her head, and saw a blaze of expression in his eyes before his mouth found hers at last and the terrible tension of the evening exploded into hunger and delight and intense, rocketing excitement. Succumbing to the rush of sensation, she wound her arms around Gabriel's neck and clung to him, kissing him back with a kind of desperation.

After waiting so long, she couldn't hold him tightly enough, couldn't kiss him deeply enough. It was bliss to be able to run her hands over his powerful shoulders, to give herself up to the taste and touch and the feel of him.

Without being aware of how it happened, Tess found herself back on the sofa, with Gabriel kissing his way down her throat, murmuring endearments against her skin. She arched beneath him and tangled her fingers in his hair and, when his hand slid beneath her top, she gasped at the feel of flesh against flesh, beyond remembering what sensible meant, beyond thinking at all, lost in a tumbling tide of desire.

A harsh buzzing sound was jarring the gentle melody from the CD player, filtering insistently through the sound of their breathing. Gabriel heard it first and he lifted his head with a frown.

'That'll be my taxi,' said Tess shakily, belatedly recognising the buzz of the intercom.

She tried to sit up but Gabriel kept her pinned beneath him. 'Stay,' he urged her. 'I'll tell him to go.'

But that would mean him going all the way down to the entrance to pay off the cab. The spell would be broken. Perhaps it already was, thought Tess sadly.

'No—I—I'd better go.'

'Are you sure?'

For a moment, she wavered, biting her lip. Her body clamoured to let him persuade her to stay right where she was, but her head, annoyed at being so comprehensively ignored up till then, reminded her sternly of all the reasons why that would be a bad idea. A very bad idea.

'I'm sure,' she said huskily.

Gabriel levered himself abruptly off her and went over to the intercom as the cab driver leant impatiently on the buzzer again. 'Five minutes,' he said curtly into the speaker, and turned back to Tess, who was gathering her things together with trembling hands.

She glanced at the table where they had left their plates and glasses what seemed like a lifetime ago. 'What about all this?' she said in a brave attempt to sound normal.

'Leave it. I'll sort it out,' said Gabriel with a twisted smile. 'I won't have anything else to do.'

At the door, he kissed her once, hard. 'I wish you'd stay,' he said.

'I…can't,' said Tess, weak-kneed and clutching desperately at her resolution.

'Coward,' he said softly.

'Maybe I am.' She forced a smile. 'But I'm a sensible coward.'

Gabriel ran a finger down her cheek. 'You weren't being sensible a few minutes ago.'

'I know,' she said, her skin seared with his touch. 'I got a bit carried away with the romantic atmosphere.' Drawing a breath, she made herself look directly at him. 'I think we should agree to forget this evening.'

There was a pause. Gabriel's hand fell to his side. 'Is that really what you want?' he said in disbelief.

'Yes.' Tess put up her chin, not sure whether she was defying him or the voice inside her that was shouting, No. No! That's not what I want at all.

'Everything will look different in the morning,' she said, keeping her voice steady with an effort. 'And on Monday I'm going to have to walk into the office and be your secretary again. I can only do that if we both pretend this never happened.'

Gabriel looked at her for a long moment before giving a curt nod. 'All right,' he said, swallowing the bitterness of his disappointment. Because what else could he say? He knew how much Tess needed her job, and he needed her. He couldn't be responsible for putting her in an impossible situation.

He opened the door reluctantly. 'We'll pretend nothing happened if that's what you want. I won't ring you and I won't discuss it, but if you change your mind about tonight, come back. I'll be here.'

Tess sat rigidly upright in the back of the cab, staring unseeingly out at the dark London streets while the memory of Gabriel's kisses raged through her. Leaving had been the only sensible thing to do, Tess knew that. She knew that she had done the right thing. But it had felt so right in his arms, so real. Much more real than this taxi with its ticking meter and its strange taxi smell and its thankfully morose driver.

Coward, Gabriel had called her, and he was right. She was afraid of falling in love with him, afraid of getting hurt the way Oliver had hurt her before. But Gabriel wasn't Oliver. He hadn't made her any promises nor told her any lies. He had offered her a night, no more. He had offered her the here and now, with no thought of tomorrow, just his lips and his hands and the feel of his body, and she had been too much of a coward to admit that was enough.

'Come back,' he had said. 'I'll be here.'

The taxi was turning into her street when Tess leant forward and spoke to the driver. 'I've changed my mind. Can you take me back?'

Grumbling, the driver turned the car round and retraced their route across the bridge and back through the heart of London to draw up across the road from Gabriel's apartment. Tess's fingers were shaking as she searched in her purse for the money to pay him. At last she located a couple of notes, and sat forward to pass them over to the driver but, even as he took them with a martyred sigh, she caught sight of someone approaching the front door.

Red hair glowed in the harsh security light as the figure pressed the intercom and waited confidently for the door to be released.

Fionnula.

Tess froze with her hand outstretched. Had Fionnula decided to make up for her earlier rejection of Gabriel? A worse thought slid insidiously into her mind. Had Gabriel rung her as soon as he'd realised that *she* wasn't going to change her mind and send the taxi away? Surely even he couldn't casually hope to substitute one woman for another within an hour?

He wouldn't let Fionnula in, Tess told herself. He couldn't let her in.

But he did let her in.

Tess watched numbly as Fionnula pushed open the door and disappeared inside. She would take the lift up to his

floor and Gabriel would be waiting for her. Would he kiss
Fionnula against the door? Would they sink onto the sofa
together? Or would they go straight to bed?

Tess squeezed her eyes shut against the thought. It was
her own fault. She should have stayed while she'd had the
chance.

Except that now she knew that leaving had been the
right thing to do, after all. It was all very well telling herself that a night would have been enough, but of course it
wouldn't have been. She would have had to face the fact
that she was in love with him, and what happiness could
there be with a man like Gabriel, who didn't want compromise and didn't want commitment, who only wanted
love to last long enough?

'Do you want your change or not?'

The taxi driver's weary demand made Tess open her
eyes. He was holding out a handful of coins, and watching
her with a mixture of suspicion and concern.

'I'm sorry,' she said bleakly. 'I've made a mistake. I
want to go home.'

'Good morning, Tess.'

'Good morning.'

Gabriel eyed her with resentment. How could she sit
there so self-possessed? When she had told him that she
wanted to forget Saturday evening, he hadn't thought that
she would really be able to do it. Her eyes hadn't so much
as flickered when he'd come in. It was as if she had wiped
the whole incident for her mind.

If only he had been able to do the same.

After she had gone, he had blown out the candles very
deliberately. He'd switched off the music and had cleared
up the debris from the meal, working with a ferocious
concentration as if trying to erase Tess's presence from his
apartment. He had wanted her to stay too badly. Things
had been going too far, too fast. Gabriel had known that

they had been in danger of getting complicated. Worse, he had been in danger of getting involved.

No, it was just as well Tess had gone when she had.

That didn't stop him leaping for the intercom when the sound of the buzzer ripped through the empty apartment. She had come back after all!

'Come on up,' he had said, and afterwards he had cringed when he'd remembered the ridiculous smile that had spread over his face. 'I'll meet you at the lift.'

Impatiently, he'd waited for the doors to slide open. 'I'm so glad you've come—' he'd begun and had then stopped, because it hadn't been Tess who'd stepped smiling seductively out of the lift. It had been Fionnula.

Gabriel shuddered at the memory of the scene that had followed. If anything had told him how he felt about Tess, it had been the bitterness of his disappointment. It had been some time before he'd heard a word Fionnula had been saying. All he'd been able to take in had been the fact that Tess hadn't come back after all.

He'd spent most of Sunday looking at the phone. Gabriel had lost count of the number of times he'd picked it up and begun to dial her number before cutting the connection. He had said that he wouldn't call her. Tess could have stayed if she had wanted to, and he wasn't going to humiliate himself by crawling after her.

If she wanted to pretend that nothing had happened, that was fine by him. There was no way Gabriel was going to let her guess the turmoil raging inside him. He had never felt like this before, and he didn't like it.

Things might have been different if Tess had shown any sign of confusion when she'd seen him that morning, if she had given the slightest hint that she even remembered kissing him but, as it was, Gabriel decided there and then that he had to get away for a while. It was all very well for Tess to say that they should just forget what had happened, but how could he forget when she was right there every day?

Gabriel didn't care if it looked as if he was running away. He had been neglecting his offices in the States, and it was high time he paid them some attention. There would be so much to do over there that he would have no time to think about Tess.

That was what he told himself, anyway.

'I want you to get me a seat on this afternoon's flight to New York,' he told her.

He watched her closely to see if he could detect any sign of disappointment in her face, but she only asked calmly when he would be coming back.

'I haven't decided yet,' he said tetchily. 'Get me an open return.'

'What about your meetings this week?'

'Reschedule them.'

'Very well.' Tess looked up at him over the top of her spectacles. 'Do you expect to be gone more than a week?'

'Possibly,' said Gabriel. 'Why?' He tensed. Was she going to say that she would miss him?

She hesitated. 'I think I should tell you that I will be handing in my resignation later today. I'll work out a month's notice, of course, but you might like to set arrangements for finding a replacement in train before you go.'

It was as if she had kicked him in the stomach. Winded, shocked, Gabriel stared at her. 'You're leaving?' he echoed numbly.

Tess swallowed. 'Yes.'

'Is it because of what happened on Saturday?' He hadn't meant to mention it, had been determined not to, in fact, but the question was out before he could stop it.

'No,' she said, but her eyes didn't quite meet his. 'We agreed that wasn't important.'

She might have agreed it, Gabriel thought bitterly. His own feelings apparently didn't matter.

'Then why?' he asked in a hard voice.

'I've been offered another job,' she told him. 'A good job. I'm going to be office manager. I've been wanting to get away from a secretarial role for some time, and this is the perfect opportunity for me to develop my career.'

Gabriel's jaw worked furiously. If she didn't want to be a secretary any more, there wasn't much he could offer her as an inducement to stay, was there? 'I suppose you'll want a reference before I go?' he bit out.

'That won't be necessary,' said Tess composedly. 'Steve knows me well enough.'

'Steve? Steve Robinson?' Gabriel was very white about the mouth. 'Is that who you're going to work for?'

'Yes.'

'I see.' He was gripped by such a murderous rage that he could hardly speak. She was going, leaving him for Steve Robinson! 'Well, I suppose I should congratulate you.' He managed to get the words out somehow.

'Thank you.'

Gabriel turned blindly for his office. 'You'd better get onto personnel. Tell them to advertise the post right away. I want someone suitable to start as soon as possible.'

Tess looked after him, her eyes stinging with the tears she had kept so tightly under control while she'd been talking to him. Was that all she meant to Gabriel? A suitable secretary who could be replaced if necessary, the same way he had replaced her with Fionnula on Saturday?

She was glad he was going away. It would make it much easier to get through the next four weeks. After making her decision on Sunday, she had called Steve right away, but deep down she knew that it was already too late. She was in love with Gabriel, and nothing she could do would change that now, but at least the new job gave her the chance to walk away from him with her pride intact. That was something.

Not much, but something.

Six weeks later, buffeted by vicious gusts of wind and rain, Tess wrestled with her umbrella in the meagre shelter of the bus stop before giving up the unequal struggle and deciding that she would just have to get wet. Turning up her collar, she set off to walk home, her shoulders hunched against the rain. It was dark and cold and miserable. The only thing to be said about the weather, Tess thought bleakly, was that it matched her mood perfectly.

She had been office manager for two weeks now. Her office was nice, the people were friendly, and the job was busy and stimulating. At last she had the challenge she had thought she'd wanted.

Except that the challenge wasn't in running a strange office. The challenge was forgetting Gabriel. Tess had hoped that it would be easier by now, but the less she saw him the worse it got.

The last few weeks at SpaceWorks had been agony. In the end, Gabriel had stayed in the States for nearly three weeks, and he'd only been back for a day to approve the choice of his new PA before setting off for Frankfurt. Tess didn't know whether to be glad or sorry that he had missed her leaving party. He had sent her an e-mail, thanking her for her help and wishing her success in her new job, but the message had been so impersonal that Tess had wanted to cry when she'd read it. He had sent her some flowers, too, but they didn't mean anything. One of the other secretaries had confided that Gabriel had asked her to arrange them while he'd been away.

Time and again, Tess told herself that she had made the right decision, but it didn't ease the dull ache in her heart that sharpened like the grinding of knives whenever she remembered the time she had spent with Gabriel—which was every unoccupied moment. She couldn't think about anything else. Over and over, she relived the feel of his arms around her, his lips on hers.

At night, she lay in bed and tortured herself by imagining how different things might have been if Gabriel had persuaded her to stay that evening in his apartment. They would have woken up together, the way they had done once before, but this time he wouldn't have frozen in horror when he realised just who he was kissing awake. They could have spent Sunday together, a long, lazy, luxurious day making love, could have gone into the office together on Monday.

And then what? Tess's dreams always stopped at this point. She couldn't imagine calmly going back to typing memos and organising meetings and booking tables for him at Cupiditas. A night, maybe two, was all she would have had. Why would he have wanted her for longer than that, when he had someone like Fionnula, who was so much more beautiful in the cold light of day, and who didn't demand anything more than he was prepared to give?

No, it would have been impossible, Tess reminded herself drearily. She had been right to leave. She just hadn't thought it would be so hard not even seeing him.

Head down, she hurried down her street while the wind tore her hair out its clips and the rain lashed against her face. Her eyes were screwed up against the wet, and it wasn't until she pushed open the gate that she realised that someone was waiting for her on her doorstep.

It was Gabriel.

The sight of him stopped the breath in Tess's throat and drove all feeling from her like a blow. He was hunched, like her, against the rain, dark hair plastered to his head and his face dripping. She stared at him, hardly daring to believe that he was real and not some mirage conjured up by her desperate longing.

'Tess,' he said, as if his throat hurt him, and the sound of his voice sent sensation whooshing back in a dizzying rush to Tess's head and to her heart.

'Wh-what are you doing here?' she croaked.

'Waiting for you.'

'In the rain?' she asked, still dazed.

'I wanted to see you,' he said. 'I knew you'd come home eventually.'

Tess hardly heard him. She couldn't get beyond the wonderful, glorious fact that he was there, right there, waiting for her.

Belatedly, she realised the rain was streaming down his face, and puddling around their feet as they stood there. 'You'd better come in,' she said.

Gabriel stood back while she unlocked the front door. She seemed to have lost all control of her hands, and she fumbled with the key, almost dropping it several times. It took ages to get it into the lock, but at last she got the door open and switched on the light.

He stepped into the hall behind her. Under the harsh electric glare, Tess saw for the first time that he was looking tired and drawn. 'I'll take your coat,' she said awkwardly, and then exclaimed as she felt how heavy it was. 'It's sodden!'

'I was standing out there for nearly two hours,' said Gabriel. 'I thought you would be back before now.'

'I was working late.'

'On a Friday night?'

Without him, there had been nothing to come home to, Tess remembered. She hadn't known that he would be there, waiting for her in the rain.

'Oh, well…you know…' Awkwardly, she opened the sitting room door. 'Come and sit down.'

Gabriel sat in the armchair, leaning forward, wiping the rain from his face with the flat of his hands. Tess longed to be able to do it for him, to touch him, to feel the warmth of his skin, to convince herself that this was real, that he was really there. Instead, she fidgeted around the sitting room, pulling the curtains, putting on the lamps, kneeling to fiddle with the gas fire.

It was Gabriel who broke the silence. 'I saw Harry yesterday,' he said, sounding as ill at ease as Tess felt, and she looked up sharply. She had kept in touch with Leanne but she hadn't heard from her for a while.

'He's all right, isn't he?' she asked in concern.

'He's fine. Greg's over,' Gabriel explained. 'I took him to meet his son.'

'Oh.' Tess looked a little doubtful. 'How did that go?'

'OK, I think. Greg was on his best behaviour. He asked Leanne to marry him—in a burst of chivalry, I guess—but she said that she'd rather just be friends. Leanne's no fool,' he went on. 'She knows how unreliable Greg would be as a husband and, now that she's finally accepted an allowance, she's got some financial security. She won't need to leave Harry again.'

'I'm glad about the allowance,' said Tess. 'Is Greg paying that?'

'Leanne thinks he is,' Gabriel answered obliquely.

Tess nodded slowly, appreciating the situation. There was a lot you could say about Gabriel, but never that he wasn't generous. 'That's good.'

After the burst of conversation, another strained silence fell, broken only by the hiss and flicker of the gas flames.

'Is that what you wanted to see me about?' she asked at last.

Gabriel ran a finger around his collar. 'No... Well, partly, I guess... I thought you would want to know about Harry and—but no, it wasn't that.' He admitted the truth abruptly, 'I just wanted to see you.'

He swallowed. 'The thing is,' he said, 'I miss you.'

'You've only had your new PA for two weeks,' said

Tess with difficulty. 'It's bound to take a little time to get used to her.'

'No, you don't understand. I miss *you*.' He stopped, hearing the inadequacy of his words, but all he could think of was to try them again a different way. 'I *miss* you.'

Still kneeling by the fire, Tess heard the slow slam of her heart against her ribs. She couldn't move, couldn't speak. She could only stare at Gabriel with dark, dazed eyes while hope trickled tentatively along her veins.

'That's why I came.' Now that he had started, Gabriel couldn't stop. 'I had to tell you that there hasn't been a day since you left when I haven't missed you.' His voice deepened. 'There hasn't been a day since we kissed when I haven't wanted you.

'I told myself that I would forget you in the States, but I couldn't. I couldn't stop remembering, I couldn't stop thinking about you. I hoped it would be better when you'd gone, but every day has been worse than the last one. I keep looking for you, listening for the sound of your voice, and I've realised that it's you that I need, not a secretary. I could get a new secretary, but I couldn't get a new you.'

He risked a glance at Tess, but she was still staring at him as if she couldn't believe what she was hearing, and he ploughed on before she had a chance to laugh in his face and tell him that he was too late, that she was quite happy with Steve Robinson and her great new job.

'I know you're OK on your own,' he said. 'I've always been OK on my own, too. I guess I still would be if you don't... I'll survive, anyway.' He swallowed. 'I just wondered whether we might be OK together. I thought we might be more than OK. I thought we might be happy.'

He paused then, and his smile twisted. 'I guess this sounds crazy. I'm the boss from hell, aren't I? I don't expect you to believe me straight away, Tess. All I ask is a chance to make up for all the times I've shouted at you or snapped at you or made your life difficult. I thought if maybe we could go out, we could start again,' he said, sounding less sure of himself than Tess had ever heard him.

He tugged at the knot of his tie as if it felt too tight, and took a breath. 'I guess I'm just trying to ask if you would like to go out to dinner.'

It was so little to ask that Tess almost laughed. She couldn't believe that this strong, successful man should be stumbling awkwardly over his words, that he could be so blind. Didn't he know how much she loved him? Couldn't he *see*?

'Dinner?' she repeated, a smile trembling on her lips. 'Now?'

'Yes.'

'You mean like on a date?'

He set his jaw. 'Yes.'

She could feel warmth spilling through her like sunshine. 'Where were you thinking of? Cupiditas?'

'Wherever you like.'

Tess pretended to consider it, then shook her head. 'I'm not really hungry,' she said.

'We don't have to eat.' An edge of desperation crept into Gabriel's voice. 'We could go to a bar, to a movie. We could do anything you want.'

'I don't want to go out,' she said, and he stared at her for a moment before his shoulders slumped.

'Sure, I understand,' he said flatly. He shifted forward in the armchair, making ready to stand up. 'Thanks for listening, anyway. I just had to tell you how I felt, but I'll get out of your way now.'

He looked so defeated that Tess was sorry she'd teased him. 'Don't go,' she said softly as she got to her feet and went over to him.

He stared blankly up at her as she bent to lift his hands out of the way. Slack with surprise, he let her push them aside as she sat down on his lap and put her arms around his neck.

'I don't want to go out with you,' she whispered against his mouth. 'I want to stay in.'

'Tess,' he mumbled incredulously as she kissed him. 'Tess…' Recovering from the shock, his arms encircled her while his lips moved wonderingly against hers. 'Tess, what are you saying?'

'I love you,' she told him, kissing his cheek, his jaw, his mouth once more. 'I love you,' she said between kisses. 'I love you. I need you. I've missed you, too.'

Suddenly afraid that he was dreaming, Gabriel twined his fingers in her wet hair and held her head still so that he could look deep into her starry eyes.

'Say that again,' he said urgently.

'I love you.'

'But you can't love me. I'm grouchy and crabby and selfish… I've never done anything to make you love me.'

Tess smiled lovingly at him. 'There's no accounting for it,' she teased him, 'but there it is. I do. I think I've loved you since the day Harry arrived and we changed his nappy together.'

Almost giddy with relief, Gabriel began to laugh. 'I've got more romantic memories than that,' he said. 'Like waking up with you the next morning…do you remember that?'

'I remember,' whispered Tess, winding her arms more tightly round his neck so that their mouths could meet in a long, sweet kiss. 'I didn't want you to stop,' she confessed with a blissful sigh.

Gabriel smiled wickedly against her throat. 'Next time I won't.'

'Is that a promise?' she murmured, her lips moving provocatively along his jaw.

'It's a promise,' he said, his voice ragged with desire, and his arms tightened around her, enfolding her, loving her, his hands moving possessively over her as they kissed, and kissed, and kissed again.

It was some time before Tess could speak. Breathless with happiness, she laid her head on Gabriel's shoulder and snuggled into him, resting her face against his throat. 'I wish I'd known.' She sighed contentedly, thinking of the long, miserable nights she had spent trying not to cry. 'Why didn't you tell me you loved me?'

'I didn't know myself until that evening you came round to cook the romantic meal. It felt so right to kiss you then, I couldn't believe that you didn't feel anything, but on the Monday you were so unapproachable that I thought you must be regretting it. And then when you told me you were leaving…' he grimaced at the memory '…it seemed as if you just wanted to forget the whole thing.'

'I was just terrified that you would guess how much I loved you,' said Tess.

Gabriel smoothed the hair away from her face as he kissed her once more. 'Then why didn't you stay that night?'

'I was a coward, like you said but, if it's any comfort, I regretted it all the way home.'

'I wish you'd come back.'

'I did.'

He lifted his head in surprise. 'You did?'

'I saw Fionnula going into your apartment, and decided she must be on her way up to see you.'

'She was.' Gabriel told her how he had rushed to let Fionnula in. 'I thought it was you,' he remembered. 'When I saw her, I realised just how much I'd wanted you to come back. I knew then that making love wouldn't be enough, after all. I wanted you to love me the way I loved you.'

Tess sat up so that she could look into his eyes. 'I do,' she said, and kissed him softly.

'All that time we've wasted,' Gabriel pretended to grumble, when they could speak again.

'We won't waste any more,' she consoled him. 'We've got the rest of our lives together.'

'Is that a promise?' he said, taking her face between his hands.

'It's a promise,' she said.

'How long do these promises of yours last?' Gabriel asked, and Tess smiled as she kissed him again.

'A promise is for ever.'

Mills & Boon® have teamed up with
Prima Magazine to launch a
brand-new co-branded series called
Prima New Beginnings.

Each of the warm and captivating
stories in the series features women
facing up to the glorious unpredictability
of life – stories that are relevant for
every woman who has ever sought
a new beginning.

Two compelling **Prima New Beginnings** *titles
are available each month at the amazingly
low price of only* **£3.99** *each*

Available at WHSmith, Tesco, ASDA, and all good bookshops
www.millsandboon.co.uk

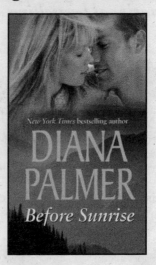